The Honour of the Knights

The Battle for the Solar System : Book One

Stephen J Sweeney

For Dad

— Prologue —

I t had taken only a matter of hours for the Kethlan system to become a tumbling sea of debris; the twisted and burnt out remnants of a once glorious Imperial nation. An empire whose costly mistakes would for many years to come echo into every corner of the known galaxy. And with those mistakes would come death to billions of innocent, unsuspecting lives.

A starfighter hurtled through the scattered metal, the pilot desperate to find a way to stop himself from joining the ever growing population of this interstellar graveyard.

Jacques Chalmers was not alone in his frustration with the current situation, but he was doubtless one of the most panicked. He tried to steady himself as he began cycling once again through the available display options for his starfighter's radar system. His anxiety continued to grow with each passing second, every change of the screen doing nothing to abate it. He stopped midway through the calibration and glanced out of his cockpit.

The scene was the same as it had been a few moments ago and it brought him no comfort. He couldn't count the number of capital ships that dominated the Enemy's front line. Twenty? Thirty? Fifty? In his years of service to the Imperial Naval Forces he had never seen anything like it, not even in archive war footage. The enormous forms of the battleships loomed like giants atop a hill, staring down upon a tiny village below. Then there were the Enemy starfighters themselves: hundreds at least, swarming about like a huge wall of locusts.

Knowing that he had already been flying straight for longer than was advisable, Chalmers altered his course to attempt to throw off any pursuers.

Not long before he had been standing on the flight deck of his deployment carrier, amongst the other pilots, his heart pumping in his ears, his hands sweating as he awaited the order to board his fighter.

Chalmers saw his friends run forward as their names were called out, scrambling into cockpits, pulling on helmets and performing last minute safety checks. Though most hid it well he was convinced they were all as nervous and scared as he was - knowing they could well be speeding only to their own deaths. As he watched his friends' fighters hurtle down the catapult his commanding officer had addressed the last remaining pilots still standing on the flight deck.

"Right, listen up," he started. "This is where we must make our stand. The Enemy cannot be allowed to advance any further. Tonight we fight the battle for Kethlan and for the Imperium; the battle for our survival. Hundreds of millions of lives are depending on our actions here. Make them proud!"

Hundreds of millions? thought Chalmers. *Is that all that's left? A few months ago it was billions.* This day had crept ever closer as cities, planets and then entire star systems had fallen to the Enemy; to those damned Pandorans; to the Senate's mistake. How many of his friends had he lost over these last few terrible months? Had they died fast or were they now suffering a fate far worse..?

As his CO continued to pump them up for the critical battle, Chalmers' head was filled with visions of row upon row of black-clad soldiers. A white emblem resided on their right arms and left breast, an all-encompassing full black helmet upon their heads, its smooth form negating all facial features. Two bright red oval spheres were set into an eye level groove that ran all around, the "eyes" themselves slanted into a menacing and intimidating scowl. One of the soldiers turned to face him, the ruby-like eyes seeming to pierce his very soul. He felt his hand tighten on the flight helmet he held, swallowing hard.

"Daniels! Peterson! Foster! Brown! Rye..." a voice called out above the other sounds that filled the flight deck. Feet moved and Chalmers felt his stomach lurch. His name would be called soon. He felt a sense of doom. If the Empire could not stop the Enemy before, what hope did they have now? The Enemy's power had grown exponentially and they had crushed everything in their path with harrowing little effort. Chalmers was feeling forced to accept the truth: they were all that was left of the Imperial Naval Forces. This was a battle that could not be won; not now, not ever.

"... Tyler! Flynn! Chalmers! King! Golden! Blair..."

At the sound of his name, Chalmers felt himself move robotically, his mind screaming in protest against what his legs were doing. He ran over to the waiting starfighter, threw on his helmet and begun ascending the ladder into the cockpit.

Zombie-like he sank down into the seat, watching as if from outside his body as his hands buckled him in, his fingers flip switches, press buttons, acknowledge questions and confirmations on the screens before him. Moments later his craft was taxied to the catapult and before long he'd found himself out in space and into the thick of battle.

At that moment, his worst fears had not only been altogether realised, but far exceeded.

Chalmers cancelled the radar calibration screen and instead opened a communications channel to his parent carrier.

"*Centaur*, this is First Lieutenant Chalmers." He could hear the fear and tension in his own voice as he spoke and could not control it. "Has there been any update to the radar situation?"

"That's a negative, Chalmers, we're still working on it."

Centaur's answer did nothing to ease his distress. "Any contingency plans? I can't see what the hell I'm supposed to be shooting at out here!"

"Again, that's a negative. Ops believes that enemy craft are masking their vessel signatures. We're working to decode it ASAP. We will keep you notified. *Centaur* out."

Chalmers again looked down at his radar screen in frustration. In a normal combat situation the radar would differentiate between the participants with simple colour coding: green for friendly, red for hostile and white for unknown. His radar had been functioning as normal when he had launched, but only a few minutes into the battle every item on the screen had turned green. In that state it made it impossible to decipher hostile targets from friendly ones. To make matters worse his opponents were flying the same craft as he and his squadron, so that even at visual range he could not be certain whether he was about to open fire on friend or foe.

"Jules!" he said, opening a communications channel to a life long team mate. He attempted to keep his voice steady as he spoke, trying his best to avoid drawing any of his allies into his own personal hell. "Is your radar any good?"

"Jacques!" the familiar female voice came back to him, sounding grateful to hear from a friend. "Where are you? I'm flying blind here! I can't see a thing!" The anxiety and distress was clear in her own voice. Chalmers had known Jules for years, she was almost like a sister to him. For him to hear her in such a state horrified him. He longed to open a video link, to look into her eyes and tell her that everything was going to be okay, that they would both get through this. But with his fighter in its current state he dared not touch anything for fear it would make matters worse.

As he tried to think of how best to relay his present location to his team mate he noticed that the radar had tagged the craft he was speaking to; a thin, blinking white rectangular box outlining the green triangle. For a brief moment his anguish subsided and he brought his craft around to face Jules' fighter. He could see her weaving and twirling in a similar fashion to his own meandering and confused flight, the cannons of her fighter as quiet as his own.

"Jules, check your radar. I'm..." Chalmers began. Jules' starfighter exploded before him, a pair of fighters peeling away from the wreckage that spread out like a firework. His small glimmer of hope melted as soon as it had first appeared and he felt the words he was about to speak become lodged in his throat. Though he had witnessed it so many times before, to see two fighters identical to his own open fire on and destroy an allied craft was still an awful sight to behold. It was not like combat against foreign craft, those of the Confederacy or Independent Nations, for instance. This was more personal, as though one was watching dear friends turn on each other again and again. For longer than was wise he sat staring at the sparking, spinning metal that continued to spread out. Chalmers took it as sign that the destruction he had witnessed over the last few months was edging ever closer to engulfing him.

"No..." the pitiful sound of his own voice finally escaped him. He felt his throat close up, but forced back the tears he could feel welling up and threatening to blur his vision. His fighter gave a heavy jolt as he was hit from behind and he banked hard, seeing a stream of bright green plasma streak past him.

In the wake of the attack he tried to think. He could wheel around and go after the closest craft to him, hoping that he was opening fire on a hostile. However, he risked killing a friend who had assumed that *he* was the Enemy. A voice from his comms system drew his attention,

"All available support, this is *Minotaur*. We are sustaining heavy damage. Requesting immediate assistance!"

Chalmers felt the panic rising further within him and fought to control it. *INF Minotaur* was the Imperial flagship; a symbol of the Empire's glory. Historically its very presence within a conflict zone was enough to spur the Imperial combatants on to victory. But a desperate request for help from the great battleship could only lower morale. He could not allow such a thing to happen. He pushed recent events behind him and looked around for the great capital ship. Even though he could not identify it on the cluttered mess of green that was his radar, its sheer size meant that he would have no trouble locating it with his own two eyes. He saw it hanging high above the planet Kethlan; the former Seat of the Emperor and the planet where he himself had been born.

He changed his heading, raising his velocity to maximum and sped forward. Even at this distance he could make out the explosions ripping across the hull, blooming before dissipating. *Minotaur's* laser and plasma cannons were firing indiscriminatingly in all directions, whilst volleys of return fire impacted further on its surface, the battleship's shielding all but destroyed.

As he drew closer to the once proud symbol of Imperial might, he came to realise that he was looking at the future. The official line from the Empire to their galactic neighbours was that they were entrenched in a civil war. To those within the Imperium itself the truth was far more shocking. Over three quarters of the Imperial armed forces had so far been defeated, more than a dozen of its star systems having fallen to the Enemy. Unless they could halt the advances of the Enemy here and now it would not be long before the Imperium was lost forever, confined to the annals of time; and then the rest of the galaxy would follow. He wondered if the true story had come out, whether the Independent Worlds or the Confederacy had seen through their spin.

Though it had taken him longer than he wanted, even at full speed, he was within visual range of other fighter craft. As he entered the thick of combat, it dawned on him that he did not need his radar any more, he had only to aim for any craft that was firing upon *Minotaur*. He could see several dozen starfighters attempting to tackle *Minotaur's* attackers, their work cut out as they struggled against the far greater numbers of heavier fighters the Enemy flew. The lightly armed and shielded Jackals that he and his team mates piloted were almost all that remained of their complement, the majority of their own heavy class fighters having been destroyed in combat months earlier. Though the Jackal was faster than the other starfighters and able to out-manoeuvre them, Chalmers was aware that in his current state of shattered nerves he would need a lot of luck if he wanted to exploit such capabilities to his advantage.

Picking out a target the Imperial fighter pilot aligned himself with the aggressor and opened fire. The shots sailed harmlessly past their target, leaving Chalmers to curse and attempt to calm himself down so that he could aim straight. His right hand was shaking. He took hold of it in his other and flexed his fingers. He tried to convince himself it was still possible that the Imperial forces might all somehow get through this, that they would secure a victory here today; that they could at last turn the tide and the nightmare that had started five years ago would end.

A steady bleeping from his on-board computer system dragged him from his dreams of hope. He recognised the sound as the lock warning and instinctively looked to his radar for the location and speed of the incoming threat. At the same time that he remembered his radar was useless to him an explosion rocked his fighter, the sound of the missile lock warning cutting out, to be replaced by another, far more urgent tone. Though having rarely heard it before, Chalmers knew just what it meant. His starfighter's speed dropped off and the craft began to tumble, the engines no longer functional. Both his computer screens were flashing the word "EJECT".

Chalmers reached up for the ejection control, fingers wrapping around the handle. But he stopped short of pulling it, turning his attention once more to the scene outside. Bright green bolts of plasma flew in every direction; thick red, yellow and blue pulsing lines of various beam weapons sweeping around elsewhere; trails from missiles curling about the chaos as they hunted down their targets. Fighter craft circled *Minotaur*, continuing to open fire on the stricken battleship and each other. *Minotaur's* cannons were silent. He knew it was only a matter of time before it was completely destroyed.

From the bridge of the Imperial carrier, *INF Chimera*, Fleet Admiral Zackaria watched the last minutes of *Minotaur's* service to the Imperium unmoved. The destruction of the enormous battleship and the tremendous loss of life brought him no sadness nor regret. He turned to his second in command and spoke to him in a strange tongue. *Minotaur* was lost; it was useless to them. Let it burn. If they could not have this battleship, then they would just acquire another. One that was not so fragile; one that reflected the majesty of the Imperium; one that would help them to complete the Mission.

Commodore Rissard spoke his understanding of the admiral's request and moved to comply with it. Their short exchange over, Zackaria turned back to the scene of the soon to be concluded battle and continued to watch in silence.

"May... M...day!" Chalmers' weak comms crackled as *Minotaur's* final fleeting requests broadcast out to the overwhelmed Imperial forces. Though his fighter's screens were still flashing their suggested course of action, Chalmers knew there was no point in ejecting; he was dead already. Escape pods could be seen jettisoning themselves from *Minotaur*, their occupants doing nothing but prolonging the inevitable: prisoners would not be taken, lives would not be spared.

For him there was nowhere further to run. Not that running had ever been an option. From this Enemy you could not run and you could not hide. With the acceptance of his death, Chalmers' panic finally subsided. He would soon be at peace with his friends. With that he released his grip on the ejection handle and let the tears trickle down his face.

I

— An Uninvited Guest —

N early six months had passed since Chalmers' death, the fall of Kethlan and the destruction of the *Minotaur*; and on the other side of the known galaxy, Simon Dodds was awoken by the sound of someone, or something, thumping on the porch door of his parents' house. At first he thought that the three loud thuds had been the result of the unlocked front door banging in the wind. Glancing out of his bedroom window, however, he saw the branches of the apple trees standing peaceful and serene in the moonlight of the cloudless night. Ignoring the disturbance, he turned over to catch some more sleep before the inevitable onset of his father's daily routine of dragging him out of bed to help work the fields, or deal with the orchards' tedious administration. Despite the fact that Simon was only staying with his parents for a short time - if one could count six months as short - his father was not about to permit him free food and lodgings without making him pull his weight. Maybe today he could try disappearing into town and hiding out in a bar for a few hours.

He had just shut his eyes again when another two thuds came from below, followed by the unmistakable sound of a man's distressed voice crying out for attention. It was followed by the sound of loud, uneven feet clumping down the porch steps and then scraping up the well worn dirt track leading away from the house.

Now more or less awake, Simon took a look at his bedside clock. The illuminated green numbers informed him that it was just past four thirty; too early for any of the orchard's hired help to be turning up. With great reluctance he threw back the covers and pulled himself out of bed, making his way to the window. His bedroom was located at the front of the house, more or less above the front door. He shoved the window all the way open and leaned out to investigate the source of the noise, which had since ceased.

No sooner had he stuck his head out the window when he spotted a figure sprawled on the ground, halfway up the track. He leaned further out and took a quick look around the surrounding area. Seeing no one aside from the body he drew back inside, turned around and gave a start.

"Who is it?" his father asked him. Gregory Dodds, also awoken by the commotion, had wandered into his son's bedroom. Simon noticed that he clutched a shotgun in one hand, no doubt in preparation for whomever he believed was attempting to break into their property; it wouldn't have been the first time. His father had already activated the weapon, a digital counter towards the rear of the gun gently illuminating the man's chest with a soft blue light.

"There's someone outside," Simon said.

"Where?"

"Halfway up the track, face down in the dirt."

Simon's father shoved past to see for himself and, just as Simon had done, took a quick glance around to see if there was anyone else about. Satisfied that the figure was the only probable source of the disturbance that had woken the family he turned once more to his son.

"We'll go and have a look. I'll have your mother get ready to call the police."

Simon nodded in agreement. "Here," he said, reaching out to take the shotgun from his father.

His father pulled back, pushing Simon's hand away from the weapon and giving him a distrustful look. "You've got to be joking!"

"I'm not going to shoot you in the back, Dad," Simon said. "You've got to start trusting me again."

"Just put some clothes on," Gregory answered, leaving Simon's room.

Simon pulled on the previous day's clothes, that he picked up off a chair, and laced up some boots before joining his father on the upstairs landing. By all appearances his father had made a similar decision with his attire and the pair made their way down the stairs and opened the front door.

The figure in the dirt remained motionless. Leaving his father to guard the front door, Simon hurried up the track and knelt down next to the body.

"Hey," he said, giving the man a gentle shake about the shoulder. The man let out a groan and Simon wondered if he was a drunkard who had staggered up to the house searching for a place to sleep. He then discovered that the unpleasant, sticky wetness he felt on his hand was not vomit or alcohol; it was blood.

"He's hurt!" Simon called to his father, looking at the blood and dirt that clung to his fingers. His father quickened his step, joining his son by the body. Simon became aware of the man's attire and realised that he was wearing a somewhat loose fitting Confederation Stellar Navy flight suit. He rolled the man over on to his back carefully, discovering the front of the suit to be torn and bloody.

"One of your bloody lot," his father muttered, kneeling down.

"Looks like he's been shot," Simon said. Even though it was still before sunrise, he was able to make out the dark patches of blood glistening on the suit. The wounded man's eyes fluttered open and his gaze fell upon the two that knelt over him. He tried to speak, but the effort seemed too great, only a whisper escaping his lips.

"Hey, you okay?" Simon asked, speaking in a loud and clear voice. The man gave him no response, his eyes starting to close again.

"Can you stand?" Gregory asked, but there was no reply. "Let's get him inside the house," he suggested. Simon watched as he trotted back up the worn track to relieve himself of the shotgun, before returning to his side.

"Ready?" Gregory asked.

"Ready."

Simon lifted the man under the arms, his father taking his legs, the pair ignoring the groans from their unexpected guest. They made it back to the house, Simon noticing for the first time the dark red blood stains on the outside of the door where the man had thumped on the white painted wood.

"Oh God!" Simon's mother breathed as they struggled through the door and carried the man into the living room. She had pulled on a thin dressing gown over her night dress. She was a tall woman, with blonde hair and, at this moment, a shocked expression. A cat, that had been enjoying a blissful doze on a chair, lifted its head and then shrank back as it saw the stranger in the men's arms. It jumped down from its resting place and darted out the room, past the three men, the bell on its collar tinkling as it went.

"Sally, shotgun's just inside the porch, could you fetch it inside?"

Gregory said.

"He's been shot," Simon added as he and his father deposited the heavily breathing man on to the couch. Sally did as Gregory requested, bringing the shotgun inside and propping it up against a wall in the hallway, the ammunition counter projecting a blue hue on to a small spot on the wooden floor where it was placed. Sally moaned as she saw where the two men had set the man who had woken them.

"Greg, you're going to get blood all over the couch," she said.

"Well, we can't exactly just dump him on the ground," Gregory said.

Simon noted a couple of splotches of blood on the wooden floor.

"We need to get him comfortable."

"Who is he? Where did he come from?" Sally said.

"He's CSN, Mum," Simon said. "Do you know where the first-aid kit is?"

"Hello? Can you hear me? What's your name?" Gregory was still trying to get a response.

"It's "Dean", Dad, it says so on his suit," Simon said, pointing out the lettering on the left breast beneath the squadron logo. "Mum, first-aid? He's bleeding pretty badly," Simon prompted his mother who was staring at the injured man.

"I'll call an ambulance," Sally said.

"And you can call one of your friends at the Navy straight after," Gregory added to Simon. "There's got to be a number for this sort of thing, right?"

"N... No! Don't!" the stranger named Dean cried out, looking around for who was speaking. The three jumped at his voice.

"You need medical treatment. We have to get you to a hospital or a doctor," Sally said, looking about the living room. "Where's the handset?"

"The handset?" Gregory said.

"For the phone."

"I don't know. It's probably fallen down the back of the couch again. Just use the video screen in the hall."

"No... no doctors! No Navy!" Dean protested, finding strength to talk. "Let... let me stay... here! Please!"

"Hey, calm down," Simon said. "You're in shock."

Dean looked quite distressed as Sally left the living room and walked out of his view, his breathing becoming erratic.

"Where's the first-aid?" Simon asked his father.

"Your mother knows," Gregory answered. "We'll get it after she's called the ambulance."

"Simon," the young man heard his mother call from out in the hall. He left his father with Dean and found his mother floundering in front of the video phone that hung on the wall. "I can't remember how we do this. That's why I wanted to use the handset instead of this stupid thing."

"Just tap the screen anywhere and then press the "Emergency Services" icon," Simon prompted. He positioned himself within the doorway of the living room, so that he could both keep an eye on their guest and jump in to assist his mother should she need it.

Sally tapped the touch-sensitive screen to bring the phone out of its sleep state, the device lighting up and displaying icons and options. She stabbed at the "Emergency Services" icon and hugged at herself as the screen informed her the video phone was connecting. Before long it did so. From his skewed angle of the screen, Simon could just make out the headset wearing blonde woman who answered the call.

"What service do you require?"

"Ambulance," Sally said, then hastened to add, "We've got a man here suffering from gunshot wounds."

"What's his condition?" The woman's fingers tapped away at an unseen device.

"He's bleeding quite heavily. Not sure how many times he was shot, but he can't walk and can barely speak. We had to carry him into the living room from outside the house."

"Are the wounds the result of a projectile or energy weapon?"

"I... er... I don't..."

"Are there any burn marks? If it was an energy weapon then in most cases you'd be able to smell the burnt clothes and wounds."

Sally glanced over to Simon.

"Bullets, Mum," he said.

"Bullets," Sally repeated.

"Okay, thank you," the operator confirmed, maintaining her calm. Simon could see his mother ringing at her dressing grown quite hard.

"Has he been shot in the arms, legs, torso, or head?" the woman wanted to know.

"His body. The chest, it looks like."

The woman at the emergency services tapped away and then paused, looking down at something for a few moments, a curious expression on her face. "Could you hold the line for a minute, please? Thank you." Her image disappeared, to be replaced with the medical services logo.

"Simon, she's just hung up," Sally said.

"Are you sure?"

"It's gone back to this," Sally indicated the logo occupying the display. Simon was about to start over to investigate when the operator who had answered the call re-appeared on the screen.

"Could you confirm your name and address?" she requested. Sally did. "Okay, good. Someone will be with you within the next thirty or forty minutes. Now listen carefully: please don't move the victim since you could cause him additional trauma. The bullets may have missed vital organs, so we don't want to do anything that could result in further injury. The biggest risk to their life will come from loss of blood. If you are able, dress the wounds and try to stem any blood loss. It could make the difference between life and death. Don't move him from the house or attempt to bring him to us yourself." The operator hung up.

Sally swore and came back into the living room.

"What's wrong?" Gregory asked.

"They're not going to be here for another thirty minutes, at least."

"Thirty minutes?" Gregory said, horrified.

"*At least!*"

"We'll have to take him ourselves," Simon said.

"No, they said not to move him, it could make things worse," Sally said, wringing her hands. "We're going to have to do the best we can for him until they get here. I'll find a first-aid kit. Simon can you call the Navy?"

"No, he said not to," Simon said, shaking his head.

His mother stared at him in disbelief for a second. "Simon..."

"No, I can't. He asked us not to contact them. Didn't you hear him?"

"Simon, don't talk to your mother that way," Gregory said, a scowl on his face.

"I'm just following protocol, Dad," Simon answered.

Gregory glared at his son. "Oh, so *now* you decide that it's time to start doing as you're told..."

"I always do as I'm told."

"You could've fooled me..."

"Oh for God's sake, stop it you two, just stop it!" Sally said. "Don't start having *that* conversation again, especially now. I've heard it every day for the last five months."

"I'm just trying to do the right thing," Simon said.

"And why couldn't you have done the right thing *then*?"

"It was an *accident*, Mum. Those people were just there. It's not as if I decided to shoot them all on purpose. I didn't go out of my way to take their lives."

"And now you're just going to let it happen here instead," Sally said, choking back tears and pushing past Simon, leaving the living room and the three men behind her. Simon watched as she walked in the direction of the kitchen and began pulling things out of cupboards in a search for sufficient medical supplies. He began to start after his distressed mother.

"Simon, wait there a moment," his father called. Simon turned back to the scene in the living room, watching his father undoing Dean's flight suit and trying to get a better look at his injuries. The extent of the damage was clear even before the white vest Dean wore beneath the suit was pulled up. Two dark holes were prominent in Dean's chest, blood still seeping out with each breath. Gregory stood and walked over to Simon.

"Why doesn't this guy want us to call an ambulance or the Navy?" Gregory asked.

Simon shrugged. "It's possible that he's involved in some kind of covert operation."

"Covert?" His father screwed up his face. "You mean he's meant to be doing something in secret?"

"Yeah. Or with very little exposure. Whatever it is, he doesn't want certain people within the Navy finding out about it." Simon looked at Dean, who was still taking heavy gasps of air.

"Well what does he expect *us* to do with him?" Gregory asked in somewhat accusing tones. Gregory studied the man for a moment. "Do you know him?"

"No," Simon shook his head. "I've never seen him before in my life. Honest," he added, seeing the unconvinced look his father gave him. They returned to Dean and knelt down next to the couch.

"Looks like he's been shot in the chest and shoulders. You stay here with him. I'll help your mother find some bandages and something to plug up the wounds."

Dean was staring up at the ceiling and breathing hard, struggling to catch his breath. Simon decided to try and discover what had happened whilst he still could.

"Don't worry, mate, everything's going to be okay. You'll just have a few scars to show your friends."

Dean said nothing.

"Confederation Stellar Navy, eh? I'm in the service myself, although it's a little complicated right now."

Just in case you're wondering why a twenty-nine-year-old is still living at home with his mum and dad, Simon thought to himself.

Dean still said nothing, his eyes remaining fixed on the ceiling.

"*Yellow Dogs*?" Simon noted the emblem of a cartoon dog, tongue lolling from its mouth, on the outside of Dean's flight suit. "Not heard of you guys. I usually fly with the *White Knights*."

At Simon's words Dean turned his head to look at the young man, his eyes filled with anguish.

"A... TAF... ject..." he tried, the effort of speaking appearing quite great.

"What?" Simon drew closer. "Say that again." Simon could hear his mother's distressed voice carrying through from the kitchen as she spoke to his father, evidently quite upset by what she had been dragged into.

"... you don't know who's done this to him. They could come around here looking for him," she was saying.

"We didn't see anyone else outside," Gregory said.

"But how did he get here? Did he drive? Where's his car?"

"He's a pilot. Maybe he parachuted?"

"So where was his parachute? Where did his plane or whatever it was come down?"

"I don't know, Sal."

"We don't even know if he is who he says he is. For all we know he could be one of those terrorists from Mitikas. You know how it starts - they come over here one by one and then start blowing each other up."

There was a clatter and then a heavy crash, followed by cursing from his mother.

"That man is going to die unless he gets to a hospital."

Simon forced himself to filter out the rest. He was intent on discovering what had happened to Dean and how he had come to be there. The wounded pilot reached out and placed a limp hand on his shoulder.

"A... T.. AF... operation..." the man tried again.

"You ejected from your TAF?" Simon asked, trying to make sense of what Dean was saying. If he'd ejected from his TAF how did he get all those bullet wounds? Had someone managed to shoot him while he sat in the cockpit? That didn't make any sense. Bullets would have a hard time getting through the toughened canopy, let alone the energy shields surrounding the fighter. "Where did you come down?"

The man started coughing and took another deep breath. "Imperial war... wrong..." was all he could manage.

Simon didn't know what he was talking about. The Imperial civil war was wrong? Of course it was, lots of people had lost their lives in that unending conflict. Dean was making very little sense.

"Right Simon, give me a hand here." Gregory reappeared in the living room, carrying a small red first-aid box and a much larger medical kit. He dumped them both on the floor at the foot of the couch and together the pair did their best to bandage the man, but they both knew that he would die without proper medical attention.

As Simon bandaged the bullet wounds in the man's chest, in a futile attempt to stem the flow of blood, he noticed his mother in the doorway. She was still distressed and he could make out the tears sliding down her face. He was well aware of what she must have been thinking: one day it might be her son in the same position, being patched up by friends, or strangers, as they did their best to prolong his life for what might well prove to be only a few minutes. He smiled back at her, to let her know it would be okay. Following naval protocol or not, he now regretted the way he had spoken to her. Dean could not have been much older than himself, something which had likely compounded her anguish.

The wounded pilot never took his eyes off Simon as he and his father tried to make him comfortable and stable.

"*Sudarberg*," Dean said all of a sudden, still staring at Simon.

"What did he say?" Gregory asked, the two men ceasing their messy bandaging to listen.

"*Sudarberg*?" Simon asked, leaning closer to Dean.

"Y... yes. Stay... a.. aw.. way."

"Where's *Sudarberg*?" Gregory asked.

"I don't know, I've never heard of it. Where's *Sudarberg*? Why should I stay away from it?" Dean didn't answer, but panted, struggling to swallow.

"This guy is going to die unless we can get him to a hospital soon," his father remarked. Simon looked over their attempts to preserve the man's life, their efforts far poorer than what he had originally envisioned. Whilst the medical kits contained a number of dressings, bandages and solutions designed to stimulate rapid coagulation, they were not enough to contend with Dean's kinds of injuries, nor his sustained blood loss. They persevered for a while longer, until Gregory threw in the towel.

"Right, Simon, call your friends at the Navy," Gregory said. "We've been at this for ages now and that ambulance could still take quite a while to get here. The Navy might be able to get here quicker. Whatever this guy is worried about, I'm sure its not worth dying over."

Simon conceded to what his father was saying and, pushing protocol aside, he made the call. He then sat with Dean attempting to get a little more information out of him whilst they waited for help to arrive. But Dean was done talking and less than twenty minutes later he was dead.

"Where exactly did you find him?" A representative of the Naval Investigation Services was asking the Dodds family. It was quite late in the morning and several men and women were carrying out final investigations of the perimeter of the family home. The ambulance that had been called never arrived. Instead, a military medical transport had showed up, a number of heavily armed personnel accompanying the medical team into the house. In addition a large area around the house and orchards had been sealed off, the workers arriving at the orchard being turned away.

"He was lying there, face down on the ground," Gregory said, pointing at the spot where they had found Dean. "How much longer is this going to take? You've been here for bloody hours. I've got pickers and harvesters waiting to get to work."

"I just need to ensure I have all the details down, Mr Dodds," the rep said, tapping away at a hand held device with a stylus. "After you found him, what did you do next?"

"For the love of God, are you deaf?" Simon's father glowered.

"Dad, don't worry, I'll deal with this," Simon said, seeing his father's last thread of patience about to snap. "Go and check that they're not destroying the house." His mother and father departed and Simon turned back to the representative. "We brought him inside and called for an ambulance. The medical services told us it would be over half an hour before they could get to us, so we attempted to patch him up ourselves."

The man nodded. "According to your call records you waited a good twenty-five minutes before placing the call to the nearest military hospital, regarding Lieutenant Commander Dean's condition. Why did you wait so long?" He kept the device in his hand held up. Simon suspected it was recording everything that was being said.

"I considered that he may have been taking part in a classified mission and I needed to be sure I wouldn't be putting the operation or other participants at risk by drawing attention to his presence." Simon stopped short of telling him about Dean's objection to the call for an ambulance or other medical assistance.

The rep, however, seemed satisfied. "Okay, that's fine. I can appreciate that it was a difficult position you found yourself in, but you made the right decision. I believe you're currently in the service of the Confederation Stellar Navy yourself?"

"That's right."

"Could you please state your full name and rank?"

"Second Lieutenant Simon Dodds," Simon said.

The man tapped away at the digital assistant in his hand and waited for it to retrieve the information he was after. "Hmmmm. Says here that you've been a pilot for several years and that you are currently on suspension from active service; reinstatement not due for at least another six to seven weeks, pending the outcome of further hearings." He tapped at the device and then whistled. "Court marshalled back at the beginning of December on two counts of involuntary manslaughter, as well as disobeying orders during…"

"Yeah, yeah, we get the picture," Simon interrupted.

"So, that all correct?"

"Yes," Simon said, trying not to glare.

"May I ask where you've been and what you've been doing for the last four and a half months?"

"I've been working here."

"Doing what, exactly?"

Simon looked around, then back at the man in disdain. "What the hell do you think? I've been picking apples!"

"Cool it, Lieutenant." More tapping. "You've not been anywhere else? Not left the country or the planet?"

"No."

"Fine," the representative said. "Did Dean speak much before his death?"

"Only to tell me that he had ejected from his Tactical Assault Fighter, though I never heard it come down. It's pretty quiet around here, so I'm sure it would have woken me up. He didn't manage to tell me how he got all those bullet wounds either."

"The TAF has been taken care of," the man stated, eyes focused on the digital assistant.

"Where did it come down?" Simon asked, looking around a little confused. He half expected to see a plume of smoke rising from somewhere in the distance. "Not in one of the orchards?" If the TAF had come down, then wouldn't there be some sign of its crash? And come to think of it, where *was* Dean's parachute?

"No, don't worry. There's no need to be concerned about that. Like I said, it's been taken care of." The man raised his eyes from his PDA. "You're sure he didn't say anything else?"

Simon felt as though the man was trying to suggest that he might be trying to hide something. "No."

"Okay. Thank you for your co-operation, Lieutenant. You can let your family know that we will be departing shortly," the man said before powering down the PDA and slipping it back into his jacket. He pressed a button on a device in his ear and spoke to confirm he was finished.

Simon started off to re-join his mother and father, who were hovering by the porch and trying to see inside the house.

"Excuse me, Lieutenant," the NIS representative called out to him, before jogging over to join the three. "Just one thing before we go..."

The three listened as he made one last point clear: no one had come to the house that night and none of them had ever heard of a man by the name of Patrick Dean. Once they understood and agreed with what he was telling them, he then informed them, in rather pleasant tones, that they would have their couch replaced later that day, or early the next. Their living room had also been thoroughly cleaned, leaving no trace of the incident.

"Bloody pain in the arse," Gregory grumbled as he and Simon tried to locate and organise any orchard workers who may have decided to return to work that afternoon, following the Navy's departure. Simon did not comment, the whole experience seeming a little surreal to him at this point. "Let's hope that it'll be another ten years before we see that lot again."

The CSN returned just two weeks later.

II

— An Unwelcome Visitor —

Although the CSN's reappearance at the Dodds household was by no means discreet, the first Simon knew about it was due to the sound of his father cursing at the top of his voice and striding with great displeasure towards the Confederation transport craft that had landed close to the house. It had touched down in one of the orchards belonging to the family, damaging the valuable crop and sending his father into a rage.

Simon had been sitting in the study at the time, pushing a pen around various pieces of paper. At the sound of his father's cursing he left the house, seeing the CSN representative that was making his way up the track; the man removing a white envelope from within his jacket. Simon's father strode past him, caring little for what he had to say and only about what was happening to his field.

"Second Lieutenant Simon Dodds?" the man in full naval dress and sporting a pair of dark glasses asked, as Simon hurried after his father.

"Yeah?" Simon answered, both men now following Gregory down the track in the direction of the transport.

"This request came in from CSN HQ for you today. I should advise you that it is urgent." Simon took the envelope from the man and removed the single piece of folded paper within. Though the letter was brief, the message was clear: it called for his immediate return to duty. His suspension was over, even though he had only served five months of the six he had been handed. Odd. Suspensions often ran far longer, whilst the Confederation Stellar Navy considered reinstatement of personnel. Stranger still was that the request had been made in the form of a personal letter. A video call was far more usual. The Navy's presence at the family home, to hand deliver said letter, further compounded the supposed urgent nature of the request.

"Do I have to leave right now?" Simon asked, lowering the letter.

"No," the man shook his head. "But I'd suggest you be prepared to do so early tomorrow morning."

"Was the request made on behalf of anyone in particular?" Simon said, turning the piece of paper over a few times.

"I believe it was Commodore Parks," the delegate said.

Simon looked again at the letter, trying to extract some more information; trying to read what was not there. As he did so he vaguely heard the messenger telling his father that the family business would be compensated for any untoward damage to his field.

"A CSN inspector and maybe even a government inspector, if need be, will be dispatched to assess the possible damage."

"No, that's not good enough," his father bellowed back at the dark glasses wearing man, who raised both hands in a defensive gesture. "That's an *organic field*! We don't use chemicals, *or* machinery to pick the produce. We do *everything* by hand! And you have gone and contaminated the entire region with your blatant disregard for the honest working man..."

Workers handling various pieces of farming equipment and clutching baskets brimming with apples were looking from their employer to the naval delegate.

"As I said sir, I am sorry for any damage that we may have caused..."

"And yet you are still not shutting off those damn engines!" Gregory said in disbelief, throwing his hands up in the air. The shuttle's engines were burning the grass behind it and Simon could only guess at the long term effects it might have on the crop.

The Dodds family owned several orchards and were proud to be one of the few remaining large scale organic farms remaining in Ireland. Much of the produce was sold to be used in premium organic juices. Others worked their way into stores throughout western Europe. Though rather impressive, Simon had had enough of apples for the time being.

He spent much of the afternoon stuffing clothes into a bag in preparation for his departure early the next morning. His father's voice had drifted up the stairs to his room as he did so; the man expectant of not only a very large cheque from the CSN, but an even bigger apology.

Gregory was still seething over the CSN's visit to his orchard when Simon joined his parents at the table for dinner. The true extent of the damage had become clear once they had departed and it wasn't good. He shot Simon a dark look as he settled into his chair, the young man quite aware that his father was holding him partly responsible for the events of the past couple of weeks.

"You know they only want you to come back and sign something so they can get shot of you," Gregory muttered.

"I doubt that," Simon said, taking a sip of orange juice.

His father tutted. "Well, even if they don't you should give it up anyway; get yourself a proper job."

"You don't have to go, you know. You could just stay here," his mother commented as she deposited three plates of chicken, rice and salad on the table.

"Your mother's right," his father muttered again, not giving Simon a chance to speak. "You should have just worked here instead of joining the Navy. You wouldn't have to worry about promotions, gruelling exercises, crap food or even chances of getting killed. You could be giving out the orders instead of receiving them. Other people would be doing the work. I've been there, Simon. It's not worth it."

Simon paused in the process of cutting into his chicken and set his knife and fork back down on the table. This again. "Dad, you were never in the Navy," he said, rolling his eyes. It was the same thing his father had said to him the day he had told them of his plan to become a pilot in the CSN. He sometimes wished he had a brother or sister, if only to have someone on which to deflect unwanted attention.

His father waved his glass of red wine dismissively, but said nothing.

"And the request is urgent," Simon reminded him, not touching his food until he could gain some sort of support for his decision.

"You'll be back here in a few days," his father said, sipping the wine and reaching for a small granary roll.

In truth, his father was not being negative about Simon's ability, or intentions to continue his career within the Navy; he had just become used to having Simon around for the last few months. Simon had been in the Navy for close to ten years and his mother and father had missed seeing him grow into an adult.

Or at least that's what his mother had told him as she stood at his bedroom door that night, after his father had turned in. At that time a small part of Simon did not want to leave, having become comfortable back at the orchard, with his family close by. But a bigger part of him was set in the decision to return. Even his father's attempt at emotional blackmail could not dissuade him from responding to the CSN's request. Though he could just as well have refused it and then terminated his service, he did not. He owed it to himself to put things right.

Simon made his goodbyes and left first thing the next morning, the transport waiting for him further down the road this time. He had been summoned not to another planet in Sol, but to another star system within the Confederacy know as Indigo.

The interior of the transport was like that of a small private jet, if not quite as luxurious. A small screen, fixed to the left of his seat, displayed their planned route, overlaid across the galactic map he had seen so many time before. A great number of inhabited and uninhabited star systems were dotted all over the chart: the Confederacy, home of Earth, lay on the right hand side, its systems grouped quite closely together; though there were a few stragglers here and there; the Mitikas Empire, on the left, comprised a far greater number of systems, all snuggled together like fish that had been dragged up in a net; and then there were the Independent Worlds, running between the two huge nations like a gulf or a river, keeping them apart and acting like a buffer of sorts. Here and there throughout the declared independent space, star systems were marked as belonging to the Empire from where it had spidered out and captured some during the latter days of its expansion.

His eyes lingered on a few of the systems that were labelled in a larger type than others: Sol and Alpha Centauri within the Confederacy; Alba, one of the more powerful and prosperous of the Independents; Krasst and Kethlan of the Empire, their lettering and stars rendered in red hues. For some reason the colour looked a little ominous, compared with the whites and blues. He turned his mind to other things.

With the knowledge that the system he was travelling to was several hundred light years from Earth, Simon was confident that his reinstatement was assured. It was a long way to bring someone only to tell them that their service within the Navy was no longer required. And surely the only reason they were bringing him all the way out there was because they needed him back as soon as possible?

But during the trip Simon had found himself still arguing against his father's alternate explanation for his summons back to duty: what if he really was going to be discharged? Even though at the end of his hearing five months ago he had been handed a suspension due to "lack of evidence" - the testimonies of four eye witnesses, for some reason, did not count - he was still not one hundred percent sure. It was possible that the committee and top brass needed him to come all the way out there so they could discharge him in the correct manner, being too busy to travel themselves.

Simon had looked out at the stars whilst his transport craft had awaited clearance to jump from Sol to Indigo and thought back upon the events that had led him to where he was in now.

It was whilst flying with his own wing, the *White Knights*, and under the command of Commodore Hawke, a man whom he had failed to see eye to eye with ever since the first time the two had met, that Simon had disobeyed a direct order, with disastrous consequences.

On a tiny Confederation planet, little larger than Sol's own Pluto, a large separatist faction from an Independent World state had secreted themselves. Despite knowing the planet to be home to many planetary explorers and independent research groups, the Confederation had allowed them to do so, intending to strike and bring to an end their repeated acts of aggression once they were all together. When the time had come the Confederation's armed forces had launched a large scale operation with the intention of simultaneously evacuating the explorers and eliminating the enemy. As night had fallen landers had touched down and ground troops and vehicles had streamed out. Large drop ships broke the atmosphere and deployed fighter craft, Simon and the *White Knights* amongst them.

Though it had started well the operation ran into difficulty when reinforcement enemy fighters had arrived in the conflict zone without warning. Following their appearance Hawke had ordered the air support to pull back. He was concerned that the additional aerial combat would have a detrimental effect on the success of the mission, endangering the ground teams as the risk of friendly fire to and from the surface increased.

As the squadrons pulled back, Simon had witnessed two of his wingmates being brought down and, frustrated with the way things were going, had looped back around to try and prevent further losses. His efforts had resulted in his own fighter sustaining heavy damage and dropping from the sky. He had ditched not far from a rescue point. In the confusion - and with the desire to get back from the advancing enemy lines as quick as possible - Simon had retrieved a weapon from a downed soldier and headed back towards the extraction zone.

Along the way he had been surprised by a group of men and women who had run into him. His own survival instinct had kicked in, causing him to open fire. It was only after blood had splattered the ground, soaking into the dark sand, colouring small rocks and pebbles, and covering the bodies of his victims and the hands of those that were trying to help them that he realised who he was shooting at.

For the unlawful killings of Poppy Castro and Stefan Pitt, the blatant disregard for orders, and the loss of a Tactical Assault Fighter he could have flown home, the court marshal had suspended him from duty for six months. He had returned to Earth, tail between his legs, to stay out the time with his parents and get away from everything.

The whole experience was one that he never wished to go through again.

After several hours his transport arrived in the Indigo system and not long there after docked at Xalan Orbital Station where he was to meet with the senior command.

Time to be known as Dodds again, Simon thought as he picked up his belongings. An attendant met him as he exited the transport and led him from the landing deck to a lift and, from there, down the various corridors to his appointment. The escort rushed him along, giving Dodds no time, or place, to stow his bag.

"Second Lieutenant Simon Dodds to see the Admiral," Dodds' escort informed one of the two female security guards standing outside the meeting room. She communicated the message to another standing within. The door was opened.

"Fleet Admiral Turner is waiting for you inside," the woman said, gesturing for him to go forward.

"Admiral Turner?" Dodds repeated, feeling his mouth go dry.

"Yes, sir. Fleet Admiral Turner."

They didn't bother to put that *into the letter,* Dodds thought, before realising his jaw had become slack and that his mouth was hanging open. He shut it and cleared his throat. "Thank you," he said and entered the meeting room.

Walking up to the front he set his bag down, removed his cap, and saluted the three men seated behind a long, well polished wooden table.

"Second Lieutenant Simon Dodds reporting as requested, sir," Dodds presented himself. He stood before the three men in full naval dress: a pair of dark blue trousers and blazer with gold trims and buttons. On his feet he wore a pair of well polished black shoes, which he had become quite conscious of in the last couple of minutes, for some reason. Perhaps it was because of the clamorous clopping they made as he walked, announcing his arrival much more than he would have liked.

There was no answer from any of the men behind the table. The admiral, seated in the middle, continued his unhurried leaf through a number of pieces of paper in front of him, apparently deciding to make him wait on purpose.

Simon recognised all three of the men in front of him: Commodore Parks and Commodore Hawke sat either side of Turner, both waiting patiently for the admiral to begin. Behind the desk, a window that made up the entire back wall permitted Dodds a view of the twinkling stars outside. He forced himself not to be distracted by the sight. Aside from the four men only two others occupied the room, both armed security personnel by the closed door at the other end, rifles drawn and pointed down.

He waited some more. Turner continued to turn pages. Dodds started to get the impression that what was about to be discussed was quite confidential. After some time Turner looked up from his reading, gathering together the papers.

"Before we begin, Lieutenant Dodds, I have a question I want to ask you." The admiral clasped his hands together on the desk before him.

"Yes, sir," Dodds said.

"Tell me: what does the name "Lieutenant Commander Patrick Dean" mean to you?"

"He's a TAF pilot, sir. Flies with the *Yellow Dogs*. He was recently injured in the line of duty," Dodds said truthfully.

"Wrong answer, Dodds," Turner said with false patience. "I'll ask you that again. Who is Lieutenant Commander Patrick Dean?"

Dodds noticed that all three of the men were staring fixated at him and he became thankful for the cap that he held by his side, his grip tightening on it. He grasped the direction that the admiral's question was leading him and, remembering what he had been told the morning of Dean's death, supplied his next answer.

"I don't know, sir. I've never heard of him."

"Excellent. Neither have I," Turner said, sitting back up straight. The man appeared satisfied with the point he was making, it now very clear in Dodds' mind. "Shall we get this under way then?" the admiral asked of the two other officers before turning back to Dodds.

"There are three reasons why you have been brought out here today, Lieutenant," began Turner. "None of which should be allowed to go to your head. First and foremost: it is after considerable discussion that we have decided that your suspension from duty has been met. You should have had sufficient time during this period to reflect upon your actions and realise just how serious and costly your mistakes were."

"Yes, sir," Dodds said, straightening. "During my suspension I spent a lot of time..."

"Secondly," Turner continued, raising his voice whilst at the same time telling Dodds to silence his own, "Naval human resources are at an all time low and we need every man and woman we can get a hold of. You may be aware of the on-going problems we are facing securing Confederation interests against increasing insurgency, as well as the not so insubstantial threat posed by the Imperial civil war. The war is now causing unrest in a number of Independent World star systems; unrest and disturbance that could eventually spill over into Confederation controlled space. Should that happen we can be assured that immigrants will come pouring into many of our own systems, bringing refugees, criminals, bounty hunters and even more insurgents along with them. In order to pre-empt such an event we need to increase naval presence along our borders."

Dodds saw the map he had studied for the last few hours once more in his head, focusing in on the former Independent worlds that had been swallowed up by the Empire. He could not quite imagine the same thing happening in reverse to the Confederacy, as Turner might well be suggesting. He might not know a great deal about the history of the galaxy, but he assumed that the Confederation was a little more stable than most other places; considerably more so than some of the Independents.

The image evaporated as Turner continued speaking. "This is a point that needs to be understood by all Naval personnel: the relationship between the Imperial Senate and the Emperor is now strained beyond repair and as such the Confederacy, as well as number of Independent nations, have begun the recall of all diplomatic staff. You may hear talk of parts of the Empire having been *bombed back into the stone age*, but for now the Confederation will *not* be sending forces into any part of the region in an attempt to bring about stability."

Dodds had heard about the issues that were plaguing the Empire, the events now a regular feature on news broadcasts. The trouble was that, since it had become such a regular feature of the news, he had almost stopped paying attention to it altogether. It was like background noise to him.

His eyes swept over Parks and Hawke sitting either side of Turner. Each both looked straight at him, as Turner did, their faces inexpressive. They were both in their forties and of similar height, although Parks looked thinner than Hawke, both in the body and face. Strands of silvery grey hair were quite prominent throughout Parks' thinning black hair, but absent from Hawke's. Turner by contrast was quite an old man. Dodds thought he was somewhere in his early sixties, close to retirement age.

Dodds had noticed when he entered the room that Parks seemed to have aged a good ten years since he had last seen the man, looking older than Hawke, despite being six or seven years younger. Strangely Hawke appeared much healthier by comparison. Fresh faced, the man was almost glowing.

"And finally Lieutenant it is my privilege to inform you -"

Dodds detected a hint of sarcasm in the admiral's voice.

"- that you have been recommended and subsequently selected for participation in the Navy's latest technological endeavour. It is not a decision that I entirely agree with -"

Parks turned his head only a minute amount to acknowledge the accusing look he was given by Admiral Turner.

"- but your flight profile along with your *usual* ability to work well within a team made you fit the bill."

"Thank you, sir," Dodds said. "It will be an honour to take part."

Turner gave an unconvinced snort, then said, "Tell me, Lieutenant, has anyone discussed with you anything about the ATAF project?"

"No, sir. No one has ever mentioned it to me."

"As it should be," Turner said. "The project is strictly on a need-to-know basis and, as of this moment, you are not to discuss it with anyone not directly involved in the evaluations. I must warn you that to do so would result in a punishment far worse than a mere suspension from service. Am I making myself clear?"

"Yes, sir."

"Good. I believe that is all I wish to say," Turner concluded, sliding the papers in front of him back into their folder. "I did not intend for this to be a long meeting, so I will wrap things up here. Unless there is anything further that you wish to add, Commodore?" He looked to Parks who shook his head. "Commodore?" His attention turned to Hawke.

"I must once again reiterate my objection to this man's reinstatement into active service, Admiral!" Hawke spat. "The man is a cocky, arrogant insubordinate who is a danger to himself, his squadron and the Navy's very reputation."

Dodds gave an inward sigh. It felt as though the commodore had spent several hours before the meeting rehearsing the line, so as to deliver it without error for maximum effect. The moment Dodds had entered the meeting room and seen Hawke seated alongside Turner and Parks he knew there would be problems.

"I do not doubt for even one second that he will continue to mock the chain of command within weeks of being back in control of a starfighter,"

Hawke went on, glaring at Dodds. "It would be better for all of us if the man were reassigned to logistics where he..."

"Yes, that will do, Commodore, I am fully aware of your objections," interrupted the admiral, waving him down. "Thank you for repeating your original statement, but I read it clearly the first time."

Hawke turned back to look at Dodds, a dark scowl across his face. "No, I have nothing further to add, Admiral," he finished dryly.

Dodds felt a small sense of relief swell within him. How Hawke loved to gloat. Should Turner have agreed with the man's suggestion, Hawke's eyes would have been filled with that subtle, malicious satisfaction; the very same pleasure that Dodds had seen register during his court marshal, the moment the guilty verdict had been brought against him. But not now. He had been denied such delight today and would have to find it another time, in another place. And preferably with someone else.

Dodds' eyes were drawn to a crimson-red substance that was gathering just above the commodore's top lip and noticed that Hawke's nose had started to bleed. Hawke too became aware of the flow and rummaged around in a pocket for a handkerchief, producing it just as a drop of blood slid down from his nose and splattered without a sound on to the table in front of him.

Dodds watched the man place the handkerchief under his nose and tip his head back, attempting to control the flow, though Hawke kept his eyes on him as he did so. It was not as though his nose was gushing, but it was obvious it was more than a few drops. Dodds found it strange that, though Parks and Turner looked over to the man to see what the cause of his sudden discomfort was, they gave it no more than a common courtesy before they turned back to the starfighter pilot stood before them.

"Good. We must press on gentlemen, time is not a commodity we can currently afford to waste," Turner said. "Lieutenant Dodds, I am hereby returning you to duty. Commodore Parks will brief you shortly." He gestured to one of the guards standing by the door who strode forward to Dodds' side. "Mr Sears here will escort you to a suitable waiting room where the commodore will meet you. You are dismissed, Lieutenant."

"Thank you, sir," Dodds said, saluting before replacing his cap, picking up his bag of meagre belongings and making to leave.

"Lieutenant Dodds," the admiral's voice called to him as he crossed the room.

"Sir?" Dodds stopped halfway to the door and turned around to face the table again.

"With regard to the statement that Commodore Hawke gave: whilst the Navy does indeed need every good pilot it can get I will have absolutely no qualms whatsoever with immediately dismissing from service any pilot whose actions put the lives of others at risk; or whose reckless actions result in critical mission failures, directly or indirectly. Do not let your selection into the ATAF project and the early end to your suspension make you believe you are invincible, Lieutenant. The day you do a good job I will be the one to let you know. Do you understand that?"

"Yes, sir. Fully, sir," Dodds said, saluted once more and left the meeting room.

III

— Reunion —

D odds jumped to his feet as he heard the door of his assigned waiting room open, almost spilling the glass of water he held. He stood to attention and saluted Parks as the man entered.

"At ease, Lieutenant," Parks said. "Welcome back, Dodds; and welcome to the Indigo system, I might add."

The room the pair stood in granted its occupants an appreciative view of the planet below them, something that Dodds had spent the last half hour staring out at. He often made a habit of looking out at the stars, sometimes just for the view, but frequently because it helped him to think. He found the often tranquil views to be rather therapeutic.

"I trust you had a good journey here?" Parks said.

"Uneventful," Dodds shrugged.

"You stayed out your entire suspension on Earth?"

"With my parents. I was giving them a hand with the business."

Parks nodded and his eyes gave the young man a once over. "Good to see you didn't come back soft and completely out of shape after all that time away. Too many do so after a few weeks of leave." Parks came to stand with Dodds by the window and nodded to the planet far below. "Xalan. Where you will be spending the next three weeks training for the ATAF project. Myself and Admiral Turner will also be stationed there during that period to oversee your progress."

"Who else will be there?" Dodds asked, figuring that he would not be the sole participant in the training program. He had a hunch that his old wingmates were on the surface.

"Aside from yourself and the *White Knights*, there will be two other teams of five who you will be undergoing the evaluations. At the end of the three-week period the team who has successfully completed the evaluation, and passed the final examination, will be the one that will go on to pilot the ATAFs."

"Got it," said Dodds. Sounded easy enough.

Parks paused, then said, "This isn't an individual exercise, Lieutenant. Your success or failure during these tests will be governed by your ability to work as a team *and follow orders.*"

Dodds could feel Parks' stare boring into him even before he turned around to meet it.

"Don't screw this up, Dodds," Parks said in a stern voice, his mood now a lot more serious than when he had first entered the room.

"I won't, sir," said earnestly. Though Dodds enjoyed a good relationship with Parks - or maybe it was that the commodore just tolerated him better than most others - he was still only prepared to cut the young pilot so much slack.

"I sure hope you mean that, Lieutenant," Parks said, walking towards the door. "Now, whilst you're here you may as well attend a medical examination before leaving for Xalan. Your team mates arrived a few days ago so they will be able to show you around. You should also know that since your departure we've lost Wells to an accident during training, as well as your own replacement. de Winter will introduce you to your new team mate when you arrive at your assigned housing block." The door slid open as Parks approached. He hovered in the doorway, looking back at the second lieutenant who hadn't moved. "Come on. Get your gear together, Dodds, we have a lot to get through before we leave."

Dodds picked up his bag and followed the commodore out, his head swimming with thoughts. It seemed a lot had happened since he had been away and the multiple deaths within his flight group had hit home. Not least because of the casual manner in which Parks had told him about it, as if there were greater concerns than keeping pilots alive. He wondered what other pieces of information the commodore might be holding back.

● ● ●

Wednesday, April 23rd, 2617

We've been stationed here at Xalan for three days now and I'm beginning to feel more settled. There hasn't been a lot happening so far, but Estelle is making us hit the simulators for hours on end. She's really cracking the whip, but I know this is a big thing for her. She had us on them for sixteen hours yesterday, first thing in the morning until last thing at night, with barely any time for lunch. I had to just get in there, shovel it down my throat and get back into the simulator suite. I thought Estelle was going to choke at the speed she wolfed hers down! She was acting like she hadn't eaten for weeks and like she didn't know where her next meal was coming from! She did the same thing at dinner too! I'm sure that's not healthy. But there again something like this is a once in a life-time opportunity and she's determined to do whatever it takes for us to be the first to test out the Navy's latest creation. I can't say exactly what it is here or suffer the consequences.

We are getting our first briefing this afternoon and then tomorrow we'll start our formal training. I don't know any of the pilots from the others teams, but Estelle seems to know a girl called Andrea. According to her we were at flight school together years ago, but I don't honestly remember. I haven't seen her about since our arrival, but apparently that's intentional since they don't want the teams to all be mixed together.

We're in a mixed dormitory here, no separate rooms, so looks like we won't be getting any ritzy treatment even though we're involved in a special project. Luckily the room has been designed to accommodate quite a few people, and since there are only four of us we have plenty of space; so at least that won't be a cause of any tension.

Enrique is just getting on with it, as he does. With everything that's going on, he's not really found the find time and space to practice his martial arts or the other things he does. He was a bit put out that there might not be anyone to partner with whilst he was here. Being a research facility there are of course some people here, but I think Enrique was bothered about "hitting nerds" as he put it.

Chaz, the new boy (he's actually a bit older than us, only known him a few weeks), said he'd spar with Enrique when they both got some free time, but Estelle soon put a stop to that. Think she's getting paranoid that one of them would hurt each other and then not be able to compete efficiently.

I'm still not too sure about Chaz. When he first turned up he introduced himself and dispensed all the normal pleasantries, but wasn't too keen on giving anything else away. He keeps his cards very close to his chest. As far as I can tell it was Commodore Parks' idea to assign him to our team. We, of course, didn't get any say in the matter and Estelle was quite concerned. But during the routine flight exercises before our transfer here he seemed to be a good fit. He's quiet though and seems to spend a lot of his time reading. He doesn't smile a lot either. I don't honestly imagine I'd have too much to do with him if he had not been assigned to the White Knights. He seems to be somewh...

As Dodds entered the room he saw Kelly Taylor stop writing in her digital journal, and look up.

"Dodds!" Kelly said. Dodds had changed out of his uniform for the medical examination. He now wore a blue naval shirt and dark slacks. The smart uniform that his mother had pressed and ironed in preparation for his meeting with the three of the CSN's top brass now lay crumpled somewhere at the bottom of his bag. He had worn it twice in the space of six months, for the purpose of formal meetings, and was not keen on putting back on again any time soon.

"Hi, everyone," Dodds said, slinging his bag on to a nearby bed.

"Hey, Dodds!" A tall, sandy blonde haired man over the other side of the room got up and strode over to greet his friend. Dodds noticed when he entered the dormitory that Enrique had been propped up against the back wall doing press ups on his head. He was dressed down in a white vest and thin trousers and Dodds guessed that he was doing the exercises to let off some steam. Another man, whom Dodds did not recognise, lowered the book he was reading to get a look at the long absent team member.

"Hey, Enrique, how you doing?" Dodds said, extending a hand.

"They said we should expect one more person to join the team, but I didn't expect to see your ugly face around here any time soon," Enrique said with a chuckle, greeting his friend with a shake of hands, an embrace and a hearty slap on the back. "Made it back okay then?"

"Just," Dodds smiled. "I think I would have been on the next shuttle to Earth if Hawke had had his way. Hadn't been back hardly five minutes before he was on my back."

"Don't let him wind you up, mate," Enrique said. He too had suffered his fair share of encounters with the commodore in the past, though in most cases on account of Dodds, one way or another. If Hawke possessed a list of personnel in the CSN that he most disliked, the pair could be certain that they would be tied for the top spot.

"Hey, how you doing, Kelly?" Dodds asked of the young woman who was untangling her legs and crawling off the bed she occupied. Kelly Taylor was a girl of average height, with a short face, long brown hair and brown eyes. Dodds often found her quite cute.

"I'm well, thanks," Kelly said embracing him and giving him an affectionate kiss on the cheek. "Nice to have you back."

If things had changed a lot within the Navy during Dodds' absence, then at least he could take comfort in the fact that his friends had remained the same; although the team had shrunk from its initial ten members down to five, and there was now a new addition.

"Where's Estelle?" Dodds asked.

"She'll be back in a minute. Think she went to check the simulation stats or something," Kelly said, rolling her eyes.

"Oh, this is Chaz, the latest additional to the *White Knights*," Enrique indicated the dark skinned man who still lay on his bed at the far end of the room, reading. After briefly acknowledging the appearance of Dodds he had turned his attention back to his book, looking quite uninterested in what was going on. Now, he put the book down and jumped from the top bunk. Dodds saw that Chaz was not only very tall, but built with it. He also appeared to prefer to shave his head.

"Pleased to finally meet you, Dodds," he said, joining the others. "My name's Koonan; Chaz Koonan. Only been with the team for a few weeks, but I've heard a lot about you."

"Nothing good, I hope," Dodds replied with a wry smile, shaking the massive hand that Chaz extended towards him.

"Estelle assures me that you're a fine pilot," Chaz said, dodging Dodds' attempt to engage him in some comedic banter. There was something in the man's voice that Dodds could not put his finger on. It was not unfriendly, but somehow neutral and a little indifferent.

"Where have you been transferred from?" Dodds asked.

"That's a long story..."

"Yes, and not one we currently have time for," a voice came from the doorway. A slender woman with long, jet black hair that fell over her shoulders stood at the entrance to the dormitory. Her attire was a close match to that of Enrique's, a small white vest and black trousers. In her hands she clasped a number of sheets of paper.

"Hi, Estelle. How are you?" Dodds said.

"I'm well," she answered, somewhat pertly.

"Good..."

"Uh huh. Could I have a word with you out here?" she indicated out the door and then left the dormitory. Dodds looked at the others, who shrugged and then dispersed back to what they were doing before he arrived. Frowning, Dodds followed Estelle out of the small housing block they had been assigned to, incensed at the way she had spoken to him within the first minute of being reunited.

"Hey..." Dodds called after her, stepping out into the warm morning sun. Estelle turned around to meet his confused expression, her own a picture of happiness. She walked back to him and put her arms around the man, giving him a tight hug.

"I've missed you," she said. "I didn't think you were ever going to come back."

Dodds didn't know what to do, though a few moments later he hugged her back.

"After you were suspended from duty I figured you'd give it a couple of months and then hang up your boots. You've not been in touch at all." Estelle broke their embrace, looking up into his face with a warm genuine smile, her dimples showing up as she did so.

Dodds said nothing.

"Did you miss me?"

"Well... sure I did."

"So why haven't you been in touch?" She swept some of the hair that had fallen over her face out of the way.

"I needed time to think. I just wanted to get a clear perspective on my life. What was all that about?" Dodds asked her, referring to the way she had yanked him away from the others whilst they were in the process of catching up.

"Sorry," Estelle said. "Right now I want everyone to stay focused on what we're doing here, not caught up in emotional reunions that could have a negative effect on our progress and training. But it is good to see you," she added as Dodds pulled a face. Estelle had a tendency to put her career before her friends, something that appeared to not have waned at all during his absence.

"Let's walk," Estelle said. "I'll show you around and bring you up to speed." The pair started down the brick path that led to their housing block, the walkway splitting and snaking its away all about the research campus to other buildings and areas contained within.

"Good to be back?" Estelle asked.

"It is, actually," Dodds said with a bit of a sigh. "I spent five months on Earth with my parents, picking apples."

"How's the business?"

"Steady. They think they'll have a good harvest this year," Dodds stopped short of telling Estelle about how his parents had suggested he consider a career change to work their fields instead of returning to the Navy.

They made their way down a set of wide stone steps, leading down to the lower areas of the campus and towards the main research buildings. The vast majority of the construction was made up of tall glass buildings. Small trees and lamp posts lined the paths they walked, complimented by grass.

Men and women dressed in everything from suits to casual entire and white lab coats walked past them, chatting to one another, drinking from polystyrene cups and going about their business.

"How's it going here?" Dodds asked. Parks had not been too forthcoming with details, only to let him know of the briefing that afternoon and the start of the program the following day.

"A little better than I expected, although there's still room for improvement," Estelle said as she leafed through the sheets of paper she was carrying. Dodds saw that the pages were packed full of graphs, pie charts and other statistical information, each headed with a different pilot's name. He noticed she had already attacked them with a red pen, circling various numbers and writing scruffy and hurried notes. "We've only been here for a few days, but the training starts first thing tomorrow morning. You'll have to get into a simulator for the rest of the day to get back up to speed."

Dodds frowned. "I'm not sure I'll be as bad as all that."

"No, Dodds, you will be," Estelle said. "There was a guy a few years back who broke both his legs. When he eventually got back into the seat it took him weeks to get used to it again. It's not like riding a bike."

Dodds wasn't so sure. He had doubts that his time out of the cockpit, and away from the stick, would have impacted his flying standard as much as Estelle was suggesting.

"What did you think when they picked us to come here?" Dodds asked, changing the subject.

Estelle gave a small chuckle. "When they first told us that we were being transferred I was worried we were going to get posted to border patrol duty."

"That wouldn't exactly have been much fun."

"Yeah. I couldn't think of anything worse. They've been shifting people over to the Temper system a lot lately. When did you actually get back?"

"Just this morning. I received a request from Commodore Parks to return to duty yesterday."

"That was quick," Estelle said, "You must have been pretty keen to get back here."

Dodds started to saying something, then stopped walking.

Estelle studied him for a moment as he looked about. "What?"

Dodds sighed, then shook his head. "But I had to, didn't I? I have to make amends."

"Hmmmmm," Estelle scowled for a moment.

"I'm being serious, Estelle. Hardly a day goes by where I don't think about what happened."

Estelle said nothing, but looked about the campus. She soon turned back to him, now appearing a little sympathetic. "How do you plan to do it?"

"I don't know," Dodds shook his head again. "I'll find a way."

"Well, if you ask me you could try just following orders."

So I keep being told, Dodds thought.

Estelle said nothing more on the subject and the pair continued walking.

They both knew that, whilst he was a good pilot, Dodds had a tendency to be reckless, and it was that recklessness which from time to time led to undesirable consequences.

Estelle began to point out some of the buildings on the campus: the housing blocks for the on site staff; a number of research buildings that they were not authorised to enter; a large lecture theatre, where they would attend the ATAF presentation; and a few large, square buildings that housed the simulators.

"Anything interesting happen whilst I've been away?" Dodds asked.

Estelle chuckled. "You mean aside from what happened to *Dragon*?"

"What happened to it?"

Estelle stopped walking. "You mean no one's told you?"

Dodds' initial belief that Estelle was about to regale him with some useless trivia about the enormous battleship was quashed by the look on the woman's face. "Told me what?"

"It's been stolen! It hasn't been seen or heard from for months!"

"*Dragon*? The battleship?" he looked at her sceptically for a moment. "You're being serious, aren't you?"

Estelle nodded. "Didn't Parks tell you?"

"He seemed... distracted," Dodds said, remembering how, after the two had departed the waiting room, Parks had seemed eager to return to other business, saying very little. "He didn't speak to me about anything other than getting through my medical and getting me down here. What happened?"

"It disappeared a few weeks after your court mar... after you left," Estelle said. Dodds noted how she doubled back and skirted around the touchy subject of his court martial. Though she had not been on trial herself, he knew the many hours sitting in the court room delivering evidence and being cross examined was not an experience she had relished, wanted reminding of, or ever wanted to go through again.

"It just disappeared?" Dodds said. "That ship's not exactly small or defenceless. Did someone just take it out of dry dock?"

"It happened in Independent space, near the Independent-Imperial border. From what I've heard it was a hijacking."

"What the hell was it doing all the way out there?" Dodds asked.

"No one knows. Seems that information is classified," Estelle said.

They came to a tall, circular fountain, water spraying out of the top. Estelle and Dodds joined a few people sat around it, enjoying a mid-morning break from their work, reading and chatting to one another. The two CSN pilots made sure they put a good amount of space either side of them so they could talk with a little more privacy.

"How do they know *Dragon* was hijacked and nothing else happened to it? Were there any witnesses or survivors?" Dodds asked.

"Only one: Commodore Hawke. He was captain at the time. And *no*, Dodds, he wasn't involved," Estelle put in, as Dodds roll his eyes at the mention of the man's name. "They found him drifting through Confederation space in an escape pod a week after they lost contact with the ship. The pod didn't have any food, water or medical supplies, and the stasis capsules had been smashed up. Hawke himself had been badly wounded and suffering from blood loss. He was lucky to be alive."

"No one else survived?" Dodds asked, mystified. Though he had never laid eyes on the vessel himself, having only seen it in archive footage and photographs, he knew enough about the Confederation Solar Navy's flagship to know that the event of its theft was quite worrisome. *Dragon* was the largest and most powerful starship in existence, second to none. Owing to its size, fire power, starfighter and troop capacities, its mere arrival within a battle zone had been known to cause the opposing forces to make a hasty retreat or even surrender. Attempting to fight it was usually never worthwhile. It was so heavily armoured and shielded that the best defence against it was to be nowhere near it. If a battle was unavoidable, other capital ships, such as frigates and carriers, stood a much better chance of survival due to their own increased capabilities, though it would still be a somewhat one-sided battle. Dodds knew of only one other ship that stood a chance of taking on *Dragon*: *Minotaur*, flagship of the Imperial Naval Forces.

"No, there weren't any other survivors, he was the only one," Estelle said, keeping her voice low.

"Did Hawke tell anyone what happened?"

"He says he can't remember much before waking up in the escape pod. He recalls a large boarding party appearing out of nowhere and storming all the major divisions simultaneously. *Dragon* was operating with a full complement, but they were completely overcome. Hawke believes they were in jump space at the time, so no one is sure just how accurate his story is."

"They were in *jump*? No, that's... well, it's not impossible, but it's extremely dangerous. They could have stranded both themselves and *Dragon* in the middle of nowhere."

Estelle nodded. "I find some of it hard to believe."

"You're not the only one. Exactly how did they get aboard in the first place? Who were these people?" They spoke for a while, discussing the possibilities, none of which Estelle had not already considered herself. They concluded that it may have been a faction from the Imperial civil war, though given *Dragon*'s almost legendary status throughout the galaxy, even that seemed rather far fetched.

After some time Estelle suggested to Dodds that they should leave the fountain. They started walking along the brick pathways, Dodds noting the sizeable wall that ran the entire perimeter of the campus, effectively shutting it off from the outside world. Though he had only been at the research centre a little under an hour, Dodds had counted no less than ten pairs of armed personnel patrolling the grounds. The young pilot said nothing as they continued to walk, still trying to put together the pieces of a large and complicated puzzle.

"Would have made your day if Commodore Hawke hadn't returned either, wouldn't it?" Estelle commented.

"You can't say you're very fond of the man yourself," Dodds replied. Estelle had had her own brushes with Hawke, either as a result of her own actions or because of those under her command. Owing to her nature she was much more adept at handling such meetings, although those methods quite often came under many variations of "Yes, sir!", "No, sir!", "Sorry, sir!", and "It won't happen again, sir!".

"I find it's best to try and stay on the right side of him," Estelle said.

"Which side would that be?" Dodds enquired.

"Just follow the chain of command, Dodds." Estelle's voice was close to taking on a tired and irritable tone. "And please; don't either you or Enrique start leading each other astray. This is a fantastic opportunity we've been granted and we should all act like true professionals."

Dodds decided it was time to let the topic lie. "So, what's the new guy like?"

"Chaz?"

"Yeah. I spoke to him before you arrived. He seems a little... distant?"

"He's very quiet," Estelle mused. Dodds got the impression she was still trying to figure the man out for herself. "He's a good pilot, not as good as you or Kelly, but he still gels well with the team. He used to fly with a group called the *Copper Beetles*. His team have been shuffled around. They assigned him to the *Knights* and the others were transferred to Earth."

"Guess I'll get to know him better during the training then," Dodds remarked.

Estelle shook her head. "Wouldn't bet on it. He's been with us for three weeks and that's all I've managed to get out of him. He's nice though, if a bit grumpy. Likes to read too."

The pair had walked a fair way and Estelle suggested they head back. Dodds asked Estelle what she knew about the ATAF project, but it seemed that her knowledge on the subject was as good as his.

Returning to the dormitory they found that Enrique, Kelly and Chaz were back in their original places. The accommodation of the campus was better than Dodds was used to: the dormitory was bright and spacious and, from the looks of things, sported much cleaner and improved washing facilities. He grabbed his bag from the bed and began to sort through is belonging, pulling things out and dumping them onto the mattress.

Estelle cleared her throat in an authoritative manner. She shuffled through the papers in her hands and then addressed the group as a whole,

"Okay everyone, listen up. We've still got a lot to do before tomorrow morning. The simulator results are extremely positive and we're all doing much better than we were yesterday on the advanced courses, but there's still room for improvement. We can get times down, minimise ally and ammunition losses... Kelly, could you stop writing for just one second until I have finished speaking, please?"

Kelly put down her digital journal, pushing it down the bed and out of reach for good measure, before giving the first lieutenant her undivided attention. Dodds feigned an irritation around his eye, looking away from his team mates as he saw Estelle's domineering side starting to creep in.

Although Estelle liked to treat those in her command as friends, she was never afraid to pull rank to get the point across. Things had not changed much with her over the past five months either then.

"After lunch and the presentation, I want us to go back over simulation courses A4, A9, A15 and A19..." Estelle continued.

Enrique groaned and looked to the windows, at the warm afternoon sun that was streaming on through.

"We're not here on vacation, Enrique," Estelle snapped at the man. "In fact, Dodds, you need to get on those sims ASAP to work out the rust. Enrique will go with you and give you a hand setting up."

Enrique stifled another groan and pulled himself to his feet. "Come on, man, let's go," he indicated to Dodds as he walked over to join him. Estelle flourished a red pen.

"I've not been over everything," she said, tapping the papers. "But I'm sure after I'm done with these we'll be able to..."

"I'll go too," Chaz announced, swinging his legs off his bunk and jumping down. "I've never flown with Dodds before, so the sooner I see what he can do the better we can exploit our strength and cover our weaknesses."

Estelle held a bemused look as the big man hurried towards Dodds.

"Yeah, good point," Kelly said. "I think that having more familiar wingmates will help Dodds to get back up to speed much sooner than... uh... unfamiliar ones." She hopped off her bed, and squeezed herself between Enrique and Chaz to get to Dodds, taking one of the man's arms and herding him out the quarters. "No time to waste, now!"

Behind them, Enrique and Chaz hurried along and the four bustled out the dormitory, past Estelle who watched them go with a flabbergasted expression on her face.

"I'll meet you in the simulation suite just before lunch," Estelle called after them as they disappeared down the corridor towards the exit of the housing block.

"No, don't worry, we'll meet you in the refectory," Kelly called back without turning around. "That was a close one," she said in a low voice.

"Yeah, tell me about," Enrique said, then turned to Dodds. "Seriously, mate, I can't believe she used to be your girlfriend."

IV

— May the Best Man Win —

The simulator suite to which Dodds was escorted was contained within a large square glass building, its central expansive floor home to a large number of the systems. Each simulator itself was self contained, to guard against any visual distractions. The interior of each was an exact replica of the designated craft, with readouts and consoles all working as expected.

For the most part the shiny white suite floor was devoid of anything except for the modules, whilst a high gallery of observation rooms and offices ran around the perimeter. Staff milled around inside, performing various tasks. After explaining their requirements to a staff member, Enrique and Dodds made their way over to a TAF module.

Dodds sat down in the seat and buckled himself in, the screens inside powering up to display a convincing astral scene all around him. The HUD activated and control consoles lit up as they prepared themselves. A sense of familiarity came back to Dodds. He reached forward and expertly configured the fighter's HUD to the way he preferred, before informing the simulation operator that he was ready to begin.

To his dismay Dodds found that he was, just as Estelle had predicted, somewhat rusty on the simulator. The months away from duty had led to him forgetting some of the more intricate principles of space flight and combat, and he found himself stalling from time to time. But he focused and an hour later he well on the way to returning to his original form. He embarked on a series of courses, each designed to work on various aspects of his skills, from flight handling to basic target practice. After sometime Enrique, Kelly and Chaz joined him on a simple training mission, working as a team to fulfil various objectives.

Dodds discovered during the course of the exercise that Chaz's alleged silence made the transition to the cockpit, and whilst the others would engage in all kinds of genial banter and teasing, Chaz's voice lent itself only when it was required of him. Despite this, Dodds found that the man was an accomplished pilot and worked well with the rest of the team.

The mission took the best part of an hour to complete, by which time they were all grateful for a break and some food.

Making their way into the refectory after Estelle joined them, Dodds felt quite out of place, the five pilots being the only military personnel present. The tables were packed full of casual and suit attired staff, a smattering of white coats here and there. More walked around carrying their meals on trays.

"Is there anyone else here?" Dodds asked as he sat down to eat whatever delights Xalan's research staff were given for lunch. He had yet to see any other servicemen and couldn't help but feel that he was missing out on something.

"Two other teams," Estelle said, confirming what Parks had told him earlier, whilst holding up a fork full of mashed potatoes, dripping in gravy. "But we're being kept apart; something about the segregation enabling us to function better as a team and provide us with fewer distractions."

"Sure it will," Dodds replied as an attractive, petite brunette brushed past his chair, their eyes meeting for a brief moment. She looked away, but smiled as she continued walking.

Estelle tutted before going on to question Dodds as to his performance on the simulators for the rest of the meal, asking every conceivable question about his progress. She was quite disappointed to discover he had not brought back any analytics.

Finishing, the team stashed their trays on a rack and left the refectory, Estelle steering them in the direction of the central lecture theatre to attend the presentation.

The lecture theatre, like the other areas of the facility Dodds had visited that day, had a far larger capacity than their needs demanded. Positioned centrally in the rows of red steepled seating, and close to the front, were ten other people, who must have been the other teams.

"Ah, you must be... um... you are.. the *White Knights*?" a voice boomed out over the theatre speakers. A tall suited man stood behind the podium at the front, with his back to a large screen covering the wall. To one side of him sat two other men, one of whom was Parks. "If you're all ready then... er.. please take your seats and I will begin the... the presentation."

"Come on, come on," Estelle muttered, ushering her team into their seats.

"Estelle, we're early, relax," Dodds said.

"Yeah, about fifteen minutes early," Kelly said.

"Yes, but the other teams are already here," Estelle replied, before insisting on dictating the seating arrangement so that she could sit herself in the middle of the team.

Dodds was already beginning to feel sorry for the others, having had to put up with her perfection-seeking attitude for three intense days already. Sadly he knew that with their formal training starting the following day, it was going to get a lot worse before it got any better. And should they succeed in the evaluations and have the opportunity to pilot these new starfighters, Estelle could become unbearable.

"Now," began the lecturer, "may I first welcome you to the Obex Research Centre here on Xalan and er... tulate... all..." His words became inaudible through his mumbling. The speaker looked around as Parks said something to him. He cleared his throat and went on.

"...congratulate you all on your selection to become the first to pilot the Confederation's newest and most advanced starfighter... um... My my my name is James Ainsworth and... er... I am the chief engineer on the ATAF project. This is Scott Mansun," he indicated to the man seated just behind him, "the project leader, and you all know Commodore Parks.

"Right, um... I know you'll probably have a lot more questions, b... but, if you could hold off from asking them... erm... until the end of the presentation, and then Scott will... will gladly take them."

"Probably a good idea," Dodds whispered to Enrique, sat next to him.

Ainsworth studied the podium for a moment, appearing unsure about how it operated. He pushed a button and then jumped when it did not do as he had expected: his microphone cutting off and classical music beginning to stream in through the hall's speakers.

"Oh God, this is going to take hours..." Enrique murmured, as a befuddled Ainsworth, aided by Mansun, attempted to regain control of his presentation. There were some stifled chuckles from the other teams and Dodds wondered what Ainsworth must be like when the lecture theatre was full.

Ainsworth was a tall, thin looking man with pasty white skin. His head was covered in lank, long blond hair that fell just short of his shoulders. A gold earring sparkled in the light as he turned his head. Dodds got the impression that he was the sort of man who had never quite found the strength to sever his ties with his earlier hedonistic years, even after embarking on what seemed like quite an illustrious career.

"I... I'm sorry about that," Ainsworth said as the music ceased. "I'm not used to this theatre." With the presentation back in his control, Ainsworth pressed the correct buttons on the podium and the lights began to dim.

Dodds looked over at the other teams as the light level lowered, seeing that, unlike the *White Knights*, the other two teams were both single-sex. Five men and five women were seated together and Dodds wondered if this was again part of the team selection. Maybe the Navy wished to discover if a single-sex team was more suited to the project and its long term goals. But there again it could just be pure coincidence.

There was not one face amongst the team of women that he recognised. One turned her head in his direction, a contented smile on her face. She did not meet his eyes, however, and faced back to the front. He guessed she was doing the same thing that he was: sizing up the competition. Neither did he recognise any of the men; two olive skinned men seated at the end of their row whispering to each other.

The lights didn't shut off, but instead dipped only to a level in which they did not drown out the presentation screen at the front. Dodds hoped that he would not find himself with an elbow in the ribs from Estelle after falling asleep. He felt as though he was in a warm, comfortable cinema and he sensed the impending danger, even more so after such a filling lunch.

"Ladies and gentlemen, I give you the Advanced Tactical Assault Fighter, more commonly known as the ATAF," Ainsworth began. "It is the... er... spiritual successor to the standard Tactical Assault Fighter which you all know so well, though with many enhancements as... as we are about to see.

I'm sure that you will find the following presentation t-t-to be both very informative and impressive."

The presentation started, the screen showing a sleek, black starfighter moving against a backdrop of planets, nebulas and starships. It appeared to be a mixture of artists' impressions and real footage of the fighter, as it weaved its way around other Confederation starfighters.

There were no official markings or identifiers on the craft, the black armour complimented only by silver trims on the wings, fins and body. Despite being more or less black, the definition of the fighter was not lost against the inky darkness of space, the armour catching the light and softly reflecting the environment about it.

With the introduction over, Ainsworth went on to speak at length about the new fighter. He was keen to point out that the ATAF, though descended from, was quite different from its TAF cousin and was not just "a TAF with more guns", as he put it. Over the next two hours he detailed each and every aspect of the craft, focusing on enhancements which he thought the pilots would find most appealing: a HUD that featured a predictive targeting matrix, allowing the pilot to aim for where their opponent would be, rather than where they were; an arsenal that was made up of significantly more powerful armaments than its predecessor; a much higher acceleration rate and top speed; and a shield generation unit that was many times more efficient.

The detail of the each enhancement was accompanied by video footage, some of it set planet side, the rest in space. Whatever the backdrop, most involved something exploding in rather dramatic fashion.

With his presentation concluded, Ainsworth thanked his audience and moved away from the podium. No one had attempted to ask any questions, but Dodds noticed that all around him people were gaping; all that was, with the exception of Chaz. The big man had sat through most of the presentation with a deadpan expression on his face, slouched down a little in his seat and his arms folded across his chest. He didn't look all that interested or even impressed at what he was being shown. Dodds wondered why. At the very least, he would have expected to see a flicker of curiosity. Maybe he held the same point of view as Dodds: something about this didn't look right.

"Dude, I'm finding this a little hard to swallow," Dodds whispered in Enrique's ear.

"Which part?"

"Which part? Well, where do I start? The bit about the accelerator or that that flimsy looking crate is better shielded than most of our carriers."

"It's just the next evolutionary step up," Enrique said. "They make these sorts of advancements all the time. You can bet they're already working on the successor to that one in a lab somewhere else too."

Dodds frowned.

"You've gotta admit, those things look pretty sweet," Enrique added, with a nod towards the screen.

"You know, my Dad has a saying - *Never believe everything you hear, and only half of what you see.*"

"I don't think this is one of those cases, mate."

"Okay, well, imagine this..." Dodds started. With all that they had heard that afternoon this starfighter, when compared to any other, was in essence the equivalent of taking an ordinary ground soldier and strapping a tank cannon to their back. Said soldier would then be given a belt holding two dozen grenades, before being presented with two shotguns, two pistols and two machine guns. Not only would all the added weight be of no consequence to their ability to walk or otherwise move, nor in any way hinder their performance on the battlefield, they would be able to run at the speed of a top class athlete and survive being shot many, many times before they were at last brought down.

Dodds hoped the image of such a man leaping, somersaulting and sprinting through a torn, urban landscape would look so ludicrous, as to sway Enrique's opinion. It didn't.

"Questions?" Mansun, having taken to the podium, asked. A flurry of hands went up, none of which belonged to Dodds.

"Yes, you. The young lady in the middle there." A rather striking, tall woman with curly blonde hair stood up.

"First Lieutenant Andrea Kennedy, *Red Devils*, sir," she introduced herself. "I'm aware that I'm probably about to ask the same question as everyone else -" she looked around briefly "- but I have to know: how it is possible that you have managed to outfit a single man starfighter with a plasma accelerator? I mean, we're talking about a weapon that is usually only found on cap ships and orbital defence platforms; something capable of cleaving a passenger vessel in two, with ease. The power requirements must be astronomical!"

Yes, how did *you do that?* Dodds wondered. *That's not technically possible.* A part of him was intrigued, but another part of him was feeling a little uneasy. A three-dimensional image of the ATAF was continuing its idle rotation on the screen behind Mansun and he couldn't help but feel that he was looking upon something that shouldn't be; shouldn't *need* to be.

"I thought you might want to know that," Mansun answered Andrea with a wry smile. "But unfortunately I can't provide any more information right now. Let's just say that we have access to some of the best architects and engineers that the galaxy can currently offer. As a comparison you must remember that we are also able to travel a distance of many hundred light years in the space of only a few hours, something that was also considered impossible, until you knew the trick."

"Well, I have to say that I'm *very* impressed," Andrea beamed. "You and your engineers have done an absolutely incredible job."

"Thank you," Mansun said.

"And may I just add, on behalf of myself and my team, that it will be an honour to evaluate the Advanced Tactical Assault Fighter for the benefit of the Navy," Andrea said, with another radiant smile that was now mimicked by her team mates. "Thank you for giving us this opportunity."

Mansun gave a small chuckle, but did not answer. The project leader clasped at the back of his neck with one hand and turned in the direction of the still seated Parks. He was clearly a little embarrassed and was attempted to avoid eye contact with his admirer.

Dodds looked over at Andrea again as the woman settled back down into her seat. He found her quite beautiful, with sharp features and smooth white skin. Even now, she continued to wear that very attractive smile.

Mansun gave a cough and collected himself. "Any other questions?" he requested. "If not then I will wrap up this portion of the presentation and move on to the program for the next three weeks." A few more hands went up from all three teams, with various questions aimed at elaborating more on various aspects of the starfighter. After answering a good number, Mansun decided it was best to press on, lest they spend the remainder of the afternoon stuck in the lecture hall.

"I'm sure any other questions that you may have will be answered once the training begins tomorrow morning," he concluded and began to discuss the schedule for the following days' training and eventual graded evaluations.

Leaving the theatre, herded once more by Estelle in her eagerness to get back the simulation suite, Dodds was left with one question that he had refrained from asking. It seemed to him that the Confederation was preparing to push the bounds of military force and technology in ways that had not been heard of for centuries; even more so during peacetime. His question was "Why?"

Dodds found the initial few days of the training quite straightforward. The group arrived at their simulation suite and were taken through a number of basic flight programs. The simulated ATAF cockpit layout was quite similar to that of a TAF and it did not take long for the team to get used to it.

Contrary to what Ainsworth had said, Dodds did feel that he really was flying a "TAF with more guns", and it was not long before Estelle began pressuring the group to move on to more advanced techniques.

As the days progressed the learning curve began to increase, until they came to realise that more than a week had passed and they were beginning their first ungraded training exercise. As with the standard simulator tests they were required to undertake a series of missions, though within vastly inflated constraints: a simple dogfight against six opponents ballooned into a struggle against over three dozen; the enemy supply line hit morphed into a strike run against an Imperial frigate, complete with escorts; and their own escort mission transformed into a monstrous operation involving the protection of a crippled carrier against an onslaught of opposing forces.

Had the *Knights* been flying anything other than ATAFs many of the tasks would have proven next to impossible. As it was, the benefits provided by the fighter permitted the pilots a much greater fighting chance; though not always.

"A rather unrealistic combat simulation," the training supervisor assured them upon the team's first failure. "Doubtful that such a situation would ever arise in real life. When you're ready, you can attempt the mission again. Remember that most capital ships have some structurally vulnerable points. If you focus your attacks against those, then you should be able to bring it down with relative ease."

Dodds clambered out of his module, the scene of the carrier breaking up still projecting itself about the interior. The cannons of the frigate they were supposed to be defending it from were still ravaging the surface as he joined Estelle by the training supervisor.

"Can we use the accelerators?" Estelle asked, trying to do something about her ruffled hair. Even though they had failed on their very first attempt it was clear she was already becoming frustrated, wanting nothing more than to succeed on the first attempt, with flying colours. Dodds felt his shoulders sag and he turned wearily to Enrique, who let out a sigh, lowered his eyes to the floor and shook his head. Kelly also appeared drained, even more so than Chaz, both of their eyes starting to turn red. The strain of the non-stop exercises, staring at a screen for well over an hour at a time, and having to concentrate hard on everything was taking its toll. It was a long time to sit in a cockpit, simulator or not, without a break.

"No, I'm sorry," the training manager shook his head. "But whilst they were a part of your initial training and familiarisation, the accelerators aren't a part of these ungraded exercises, or the final evaluations, I'm afraid. Should you successfully complete the evaluation, and set yourselves apart from the other teams, then you may have a chance to use them during real life training."

Estelle made sure the *Knights* succeeded on the next attempt.

After many hours spent in the modules, the final few days were upon them and arriving at the simulation suite the group were met by Commodore Parks.

"Good morning, *Knights*," he greeted them.

"Good morning, Commodore," Estelle saluted.

"As you were. As I'm sure you're well aware, today will see the beginning of your last three days at this facility and also the first day of your graded evaluations. Regardless of the outcome of these tests you will be transferred to Xalan's Orbital to await further instruction. Your destination from there will be determined by your performance here; and I have to say, Lieutenant de Winter, that so far your team has performed far better in these evaluations than any of the others. I am expecting good things from you over the next few days. Good luck, *Knights*."

"Thank you, sir," Estelle said, saluting the commodore once more as he left the suite. Estelle turned to her team, her eyes bright.

"Okay, everyone. This is it. Let's give it all we've got."

Four days later the *White Knights* stood before Parks, Ainsworth and Mansun in a meeting room aboard Xalan's orbital station. As they waited before the commodore, Dodds glanced momentarily to Estelle, seeing the woman almost bursting with pride. She caught his eye and gave him a wink.

Parks looked up. "I will keep this brief," he began. "Your performance throughout the entire evaluation period has been nothing less than exceptional; you exceeded expectations in almost every exercise."

"Thank you, sir," Estelle said.

Parks' face remained expressionless. "However, compared with the final test results of the other teams, you did not perform as favourably. I realise that this is not the news that any of you wished to hear after all the effort you have put in, and on no account should you hold each other to blame for this," his eyes flickered to Estelle. "I'm sorry to say that as far as your participation in the ATAF project is concerned, you will not be proceeding any further."

Estelle was devastated, that much was obvious to Dodds, even above the poker face that she had practised for years. Inside she must have been distraught. Enrique and Kelly disguised their feelings less well, disappointment written all over their faces. Rather strange however was that despite the fact that Chaz had put one hundred and ten percent into the ATAF evaluations, the big man didn't seem bothered about the end of their participation in the project. In fact he almost looked – relieved?

Parks continued. "This is by no means a reflection on your abilities; unless you were of a high calibre, you would not have been selected in the first place."

"Thank you, sir," Estelle said, somehow managing to keep the disappointment out of her voice.

Dodds, Enrique and Kelly echoed her words. Dodds had half expected another speech from Estelle, mimicking Andrea's speech in the lecture theatre and thanking the commodore for the opportunity to have taken part, but she said nothing more.

"Guess we're all heading back to Gabriel then?" Enrique said, half to Parks and half to his team mates.

"Actually, Mr Todd, from here all five of you will be transferred to the Temper system..." Parks began.

"*What?*" Chaz said.

Dodds jumped at the sound of the man's voice. Not least of all because he was not that used to hearing it, but also because of the sheer anger that seemed to flow from the man like red hot magma. He turned to look at the man, though he subconsciously leaned away. Chaz's eyes were narrowed, his face furious. He was almost shooting daggers at the commodore sat before him. Dodds glanced to his team mates, noticing that they appeared every bit as surprised at the man's sudden outburst. Kelly, in particular, looked like a scared rabbit. On the other side of the desk, a shocked Ainsworth had begun tense fidgeting, looking with apprehension over to Mansun.

"The *border*?" Enrique said, once the shock of Chaz's outburst had subsided enough for the added impact of the new destination to sink in.

"Yes, Mr Todd, the Confederation-Independent border," Parks continued, ignoring Chaz. "As you have been told before we are currently suffering from a lack of personnel, and thus an inadequate supply of experienced starfighter pilots. You also need to remember that we are still counting the cost of the theft of *Dragon*. It's not just the loss of the battleship that's troublesome, but the disappearance of virtually all who were serving aboard. Those numbers include several hundred starfighter pilots, all of the highest calibre that the Confederacy could offer; a figure that, as I'm sure you can well imagine, doesn't replenish itself overnight, nor even within six months.

"Your experience and skills will therefore be invaluable within the Temper system. Given all that we cannot afford to have you stationed anywhere else at this time."

"This is just in the short term, sir?" Kelly ventured.

Parks shook his head. "No. Until further notice you will be posted to Spirit, where you will fall under the general command of Captain Meyers. Preparations for your departure to the system have already been made, and your transport will be ready to go within the next quarter of an hour. Please ensure you are ready to leave at that time." The man's voice had an edge of finality to it.

Spirit. Dodds racked his brain to remember it. He then discovered why he had buried it so deep: the planet was supposedly run down and dilapidated, nothing about it at all very appealing, not even the "notable" parts. Certain Confederation planets that were home to military interests were wrapped with a large orbital ring. Spirit's had been under construction for many years, but had never been completed. It had fallen into disrepair as a result. The orbital station that hung above the planet was all there was to service the CSN's needs and was almost unable to handle the demands placed upon it. Dodds suppressed a feeling of horror. What had he agreed to come back to?

Mansun stepped forward. "On behalf of the research and development teams at Xalan, I would like to thank you all for your work in helping us evaluate the ATAF," he said, shaking their hands in turn. When he came to Chaz he let out a yelp, a clear look of discomfort on his face. Chaz's eyes were still narrowed and he looked to have a very tight grip on the man's hand. Mansun retreated back, nursing his injured fingers.

"Yes, I... er... would also like to thank you," Ainsworth said. "Erm... than... thank you." He gave a little wave, but refused to move away from the safety of the desk. Parks looked to him, but Ainsworth only gave a very slight shake of his head.

Parks turned back to the *Knights*. "Before you go: I shouldn't have to remind you that even though you are no longer active participants within the ATAF project the project is still classified," he stated bluntly. "As before, none of you are to discuss your involvement or knowledge of the starfighter; it doesn't exist. Your personal records and other assignment papers will state that you have just transferred from Wolf 359 where you were working to ensure continued security of Naval interests.

"That is all, *White Knights*, you are dismissed. You will be informed when your transport arrives. Until then please remain in your assigned waiting room; security will see you out. If there is anything you need before your departure then please inform a member of personnel."

The same tone of finality was still present as Parks finished and Dodds could not help but feel as if the commodore was blaming them for something. With some reluctance the *Knights* saluted and turned to leave.

"Man, I can't believe they're sending us to Spirit," Enrique grumbled.

"It must be some sort of mistake," Kelly said. "They surely won't keep us there for more than a few weeks..."

"Is there a problem, Mr Koonan?" Parks' voice came from some way behind.

Dodds looked around to discover that whilst the others had walked towards the door, where a couple of members of security were waiting to escort them away, Chaz had remained rooted to the spot. He was staring down at Parks and, from the concerned look on Ainsworth's face, he was not in the best of moods. Mansun too had taken a small step backwards in retreat, away from the big man who seemed to be radiating fury.

Enrique started back, but Kelly grabbed his arm, holding him with the others. From what Dodds had gathered, whilst Enrique maintained a better relationship with Chaz than anyone else, it was doubtful that he would be able to handle the man in his current state. The two security guards exchanged a quick look with one another, and their hands poised over the pistols at their belts, ready to move in in case of trouble. Parks remained sat at his desk, twiddling a pen in hand and staring unflinching back up into Chaz's enraged expression, his own quite still and impassive.

"No, *sir*," Chaz said after a time, in a cold, bitter tone, the hands at his sides balled into tight fists.

"Good. Please don't keep your transport waiting, Lieutenant," Parks answered, now meeting Chaz's glare with a stern look of his own.

With that, and without saluting, Chaz turned on his heel and marched out the door, past his four wingmates and the two security guards. He acknowledged none of them as he went, his brow furrowed, his eyes blazing, his fists still clenched firmly. They looked around to the commodore.

"Please escort the *Knights* to where they will await transport," Parks prompted security, before turning his attention to some paperwork in front of him.

"Is Spirit really that bad?" Kelly asked Enrique, eyes on Chaz, as security led them to their assigned waiting room. Ahead of her, Dodds put his arm around Estelle, but she shrugged him off without a word, apparently preferring to wallow in her own misery. Chaz still strode ahead of the group, alone.

"I don't think that's what's upset him," Enrique replied.

V

— The One That Got Away —

W earing a surly expression, Estelle marched to the rear of the transport shuttle and slumped down into one of the seats, ignoring her fellow *Knights* and choosing instead to stare out the window. Out of the corner of her eye she saw Dodds attempting to get her attention, before giving up and settling down into a seat further up the shuttle.

With the ejection from the ATAF project and her dreams in tatters, Estelle felt that her life was just about over. The greatest opportunity of her career, gone; just like that. She tried to remind herself that there was always someone, somewhere who was worse off than she; though right now she was having trouble picturing it.

At the edge of Imperial space Natalia Grace had dragged a barely conscious, dying man down the corridors of her stricken vessel for what seemed like an eternity, doing her best to avoid the flames that continued to erupt all around her. Twice she had been forced to change her route to reach the escape pods. The smoke was starting to thicken now, making it difficult to see and breathe.

To make matters worse the man she struggled to bring with her had fought against her throughout the journey, attempting to shake her off. He had shouted at her to leave him, but she had insisted on bringing him with her. The man's clothes were bloodied, ripped and burnt in several places, the flesh beneath raw and charred. Natalia did not know the man's name and he had been unable to tell her.

Finally, she had made it to the escape pods. The ship that burned around her was not a large vessel and there were only a handful of pods to serve the crew. Here, there were just two. Both of them remained, none of the other crew - if any were still alive - having made it this far. Natalia had encountered numerous bodies along the way and it appeared that she and the man she had fought to bring with her were the last two people remaining alive on the ship.

The vessel gave a sudden, violent lurch, knocking Natalia off her feet. She struggled to stand as it continued to vibrate and shudder.

What the hell was that? she thought.

"... sh... ship's coming apart..." the voice of her unknown companion answered her thoughts, still lying on the floor where he had been deposited. Now that he appeared to be at least semi-conscious and talkative, Natalia hauled him over a bulkhead and, with some effort, managed to help him up into a sitting position. His breathing was heavy and rattling.

"... you've gotta get into... one of... those quickly," he told her, gasping and staring at the escape pods. Natalia tried to help him stand, but he cried out in pain, pushing her away as best he could.

"Please, you have to get up!" she begged him.

"... i can't," he whined back to her. "i can hardly... even breathe." He looked into her eyes. "You have to go, now."

"No, I can't go on my own!"

"... if you don't leave soon... this ship will come apart... and you'll be sucked out into space... unless they decide to finish it off before then... you know they will... you, more than anyone... should know that... this... this ship is useless... to them now... they'll come for you when they're done with the others."

Natalia knew he was right. The only reason their attackers had not destroyed the ship already was because they were tackling those who were still putting up a fight, and her own vessel was dead in the water. But as soon as they became aware that it was no longer usable, and not-at-all salvageable, they wouldn't hesitate to blow it to pieces.

"I can't go on my own," Natalia repeated, tears streaming down her face. "I wouldn't know where to go or what to do. I've never flown a ship, let alone attempted to navigate in jump space."

Through the flickering light she could see a smile spread across the man's face. "... didn't... think you wanted me for my wit or good looks," he said, attempting not to cough blood over her.

Natalia smiled back, though hers was filled with sadness. She knelt close to him and took his head in her hands, kissing him on the forehead.

"... in my top pocket is... my id card... please make sure it gets to my wife."

"I will, I promise." Natalia took the id card from him - it revealed his name to be David S. Porter - and slipped it into a zipped inner pocket of her jacket. She recalled the man now: he was always telling jokes to lift the spirits of all of those around him. He'd made her smile on a number of occasions.

She double checked to ensure that all her other important data cards were safe and secure and still with her, before opening the door to one of the escape pods and stepping across the threshold. After everything that she had been through she could not afford to get away only to leave all the reports behind. She could not remember all of what she had seen and done and many others' hard work had been entrusted to her. She could not let them down.

From the rear doors she could see straight through the pod to the cockpit windows at the front, the launch chutes of the main vessel open, revealing the vast emptiness of space beyond. It was then that she noticed the ship was spinning. Every now and again scenes of the on-going battle would enter into her view, burnt out debris from other craft tumbling by in the immediate outside space.

"... can you still see... the jump gate?" she heard Porter ask behind her, his voice weak.

"Yes, yes I can," Natalia replied. "But it looks like we're moving away from the entry point. I'm sure we were closer to it than that."

"... it's not getting... further away... it's... getting smaller because it's closing... soon it will be unusable... you'll... have to hurry."

Natalia hesitated. The thought of piloting a space craft, no matter what type, made her sick to her stomach; like attempting to cross a vast ocean, on a small raft using nothing by her own arms for paddles. Looking around the pod an idea struck her and she scampered back to Porter's side.

"... i can't come with you," he managed again, as she tried to help him up once more.

"I can put you in one of the stasis capsules!" she enthused. "You'll be fine once you're under. And once we get to the other end, we can get you some medical assistance."

Porter shook his head. "... those ones aren't... military grade... they don't work like that... they just make you fall asleep... i'll die in there... and then you'll have to put up with a rotting corpse... until you get picked up."

Natalia looked in anguish from her dying companion to the open pod.

"... the controls are clearly marked," he assured her. "... the pods are designed to be simple to use... smart girl like you... should have no trouble working it out..." he coughed uncontrollably and there was more blood.

The ship rocked again, the shaking accompanied by a terrible grinding sound.

"Go!" Porter mustered enough strength to put emphasis on the word.

Natalia rushed back into the tiny, cramped pod, past the stasis capsules that lay like small beds opposite one another, and up to the front. She studied the control panel in the cockpit and discovered it was indeed very basic and straight forward. There was even a brass plate with engraved launch instructions on the main console. As Natalia looked out for the jump point a thought occurred to her.

"How can I reach the jump point with the ship spinning?" she asked, returning yet again to the pod's rear doors. David did not answer her; he was dead. The man's eyes were closed and he was slumped forward, quite still.

Natalia felt her heart rate increase, her breath coming quick. She was alone. Wasting no further time she hurried to the front of the pod and began working through the instructions on the plate one by one, pressing buttons and activating systems in the specified order. Behind her the rear doors closed and locked. As she continued various instruments sprang into life, screens and monitors lit up and started to tail system logs, statuses of essential parts and other texts. The final instructions on the engraved plate read,

```
Press 'Release' to release locking clasps
    Press 'Launch' to fire engines
Ensure autopilot is engaged 100m from host vessel
```

Looking down the launch chute Natalia realised what she had to do and pressed the release button whilst studying the spinning scene outside. The now tiny jump point was coming into her view from bottom to top. The vessel was not spinning very fast, but her inexperience with star ships had hit her confidence. She swore as she missed the second spin... and the third. On the fourth pass of the jump point, when it was more or less central in her view, Natalia pressed the launch button. She felt the engines engage and the pod shot forward. The jump point was now smaller than ever and she prayed that by the time she reached it, it would not have closed completely.

Looking behind her, to the tiny rear door window, she caught a glimpse of what remained of the ship she had been travelling on. Compulsion overtook her and she moved over to the small viewport.

As David had said, her old ship was coming apart, small pieces breaking off all the time, severing the links between the larger sections. Around the vessel Natalia could make out Imperial starfighters weaving between other stricken craft, explosions ripping across their hulls.

Her ships, her allies, her friends. She would never see them again. The tears came afresh and through her blurred vision she caught sight of an Imperial frigate reigning over the carnage. As she watched she saw a starfighter deviate from its current course and move towards her pod. Her tears of sorrow became ones of fear and she gave a loud gasp. The starfighter approached and Natalia found she was unable to tear her eyes away from it.

Two green bolts of plasma issued from beneath its wings. Her pod was bathed in a brilliant light. Moments later the exploding, stricken vessels, the frigate, and the fighter were gone, to be replaced by the blue haze of jump space.

"I think the *Red Devils* must have cheated. You saw the way Andrea was sucking up during that presentation. She was probably doing stuff like that the whole way through the evaluation," Estelle continued to chew on the bone of the *Knights'* exit from the ATAF project.

The others said nothing, having since taken to just ignoring her. Enrique was slouched in his chair asleep; Chaz was back to his book; Kelly was taking the time to write in her journal; and Dodds was back to his favourite activity of staring out the window. The view was quite uninspiring, with nothing to see aside from jump space's blue haze.

Estelle's misery was further compounded by the fact that the transport the five now occupied was likely the last luxury they would be afforded before arriving at Spirit. It could comfortably hold twelve passengers, and was often used by high ranking officials and members of senior command. With no one having acknowledged her, Estelle slipped back into her own thoughts and went back over everything that they had done in the past few weeks at the research facility.

She could not think where they had gone wrong: her team had been up to scratch on the TAF simulators; even Dodds, following his lengthy absence from the cockpit, had performed. There was no weak link anywhere as far as she could determine. The ATAF evaluations in the simulators themselves had gone without a hitch. The team had not lost a single member during any of the missions they had flown, an act that would have without doubt been a reason for instant failure. They had not conceded very many allied casualties during the assessments - in some cases, none at all; neither had they wasted very much ammunition. All she could think about was that they had not completed the tasks fast enough. Stepping into Parks' office she had been confident that the *White Knights* would be charged with piloting the ATAFs for whatever purpose the Confederation had in mind. But she had instead seen her dreams go slipping through her fingers.

"Well, welcome to the rest of our military lives," Enrique said, shuffling in his seat, his arms folded across his chest, his eyes closed. Estelle half scowled at the back of his chair. The man was just pretending to be asleep, so as to avoid making conversation with her. It seemed that, although he too was disappointed, he had been quick to accept it.

Dodds had spent the time before the transport picked them up talking things over with Estelle and trying to reassure her that, like Parks said, it was not a reflection on her; although his efforts had done little to persuade her either way. Chaz had characteristically said nothing to the others following their meeting with Parks and had instead buried his head back in his book. No one had since questioned him about it, a heavy cloud of rage still lingering over him.

"This is your captain speaking. We are now leaving jump space," came a pleasant and cheery voice over the transport's intercom. From the way she had spoken throughout the journey, Estelle got the impression that the transport's captain was used to ferrying VIPs and didn't change the way she addressed her passengers, regardless of their rank or status.

With their impending arrival at their destination, Estelle leaned over to take a peak at Dodds, whose eye were glued to the window he sat beside.

Dodds watched out the window as the blue haze peeled away and the stars outside came rushing by. A massive, far-off transport vessel, its engines glowing with cyan hues, entered the meagre space afforded by his window and began to slow along with the stars outside. The effect was something of an illusion: the disengagement from jump space giving the impression of a rapid burst of speed.

Dodds was greeted by a view of Spirit not long after, the large blue and green ball looming in his window. As he'd heard a number of times before, the orbital ring that wrapped its way around the planet was far from complete, with sections missing here and there. Construction equipment drifted close by, looking as worn out and neglected as the ring itself. It appeared that work on the ring had been put on the back burner. As the planet slid from his view, the captain changing heading to bring the shuttle in line with their destination, Dodds could not help but feel that it was a fitting preview of things to come. After the initial excitement and great anticipation of his call back to duty, was this really what he had returned to? Maybe his father had been right all along.

As well as the ring, Dodds could make out the wheel-like form of the orbital station hanging high above the planet. It was the first station of its type that Dodds had ever seen, Xalan's own orbital station being more saucer shaped with rounded tops and bottoms like most others. The design of Spirit's station looked as though it had wormed its way out of the reject pile. Either that or it was just cheap.

Kelly, seated in front of him, turned around with an ominous look on her face, her first impressions of their destination leaving much to be desired.

"Disengagement complete," the transport's captain said as cheery as ever. "Welcome to the Temper system. We will be entering Spirit's orbit within the next twenty minutes, before landing at Spirit Orbital Station and completing our flight. I trust you will have a pleasant stay."

Estelle went back to sulking.

VI

— An Admiral's Confession —

C ommodore Parks' transport shuttle touched down on its appointed cliff-side landing pad, and the man made his way along a connecting jetty that led towards a number of tall buildings, set up against a small mountain range. The buildings that he walked towards were home to a number of research centres and offices, one of which had been designated to Admiral Turner for the duration of his stay on Xalan. Though the admiral had been present on Xalan during the three week ATAF evaluation program he had, for various reasons, remained far from the Obex Research Centre, upon a different continent entirely; the ground that Parks now trod.

Despite being home to the Confederation's main research and development facilities, Xalan was also populated by a number of thriving cities. Civilian immigration and migration was rigidly controlled. On a planet such as Xalan the Confederation were careful not to allow free movement and risk losing value research and findings to enemy, or even allied, hands.

Unlike Spirit, Xalan had no orbital ring, a standard orbital station sufficing. Even so, the planet was one of the most fortified throughout the Confederacy, a huge array of long range planetary defence platforms circling a vast distance. Many of the platforms were automated and would open fire on any unidentified object that came into range, after issuing only a single warning.

Turner's office was high up, affording him a stunning panorama of the city. It was early evening when Parks arrived and the many lights from buildings and low flying vehicles could be seen twinkling in the fading light. Occasional patrol craft passed by his office window.

"Good evening, Commodore," Turner said as Parks was shown in by the admiral's security.

"Good evening, Admiral," Parks responded, saluting.

"Please leave us," Turner looked to the security personnel who stood either side of the door inside his office. The pair saluted and left.

"Don't concern yourself with any standards of correctness, Commodore, I don't expect this to be a formal meeting," Turner said once the door had shut. "Let me apologise for having you run around so much these past few days. I appreciate that the constant back and forth can be stressful and I myself find space travel so much more convenient. No need to worry about things like atmospherics."

"That's quite all right, sir," Parks said. "Whatever was needed to get the job done." Parks had indeed been travelling a lot recently. Whilst in the Indigo system he had divided his duties between Xalan's many research centres and the orbital station, spending a fair amount of time being transported between all of them. The constant travel had begun to take its toll, but he was coping.

"Spectacular, isn't it?" Turner changed the subject, nodding to the view out of the window.

"I was about to say so myself," Parks agreed, looking out at the bright lights of the city in the distance. "How do they manage to get any work done here with a view like that?"

"That's part of the reason we move most of them underground!" Turner chuckled. "Drink?" The admiral walked over to a cabinet and removed two spirit glasses. He picked up a near full decanter of whiskey and gave it a gentle shake, with a smile. "Imperial White Label."

"How did you get that?" Parks asked, knowing that the contents of the vessel the admiral held were not only very expensive, but also difficult to get hold of.

The admiral smiled, pouring out a modest amount of the amber liquid into each glass. "It was confiscated from one of the local residents returning home. I saw it on the seizures list and decided to help myself. One signature and it was mine."

Parks raised an eyebrow at just how blasé the admiral was acting. Never in his career had he seen the man behave in such a manner.

"Anything else?" Parks asked as Turner dropped a couple of ice cubes into each glass.

"No," Turner waved a hand dismissively. "A man of my authority shouldn't abuse his position. So, knowing that, I just took the other two bottles." The admiral smirked and handed one of the glasses to Parks. He then returned to his desk, sinking down into the comfortable black leather chair with a contented sigh. He then raised his glass. "Congratulations on a job well done, Commodore," he said, before knocking back some of the liquor.

"Thank you, sir." Parks took a small sip of the whiskey, never too sure if he would ever acquire a taste for it. The Imperials tended to like their drink strong, vodka being high on their list of exports. The spirit was drunk in vast quantities by asteroid and mineral miners all over the galaxy, the most popular being a brand known as Velda; coincidently made by the same company that produced the White Label whiskey. Parks had tried some on occasion and found it to be, in his own words, "lethal". At close to hundred and fifty proof it was not a drink to be taken lightly. It was also quite flammable and, as a consequence, banned in many bars throughout the Confederacy.

"Looks like we got our men then. Or, in this case, women," Turner said cheerily. He rocked the whiskey glass in his hand, staring at the liquid within and watching the way it washed over and around the ice cubes.

Parks said nothing.

"You don't agree?"

"With all due respect, sir, I feel the *Knights* would have been a better choice."

"Don't take it personally, Elliott, this isn't a competition," Turner said with a small air of impatience. "You have to remember that at the end of the day we may in fact be doing them a *favour*."

"There was very little in it," Parks objected.

"In the *test scores*, yes. But I have doubts about their psychological profiles, Commodore and *that* is what will count. We only have nine months or so to convince those five women of the truly monumental task that we will be expecting them to undertake. For now, we may as well take the opportunity to celebrate one thing going right over the last six months. God knows we could use it with the prospect of never seeing *Dragon* again. I'd sooner have that battleship completely destroyed than in the hands of the Enemy." The last part became something of an irritated mumble. He took another drink from his glass, leaned back in his chair and looked up at the ceiling.

Parks, tired of standing, sat down in a chair adjacent to the admiral's desk. He recalled going over the results of the ATAF evaluation test scores and seeing the minimal differences between the *Red Devils* and *White Knights*. There were various aspects of the evaluation where the two teams had out-performed one another, leading to a very difficult decision. In the end, however, the *Red Devils* had just edged out the *White Knights*, leaving Parks with the painful task of reassigning the team to the border. The *Silver Panthers* had performed to a far lesser degree when compared to the others and Parks had returned them to their previous duties.

"What happens if the *Devils* refuse to go through with it?" Parks asked.

"That's why we need to be absolutely sure that they won't, Elliott," Turner said in a gruff voice. "We cannot afford to have them pull another Patrick Dean on us. That little incident set us back well over a month." He paused, staring into space, then said. "Remind me: what was the official line on that incident?"

"That all members of the *Yellow Dogs* were killed during covert operations. There were no bodies to recover because they were all vaporised in starfighter explosions," Parks recited.

"That's not a story we can spin out for another five pilots if they also decide to run," Turner said. "I don't like the idea of keeping secrets from our own men, but if it means the difference between keeping the facts away from the general public and chaos on a quite literally galactic scale, then so be it."

"And if the *Devils* do try to run?" Parks wanted to know.

"Then we will have to find another way," Turner said.

But both Turner and Parks knew that there was no real other way and the tone of Turner's voice had already acknowledged that fact. In order for the ATAF project to successfully run its course from here on out there could be very little room for deviation or stalling, meaning that both men would have to be dead certain of their every decision. But neither of them wanted to talk about it now, Parks himself figuring there would be plenty of time in the coming months. He decided to change the subject,

"I received word that the *Knights* arrived at Spirit early this afternoon, local time. They will begin routine patrols and counter piracy measures within the next few days." He decided not to bother Turner with the details of the little incident with Chaz at the time he had informed the group of their new duty. He was sure that it would not have surprised the admiral in the slightest. It could be put into a report for his perusal at a later date.

"Under Aiden and Anthony?"

"Just Captain Meyers, but the commodore will also be around as needed."

Turner nodded. "They will be in good hands with Aiden. He's a good man, if a bit soft. He seems to prefer the carrot to the stick nine times out of ten, which may be the reason he's passed over for promotion so often." Turner drained his glass. "And the *Red Devils*?" He poured himself another small measure of whiskey.

Parks declined the offer of a top up, but noticed that Turner eyed him closely, as if suggesting the drink were needed. "The *Red Devils* will begin hands-on ATAF training operations in the pre-arranged location against some holographic units. After that they will participate in simulated combat training against real pilots."

"Just so long as they don't kill anyone," Turner remarked. "I don't expect those other pilots quite know what they're in for, facing off against those fighters. They're in for one hell of a shock."

Turner drank again from his glass and Parks looked down into what remained of his own whiskey. He had decided that he really was not very fond of it and in future he would only drink it out of good grace.

Turner cleared his throat and set his glass down on the table. "Now, Elliott, I have to confess I didn't just ask you here to share a celebratory glass of whiskey. You may be aware that I have been in the service of the CSN for most of my life, something the suits in Office have come to realise too. So it is with some regret that I have to inform you that in just over six weeks' time I will be retiring from service."

"*What?*" Parks almost dropped his glass in shock.

"I know you believed that I was going to be around until the very end, but that hasn't been the case for quite some time. Sorry for the deception."

Parks was stunned. Everything now seemed quite urgent and the situation he found himself in threatened to overwhelm him. He pulled back his sleeve to look at his watch. He had lost all sense of time and was wishing that six weeks meant six months.

"But... sir, that's impossible... it's... surely it's a mistake?" Parks spluttered as he fought to control the mild terror that was rising within him.

Over the past few years Parks and Turner had worked very close together to ensure that the ATAF project would run smoothly. In the grand scheme of things they hadn't even completed the first phase of the project, the most important aspects were yet to come. Parks now felt it all to be for naught as the admiral passed all future responsibility on him.

Out of the window before him, Parks found that the darkening skies, and layers and layers of thick grey clouds, seemed very poignant at that precise moment in time. The man felt as though he had been left holding the baby, leaving him without any means of support or food, and bleak future prospects.

"I'm sorry, Elliott, and I wish there was more that I could do, but unfortunately my retirement has been forced upon me," the old admiral said in regretful tones. "I have already deferred it by more than two years, so I am unable to play that card." He rose from his chair and paced slowly back and forth in front of the window, looking again out at the beautiful cityscape. "The suits want me out. They're afraid that a man of my age will start to make mistakes and could then jeopardise the project. Ha! I may be old, but I'm not senile just yet. Whiskey?"

Parks became aware of the admiral hovering over him. He had disappeared into his own thoughts as he had attempted to digest the news that had hit him like a sledgehammer. He only nodded, seeing the whiskey as a buffer and immediate comforter. Turner topped up his glass.

"What's going to happen?" Parks asked after taking a good drink.

"You're going to finish what we started, Commodore. You're not going to give up or wind things down a notch just because I'm no longer able to participate in the project. What would you do if, for example, I were killed while in transit?"

The point was well made. Parks reflected that people often forgot that responsibility was often passed to them without fair warning. He would be able to make use of Turner's knowledge for the next six weeks.

"We still have until the end of June, Elliott," Turner added. "There is plenty of time to ensure the transition. You know most of it anyway."

Parks studied Turner as he spoke and for the first time he became aware that the admiral looked old and tired. His eyes betrayed a sense of weariness unusual in such a strong minded man. But with the revelation of his impending retirement his other features, the greyed and thinned hair, his thin face and wrinkles, no longer said "experienced".

"Everything is changing, Elliott," Turner said, a touch sadly. "We're becoming more and more like a federation every day. Current events are forcing us all to work much closer together than ever before and the government is only getting stronger for it. We're more tightly coupled now than at any time in the last century." He was sitting once more in his chair and was leaning back, staring up at the ceiling again. Parks studied him as he did so, trying to see into his mind, to hear what the man might be thinking. "And whether the independent nations like it or not, with the gradual unifications of their governments and military forces they're making steps towards becoming a confederate state. Whether or not any of these things are good, only time will tell. Whatever happens, the galaxy will be a very different place in the next five or six years."

The two men sat in silence for a time.

"Do you have any plans? For your retirement, I mean?" Parks asked. He was not very good at small talk, but felt that it could only serve to calm them both.

"Actually, yes!" Turner sat forward and smiled, now quite jubilant. "I'll be returning to Earth to see my new granddaughter. You may remember that my daughter was supposedly barren? As it happens she gave birth to a naturally conceived healthy young girl a few days ago, and I plan on being there with my family." He took another drink; he was close to finishing his second glass. "To tell the truth I'll be grateful to spend as much time with them as possible. Should none of this work out in the end then I will prefer to have spent the time left with my family, rather than in some stellar graveyard. I hope you do not think that cowardly of me?"

"No, sir."

"Good. Despite our duties some of us did find time to start a family," Turner muttered, looking into the bottom of his glass as he spoke.

"Some of us just don't seem to be able to get started," Parks muttered back. For all his time in the Navy, Parks had never found time for romance or relationships and he knew Turner could tell that he had all but given up, more important things now driving him onwards.

"Strength to carry on, Commodore. We're only human after all." Turner set his glass down on the desk, having drained it. "Admiral Jenkins will be taking over my duties following my departure. She is already aware of my situation and the status of the project. I suggest that before the end of the month the three of us take some time to get together and become more familiar with each other's core responsibilities and assignments. That should help to ensure that there are no shocks in store come the beginning of July. Until that time I will continue to retain full command over the CSN."

Parks nodded an acknowledgement, taking another sip of whiskey.

"Now, I expect you have a lot to think about and do, so I will not take up any more of your time," Turner said.

Parks rose and saluted, taking the hint. "Thank you for the drink, sir."

"Funny how a bit of bad news can take away the taste of bad whiskey," Turner chuckled.

Parks was under the impression that he had hidden his revulsion well. He made a mental note never to play poker against the admiral.

Turner, too, stood and saluted. "Safe journey. I have the utmost faith in you to see this through, Elliott. Remember that."

Returning to his transport, Parks paused to take in the view once more. The high landing jetty provided a view of almost equal beauty to that of Turner's office. There he stood for a while at the cliff edge, feeling the cool breeze of the evening wind upon his hands and face, looking out at the cityscape and the light reflecting off twin moons shimmering across the gentle waves of the calm ocean all about it.

He had seen more stunning sights during his lifetime, but tonight, at that particular moment, this was at the same time the most beautiful and most frightening sight he had ever seen: for it was a testament to the power of the human spirit, from their humble beginnings on Earth to a space faring race, spanning dozens of star systems across the galaxy; and with that a stark reminder of the penalty for failure.

VII

— Where the Action Is —

After many hours in flight, the *Knights'* transport at last docked with Spirit Orbital and the ever chipper voice of the transport's captain informed the pilots that it was safe for them to disembark. There were grumbles from Estelle as they stepped out on to the flight deck, the initial impressions of the station itself no less than what any of them had expected. From the moment he stepped out of the transport Dodds at once noticed that the station presented an air of being run down, neglected and somehow trapped in the past.

"*White Knights*?" a deck attendant enquired. Estelle begrudgingly confirmed their identity. "Follow me. There is a shuttle waiting to take you down to the surface."

Dodds started after the man with the others, catching the sound of chuckling as he did so. He looked around to see a group of service men and women, engineers and various other deck hands watched as he traipsed by, heads turning and grinning to one another. Dodds figured that the *Knights* were far from the first to feel somewhat repulsed by their new surroundings, and it must have been a great source of amusement for the current residents to see the reactions each time a new set of faces turned up.

Reaching the shuttle, Dodds slung his meagre bag of possessions inside before slumping down onto one of the steel benches that ran the length of the cramped interior. Though he tried to remain upbeat, something about his new surroundings was already attempting to break his spirit.

Touching down on the planet's surface, Dodds needed no further confirmation that their special treatment was well and truly over. Arriving at their mixed quarters, he and Enrique were dismayed to find they were crammed in with fifteen others. Their appearance at the doorway was greeted by cheers and whistles from their new bunk mates.

"Hey! It's the new guys!" came a cry from across the quarters.

"We've got ourselves a full house, boys!"

"Welcome to Action Central!"

"Hey, you! Think fast!" A ball was thrown towards Dodds. He fumbled the catch, letting it roll out of his hands and bounce around on the floor for a time, before its path was halted by the clutter it encountered there. It looked as though the base - or at least these quarters - was not big on discipline, with clothes and personal belongs scattered all about. It looked like a holiday camp for rowdy teenagers. Kelly poked her head between Enrique and Dodds, who had halted in the doorway. Estelle squeezed past all three and scanned the room.

"oh dear god," Kelly said in a low voice. "I really wish I was back at Gabriel."

"Uh huh," Enrique answered.

"Please sleep next to me," Kelly said to Enrique. Dodds noted that the men in the dormitory were already eyeing up the two women, and were being anything but subtle about it.

"Wouldn't want it any other way," Enrique said.

Dodds was in agreement. After three weeks of his own personal space, and five months back home before that, this new regime was going to take a lot of getting used to.

Estelle coped a lot better, striding in, finding a spare bed and claiming it for her own, tossing the random items that occupied it on to another nearby bed. In the hours that followed it did not take her long to discover that she was the highest ranking officer in the dormitory (something that genuinely astonished her) and as a consequence one of the least popular.

At another time, in another place, Dodds would have advised her against flexing her muscles in the very first instance, but right now he was not in the mood.

Chaz found himself a bunk, acting as always with his trademark silence. With his locker filled with clothes, boots and other personnel effects the man kicked back, pulled out his book and disappeared into the pages.

* * *

"Welcome to Mandelah Naval Base, boy and girls; and welcome to Spirit. I'm Captain Meyers and while here you will be acting under my command," the portly, ginger bearded man said.

The *White Knights* were seated within a small briefing room, alongside other new arrivals to the Temper system, some of whom shared their new quarters.

The group had been given a brief tour of the base and found that, even though Spirit had an orbital station, the overpopulation of available pilots meant that many of them had to be based on the ground. It also meant that in order to perform their duties, they would have to be transferred back up to the orbital station on an almost daily basis.

This would not have been the case if construction on the orbital ring had been completed, allowing for crew, service personnel and starfighters to be housed within, Estelle grumbled during the tour. As it stood, not even the craft that they would be required to pilot were stationed planet-side. Standard Confederation starfighters were not capable of withstanding the stresses that atmospheres would put upon them whilst attempting planetary leave or re-entry. All this, Estelle had also reminded them, slipping into a sulk, was not something that the ATAF suffered from. Dodds caught Chaz's eye and swore later he saw him crack a smile. For his moody exterior he was starting to find some mirth in Estelle's continued moaning.

Dodds suppressed a small sigh, folded his arms and tried to appear interested in what Meyers was saying. The captain was giving them an overview of what would be expected of them whilst they were stationed at Spirit.

"The Temper system is the principle route, and therefore the closest Confederation border world, to Independent World space," Meyers went on. "In general terms this means that all sane traffic wishing to safely enter or leave Confederation controlled space must do so via this system."

"Why?" a female voice behind Dodds asked. He didn't bother to look around to see who was asking the question. "I mean, we can easily travel all the way from Earth to Kethlan in a single jump if we wanted to."

"Not any longer, no," Meyers said. "Owing to recent developments within the Mitikas Imperium, the Confederation is no longer permitting jump gates, save for those along the border, to allow incoming or outgoing traffic to non-Confederate destinations."

"So everyone is having to come through here instead?"

"For the foreseeable future, yes."

"But the volume of traffic must be incredible!" the voice sounded quite taken aback.

"It is, yes, but it's a necessary precaution that the government wishes to take."

Dodds had the image of an egg timer in his head, the grains of sand being the starships that were waiting - with strained tempers - to pass through the gates and move on to their destination.

"But what about everyone else? If they have their own jump drives they don't need to use the gates. Somewhere between ten and fifteen percent of all space craft can form their own jump points."

Dodds met Enrique's eyes and raised an eyebrow at the comment from the well versed informant.

Meyers put up his hand and waved the woman down. "We'll get onto how we are tackling that in a little bit. For now, all of the Confederacy's navigation buoys are refusing to supply data on routes towards non-Confederate systems and, in particular, the Mitikas Empire. Without that data, space is once again as the sea was to early sailors on Earth: a treacherous place with little to no land marks."

"Until they learned to use the stars to navigate," another voice chipped in.

"True," Meyers began to chuckle. "But you'd have a hell of a time doing that up there." He nodded towards the ceiling. "Now..."

"Excuse me, Captain, but what are the government taking precautions against?" yet another voice piped up.

"Mass immigration," Meyers said simply. "The increased instability of the Imperial systems has led to a greater amount of traffic coming into Temper, and from there into further sectors of Confederation space. Most of these are traders attempting to find new avenues of business now that their old ones have closed. Unfortunately, organised crime is also suffering the same loss and you can bet that they will also come flooding in with them.

Now..."

"Sir?"

"Yes?"

Dodds found that Meyers was proving to be incredibly patient, given the continued interruptions. He'd heard that the man was like that though: very pleasant and accommodating; and that was also why he was still a captain and not a commodore. Heads turned around, following Meyers' eyes. Dodds looked about this time, seeing an olive skinned man with a puzzled expression holding his hand in the air. For a moment Dodds thought he recognised him as one of the five men from the lecture theatre all those weeks ago, but realised he was mistaken. Meyers scratched at his beard as the man spoke.

"I'm sorry, Captain, but this sounds like a job for the local police, not the Navy."

"True, but the police forces throughout Temper have come under increased stress whilst attempting to handle this issue and have requested our assistance. You should be aware that it could also soon no longer be a matter for the police; remember that this is also a game of politics: whilst relationships are now good with previously troublesome Independent World systems, a show of strength is no bad thing."

"Sounds like they're turning us into the flood barriers," Dodds heard Enrique whisper to Kelly. He noticed Kelly appear to snap awake, as if she had been daydreaming. He could relate: he was drifting in and out of the room himself, trying to think of a way he could escape to somewhere more interesting and not involving apples.

"So we're going to be making pre-emptive strikes against known pirate bases and insurgent strongholds?" the questioner asked, his face brightening at the prospect for some action. At the man's words the assembled pilots all became much more awake and alert. Dodds imagined that they, like him, were visualising scenarios in which they were performing important and heroic services to the Confederation, none of which went unnoticed, and all of which resulted in a great deal of action, grand recognition, and well deserved promotion.

"Not at this point, no," Meyers said, almost as if he was apologising. "For the foreseeable future you will all be assigned regular patrols within the

Temper system."

"Oh dear God, please just kill me now," Enrique said under his breath and slid down in his seat.

"Make that a double," Dodds requested, his own dreams of valour vanishing before his eyes. It was as if some twenty four hours previous he had been quaffing the highest quality Dom Pérignon, but was now being force-fed cheap plonk. Estelle, seated in front of the pair, turned around and shot them an angry glare that said, "Sit Up, Shut up and Put Up". Enrique and Dodds pulled themselves both upright and attempted to stay focused.

Meyers, with the aid of a map of the Temper system, went on to list patrol routes, potential trouble hot spots, (*Yeah, right,* Dodds thought to himself) and schedules.

"*White Knights?*" Meyers asked as he ended the briefing with the flight roster.

"First Lieutenant Estelle de Winter, *White Knights,*" Estelle said, standing up and saluting.

"I wonder where she learned that one?" Dodds muttered sarcastically to Enrique, lowering his voice a lot more this time so as not to enrage his superior.

"Lieutenant, you will be performing your first patrol tomorrow afternoon at fourteen hundred hours. All route information will be provided to you on Spirit Orbital before the start of your patrol. You and your team should be ready one hour prior to commencement for transfer to orbit. So, thirteen hundred hours at landing zone D.

"That is all boys and girls. Please ensure you check the flight roster regularly, as it will change. Dismissed."

● ● ●

Tuesday, June 10th 2617

I have to confess that I am actually enjoying my posting to Spirit a lot more than I first thought I would. When we were initially transferred here I thought it would prompt the end to my time in the Navy and I would hand in my resignation. I'm glad that I didn't as I would only have been disappointed with myself upon returning home. I haven't been in contact with my family for a few weeks now, not since arriving. But I don't expect they will be concerned.

When I first arrived here it was like my first day in the service all over again. That's what too much pampering will do to you, I guess. I figured that Spirit would be a dull, lifeless rock with nothing to keep me sane between the endless patrols. As a matter of fact there is quite a lot to do here and I've taken up running and some other activities with Enrique and Dodds. The planet is quite temperate, not as hot here as I would like (shouldn't expect it to get any hotter than 22c, I'm told) but it could be far worse.

We get most of our evenings free here, though not the weekends any more. The schedule of the patrols means that our days off vary, but we usually don't have to do more than five days on the trot. We don't have to patrol at night either, because those stationed on the orbital handle that, although some of our patrols do end rather late and then we might have an early one the next morning. Today I've got another day off after four days of patrolling. There are a few towns nearby, but I couldn't be bothered to head into any of them. I felt like just unwinding and doing a bit of a work on my journal, so I went for a walk instead.

I've never been stationed on a planet that had an orbital ring before, at least, if I was, I don't remember being so. It's only half finished, but it is quite a beautiful and surreal sight. On clear days you can make out the ring from the ground, high in the sky. It's in a geostationary orbit, so it's pretty much the same thing every time, but it's still amazing to look at. Night times are spectacular, with portions of the ring lit up in the sky. I expect that once it is finished then it'll be even more so (although that's probably wishful thinking since I'm told it probably won't be for quite some time).

Chaz seems to have come out of his shell a bit. They have a number of boxing and other martial art type classes here, so he and Enrique often go there together to practice. I'm not sure if there is much left for Enrique to learn, but he tells me that Chaz is helping him to hone some of his skills, so I guess there's a lot more to it.

He's still a touch grumpy though and doesn't have a lot to say, so you could probably imagine my surprise when he came over and spoke to me. I was sitting on my bed writing and he asked me if I wanted to go for a run with him. He hardly said a word to me while we were jogging, but we held a good pace together and he slowed when I needed to (I really need to work on my stamina). We spoke briefly afterwards, but it was mainly about the run. I decided not to talk about anything else though, didn't want to burn any bridges. We're still not sure what got him so upset with Commodore Parks. I saw that he got another one of his video disks a couple of days ago. He also received one when we were stationed at Xalan, but became really defensive when we asked him about it. I'm intrigued as to what's on them, but we've decided it's best not to ask him about it, just in case he stops talking to us again.

I do feel sorry for Estelle though. We might be enjoying ourselves here more than we expected to, but Estelle sees herself as being stuck in a rut. I think she put in a request for a transfer, but it was denied. I hate to sound selfish, but I'm glad. She's one of my dearest friends and I would hate to see her go. I can sort of understand what she's going through though. She really had her heart set on things back at Xalan and the transfer here (especially given Spirit's reputation) must have nearly killed her inside.

"Kelly?"

The word drifted through Kelly Taylor's head as she continued to work, failing to registering. It being her day off she had spent most of the day writing, the stylus strokes of her normal handwriting being transformed into characters on the screen. Just now something had broken her concentration and she struck through the word she had written to erase it, trying to regain her train of thought.

"Kelly? Hey!" an impatient voice called out, making the young woman jump. Kelly looked up from where she sat, cross legged on her bed, to see that Estelle had been demanding her attention.

"Sorry, Estelle, what did you say?" Kelly asked. She then noticed that Estelle was wearing her flight suit and felt a small twinge of panic in the pit her of stomach.

"I said hurry the hell up because you're going to make us late for our patrol! Our transport is waiting to go!"

"I... I thought we had the day off?"

"No, that's tomorrow! They changed the schedule this morning! Come on Kelly, you've only got a couple of minutes to suit up! We've got to get to landing zone G and that's not exactly next door!"

Kelly swore as she jumped off her bed and hurriedly began packing up her belongings. She cursed herself for being so busy that day reviewing her journal, correcting spelling and reading through past entries that she had neglected to check the patrol schedule. She tugged open her locker, pulling out her flight suit and boots, tearing off her clothes and throwing them to the floor.

She struggled to get into her flight suit as fast as possible, managing to get one leg in and then starting on the next. The flight suits were skin tight and did not slip on very easily; it was like trying to put on a wetsuit...

"Stop bloody staring, you perv!" Estelle's voice came. Kelly followed Estelle's icy glare to a man who had been reclining on his bed opposite, reading a book. He had since lowered it to take a look at Kelly as she stood in her underwear, but with Estelle glaring at him, he was once again returning to his reading material. Kelly saw Estelle turn back to her once more, her eyes still narrowed, and quickly turned away to concentrate on getting ready. She didn't want to hear any accusations roll off Estelle's tongue right now, she was more than capable of imagining what they might be, having heard them on occasions before: wondering how Kelly could be such a good pilot and yet so absent minded at other times, spending too much time scribbling in her journal when there were more important things - such as this - that she needed to pay attention to, and questioning why she kept a journal at all; no good would ever come from all the constant writing.

Thankfully, Kelly was just about done.

"Do the rest on the way," Estelle suggested whilst Kelly's fingers attended to the various clips on her boots. Her boots more or less fastened, Kelly picked up her personal belonging and threw them in her locker before securing it. Although she got on well with the others in their shared quarters, she did not know any of them well enough yet to trust them. She had also written little comments about each of them in her journal that she thought they'd be better off not seeing.

"Okay, ready." Kelly said, turning back to Estelle.

"Kelly, where's your helmet?" Estelle said.

Kelly looked at the floor, then her bed and realised that she'd left it inside the locker. She yanked it out and then secured the locker once more.

"*Ready?*" Estelle asked once Kelly finally appeared to be done. She did not wait for an answer before indicating that they had wasted enough time already.

"Where are the others?" Kelly asked, as the pair hastened down the various well lit corridors, dodging other inhabitants of the base as they sort to ensure they made it to the transport in time.

"They're there already. I came back to find you."

"Sorry."

"Just don't make a habit of it."

They stepped out of the barracks, into the open air, where they stepped up their pace in order to reach the assigned pick up point. The shuttle craft awaited their arrival, but Kelly could see the air around the engines shimmering, indicating that it was prepared to set off the moment the two women were aboard.

An air marshal stood by the side door watched their approach. "de Winter? Taylor?" he asked the pair as they arrived at the transport.

They nodded, somewhat out of breath.

"Good. Get inside. We almost had to go without you."

The door shut and bolted behind them and they sat down on one of the two steel benches running either side of the length of the craft.

"Hey," Kelly said to the rest of her team, once she managed to get her breath back. The shuttle was full today, all thirty places taken up. Kelly reached up and pulled the restraining harness down around her. The transport was far less glamorous than the one they had used when they had been ferried too and from Xalan, being a lot more cramped and uncomfortable with no view of the outside world.

"Journal?" Enrique, whom she had sat next to, whispered in her ear. She gave a sheepish nod in reply. It wasn't the first time - and unlikely to be the last - that her hobby had almost landed her in serious trouble.

"Prepare for takeoff," the transport's pilot called back at them. The craft shuddered as the engines engaged and Kelly felt them leave the ground. The shuddering increased as the transport lifted them into orbit. She always hated this part. Even after several weeks of having to do endure it, it still did not get any better. Around her others had a tight hold of their restraining bars, some with their eyes closed. She joined in. The journey to the orbital station was not long, and a short time later the restraining bars were disengaged.

"Today you will be patrolling route Delta D-15," the Officer of the Deck said as he handed Estelle an electronic map of the route around the Temper system. "You should ensure that you hit all four check points at least once an hour."

Dodds stole a glance over Estelle's shoulder at the route map to see if there was anything interesting on their patrol that day; even a minute piece of information that might make the next four hours a bit more bearable. There was nothing. For Dodds the patrols were now becoming a chore; a regular job that he dreaded going to each morning and which did nothing except take up his free time. He desperately wanted something to happen to break the monotony of the hours he spent in the cockpit. He had twice had to endure just over six hours in the seat, doing nothing but watching a jump gate and its uninteresting traffic flow, with little more than an hour's break. It was just as he had feared after Meyers' briefing all those weeks ago and he had been mentally and physically exhausted after both of those. It was like being tortured to death.

The flight deck of the orbital station was never silent. Starfighters were for ever being returned to their bays or taxiing to the catapult, preparing for launch. Engineers and technicians were working to repair wear and tear, as well as performing general maintenance. Munitions handlers were moving heavy laden trolleys around the deck, so that they could be loaded on to fighters.

A number of different craft occupied the bays here, the TAF being the most common. Next there was the two seater Ray. Though the fighter was less nimble than the TAF, it benefited from greater defensive and offensive capabilities. On their patrols Chaz and Enrique would usually fly one together, availability allowing. Otherwise their flight group consisted exclusively of TAFs.

Several Rooks occupied other bays, though none of them had moved in all the weeks that Dodds had been stationed at Spirit, the fighters' main purpose said to be the defence of the station itself. The Rooks were almost never allocated to patrols, the easier to maintain TAFs and Rays being given that duty. Dodds was not fond of the Rook himself, the craft feeling far too bulky and sluggish in flight. It felt even worse in combat, where lighter and faster starfighters could outmanoeuvre it. Even so he had, at one time, looked upon the Rook in awe; there had been no denying it was a powerful craft. He now gave them little more than a sideways glance, aware that the crown belonged to another.

"Hot out there today?" Enrique said, as Dodds and Estelle continued to study the route map.

"Been all quiet so far, sir," the officer replied.

The response did not surprise Dodds. *Should have applied for that damn transfer*, he thought. Though after Estelle had been denied her own request to seek adventure and excitement elsewhere - actually, in her case, recognition - he was pretty certain he knew what the answer to his would be: remain at Spirit until further notice. He was just going to have to lump it for the time being; he was not about to return to Earth with his tail between his legs.

Around Dodds others were finishing their patrols. He watched with envy as the appreciative pilots removed their helmets and left the flight deck to return to their quarters for a well-earned hot shower. He looked forward to being in their position later on. At least today's patrol was only three hours long.

He watched as Estelle clicked through the map a few times, scrutinizing each segment before handing it back.

"Thank you," she said.

"Everything good?" the flight officer asked.

"Yep."

No, thought Dodds.

"Okay, we'll see you back here at twenty hundred hours," the flight officer replied, before heading off.

Only if I don't die of boredom in the cockpit first.

"Right, Kelly, I want you out there first," Estelle said. "Takeoff and then hold position outside the orbital until we are all assembled. Got it?"

"Yes, Lieutenant," Kelly said, shuffling off towards her waiting TAF.

"Best to make sure that she's actually with us and not bumbling about some place else," Estelle muttered to the three men stood on the deck next to her. The four watched as Kelly's TAF accelerated down the catapult.

"Who's acting wing commander for this patrol?" Dodds said, as Estelle began to make for her allocated TAF.

"I am, Dodds," Estelle answered with a flat, tired voice.

What a surprise, Dodds thought gloomily. On a patrol it was hardly a significant duty, but one that might help to lift his spirits a little. He thought of the irony of the name of the planet he was based. *Two hundred and thirty five minutes to go. Two hundred and thirty if I'm* really *lucky.*

An attendant signalled to Dodds that his TAF was ready and the young pilot traipsed his way over to the starfighter. One day of proper action was all that he wished for as he stepped up into the TAF's seat.

He secured his helmet, buckled himself in and then gave a thumbs-up to Enrique and Chaz, standing down on the flight deck, watching him. The two men were waiting for the all clear to board the Ray they had been assigned for the patrol. Enrique gave Dodds a thumbs-up in return. Chaz gave him an almost invisible nod, Dodds only catching it because of knowing what to expect of the man.

With his TAF taxied up to the catapult Dodds waited to be granted clearance to launch. Staring down the illuminated tunnel, to the dark space outside, Dodds tried to gear himself for the next few *thrilling* hours ahead. He now understood why Temper was often referred to as "Action Central".

"Lieutenant Dodds, this is Tower: you're clear for takeoff," a woman's voice came over his cockpit's intercom.

"Yeah thanks, Tower," Dodds replied. "I'll be sure to let you know if anything interesting happens; like we come across *Dragon*, hidden under a load of black tarpaulin."

Please, just remind me I'm alive, he begged, as his TAF hurtled down the catapult and out the station. *At least for just one day.*

"He's coming back around!" Dodds cried, as the fighter he had been tailing barrelled and then circled around over his head. Dodds dipped his TAF out of the way before rolling around to continue his pursuit.

"I'm on him," Kelly called, bringing the craft into her sights. She adjusted her speed to hold it there for as long as possible, so as to give her on-board computer time to lock a missile. Her opponent's movements were all over the place, swerving this way and that, Kelly herself doing her best to counter its erratic nature. She had only to keep the craft within her HUD for a few moments longer and then the missile would be ready to fire... The fighter accelerated away suddenly, shaking her off and diving straight down towards Enrique and Chaz who were already tailing another of the group's opponents.

The *White Knights* had been halfway through their patrol when they were alerted to a set of unidentified vessels travelling through their assigned route. Speeding into the vicinity they had sighted their quarry, the three craft bunched up close together and appearing to be in a hurry. Their trajectory put them on course with a jump gate that would take them deeper into Confederation-controlled space, and the speed and formation of the craft suggested that they were trying to pass through undetected.

Estelle's requests for identification, destination and business purpose had been ignored, the three fighters maintaining their tight formation, but increasing their speed. Estelle had challenged them twice more before the craft had turned hostile. Based on their vessel of choice – a Dart, a cheap single seat, general purpose craft with innumerable available variants - she had concluded that they must be wanted criminals. She had gone on to order them to surrender several times before Dodds reminded her that it did not seem like they were the talkative type.

Kelly's eyes narrowed. Though the Dart that was once again in her sights benefited from upgraded offensive and defensive capabilities, she maintained that the only real advantage the long bodied craft held over her TAF was its speed. Her on-board computer jingled and she loosed the missile even before the lock verification had time to flash across her HUD. It sped away from her, trailing blue and white particles as it twisted and curled to keep up with its target's frantic attempts to evade it.

That makes up for being tardy, I suppose, Kelly thought to herself as the Dart exploded before her in a shower of debris.

"Target down," she reported.

"Good work, Kelly," Estelle came back. "One down, two to go."

"Got one right behind me," Dodds said, feeling his TAF vibrate as particle bolts slammed into the rear, the shielding absorbing the hits.

Estelle made a quick assessment of the situation and standings. The death of their comrade had had a detrimental effect on the performance of the two remaining Dart flyers, whose flight had become far more sloppy, their confidence shaken.

"Enrique, Chaz, stay on your target; Kelly you assist them. Dodds, help me with the other one."

"Got it," Dodds confirmed.

The four Confederation fighters divided as Estelle had ordered and set after their targets. The Darts weaved and dived as the *Knights* tailed them, frequently coming close to collisions with their pursuers as they made snap changes to their headings. Plasma and particle rounds flew in every direction as the two sides attempted to bring one another down, none quite managing to hit home.

"Damn this crap HUD!" Dodds said as the Dart evaded another burst of his guns. After three weeks of benefiting from the ATAF's predictive targeting capabilities he now felt crippled without it, as though he was handcuffed to his seat. It was clear that the advantages the starfighter offered had spoilt him and he was finding it difficult to readjust. It dawned on him that this was the first time he had been in a combat situation - simulated or otherwise - since the evaluation program back on Xalan. The Dart skimmed through his sights. He fired and missed again.

"Why the bloody hell haven't they loaded the ATAF's combat software on to this damn crate?" he said.

"Careful there, Dodds," Enrique said. "You're beginning to sound like Estelle." He took his eyes off his systems for a moment, trying to guess which of the three TAFs he could snatch a glimpse of through the Ray's canopy might be Dodds.

"Shut it, mate, this is really starting to annoy me!" Dodds retorted.

The frustration in the voice made Enrique start to chuckle. He looked over at Chaz, sat next to him, whose face split into what Enrique recognised as a rare smile. It vanished almost as soon as it had appeared, the big man diverting the Ray's heading as the missile-lock warning sounded. His attempt at evasion came too late and the Ray rocked as the missile slammed into the topside of the fighter, both men feeling the heavy vibration coarse through their bodies.

"Sorry," Enrique said for allowing himself to become distracted, before refocusing on the battle. Chaz called up a damage report. It indicated that both the top and frontal shield quadrants had collapsed, but were recovering slowly. As the missile had detonated the force of the explosion had driven its way through the shield and to the Ray's armour beneath. The damage incurred by the armour had not been insignificant, but not as critical as it had felt.

"Are you two all right?" Estelle asked.

"We've sustained moderate damage. Shielding is running at sixty percent efficiency," Chaz reported back. "Nothing we can't handle."

Estelle glanced at her radar, seeing a red triangle sitting right in the middle; almost right on top of her. A moment later the four pale grey rear fins and bright cyan glow of the Dart's single engine swept across her cockpit view. She immediately gave chase.

As she closed in on the fighter she saw something detach itself from one of the fins, the object arcing up around it. She swore as too late she realised what was happening, her on-board computer sounding the warning for only a couple of seconds.

Such was the range from its target that the missile completed its manoeuvre within a matter of seconds and slammed headlong into her TAF, creating a blinding white flash as the explosion blended in with the bright blue splinters from her collapsed shielding. The starfighter rattled with the impact, jostling Estelle in her seat and making the young woman lunge for the ejection handle. The expected prompt to bail out never came, however, the rattling ceasing a short time later.

"Estelle!" Dodds' voice sounded in her comms.

"I'm okay, I'm okay," Estelle replied, thankful that her voice had not betrayed the terror she had felt upon seeing what she believed was her own death hurtling straight towards her. Out of the corner of her eye she saw an explosion.

"Target down," Kelly once again reported. The Dart that had attacked

Enrique and Chaz had pulled out of its dive and flown right in front of her, bringing itself dead on to her heading. It had aligned within her cross hairs and Kelly had only to pull the trigger. Her TAF's cannons had fired four times, the first pair of bolts slamming into the rear of the ship, followed by the second. The third pair completed the task whilst the fourth had disappeared into the explosion, striking remnants of the destroyed fighter.

"Hey, leave some for the rest of us," Dodds said.

"This isn't a game, Dodds!" Estelle barked back. "Concentrate on taking down that last fighter."

With his companions dead, and now even more out-numbered and out-gunned than ever, the final Dart pilot swung around, put full power to their engines and began to flee from the naval pilots as fast as they could, resuming their attempt to reach the far-off jump gate.

The four fighters gave chase, each attempting to bring down the final fleeing craft. The Dart was fast, faster than the *Knights*, and it would soon be out of range of their guns; but not their missiles.

Estelle's targeting computer jingled. She declared her lock. The others acknowledged her. The missile armed and fired.

At the same instant her comms crackled into life. "I won't go back there! Please don't make me go back! I beg you!"

It was not a voice that she at first recognised and as the small red triangle on her radar screen started to blink, Estelle realised that it was coming from the fighter she had just fired at. "They can't be stopped! They'll kill me! They'll kill you! They'll kill all of us!! Please, just let me go! I just want to get away from them! PLEASE!" the voice continued as the missile devoured the distance between itself and the target it sought.

Something inside Estelle made her regret firing. There was terror in the man's voice; a terror that, for some unexplained reason, caused her a great deal of discomfort. It was the kind of terror that sounded as though it had been ingrained into the man's very soul. She looked down at the TAF's controls, seeking a way, any way, to put a stop to the missile that was seconds away from destroying its target. She found none and looked back to the final floundering manoeuvres of the Dart as the missile closed.

The craft exploded, killing its helpless occupant and leaving Estelle with questions that might now never be answered. She slowed her TAF and stared ahead at the tumbling clutter of alloys. The others joined her, Dodds and Kelly coming along either side, though not close enough to identify the faces within the helmets.

"Nice shooting, Estelle," Dodds said, although his enthusiasm came across as somewhat subdued and muted, the rush of the battle dampened.

"What the hell was that all about?" Kelly asked.

"I... I have no idea," Estelle replied. It sounded too real to have been a bluff. The man's final words had been almost hysterical and they were still going around in her head,

"I won't go back there..."

Go back where?

"They'll kill me! They'll kill you! They'll kill us all!"

Who was going to kill him? Who were the people in the Darts? Why were those they were fleeing so intent on attacking the Confederation and her allies?

She was regretting her actions and now wanted nothing more than to have brought the man back to Spirit for questioning. She looked to her radar and saw Enrique and Chaz pulling up beneath the three of them. "How you guys doing down there. Any further damage?"

Silence.

"Chaz? How we looking," Enrique prompted.

"Same. Minor structural damage. Shielding is still at sixty percent," Chaz replied.

"You okay, man?" Enrique's voice came after a pause.

"Yeah," Chaz answered. "Just need to make sure we're good for the rest of the patrol."

Estelle noted that the man sounded somewhat distracted. She began to ponder.

"What now, Estelle?" Dodds asked after a moment.

"We... er... transfer a report of our findings and the battle back to Spirit Orbital," she said, watching as what remained of the Dart continued to tumble, short and explode ahead of her. "Chaz, Enrique, could you... please send them a detailed report of your damage so that... they... er... so they can be prepared to handle it effectively upon our return. Kelly, ensure you have a record of the fighters you took down; just their USIDs will do. After we're done... we'll continue with the patrol. We still have a while before quitting time."

Estelle turned to one of the TAFs, the pilot watching her closely. She saw them turn back to the front and then heard a private channel open.

"Are you okay?" It was Dodds.

"I'm fine, Dodds."

"Really?"

"Yes. Please set yourself back on the patrol route. I'll join you in a moment, I just need to make a note of something," Estelle said before cutting off the link. She watched as Dodds pulled away from her, Kelly following after him, before placing her comms on mute and putting on her over her chest. She could feel her heart thumping hard. The words of the man were still running around in her head.

"Calm down, Estelle. Calm down," she said to herself, exhaling a deep breath. "He only did it to freak you out and you took the bait. You didn't have to bail out and you've had worse than that before. Calm down. Finish the patrol, get home, have some food, a drink and a good rest."

It was the first real combat she had experienced in months, but it somehow felt a lot more real than usual. She closed her eyes and counted slowly to ten, distancing herself from the event.

"Everyone ready?" she asked once she believed she had given them adequate time to send their reports. The others reported that they were and Estelle led them back along the patrol route.

VIII

— The Cardinal and The Thief —

N ot long after returning to their designated route, the *White Knights* received new orders: they were requested to assist *CSN Cardinal*, a mobile research facility vessel, which had been attacked and boarded by a raiding party. As the *Knights* arrived within the vicinity of the *Cardinal* they found it drifting, damaged, and apparently powerless.

"Have you ever seen that ship before?" Estelle asked of her team. There was a resounding answer of "no" from all as they approached. Large quantities of debris drifted around the area, some of which appeared to belong to the *Cardinal*, the rest no doubt the remains of whomever had attacked her. From the looks of things the *Cardinal* had been equipped with some offensive weaponry and had made a conservative effort to defend itself.

"I'm unable to establish a comms link with *Cardinal*," Chaz reported. "Failure on all standard protocols."

"I'm going to head in and give the ship a quick sweep," Dodds said.

"Dodds, wait," Estelle said, as she saw him begin to pull away from the rest of the group. "Our orders are to secure the area and wait for backup to arrive." Though there did not appear to be any other craft in the area, Estelle ordered the others to hold their current position and keep a watchful eye on their radars.

Sometime later two Confederation search and rescue vessels arrived; they only recognised one: the *Merekat*.

"Area is secured," Estelle informed the captain of the *Merekat* as the search and rescue vessel approached the *Cardinal* and pulled up alongside it. The other vessel held back, waiting to serve any support requests.

"Affirmative, de Winter, we're going to send over a landing party. Please continue to monitor the area," the captain of the *Merekat* said as his ship closed on the *Cardinal* and deployed a boarding tube.

"Think anyone is alive in there?" Dodds asked of his wingmates.

"From the looks of things they're all dead," Kelly said. "We probably got here a little too late."

"At least they put up a decent fight," Dodds commented.

"Not good enough though," Estelle answered, raising her eyes up from her radar and looking at the lifeless ship they had been requested to assist. She watched as another piece of wreckage drifted toward her TAF before bouncing harmlessly off the shielding. She could see, somewhere further off, what appeared to be the remains of a small vessel, perhaps a one-man fighter craft of some sort. She assumed the *Cardinal* must have been attacked by a small group of raiders, each in their own individual craft. She dropped her eyes back down to her raider and wondered what might be going on inside.

"What are you doing?" Enrique asked Chaz. The big man was fiddling with the Ray's on-board computer, his fingers tapping away at the small keyboard underneath one of the screens.

"Finding out what's going on," he said. He continued pressing buttons and tapping at the screen, the computer issuing an occasional bleep in response. Enrique didn't recognise anything that was being displayed on the screen Chaz was accessing. The general lack of finesse in the layouts and aesthetics of the data representation suggested that the man had accessed something that was only to be used by maintenance and systems workers, and was not supposed to be readily available to the pilots.

A moment later voices filled the cockpit and Enrique gave a start.

"This is Williams. Docking tube fixed and stable. Moving towards airlock," a voice came.

"Copy that, Williams. Scans indicate some internal damage to the *Cardinal*. Proceed with caution," another voice answered.

"Will do, Captain. We will maintain an open channel," Williams said.

"What's that?" Enrique said as he listened to the chatter.

"It's the communications link being used between the boarding party and *Merekat*," Chaz said.

Enrique took a moment to understand. "Wait, hold on. Did you just hack..." he began, stunned by what the man had just done.

"Shhh! Listen."

Enrique fell silent and the two men listened in to the conversation between the boarding party and the *Merekat's* captain.

The party leader, Williams, stood by the *Cardinal's* airlock door turned to a member of his team. "Kate, would you do the honours?"

Kate produced a small portable device and connected it via a number of cables to the exterior airlock control panel. The door lock gave a short buzz, a little red light on the control panel changing to green.

"Open, sir," she said, stepping to one side.

"Excellent. Right, remember everyone: no energy weapons," Williams told his team. "We want to minimise damage to the interior if we encounter any hostilities."

His team was made up of seven, clad in dark blue, lightly armoured suits and wearing protective helmets. On their feet they wore magnetic boots that could be activated in low and zero gravity situations. Most of their larger weapons were also equipped with a torch, for circumstances where they might have to work in the dark. Aside from the weapons, the team also carried maintenance gear, and medical supplies.

The seven men and women stood to either side of the airlock, so as not to expose themselves to anyone who might be waiting on the other side. Williams gave Kate the signal to opened the airlock, and as the door slid open they were met by nothing except for an empty corridor, pitch black save for where the falloff lighting from the boarding tube illuminated the entrance.

"Archer, Fisher," Williams indicated to the two men closest the entrance to enter first. One after the other they ran in, shining their torches around the immediate area. They determined that the corridor was empty, but even so they stalked forward cautiously, still met by neither opposition nor crew members.

"Clear," Fisher declared. The rest of the team entered the thin corridor. Another member removed a device from his belt and scanned the area.

"Minimal power on this deck; gravity and life support are functioning as usual. There does appear to be more power in the direction of the upper decks, though," he reported.

Williams nodded. "Pair up and spread out. Get in touch as soon you encounter survivors or hostile forces."

The group paired off as ordered and proceeded to explore the darkened lower deck of the ship, carefully checking possible hiding places in various rooms and ensuring they illuminated all unreachable areas well. With the exception of a hacked airlock door - which they assumed the invaders must have used to get inside - they once again came up empty handed. The team soon regrouped by the lift to the upper deck and found the doors burnt and pock-marked by multiple weapon blasts.

"Lift is operational, sir," reported Kate and, at the request of Williams, pressed the call button. The lift arrived and the doors parted, greeting the team with the slumped body of a dead man. Blood was splattered over his clothes and interior of the lift. The multiple lights of the investigators fell upon a shotgun the man still grasped.

"This is Williams: we've found a body. Judging by the way this guy is dressed, it isn't one of the crew," Williams reported to the *Merekat*. "If the state of the lift is anything to go by, there has been one hell of a firefight in here."

"What're we looking at?" the captain asked.

"Definitely a raiding party," Williams said, edging forward and examining the dead man's body. He pushed aside the beaded dreadlocks that covered part of the raider's face, revealing a tattoo of a spider's web on his left cheek. "Cheap body armour. Didn't do him any good," Williams muttered, then, "We're proceeding to the upper deck."

The upper deck of the ship told a different story to the lower. Bodies, trails of blood and other clear signs of battle were in evidence throughout. Shorting electronics lit the dark corridors with bright bursts of spark light.

"Be careful of those," Williams pointed out some wires that hung inconspicuously from the ceiling.

Williams divided the team, instructing one half to accompany him towards the bridge, and the other to spread out along the upper deck and continue to search for any survivors. They moved with care, ensuring they ducked under the loose wires. The team encountered yet more bodies as they went, none of whom displayed any signs of life. A scattering of clothing styles suggested that the crew and their attackers had taken an equal number of casualties.

The team discovered most of the bodies on the bridge, some appearing to have died as a result of close quarters combat; the unfortunate crew of the *Cardinal* marred by stab wounds all over their bodies, some having had their throats cut. It was a horrific scene.

"Looks like the crew tried to barricade themselves inside the bridge," Williams reported once more to *Merekat*.

"Any sign of what they could have been looking for?" came the reply in his ear piece.

"Nothing yet, but I'm guessing they may have been scavengers. Looks like the *Cardinal* was just in the wrong place at the wrong time."

Williams and his team pressed on into the bridge in an attempt to gather more information. Following a short inspection of the bridge area, Kate began examining the ship's logs.

"Some data has been downloaded from the computers," she said, running through them. As she spoke a screen next to her sprang into life and began churning out information.

Estelle's eyes flashed down to her radar.

"Estelle!" Dodds started.

"I see it!" Estelle said.

From beneath the *Cardinal* a small craft emerged. Being so close to the ship it had escaped notice by both the radar systems and the *Knights'* own eyes. But with the activation of shielding, computer system and engines, the vessel announced its presence to all in the vicinity as it accelerated away from the *Cardinal*, keeping in line with the ship's original heading.

Estelle cursed herself for not performing a proper sweep of the *Cardinal*.

"I'm going after it," Dodds said.

"Stay put, Dodds," Estelle answered.

"I can catch it," Dodds insisted, manoeuvring his TAF toward the escaping craft and preparing to give chase.

"Lieutenant, you will hold your position. That's an order!" Estelle barked. With her own orders and duties clear in her head she was not prepared to allow Dodds to play the hero. Dodds had met with disaster the last time he had done so and Estelle was not about to let him go through all that again; for his sake as well as her own.

Dodds backed down, though not without further grumbling.

Estelle contacted *Merekat*. "*Merekat*, this is de Winter. Unidentified craft has been spotted departing *Cardinal*. Please advise." After destroying the Dart earlier, she was not prepared to allow another error of judgement lead to an action that she would later come to regret.

As she awaited the answer from *Merekat*, the space ahead of the escaping craft began to distort and twist. The distortion quickly began to subside, leaving behind a steady rotating swirl. The craft sped into the swirling mass, disappearing from sight, whereupon the portal vanished and the surrounding space returned to normal.

Estelle blinked in disbelief. "What the hell just happened?"

"I don't know," Dodds said, taken aback. "Did that ship just open a jump point?"

"No, that's impossible," Kelly said. "It's far too small to be equipped with jump engines."

Estelle looked from her radar to the *Cardinal* and back again, trying to make sense of what she had just seen.

"*Cardinal* just opened a timed jump point," Kate informed Williams. The man walked over to investigate the screens the woman was looking at. He relayed the information to *Merekat's* captain.

"Try and determine what the destination was," the captain answered. "And be careful; an unidentified craft just departed the *Cardinal* and escaped via that jump point. If it was hostile then there may still be others on the ship. Be on your guard and take extra precautions."

In another part of the *Cardinal's* upper deck, Archer had found a number of men and women lying on the floor of a room up ahead, all bound and gagged. They all appeared to be unconscious; or perhaps dead.

"This is Archer, I may have found survivors," he radioed. "Looks like someone's tied them all up. I'm going to check the bodies and then help anyone still alive off the ship."

He started forward. The people opened their eyes as they became aware of his approach and started shaking their heads and screaming at him through their gags. It did not occur to him what they were trying to tell him until he stepped through the doorway.

Too late he saw the thin red beams of the lasers break as his hand passed through them.

"Aw, hell..." Archer began.

The explosives went off, the blasts ripping their way through the ship. A wall of fire squeezed itself down the corridors, engulfing everything in its path.

Chaz and Enrique were amongst the first to hear the sound, but it was not until fire burst forth from the bridge, forcing glass, ship parts and bodies ahead of it, that they realised what they had heard and became aware of the crisis.

"Get to a safe distance! Move! Move! Move!" Estelle shouted to her wingmates. The *Knights* swung their fighters around and pulled away from the *Cardinal* as quickly as they could, retreating back away from the ship they had been called in to help.

Merekat was not so lucky. The *Cardinal's* midsection exploded, damaging the search and rescue vessel that was still attached to it. Before long the explosion that Archer had triggered found its way to the *Cardinal's* reactor and the two ships were torn apart by the tremendous force of the blast.

The *Knights* sat motionless for a moment, watching a section of one of the ships tumbling before them. Not long after Estelle was contacted by the second rescue ship, which identified itself as *CSN Buffalo*.

Together the five craft set about searching for signs of any possible survivors amongst the carnage, no matter how futile it seemed. None were found. As had been feared, no one aboard *Merekat* had been able to get to the escape pods in time, or had a chance to protect themselves against the cold vacuum of space. The search for survivors changed to a search for bodies and, after picking up all that they could find, *Buffalo* called an end to the sweep. Finally, after recovering the black boxes from the *Cardinal* and *Merekat*, *Buffalo* signalled to the *Knights* it was ready to leave.

"There's nothing more for us to do here," Estelle informed her team. "We'll escort *Buffalo* back to Spirit."

• • •

"This is an utter disaster!" Turner grated, holding his head in his hands as he read the reports detailing the fates of the *Cardinal* and *Merekat*. Though they had yet to be fully sorted and collated, it had not proven difficult to piece together a picture of exactly what had happened earlier that evening.

Parks had returned to Xalan upon hearing the news. He now stood before Turner, waiting as the admiral went over each of the reports, knowing that they did not make for pleasant reading.

"What the hell was *Cardinal* doing there without some sort of escort?" Turner growled.

"According to Spirit Orbital they had reported a suspected case of Shizaru's Fever aboard and had performed an emergency jump into Temper."

Turner stared at him incredulously. "Shizaru's Fever? The disease that induces deaf-blindness?"

"Yes, sir," Parks said, though he found himself sharing Turner's scepticism.

"There's not been a confirmed or even reported case of that for over one hundred years. They should have followed proper procedure instead of trying to handle it themselves," Turner grumbled. "Just our damned luck that raiders would choose a research ship to hit. This is precisely why we need to step up patrols in all sectors. This event could have been easily avoided if we'd simply had more manpower."

Parks nodded, even though he knew that it wasn't a real solution; Turner was clutching at straws. The bigger issue was what had been taken from *Cardinal*. The moment word had reached him that the ship had been attacked and destroyed, Parks prayed that was all that had happened. As the reports from the various witnesses had come in, he had heard that a craft had fled the scene moments before the ship's destruction. But not before a dump had been taken from the computer systems, copied onto a data card and then, presumably, taken on board the fleeing vessel.

Parks mused. As a mobile research facility *Cardinal* had held much of the Confederation's project work, acting as an extreme kind of disaster recovery service. It therefore held a lot of important data; though none as important as those pertaining to the ATAF project, as both he and Turner knew full well. It was all there: every schema, blueprint, theory, problem, solution, purpose; the list went on.

The *Cardinal's* black box had proven to be a treasure trove of information, detailing all the events leading up to the ship's untimely destruction. As well as letting the CSN know the nature of the data that had been downloaded on to the data card, it had also revealed the destination of the jump point the thief had used to escape. And Parks had almost despaired when he had discovered it led into Imperial space. Of all the places the thief could have chosen to go.

Upon hearing the news Turner had conversed with the Confederate Administration, who had been quick to assign a number of agents to the task of recovering the assumed stolen data. The investigation was then placed at the top of the Navy's priority list and Turner had summoned Parks to Xalan.

"That fool of a raider thinks he is going to earn himself a tidy little sum by selling on military secrets," Turner growled.

"The data is heavily encrypted, sir," Parks offered.

"That's besides the point, Commodore!" Turner snapped back at him. "With the resources available to them the Enemy could crack it within a matter of months."

Turner rose from his chair, taking one of the reports with him. Parks glanced over at the cabinet by the wall. The admiral was out of White Label whiskey. Turner started to pace, mumbling aloud the summarised time line of events, as detailed by Spirit Orbital station,

1710 hours — CSN Cardinal has made an emergency jump into the Temper system and reported a suspected case of Shizaru's Fever.

1749 hours — Received distress call from CSN Cardinal. Vessel under attack by raiders.

1751 hours — Contacted nearest patrol group, White Knights, and requested they assist Cardinal.

1753 hours — Dispatched Merekat and Buffalo for search and rescue operation.

1811 hours — CSN Cardinal reports that attacking vessels have been completely destroyed but raiding party has boarded.

"First *Dragon* and now this," Turner stopped reading the log of the events and tossed the report back on to the desk to join the rest. He stood staring out the window, contemplating.

"They'd still need to build the ATAFs," said Parks, once again attempting to reassure the admiral. "That would take them several months, even after they'd deciphered the data. And as far as we have been able to determine the Enemy don't retain any knowledge of starfighter construction."

"No, they could do it much quicker than that," Turner said as he picked up another report and began going over it. "Unlike us the Enemy do not require sign-offs, approvals, security, money... They don't have to justify an enormous military budget; they don't have to gloss over expenditure or attempt to keep the project under wraps; they don't have to sit in a boardroom full of suits trying to explain, in basic terms, the long-term implications of non-action. It doesn't matter that they might not understand starfighter engineering; with the information about the ATAFs in their hands they'll certainly make the effort to learn. And damn quickly, at that too."

"If..."

"You've seen first hand what that fighter is capable of," Turner went on, ignoring the commodore. "Imagine facing several dozen of those in combat. Combine that with the Enemy's abilities and we might as well arm everyone with low grade particle cannons for all the good it would do. Then there's all the other information they will have become privy to. We would have to step up the final phase of the project without any guarantees."

Turner picked up another report, reading it to himself for a time before glancing up at Parks and quoting a passage out loud. *"Upon resuming our patrol we were contacted by Spirit Orbital who requested that we assist* CSN Cardinal, *which had come under attack. We arrived to find signs of recent combat and the* Cardinal *damaged. I ordered that the area be made secure until the search and rescue teams could arrive.*

"I see the *White Knights* were at the scene."

"Yes, sir. They were patrolling the area when they received the request to aid *Cardinal*."

"And they were unable to take down a single escaping craft?" Turner demanded to know.

"Those details are sketchy, sir. The wing leader believed she was acting within a support capacity and did not act because she was not ordered to."

"de Winter was leading the wing?"

"Yes, sir."

"She should have had that ship blown to pieces the moment it was clear of *Cardinal*," Turner growled, flipping backwards through the pages. He had received the reports less than an hour before Parks' arrival and there was much in them that he had skipped over, turning straight to the most important parts. "Apparently they also encountered some unknown hostilities on their patrol... What the hell's this?!"

"Sir?"

"This part of about some transmission!"

"The *Knights* received an unusual message that they thought was report-worthy," Parks explained, recalling reading it himself on the journey over.

Turner read back to get the full details of the transmission. Displeasure etched deeper into his face as he read on. Parks knew without having to be told what the admiral was thinking: this shouldn't be here. It all had to go. The pilot's words would lead to questions; questions which would then lead to truths; and truths that would lead to panic on quite literally a galactic scale. And then the Enemy would win.

"Remove it," Turner said, dropping the report back on to his desk. "As far as anyone is concerned those men were Imperial asylum seekers fleeing their system's civil war. They stole three ships and ran the check points in the Alba system before jumping to Temper. Their ships were destroyed after they failed to identify themselves upon request to a Naval patrol unit, which they had also attacked."

"Yes, sir. I'll have that updated for the final report," Parks assured him.

"Ensure it is, as well as the traffic and activity record at Alba."

Parks nodded.

"And have someone take the *Knights* aside and ensure they do not repeat what they heard. I don't care who you get to do it: yourself, Meyers, Hawke, or whoever. Just make sure the message is clear. We need all our bases covered on this one."

Parks nodded again. "I'll have it done as soon as we've wrapped this up, admiral."

"Good. I have to leave soon to meet with those clowns in Office and I don't wish to spend any more time with damage control," Turner growled once again, as if blaming Parks for the presence of the offending sentences. "Now, before all of this crap started, I believe you said that you had some news for me?"

"I do," Parks said with a wry smile.

Turner scowled at the commodore's sudden bright face. "I hope it's *good* news, Commodore."

"It's very good news, Admiral - Intelligence have finally managed to locate *Dragon*."

IX

— Poker, Rumours and Whiskey —

T he Officer's Club at Mandelah Naval Base was filled to capacity. Most days the Club was not as packed as it was tonight, but the actions of the *White Knights* two days previous had set in motion a series of rumours that had resulted in as many service personnel squeezing themselves into the building as possible.

Word of mouth had spread that a pilot named Kelly (first name unknown) had engaged and taken down two enemy starfighters, making their way through Confederation space. The exact identity of the "enemy" did not seem to be known and neither was it important. By further word of mouth it had become four enemy vessels, who were en route to torpedo Spirit Orbital. Kelly had been patrolling on his own when he had encountered the enemy, and had therefore been unable to fall back on any wingmates for assistance (at this point Kelly had also been identified as a man, or "one hell of a guy"). In the end he had become the sole responsibility for the defence and evacuation of a heavily packed naval transporter that was acting as the enemy's secondary target.

Even with the records available showing the true nature of events, Kelly Taylor had not breathed a single word of correction to anyone; anything for a party.

The drink was flowing quite freely that night, with much singing and dancing. The pool tables were receiving a great deal more attention than they would normally, with various wagers being played out non-stop. A tall, skinny man by the name of O'Reilly was enjoying a lot of success with the cue, many challengers attempting to break his winning streak and soon parting with their cash.

With everything going on Estelle wondered just who was watching how much everyone was drinking. Certainly not Captain Meyers, who had been absent from the base for the past two days, disappearing straight after the *Knights* had returned from their patrol. Earlier on she had seen a couple of the more senior officers perched on stools by the bar, making sure their people didn't overdo it; but they were not exactly enforcing the usual rules of responsible alcohol consumption on the others.

"... of all the places that we could have wound up in. Kelly?" Estelle said, raising her eyes from her glass and discovering Kelly to be preoccupied. "Kelly?"

The brown haired girl turned back to Estelle. "Sorry, Estelle, what did you say?"

"Too busy in your own little world, as usual," Estelle muttered, wishing her friend would listen to her ranting so she could get it off her chest. "Sometimes I think you really are just like your sisters."

Kelly recoiled on her stool. "Oh, thanks, Estelle. Thanks a lot," she said, sounding both hurt and angered by Estelle's words. "I thought if there was just one person in this world who wouldn't continue to bring that up, it would be you. Why people constantly feel the need to judge me on that, I'll never know."

A gathering of eight men and women, standing not too far from Estelle and Kelly's table, lowered their drinks to watch the scene unfolding.

"What's going on?" asked a man to the group, noting the scowl on Kelly's face.

"The neurotic one and the spoilt one are fighting," one of his drinking companions answered.

"That doesn't surprise me," said another. "I don't think there's a single person on the base that de Winter hasn't picked a fight with."

"What exactly is her problem?"

"Ego," a woman put bluntly.

"That Kelly Taylor?" one of the other men asked, with a nod of his beer bottle.

"No, that's de Winter. Taylor's the one having a go."

"Oh."

"Why, do you like that?"

"She's not bad."

"Don't bother. I share quarters with her. Really full of herself that one. Kelly's nicer, even if she's quite dizzy."

"Could someone explain to me why she is even here?"

"What do you mean?"

"Well if I were her, I wouldn't be here. I'd be spending all that money her father's got."

"You know, you're a real credit to the service."

"No, I'm just making a point. You probably would too."

"Like her sisters?"

"You know, I heard she hates them?"

"No, she doesn't hate them; they just don't get on."

"Tell you what, I wish my Dad had done that."

"Done what?"

"Been a galactic commodities trader."

"It wasn't her Dad, it was her great, great grandfather or something like that."

"You wouldn't be able to do it these days anyway. The market for that sort of thing was only around for a short time before all the larger corporations started to get in on the act. He was a smart man, you got to give him that."

"What are they fighting about?"

"I don't know and I don't care."

Several of the group turned their backs on the two women, going back to what they had been talking about before they had been distracted. One only half turned back, leaning ever so slightly in the table's direction, intrigued to hear what had riled Kelly so much.

"I can't help being who I am, Estelle. I didn't ask to be born into my family," Kelly was continuing her rant, Estelle not saying a word. "And I'm not like Susan and Gemma at all. If I was I wouldn't be here for a start. I'd be being snapped by photographers falling out of cars and nightclubs, so drunk I don't know what day it is; working my way through some football team; or joining the ranks of the no-knicker club. You know my sisters don't even know what I do? I've been with the CSN for nearly ten bloody years and they think that I'm a soldier, part of the Mobile Infantry.

"And speaking of which, you need to stop trying to make up for what happened to Jed. At least he wasn't killed and could walk away from it..."

Kelly stopped talking as the sentence left her mouth, instantly regretting her choice of words. Estelle and her brother had both taken up military careers at the same time, Estelle joining the CSN and her brother the CMI. Her brother had lasted only two years before he had returned home. An accident during a live fire exercise had resulted in a bullet shattering his knee cap and leaving him with a permanent limp. Estelle's family had been unable to afford the corrective surgery.

She looked uneasily around the Officer's Club for a moment, before turning back to Estelle. In for a penny, in for a pound; she may as well get it all out now. Better Estelle hear it from her than somebody else,

"Yes, okay, I know I can be flaky sometimes, but the others have accepted that and I don't see why you can't. And to be fair, I think that I do make up for that in the cockpit.

"Look, you need to stop wanting so much, so quickly. You said you want to one day command your own carrier, or battleship or whatever; but if you keep on making enemies here then you're not going to get there, because people will find you difficult to work with. Haven't you noticed how everyone in the dorm tip-toes around you? Doesn't that bother you? I mean, what the hell, Estelle, are you going to be a bitch your whole life?"

Estelle said nothing.

Kelly plunged on further. "And to be honest, we have had a rather intense few weeks with the training, the back and forth transfers from Gabriel, to Temper, to here, and then the constant up and down to the station. And let's not forget the little incident a few days ago. I think we deserve to let our hair down from time to time. *Lieutenant.*"

Her tirade over, Kelly started to wonder if she had taken things a bit far, Estelle still saying nothing, looking anywhere but at Kelly. She caught the eyes of a group of people standing nearby, who were quick to look away. The two women sat in silence for a time, looking anywhere but at each other and playing with their drinks.

"Sorry," they both said at the same time.

"I'm sorry," Estelle said again, sweeping her hair out of her face. "It's just that..."

"You don't want to be here," Kelly filled in for her.

"I look at all of this," Estelle gestured around herself. "And I wonder where I went wrong. We've just gone from being the pick of the best to some dingy backwater system, shut away from the other squadrons, to a place where very little happens. There don't seem to be any prospects for promotion, getting out or even any real recognition. I almost feel like the only thing left for me to do would be to quit."

"Quit?" Kelly said, stunned.

Estelle shrugged.

"Estelle, look, it's just a transitional period. We're not going to be here forever," Kelly said. Despite her words Kelly knew that Estelle would never quit, the woman was far too proud to do something like that. She'd sooner die than admit it to her family or herself. "For now this is just something we have to do. Listen, why don't you come running with me and the boys tomorrow, instead of bothering yourself with so much flag duty. It will help you to keep your mind off things like that."

Estelle opened her mouth to answer and then fell quiet. Kelly watched her, stirring her straw through the clutter of ice cubes, being all that now remained of her cocktail.

"Yeah, okay," Estelle said. "I guess I have been neglecting all you guys recently."

"Good, good," Kelly smiled. Estelle smiled back. Satisfied that even though she had been treading on very thin ice she had made her point, Kelly relaxed more. She once again looked over in the direction of Dodds, Enrique and Chaz who were sitting not far from them, on a long couch in the corner.

Estelle began to chuckle. "Don't stare at him, Kelly."

"I wasn't," Kelly said. "I was just wondering who was winning their game."

"Hmmmmmm."

"Don't you sometimes miss being with Dodds?"

"My drink's all gone, Lieutenant," Estelle said, crunching at the ice cubes with her straw.

Kelly smiled. Estelle was playfully abusing her position. She stepped off her stool. "Same again?"

"Same again. And stop looking over there," she added as Kelly walked back to the bar.

• • •

Estelle did, however, look over herself. She had noticed how Chaz was sitting with Dodds and Enrique, and a number of other servicemen, merrily enjoying the game. His usual cold demeanour seemed to have evaporated tonight, making him a lot more approachable. Even so, she could tell he was still keeping things close to his chest. Tonight he was neither being too quiet nor too loud, either of which could cause one to stand out. He was acting like a real blend-in, instantly forgettable. He also appeared to be drinking at a modest pace; and disguising that well too.

She could not figure the man out and had heard from Enrique about how he had hacked the Ray's on-board comms systems to hook into the *Merekat*. Nothing more had been said, Estelle withholding his actions from the post-patrol report. In any case, she was beginning to wonder just who Parks had assigned to her wing. As she waited for Kelly to return she did her best to watch the group of men without making it too obvious.

"You in, Chaz?" Enrique asked as he shuffled the cards once again.

"Sure."

"Dodds?"

"Yeah."

"How about you four? Who are you again?" Enrique asked the men sitting on the couch opposite him. They burst out laughing.

The group were playing poker, with Enrique acting as dealer. For the most part they were playing for fun, but one of the four men that Dodds, Enrique and Chaz sat with had decided to sneak a bottle of whiskey in with him, intending to use it as an ice-breaker. The strong liquor had now taken on a new role as a penalty for anyone who played an appalling hand. This was becoming quite a regular occurrence for Enrique, who had failed to beat any of the other players in the last few rounds.

"You know, mate, if this were a casino you'd be looking for a new job round about now," Dodds said.

"Dude, how much you 'ad?" asked the first man.

"Too much already by the looks of things," the second man said. "Clearly can't hold his drink."

"Oh, I can," Enrique defended himself. "I'm not that drunk."

"Okay, so what's our names again?" the first man said.

Enrique paused for a moment. Dodds watched him thinking, stealing a glance at Chaz who was taking a relaxing swig from his beer bottle.

"Tell you what," Enrique said. "Why don't I just call you Crew Cut, Tubby, Irish and Shy Boy."

The four men exchanged incensed looks.

"Well, you can't say they're not accurate," Enrique slurred a little.

"Oi," began Tubby, glaring. "My name's Ian."

Dodds reached out and put a hand on Enrique's shoulder. "No harm, boys," he said, giving his friend's shoulder a little squeeze to stop him saying any more. "Just some friendly nicknames, that's all."

"And besides, I've lost weight recently," Ian grumbled.

"Where did you get Irish from? The whiskey?" the one Enrique had christened said.

"Your accent," Enrique said.

"My accent?"

"Yeah."

"I'm Scottish, you cretin! I'm a McLeod!" the man growled.

"What should we call you two then?" Crew said.

"Hey, wait, I know these two," McLeod interrupted. "You're Simon Dodds and Enrique Todd: The Odd Brothers." A quizzical look crossed the faces of his three companions. McLeod elaborated, "These guys were pretty much inseparable at flight school. Never used to be far from one another. We ended up calling them the Odd Brothers because they were so much like family."

"Yeah, thanks," Dodds said, holding up his hand as if to brush away the conversation and the embarrassing memories that it invoked.

"Weren't you dating that girl, Esther or something? The one who thought the sun shone out of her arse?"

"Estelle. Yeah, that one," Dodds admitted, seeing McLeod look around briefly in the direction of the woman sat at a table by herself. "But, no we're not seeing each other any more. She said she didn't have time for me and wanted to focus on her career."

"Shame," McLeod observed.

"Why is she like that? So self absorbed, I mean," Crew asked.

"She wants to make something of herself," Dodds started.

"Yeah, that's obvious," Crew scoffed.

"No, that's not what I mean. She doesn't come from a particularly well off family," Dodds said. "She was born on one of colonies on Tilli; so you know how it is out there. They never had a lot of money and had to get by mostly on state benefits. Her parents worked whenever they could find it, but again, you've heard how it is there. She quit school early so that she could try and help bring in some cash, but it didn't make a whole lot of difference. They couldn't even up sticks: they couldn't afford to settle down anywhere else, let alone afford the cost of transport in the first place. So, she joined the Navy to prove to her family and herself that she was worth more than all of that. She sends most of the money she earns home to them."

"Ah," McLeod said.

"Hmmmm," Dodds added. Whilst he was aware that he had just dished out a great deal of very personal information about a friend to a group of men he didn't know, he was only trying to defend the Estelle that he knew better than others.

"Still," McLeod said, glancing back over to Estelle, who was taking a glass from Kelly, "Shame to have let that one go."

"Oh, she's been known to change her mind from time to time," Enrique said, with a grin.

"Well, at least until the next morning," Dodds finished. He then wagged a finger at McLeod. "Getting back to things: Yeah, I sort of remember you now too. Been a long time; nice to see you again."

"Yeah, you too," McLeod said. "Drink this." He thrust a whiskey glass, half filled with the neat liquor, toward Dodds.

Dodds withdrew and directed it towards Enrique. "You came up with the names."

Enrique reluctantly took the glass and downed it in one, coughing a couple of times before handing it back. "After this round I will be passing the dealing over to my good friend Dodds here," he drawled, scooping his beer off the table and knocking back a good amount of the contents. "I really hate whiskey," he said to Dodds.

"Aw, God no, *come on*," Ian said.

At first Dodds thought that the man was unset that he was not going to get a chance to see Enrique make a speckle of himself. He then saw that the eyes of the four opposite him were looking not at Enrique, but to his left.

Sitting next to Enrique were a couple whose public display of affection for one another was beginning to encroach far too much on the poker game and everyone's enjoyment. When the male half of the couple had asked if he could sit on the end of the couch none had expected that his companion was then going to be sitting on *him* for the rest of the evening – although, from Dodds' angle, sitting on him might not have been the best way to describe the way the woman had been clambering all over the man for the last fifteen minutes.

"Guys, guys! Seriously, Romeo, get a room!" Enrique scowled at them.

"And you're the guy to ask about that are you?" the man answered him, managing to wrench his lips away from those of his eager companion. "Don't suppose you've noticed but there's little in the way of privacy around here, them not giving us private quarters like that lot up on the orbital."

"No, I hadn't noticed actually," Enrique said. "But I think you'll find there are a few spare mattresses in the south block storage room. Shouldn't be too cold in there neither."

Dodds found himself impressed at both his friend's knowledge of Mandelah's logistical offerings and the fact that the tip seemed to do the trick. The man whispered to the woman he was with for a moment before the pair got up. He clapped Enrique on the shoulder a couple of times as they left. Dodds watched them go, his attention straying to the two women seated on tall stools at a just as tall round table, chuckling to one another.

Estelle was looking particularly cheery tonight. It was nice to see her this way, especially after the disappointment she had suffered following the termination of involvement in the ATAF project. She glanced at the men sitting around the low table and, catching his eye, smiled at Dodds. He smiled back, then returned his attention back to the game at hand.

"So, why'd you boys join the Navy then?" Crew asked as they picked up the cards Enrique had dealt and scrutinised them.

"Well," Dodds began, seeing the group's gaze fall on him. "I didn't want to do the whole nine to five thing, just didn't interest me. I wanted to get out there and see and do things, find a bit of adventure. Wanted to feel like I was a bit more than some cog in a big old machine that could work just as well without me. So at the end of the day it was either this or spend my life looking after apples."

He watched their impassive expressions for a moment and then saw Ian's face split into a grin.

"Ahhhh," Ian said, with a chuckle. "So, you wanted to join the Navy and become a hero!"

"No," Dodds said, sitting back up.

"Yeah, you did," Ian began to laugh. "You thought that if you joined the Navy, you'd get to blow stuff up, go on daring missions, earn tons of medals and get to sleep with lots of beautiful women."

"No, I just wanted to do something different, you know – give something back to the Confederacy; be a part of something special," Dodds said.

"See," Crew interrupted. "You *did* want to be a hero."

All four men were laughing at Dodds. He turned toward Enrique and Chaz, seeking support, but saw that they too were enjoying the roast; Enrique shaking his head, Chaz wearing a thin smile.

Sure, I did want to be a hero, once, Dodds thought to himself. *But I'm back here for different reasons now.*

"What about you?" Crew turned his attention to Enrique, who shielded his cards in case there was some ploy against him. Dodds looked around at his friend, curious as to how Enrique might answer the question. Few outside the *Knights'* small group were aware of Enrique's back story. Dodds was not even sure if Enrique had ever told Chaz.

When he was eight years old Enrique and his family had been returning from celebrating his older brother's tenth birthday. They had been in a car travelling along a motorway when his father had noticed a truck on the other side of the road driving erratically. Enrique's father had taken precautions, deciding to slow and switch lanes. Just as he had done so the truck had swerved, crashing through the central reservation and tipping on to its side, careering towards them. The rear of the truck had clipped their car and sent it tumbling, at speed, up the road side embankment. It came to rest back on the road, leaving a trail of broken and crumpled chassis parts and shattered glass behind it.

Emergency services had been quick to arrive at the scene. His mother, older brother and little sister were pulled from the wreckage of their car, but had been pronounced dead at the scene. Along with his father, Enrique had been air-lifted to the nearest hospital. Despite all the efforts of the emergency teams his father had died en route owing to massive internal bleeding. Enrique had survived with a broken arm.

He was raised by his grandfather, an ex-military and spiritual man, who never failed to impress upon him the fact that someone was looking out for him and that he had survived the crash for a reason. Enrique took the words to heart and, spurred on by his grandfather, had signed up for the Navy in order to protect others and do his best to save lives and keep the peace.

It was not, however, a story that he would often tell.

"Figured the Navy was something I would enjoy," Enrique said with a shrug. "And I was no good at anything else."

"Sounds like that should have been your reason," Ian said, laughing once again at Dodds.

"You?" Crew looked at Chaz. So did Dodds and Enrique, more intrigued than the man asking the questions.

"I used to fly interplanetary shuttles and landers," Chaz said dismissively. "After nearly ten years of doing that I wanted to see and do something more. The police force didn't interest me: too much corruption. So I applied to the Navy. So far I've been stationed in more than ten different star systems over the past eight years and learned to fly over half a dozen different starfighters."

"Oh, okay," Crew said. There was no sarcasm from Ian or McLeod over the explanation; Chaz, for some reason, didn't seem to warrant it.

Chaz took a slow pull from his bottle, saying nothing else.

"Girlfriend, wife, kids?" McLeod said, rolling his hand around.

"None to speak of," Chaz said after considerable pause.

"He's like your mate," Enrique supplied, nodding at the fourth man of the group, who had contributed little to the conversation. "Man of few words."

The other three went on to explain their reasons for joining up, how Crew's parents disagreed with his career choice because he was basically being granted a license to murder. He argued he was being trained to protect and that the need to take a life was a wholly real and necessary part of that duty. His parents had asked if he ever raised a thought for the people in the ships he gunned down. Ian chipped in and said that to him the enemy were faceless anyway and may as well be robots. He commented that no one thought about who they may have just killed when they destroyed their fighter. It didn't matter to them that it may have been someone's only child, a mother, a father of two, a brother or sister. At the end of the day they were the enemy and that was all that mattered.

"Getting a bit deep," Dodds said as the group lapsed into silence, a sombre bubble seeming to have enclosed the group. The cheerful mood was threatening to abandon them.

"I think I'm sobering up," Enrique said.

"Yes, let's play," McLeod pushed aside a couple of cards. "Deal me two more."

Enrique leaned forward to the little table the deck rested on and, after making a bit of a mess of the pile, managed to hand the man two more cards.

"Hey, no really, do you know what I've been hearing lately?"

Dodds looked up from his cards for the source of the voice and realised it belonged to the man who had remained relatively quiet for most of the game; the one Enrique had called Shy Boy.

"I've been told that there's no Imperial civil war," Shy said.

"What's that?" Dodds said as the others lowered their cards.

"*There is no war*," Shy repeated, emphasising the statement a little more this time.

"You mean they're just making it up?" said Enrique.

"Not entirely, but they are definitely trying to cover something up. Something really bad's happened over there and they don't want people to find out about it."

"You think they've been attacked by aliens?" asked Ian excitedly, as the others pondered the statement.

"No, not bloody aliens!" Shy said, turning to him with a look of utter disdain.

"You've got to admit that'd be pretty cool," Ian enthused, ignoring him, his eyes glazing over. "Think of the architecture and the tech and the culture; what they might look like and how they'd speak; all their history and what we could learn from them. Hey!"

McLeod had reached over and plucked the beer bottle from the man's hand. "Explorers have been up and down the galaxy for decades and haven't found anything more advanced than bacteria and a few tiny little microscopic plants," he said. "So, can the fantasy; You won't be getting your fat fingers on any hot alien babes!"

"Not aliens then?" Dodds asked of Shy.

"No, something else. But whatever it is the Confederation's getting us all ready to defend ourselves against some great invasion. Apparently the Imperium has been completely wiped out, except for a load of refugees." From the look on his face he was being completely serious.

"Who told you that?" McLeod asked, looking extremely sceptical. "And whoever it was, tell them to stop smoking so much crack and go get themselves a girlfriend."

"No, really. And something else I heard was that the Navy's been pumping money into some new top secret project. Some powerful new weapon, apparently."

Dodds forced himself not to meet Enrique's or Chaz's eyes, nor say anything, and instead concentrate on what the men were saying. He could see, out of the corners of his eyes, that the other two were doing the same.

"What project?" Crew wanted to know.

"That's all I've been told, so it could be anything," Shy said with a shrug. "All I know is that it's costing them an arm and a leg."

"Think they're building another battleship to replace *Dragon*?"

Shy shook his head. "Don't know, but apparently it's the reason why the orbital ring here hasn't been finished. They've diverted all the funding that was meant to go here into that secret project." He took a swig of his beer and then pointed his bottle at Crew. "And since you mention *Dragon* that goes along with the whole thing too."

"How so?" Dodds asked, folding up his cards and putting them face down on the table.

"Well, *Dragon*'s been stolen, right? How do you do that? You can't just walk on board and take the controls. You'd need a pretty big force to achieve something like that, and that's even before you get anywhere near it. You'd have to either be super human, or have someone on the inside." He lowered his voice before continuing, leaning a little closer to the table so that the others could hear. "And Commodore Hawke, right, how'd he survive? I mean, it's not like the man would run off into the escape pods and leave his crew to defend *Dragon* alone. I'm not exactly the guy's biggest fan, but a captain goes down with his ship; and you all know that he'd sooner die on his feet than curled up in a ball in a pod."

"Most likely he was wounded," Crew said. "The crew chucked him into the pod and shot him towards the nearest jump gate. They needed someone to get away, and top brass would be more likely to believe a warning coming from him than some delirious petty officer."

"That doesn't explain what really went on though," Dodds said, somewhat disappointed.

Shy shrugged. "No one knows exactly what was going on, but from what I've heard *Dragon* was out somewhere near the Imperial-Independent border. So whatever's going down is getting closer."

"Look, can we stop with the stupid conspiracy theories, please?" McLeod growled, as though he was beginning to find his colleague's words offensive. "There's no secret project, no mass invasion. Seriously, who's telling you all this?"

"Hey, I'm not saying anything else," Shy said, putting his hands up in submission. "I heard they killed the last guy who went around gossiping."

"Really?" Enrique asked, flabbergasted.

"No, they didn't! Grow up, mate!" McLeod said, as Dodds picked up his beer. It was becoming obvious that McLeod was feeling the story teller was now winding up his audience unnecessarily, and was starting to get bored with the yarn, seeing its facts being grounded in nothing more than rumour, speculation and hearsay.

"Yeah, they did," Shy said. "They shot him when he tried to run away and buried him in an unmarked grave. Okay, that's a bit of an exaggeration, but they certainly made him disappear. I think his name was Bishop or Nurse or Dean or something like that..."

Dodds, in the middle of swigging from his bottle, suddenly choked and spat a mouthful of beer out on to the floor. He proceeded to cough for a good while, trying to clear his throat.

"You okay?" Enrique asked.

"Yeah, just went down the wrong way," Dodds spluttered. Enrique gave him a few slaps on the back. He noticed how everyone was still giving him a strange look as he continued wiping his mouth and coughing. "Think that's true about the Imperium?" Dodds asked Enrique once he had calmed down.

"No idea. What do you think, Chaz?" Enrique deflected the question to the man sat on the far right.

"I think you boys should stop worrying and have another drink," Chaz said with clear amusement. Dodds became thoughtful. Whilst Shy had been right on one count, perhaps McLeod did have a point. Maybe the man was exaggerating to amuse himself. He returned to his cards.

"Excuse me?" a voice interrupted the group as they prepared to continue their game once again. They looked up to see a man staring at Enrique, looking somewhat bemused. A short distance behind him a young woman hovered, watching the group and the man expectantly.

"Yeah?" Enrique asked.

"I er... I hear you're the guy to talk to about getting hold of spare mattresses..?"

Don't get stressed, just keep calm. They'll shut up in a minute.

Estelle attempted to convince herself that Dodds and Enrique would cease their whispering and drop off to sleep. It was not just that they were being loud that was annoying her, but also that they were doing it after lights out and everyone else was asleep and quiet. Anything bad that they did was ultimately a poor reflection on her. She tried to ignore it for a little longer.

The Officer's Club had been emptied some time ago, everyone being shepherded back to their quarters for an immediate lights out. Estelle recalled seeing a couple of men being shouted at by a higher ranking officer. From what she had heard, whilst they had been out drinking and enjoying themselves they had missed their transport and, as a result, their scheduled patrol. Though often a calm and pleasant man, Estelle knew that Meyers would not tolerate that kind of behaviour on the base and they would without doubt be feeling the heat from him when he returned. Estelle was not keen for the same fate to befall her or her team any time soon.

"Do you think tha guy wuz right?" Dodds asked, his speech slurring.

"Wig guy?" Enrique wanted to know, communicating with his long term friend in the same tongue.

"The guyz that was talk'en about the Imperial civil war."

"Naah. He's talking out ta his arse."

"Yeah?"

"Yeah."

They both went quiet; Estelle relaxed more. A good minute or so passed. It sounded as though the conversation that had woken her had been concluded. Estelle turned over in her bed and rearranged her covers to get more comfortable.

"Yeah... bu.. but, when yous thinks about it, its makes sssense," Dodds tried again.

Estelle felt herself stiffen at the sound of resumed chatter.

"How?"

"Well for one there's.. there's that transmission we got t'other day. That bloke, right, he's was really sscared. I doubt a civil war could be that bad toos make someone as hysterical as that. He wuz running away from somethings pretty nasty, I's thinks," Dodds managed, the volume of his voice rising as he spoke.

"Okay. Anythings else, like?" Enrique wanted to know, not sounding convinced.

Both men went quiet again. Even so Estelle was feeling thoroughly wound up. She hated it when people would not shut up at night, and even if they did quieten down now, it could take her quite a while before she was settled and able to drift off.

Dodds paused to consider all the possibilities. Despite being drunk he was not about to bring up the subject of the ATAFs and the redirection of revenue into support his argument. He realised, just as he had said it, that he should not really have mentioned the Dart pilot either. No, it didn't matter. He was sure that no one else was awake to hear him anyway. He considered telling Enrique about Dean. That was weird that his name had been brought up tonight. He then remembered the warnings given him by Admiral Turner and the officer who had come to retrieve the man's body, and thought better of it.

There was something there though, in the back of his mind. Was there a connection with what he had heard tonight? Dean was doubtless a piece of the puzzle, but was there something else too? Had Dean said something that, at the time, he had missed? The amount of alcohol he had consumed was inhibiting his ability to think straight.

"Well, then there's Hawke," Estelle heard Dodds' voice offer, resuming after leading her into false promises that he and Enrique had fallen asleep.

"Yea, sho?" Enrique replied to the man in the bunk above him.

"I swears that since they pulled him out of that escape pod he's become an even bigger arsehole..."

"Go to sleep, Dodds," Estelle said. She'd had enough. The pair clearly had too much to drink and were now just spouting random nonsense. At the mention of a senior officer, and the insults that followed, she had decided that they had crossed the line. Should anyone come around to inspect their quarters and discovered them to be speaking after lights out, drunk and making derogatory remarks about the commodore, they would be disciplined; all three of them.

"Dids we wake yous up, Estelle?" Dodds asked.

"It's after lights out, Dodds."

"Ssorrys, Estelle, couldn't sleep. And we's was jus' chattin'," Enrique muttered. "We ain't doin' anys harms, right?"

"You're drunk and you're being loud," Estelle hissed back at them.

"Nos louder thans Kelly," Enrique said. The woman was snoring ever so slightly.

"I remembers when tha' girl us' ta be able t'put it away," Dodds said, regarding her from his top bunk. "Hmm, things shange..."

"Yeah, sshame she shill shnores likes a pig though!"

Both men started laughing.

"I mean it, you two! Shut up and go to sleep!" Estelle raised her voice. Others around her stirred a little in their beds.

"Whatz the problems, Estelle? Wuz got a late patrol tomorrows," Dodds said.

"Or maybe not evens one a'all, the way they muck the schedules 'bout," Enrique added.

"Yeah, exactly; nothing to do tomorrow mornin'" Dodds moaned.

"If you don't shut up and go to sleep, then I will *give* you something to do in the morning, Lieutenant!"

"Jeez," Dodds said.

"Sssherioushhly dude, I can't believe..." Enrique started.

"Final warning, Todd!" Estelle glowered.

She waited patiently for them both to settle down, feeling her heart thumping hard, her chest tight. She drifted off to sleep herself once Dodds and Enrique had fallen silent.

Chaz Koonan lay on his back, arms folded across his chest, staring up at the ceiling. Unlike Estelle, Dodds and Enrique's conversation had not roused him, as he had not been asleep. He was thinking, his head filled with memories of the past and contemplations of the future. He thought of the Dart pilot; of the conversation in the Officers' Club; and of how Parks had not kept his word, had not let him go, had broken his promise.

He rolled over and closed his eyes, knowing that tonight he would not be getting much sleep. Just like every other night for the past four years.

X

— Far From A Saving Grace —

N atalia Grace slept deeply, her slumber aided by the stasis capsule that she had crawled into over three weeks previous. The escape pod around her lay in almost complete darkness. Crumbs from biscuits she had eaten dotted the floor, a small trail leading from a storage cabinet to the cockpit chair.

Deep asleep, those last three weeks had passed unnoticed to her. No longer had she to endure the frustration and depression she had suffered during the first seven days alone in the pod. She had wept several times during that period, almost uncontrollably the whole way through jump space. Exhausted, she had settled down and slept in the cockpit seat and had, upon awakening, been greeted by the inky blackness of space and her exit from the jump.

Hope and relief had washed over her as she looked out of the pod, expecting to see familiar sights of the Independent star system she had entered. Far below her she sighted a planet, though not one she recognised. That didn't matter; she was home. A quick glance out the rear viewport revealed the jump gate she had exited, the structure not too far behind her.

The navigation systems of the escape pod synchronized themselves with her new location's navigation buoys and soon revealed her location: Iliad, an Independent frontier star system; the planet below her, Diso. According to the navigation computer Iliad was sparsely populated, but populated nonetheless. At that moment Natalia had exhaled a breath she seemed to have been holding in for months.

She had activated the pod's SOS broadcast and then explored the cramped pod. From a storage cabinet she had removed a small bottle of water and a handful of biscuits, before settling back in the cockpit's seat to await rescue. And there she had waited. And waited. And waited. But the minutes had turned to hours, and the hours to days, and all that time she saw no signs of rescue. In fact she saw no signs of *anything*. Not a single glimpse of another vessel, nor any sort of activity within the system.

She had turned to the radar system in an attempt to discover whether there was anything else around her: perhaps a research station or a ship that may have failed to spot her, her arrival in Iliad having somehow gone unnoticed.

She would have expected to have seen a number of coloured shapes indicating the presence of other vessels or entities in the area. But except for a solitary yellow marker resting at the bottom of the display that she had already identified as being the jump gate, it was empty. With the aid of a flight manual she had discovered she began tweaking settings and display options, searching for something, anything, that might help rid her of the feeling that she was alone. There was nothing.

After the second day had passed the relief she had felt upon entering the star system had all but abandoned her, to be replaced by a feeling of dread. Her escape pod continued to drift, moving away from Diso and leaving the jump gate far behind. She knew what had happened: the system had been abandoned. She had done her best to hold back the anger and frustration she had then felt, but it had forced itself out, and she had hurled the flight manual across the tiny pod's interior before cursing out loud and slamming her fists on to the console. Soon after that she had begun to weep again.

Natalia was unable to shake the feeling that all her suffering and loss had been for nothing. Her fate seemed sealed: she would die trapped in this cramped steel coffin, drifting through space.

But no, she had come too far and been through too much to give up hope now. She had looked behind her to the open stasis capsule that she had used it as a bed. She deliberated use of the capsule for a while, before turning back to gaze out at the empty space ahead of her, nibbling on a biscuit and thinking back over the events of the past months.

Her primary mission had been a complete success. Along with several other operatives she had completed a series of hit-and-run operations against essential Enemy targets in a number of Imperial systems. The team had gone in hard and fast, there being no sense in attempting to be strategic about it.

The Enemy were far better equipped, far more knowledgeable and much more combat efficient than they could ever hope to be. Her unit had suffered losses along the way, but they all knew that many of them would not be coming back.

Another fundamental part of the operation had been to collect as much information about the Enemy and their recent activities as possible. This they had also achieved, though not without the expense of many lives. The data cards holding the various reports now resided safe and secure in her jacket, zipped into an inside pocket.

With their objectives met and their mission accomplished, they had begun the journey home. It was as they approached a jump gate to cross the Imperial-Independent border that they had been hit hardest. Natalia had been stood on the small bridge of her vessel when a jump point had formed behind the convoy. From it had issued an Imperial frigate and a host of Imperial starfighters of all variety. They had attacked the instant they were clear of the point, with ferocious speed and efficiency.

One of the convoy had been destroyed within seconds and several others had been crippled moments thereafter. Her own ship had been struck by a volley of rocket fire, sections of the vessel starting to come apart. Fires and explosions had ripped through the interior, resulting in a great deal of damage and casualties. The ship had started to tumble, barely a few kilometres from the gate.

As the Enemy left the vessel to concentrate on the others who were returning fire and attempting to clear their paths to reach the jump gate, Natalia had pulled the burnt and injured navigator from his chair...

She had survived, though for how much longer she did not know. After seven days alone in the Iliad system, the pod's on-board computer had started to jingle. It had warned her that she was running low on oxygen and recommended that she place herself within stasis for the remainder of her journey. Natalia had looked to the screen and then around to the capsules. It seemed she had little choice about using them. The SOS continued to broadcast from the escape pod as it had done for the past seven days, but there was no-one to hear it.

She stood beside the capsule, staring down into the soft beige padding, which would become her resting place until she was rescued. A perfectly normal, healthy human being could survive for months in a capsule such as this, their metabolism slowed to the point where neither food nor water was needed to sustain them. Death would eventually claim them, though. Maybe not for six months, maybe not for twelve, but they would not live forever. And that was the part about it that had scared Natalia the most, because she didn't know how long her pod might drift for.

As she'd stripped, Natalia had wondered if the inside of the escape pod would be the last thing she ever saw. Would she close her eyes never to awake? She paused before relenting to the capsule's control, returning to the cockpit, powering down all the lights and switching the SOS broadcast to a low range.

She was in two minds about advertising her presence. On the one hand it could aid in her rescue, should anyone detect her ship adrift. On the other the Enemy could be drawn to it. They would without doubt see the craft on their radars and come to investigate, but whether they wasted any more time with it was another matter. She had discovered that the Enemy had begun to aggressively salvage almost everything they could find in recent months, gearing up for their next big push. In combat they now preferred to cripple their adversaries, so that the vessels could be assimilated into the ranks; only destroying those that were either of a measurable threat or completely unusable. This, she knew, was the only reason she had survived the attack on her convoy: her vessel meeting their requirements only briefly before it had started to come apart.

Through the near darkness she made her way back to the capsule and settled down inside, having checked once again that her reports were still secure in her jacket. With that little peace of mind she activated the controls that would close her in and induce the stasis.

It was Natalia's belief that switching off most of the power would give the Enemy the impression that the escape pod had been drifting for years, the power and vital system components having broken down a long time ago, the occupants almost certainly dead. She hoped that the pod would prove too small to be of any use to them, and that they would waste no further time with it and move on.

Or perhaps they would destroy it anyway, just to make sure.

XI

— Another Rude Awakening —

"**D**odds! Hey! Wake up! Wake up!"

Dodds blinked awake and became aware of three things: the first was that Estelle was standing next to his bunk, shaking him vigorously; the second that there was an alarm wailing; and the third that he had a splitting headache, a result of the previous night's drinking session having caught up with him. He wanted nothing more than to go back to sleep and wake up much later when everything had calmed down, and when it no longer felt as though someone was tightening a vice around his head.

He struggled to pull himself into an upright position, wincing at the pain in his head. He saw that all around the quarters other people were hastily pulling on boots, trousers and jackets and running out the door.

"What's happening?" he asked, feeling as though his head was going to explode at any minute.

"Enrique, do *not* go back to sleep! Don't you dare go back to sleep!" Estelle shouted at the man in the bunk below him.

Dodds leaned over, taking care not to tip himself off the side of the bed.

"Hey, come on!" Estelle called again.

"All right, don't shout, I heard you first time," Enrique complained. He hauled himself back up, where he sat hunched over, head in hands. "Aw, man. I feel like I'm going to puke."

Dodds pulled out a watch that he kept under his pillow and tried to focus on the little blue figures on the face. It was just after four in the morning; he hadn't managed more than three hours' sleep since settling down. He felt a momentary sense of déjà vu.

"What's going on?" Dodds asked again. His eyes followed the figures running out of the room and then saw the answer to his question come striding in through the quarters doorway, flanked by two other staff.

Commodore Hawke surveyed the scene in front of him with a look of disgust. "Come on! Come one! Get moving!" he barked, clapping his hands together. "You hear that alarm? That's the call to general quarters! That means now! What are you standing around for? Move, now!"

Estelle turned back to Dodds and mouthed for him to *get up, now!* Dodds looked to Hawke and saw his attention shift to the bunk he and Enrique occupied.

Hawke's eyes narrowed as they fell upon Estelle. "What the hell are you doing? Did I not just make myself clear? Have you gone deaf?" Hawke asked of her.

Even in his current state, Dodds knew that Estelle was in the one place she would rather not be at this point in time: stood next to two members of her flight group who did not seem capable of mustering the strength to pull themselves out from under the covers.

"Sir, I was..." Estelle began.

"Do these little boys need their mummy to dress them?" Hawke growled. He then looked straight at Dodds and the pilot felt his heart jump the moment the flicker of recognition crossed Hawke's face. "Dodds! I should have known! How could it *possibly* have been anyone else? Didn't feel like getting out of bed this morning? Decided you were going to call in sick?"

Estelle gave Dodds a pleading look not to answer back.

"No, sir. I just had difficulties sleeping last night, sir," Dodds said, forcing himself to answer in as much as a normal tone as he could muster.

"Well then, we'll see if we can get you a cot and a teddy bear for tonight then, shall we? Now get your arse out of bed!" Hawke shot back with contempt. With one last look around the dormitory he turned on his heel and started back down the corridor. But not before issuing an ultimatum: "Main briefing room, Dodds!" he said, pointing a stiff finger. "Three minutes!"

As he stormed out of the room Estelle began throwing Dodds' and Enrique's clothing at them, urging them to get a move on. Kelly and Chaz, already clothed, hovered close by, waiting for the two men to dress themselves. They did so as fast as they could and together the five hurried from the now empty dormitory, towards the building holding the main briefing hall.

* * *

The *White Knights* entered the packed hall to discover that all of the seating, except for that closest to the podium, had already been taken. Dodds wanted to remain at the back, out of sight, happy to join others sat down on the floor against the wall, but Estelle was already herding them to the front. The group ended up sitting almost right in front of the podium, just where Dodds and Enrique did not wish to be. The platform was occupied already by Parks, standing against a large screen that covered half of the front wall.

Parks watched with an impatient scowl as people continued to stream into the briefing hall. "Find a seat or some place to stand and settle down!" his voice boomed over the speakers.

Hawke shoved his way past those standing to get to the front, followed a lot less aggressively by Meyers. Dodds caught a glimpse of Hawke stuffing a handkerchief back into an inside jacket pocket and saw that it was once again stained with blood. He wondered in his hazy mind what was causing the man to receive so many nose bleeds. He could never remember him having done so much in the past.

Parks said, "We have a lot to get through and very little time to do it, so pay attention all of you." The voices died down and all that remained were the sounds of the shuffling of chairs and obligatory coughing. Now that he had everyone's full attention, Parks began in full.

"You should all know that several months ago the Confederation Stellar Navy flagship, *CSN Dragon*, was boarded and subsequently stolen by an unidentifiable, but strongly numbered and armed, hostile force. Following the take over it dropped off of all galactic surveillance systems and vanished without a trace."

Behind Parks the screen showed images of the enormous battleship; not that anyone who had every set eyes on the behemoth needed reminding. At over four and a half kilometres in length, it dwarfed even the Confederation's own carriers, being several times bigger than its nearest rival. *Griffin*, the largest of the CSN's carriers, was a mere eleven hundred and thirty meters by comparison. As Parks continued to speak the images on the screen behind him changed to show schematics of the battleship along with size comparisons with other large vessels. Dodds rubbed his eyes, trying to focus and keep them open.

"Without going into specifics we now believe the theft to have been the work of one of the major factions fighting in the Imperial civil war. After *Dragon* disappeared it was assumed it had either been destroyed or had been abandoned and left to drift somewhere between star systems. However, two days ago *Dragon* reappeared in the independent-declared regions of space and has begun making its way through some of the uninhabited systems there. We have been tracking its progress and believe that we are now in a position to intercept and retake the ship."

Murmurs and mumbling began around the room.

"He's got to be kidding," Dodds heard Kelly say under her breath. She was staring up at the screen, looking staggered by the news. Dodds recalled the first time he had met Kelly, back at flight school, and how one of the first things she had spoken to him about was *Dragon*. Kelly, out of all the cadets there, was the only one to have ever laid eyes on it.

She had told him of how she had been overwhelmed by *Dragon*'s sheer size in comparison with all the other battleships in the Confederation's fleet. Prior to her joining the Navy her father had managed to pull a few strings and arranged for her to be given a tour of some of the CSN's bases and major battleships; *Dragon* included. The ship was in dry dock at the time, undergoing maintenance. Kelly had found the sight astounding and had gushed about it for days. At the time Kelly had remarked that it looked quite menacing and that she was glad it was on "their side".

The ship's body was like that of a knife blade, with only the merest stub of a hilt at the rear housing three massive engines, complimented by four smaller ones on either side. The main body of the vessel drove forward into a point, two pairs of protrusions in the middle and at the rear following the overall outline of its form. There were no major vertical structures anywhere along its length - only a small number of elevations present to accommodate the bridge and incredible array of armaments that dotted the surface.

And though it was now just an image projected on to a screen, Dodds could see that the sheer magnitude of ship still staggered her today. The same sense of awe was not to be found in Dodds, however. Despite the enormity of the news, he found it difficult to be either impressed or interested as he looked up at the screen. He looked at Enrique, who was fighting to keep his eyes open. Clearly, like himself, the man was wishing he could be somewhere else.

You've really messed up this time, Simon, he thought to himself. *You've come back to try and set things right, but when it comes to something bloody important you're almost incapacitated. Congratulations, idiot.*

He slid down a little into his seat to get more comfortable. Estelle nudged him to sit up. In future he'd have to make a better effort not to sit next to her during things like this.

"Pipe down!"

The sound of Parks' irritated voice was quick to disperse the mumbling that had started.

"Based on the intelligence we have gathered, we anticipate that *Dragon* will very soon be entering the Aster system, within an uninhabited region of Independent space. Once there it will be met by a large contingent of allied forces, who will immediately commence *Operation Menelaus.*"

The screen behind Parks changed once more to show an overview of the operation he had just named, listing all involved parties and overall strategy.

"The reappearance of *Dragon* within the independent regions of space has raised many concerns within the Independent World Council. The Confederation has been working closely with the UNF over the past forty eight hours and they are fully prepared to back our move to retake *Dragon*. They will be laying on support of two carriers and a number of starfighters themselves. The main strike force will consist of *Griffin, Ifrit* and *Leviathan,* captained by myself, Commodore Hawke and Captain Meyers respectively."

"This is getting pretty serious," Estelle whispered in Dodds' ear. "They're throwing a lot of weight behind this, sending up *Griffin, Ifrit and Leviathan.*"

Dodds wished he could share her admiration. He also wished he had not helped to polish off the rest of that whiskey bottle. He pulled back away from Estelle, putting a hand on his forehead. It, like most of the rest of him, was feeling rather hot. He then found himself wishing his hand was a pack of ice. There, that was his three; and none of them had come true.

Dodds turned a lazy head around the briefing room to see that, in an almost exact repeat of the ATAF presentation the *Knights* had attended earlier that year, jaws were hanging down.

"Do not misunderstand," Parks boomed over the returning mumblings. Dodds winced.

"As I'm sure all of you can fully appreciate *Dragon* by itself in a combat situation would prove a very formidable opponent; and on this occasion we believe it to also be accompanied by two Imperial frigates and several starfighter squadrons, all of which will have to be handled and dispatched in order to successfully complete the operation. For this purpose we will be employing the use of several fighter squadrons of our own."

The screen behind him changed once again to display a representation of the fighters, grouped into squadrons. Numbers of participating types were listed next to the flat two-dimensional images. There were four classes there: TAFs, Rays, Rooks, and Hammerheads. It looked as though there were three digits next to the TAFs and two for the others, but Dodds could not focus on the exact numbers.

"Now listen carefully," Parks' voice continued over the hall speakers. "There are two primary objectives in this mission: the first, as already stated, is the successful recovery and safe return of *Dragon*. The second is the apprehension of these two men..."

The screen behind Parks changed again, displaying the two men in question. Both wore full Imperial naval dress and faced the camera head on. Neither man wore a cap in the pictures, though both were highly decorated.

"The first, and most important of these two, is Admiral Zackaria. He is the Fleet Admiral of the Imperial Naval Forces and is, without a shadow of a doubt, the one person whom we cannot afford to lose. I would even go as far as to say that the capture of this man actually *outweighs* the recapture of *Dragon* itself. We believe that he may have been instrumental in the theft of *Dragon* in the first instance and is likely to also be playing a key role in the on going troubles throughout the Imperium. Should he be aboard *Dragon* then he must not, under any circumstances, be allowed to be killed. I say again: *we need this man alive.*"

"Enrique..." Dodds heard Estelle hiss. He looked around to see Enrique sitting back up from where he had been hunched over, hiccuping. Dodds couldn't be sure whether either of the three men stood on the stage were aware of the issues he was experiencing trying to focus – certainly Hawke would already have an idea – but he thought he'd better make the effort. He folded his arms and looked at the screen, finding the black thread, red trims and silver buttons of the Imperial uniforms a little easier on his eyes than the bright white glare of previous screens.

He looked first to Admiral Zackaria, a name that was a little more familiar to him than the other; he had heard it thrown around from time to time over the years, though not certain he would be able to pick the man out of a line up. The man looked to be in his early to mid sixties, his hair more or less gone, leaving him with strands of grey. His eyes, too, were grey and possessed a hardened edge. His face was long and clean shaven, but his skin appeared rough, with wrinkles, tiny scars and marks scattered about. Easy enough, Dodds concluded. His age would make him quite distinctive amongst everyone else and he would be a lot easier to tackle than most. Not that Dodds wanted to get involved right now.

"The second is Commodore Rissard," Parks went on. "To our knowledge he is Zackaria's second in command and right hand man. He does not hold as much sway as Zackaria himself, but it would be in our interest to bring this man in too."

Rissard did not appear as old as Zackaria, closer in age to Parks and Hawke. Like Zackaria he was light skinned, but with short, thick blonde spiky hair.

"Look at his eyes," Estelle said.

Dodds did: they were unnaturally bright blue, almost as if they were some kind of implant; though maybe they were just contact lenses.

"I don't like the look of him," Kelly murmured.

Though he held a neutral expression, Dodds did acknowledge that the man looked menacing; threatening; almost sadistic. Maybe it was those eyes. A slideshow of images began, displaying the two men in various other poses: some at formal gatherings, others within parades. In a few, Zackaria could be seen with a ceremonial sword at his hip, and sometimes holding it in a rather regal fashion.

His head began to ache once more. He eyed Chaz, seeing the big man looking up the screen. He looked both very attentive and as fresh as a daisy. How? He'd been drinking too, hadn't he? He'd also enjoyed his fair share of the whiskey, as far as Dodds could remember. He wondered how the other four were feeling this morning. He expected that McLeod's head was in a comparable state to his own.

"Remember these faces, people," Parks said. "I want to be assured that even those not directly involved in the boarding of *Dragon* are familiar with all targets and objectives of this operation."

He then moved on to describe how the operation was to progress. Dodds let his attention slip a little, but listened as best he could through his suffering. As far as he could tell it was to unfold this way: the Hammerheads, together with support from TAFs and Rays, would lead the Initial Run against the two escorting frigates. Together they would knock the frigates out of action, as well as any starfighter support. Once the path was clear to *Dragon* the Confederation would deliver their coup de grâce: as with all newer capital ships, *Dragon* had an inbuilt security module that allowed for all non-essential-to-life functions to be shut down remotely. The idea had been scoffed at by *Dragon*'s design committee when the chief engineer had proposed it. He had gone ahead and implemented it regardless, arguing that it might come in very useful one day. And so it now proved.

With *Dragon* disabled, the escorting frigates out of action or destroyed, and only a handful of enemy starfighters to deal with, the rest of the mission would be a cakewalk. A large number of boarding vessels would attach themselves to *Dragon*'s hull before burning their way inside and flooding the entire ship with toxic gas. Following this, joint Confederation and Independent World teams would board *Dragon* and perform a mop up of any remaining enemy forces before handing over control to Parks, Hawke or Meyers. Zackaria and Rissard would be located and taken aboard a specially appointed shuttle where medical teams would administer treatments as required.

Should the security code fail to work then the combined CSN and UNF teams would attempt to force boarding by fire power alone. Although this was far from ideal the allied forces would at least still retain the element of surprise and again seek to take down the frigates before engaging the massive battleship itself.

Or something like that anyway...

"Dodds!" It was Estelle.

Dodds realised that he had slumped down into his seat. His chin was on his chest and his eyes were closed. He was on the verge of falling asleep. He opened his eyes and looked back up at the screen to see what he might have missed. Parks was looking right at him. The commodore paused for a brief moment before starting to talk again. He then stopped, pressing a button on the podium that killed the microphone and looked at Hawke, who had gained his attention. Following the very brief exchange he brought the microphone back up.

"Time is short, people. If we are to make our appointment we need to get things under way. You will be further briefed on the strategy upon arrival at your designated carriers."

The screen behind him changed to detail a list of assigned flight teams to carriers. Parks began to rattle off the names of the flight groups as, behind him, Meyers and Hawke got to their feet and made for the exit. The assembled personnel sat staring up at the screen, waiting for him to finish.

"What are you all sitting there for?" Parks asked in sudden anger. "At least a quarter of you should be at your departure points waiting for transports. Come on people! Suit up and get moving, now!"

The fliers jumped to their feet as ordered and made to leave whilst the commodore continued to read out names, departure points and destinations. The *White Knights* had been assigned to *Griffin* and the vast squadron making up the Initial Run, meaning they would be responsible for protecting the bombers as they engaged the Imperial frigates, as well as clearing the way for the boarding parties.

"Right, let's go people," Estelle said, standing up and preparing to lead the team out of the briefing room and prep for departure.

"You all right, man?" Dodds asked of Enrique. The man's eyes were reddened from where he had been vigorously rubbing them.

"Aw, mate, I feel like death warmed up..." Enrique started.

"You two - come here!"

Dodds turned around to see Parks glaring straight at him. The delegation over, Parks had turned his attention to a new issue: that of Dodds and Enrique. He clenched his fist as if grabbing them by their jackets and pulling them towards him. Dodds had feared this from the moment he had almost drifted off. Seated right before the commodore, it looked as if he and Enrique's various sick expressions and attempts not to fall asleep had not gone unnoticed.

Enrique and Dodds stood themselves in front of Parks as requested, though neither of them saluted.

Parks looked over the two men. "What seems to be the diffic..." he started, before wrinkling his nose. "Are you two *drunk*?" The commodore did not need to finish the sentence, nor less ask the question; the stench of alcohol emanating from the two men already provided all the answers.

"No, sir, we..." Dodds began, knowing that the very breath leaving his mouth would make it all too clear that he was either rather inebriated or suffering from a severe hangover.

"Shut your mouth, Lieutenant!" Parks snarled. He looked over at the men and women retreating out the briefing room, seeking a quick solution to his new problem. "Lieutenant Chang!"

"Sir," the man Parks had called after turned around and saluted.

"You're being reassigned. You and your team will now be a part of the Initial Run. The *White Knights* will take over your secondary cover duties."

"Yes, sir," Chang's face lit up. It was clear that he was delighted that he would now be doing an important job instead of providing menial cover for the Confederation's capital ships. Should everything go well then he and his team would be recognised for the essential role they would play, and perhaps even rewarded for their hard work after a successful operation.

Dodds looked to Estelle, about to apologise, when Parks pushed past him, getting to her first. She stood to attention as the commodore approached.

"Get your boys sobered up, de Winter!" Parks glared, wagging a finger in her face. "And get to that departure point *now*! I don't want any more screw ups!"

"Yes, sir! Immediately, sir..." Estelle started, though Parks was already marching past her and out the briefing room.

"... pair of complete bloody idiots!" Estelle glared at Enrique and Dodds as they hurried down the corridors to the transport landing zones, helmets in hand, still fastening up their flight suits. "Make sure you get into those damn shuttles!" she added as the throng of people threatened to separate them from one another.

Estelle was both bitter and broken. For the second time in just a few weeks she had been busted down, absolved of any responsibility, of any chance to prove herself of her true worth. It was starting to become too much of a regular occurrence for her.

The cool, crisp air of the early morning hit her as she left the housing block, along with the crowd. It was just past sunrise and spotlights illuminated her path, aiding the dim natural light. Ahead of her she could see the multicoloured marking lights of landing platforms, flickering in her view as they were obscured by other people rushing in front of her. It was a clear morning and the arc of lights dotted around the incomplete orbital ring could be seen high in the sky. Not that this was the time to admire such things.

As she approached the landing zones Estelle was greeted by a scene that she had only seen in archived war footage: in the sky ahead of her several transport shuttles were accelerating upwards towards the atmosphere, carrying their full complement of personnel. Pairs of strong blue engine light could be seen higher up as the transports attained the speeds necessary to achieve escape velocity, leaving subtle trails of cyan as they went. A couple of dozen transport craft rested on landing pads, hatches open, personnel being crammed inside. Hovering in the sky above were more transports, waiting for landing pads to become free so they could touch down and pick up more passengers. If the presentation had failed to impress upon anyone the importance of the operation they were about to undertake, then what Estelle was witnessing now would surely do the trick.

She had long since lost Dodds and Enrique and looked around for them as she drew closer to their designated landing zone. She then spotted a big, dark skinned man ahead of her, running to a transport as people were called forward by one of the many air marshals present. Relief washed over her as she recognised Chaz, and then Enrique and Dodds following just a short way behind him. The three, along with several others, got into the transport which was quick to seal its doors and takeoff, another transport quick to take its place.

With her boys well on their way Estelle looked around for Kelly. Where was she? Like herself Kelly was barely taller than average height and in amongst the taller men and women it was going to be hard to spot her.

Estelle felt herself being pushed forward and glancing around she found that Kelly was just behind her. The woman was looking more than a little concerned as she was jostled back and forth, and Estelle reached her hand back to hold on to her. Not only to make sure her friend was okay, but to ensure that her team made it on to *Griffin* without any problems. She could not afford yet another black mark against her name. Even after the heart-to-heart she'd had with Kelly the previous evening, Estelle found it hard not to put her aspirations ahead of her friends, a fact that had now been further compounded by Enrique and Dodds' irresponsible drinking.

Estelle took a firm hold of Kelly's hand as the throng pushed her forward. Ahead of her a transport had filled its quota of passengers and was setting off. Now at the front of the crowd, Kelly and Estelle were next.

"You all right, Kelly?" Estelle looked around and asked of her friend. Kelly looked scared for some reason. "We do this all the time. Just remain calm." Estelle attempted to reassure her that the shuttle ride was nothing to get concerned about.

"This time it just feels more real," Kelly said. "We're not going on patrol this time; we're going on the offensive."

"They have it fully planned out," Estelle said, keeping an eye on the transport that was descending from the sky. "The CSN always makes the safety of those in service its top priority."

"Even before *Dragon*, Zackaria and Rissard?"

"Even before *Dragon*, Zackaria and Rissard." Estelle shook the follow-up sentence from her head. There was always a first time.

The transport landed and an air marshal beckoned them forward. Estelle lost her grip on Kelly's hand as everyone surged forward. Parks' speech must have hit home with many.

"No, only you guys!" the air marshal said, spreading his arms out and trying to get a control of the crowd. "You lot head over to that one. The rest of you get back. I only want twelve for this one."

Looking around, Estelle discovered she had been separated from Kelly and felt uncomfortable not knowing where everyone was. She tried to rejoin the main group of waiting people.

"Hey, where you going there?" the marshal stopped her from leaving. "No time to go back now. In you get."

The man's hand was on her back, pushing her on-board the transport. Now inside, the hatch closed and locked, leaving Estelle to wonder if Kelly had made it. She felt the engines engage and took up a position on the bench, pulling down the familiar restraining harness over her shoulders. The shuttle was smaller than the ones she had grown used to over the past few weeks and held fewer people. Space on *Griffin* would be at a premium when compared to Spirit Orbital. Estelle glanced around at the others occupying the transport, at first not recognising any of the faces. She then did a double take.

"Andrea?" she asked in complete surprise.

The curly, blonde haired member of the *Red Devils* looked over in the direction of the voice and smiled.

"Estelle!" Andrea said, eyes sparkling. "How have you been?" She looked genuinely pleased to see her.

Estelle was stunned at how chipper Andrea was at such a time. "I've been good. Everything's going very well," Estelle answered.

Andrea's here? At Mandelah? Since when? Estelle wondered to herself. *Does this mean that the* Red Devils *didn't succeed in the evaluation either? Did it go to the other team?* She forgot their name.

"Are you based here? I've not seen you around," Estelle asked.

"No," Andrea said, shaking her head, her curly locks bumping against her face. "I've been continuing the training and been posted in a number of places."

That confirmed it. Andrea's team had won. Estelle realised her face was betraying her sense of jealousy. She decided not to ask any more about how the training was going; about how Andrea was getting on flying a starfighter that she should have been; about how praise was being piled on her for her great work.

She did want to know one thing though: "So, what are you doing here?"

"Special operations," Andrea replied with a knowing confident wink and a smile.

Estelle had heard enough. She sat back and closed her eyes, waiting for the transport to arrive at it's destination.

● ● ●

Dodds, Enrique and Chaz stood on the flight deck of *Griffin*, bunched up with several other personnel and crew members that had disembarked from the transport shuttles. The deck of the carrier was massive, spanning close to the entire width of the vessel itself. The adjoining launch catapult ran almost a third of the ship's length, the half octagon shaped tunnel lit at regular intervals as it stretched off towards open space.

The junior OOD instructed the new arrivals to await Parks. As the numbers began to swell the three men were joined by Estelle, and then Kelly. Dodds witnessed a brief exchange between the two and guessed that Estelle was busying herself keeping her team together and focused. His eyes flickered over the gathering of personnel and he noticed a tall woman with curly blonde hair being led away from the main assembled group. Had he seen her somewhere before? His eyes followed her for a moment before he noticed Parks approaching. The assembled group stood to attention and saluted.

"Welcome to the *CSN Griffin*, boys and girls," Parks addressed them as transports continued to arrive and unload their passengers. "The ship you are standing on is currently acting as the CSN's flagship in *Dragon's* soon to be ended absence. This is *my* ship and I expect you to remember that at all times. You should feel both honoured and privileged to have been given the opportunity to serve aboard this vessel."

Dodds felt the man's gaze come in his and Enrique's direction as he spoke the last two sentences. He watched the commodore as he began pacing in a small area, hands behind his back.

Parks went on, "As soon as we are up to our full complement we will jump to the Aster system, where we will rendezvous with the UNF's charmingly named twin carriers, *Grendel* and *Grendel's Mother*.

"From there we will await the arrival of *Dragon* and then immediately commence *Operation Menelaus*. Primary defence and Initial Run teams should be prepared to depart the moment we arrive at our destination. Secondary defence teams," - his eyes once again flicked in the direction of the *White Knights* - "should await further instructions. Squadron leaders will be briefed further before our arrival. Additionally a full breakfast is being prepared for all serving crew, so there is no need to worry about going into this on an empty stomach. For now, prepare yourselves for jump."

With his introduction and points made, Parks departed the flight deck, and the attendants began clearing personnel as part of the jump preparations.

"Have you ever seen *Dragon* in real life?" Enrique asked Dodds as they were escorted to *Griffin*'s crew quarters.

"Not in real life, only video footage." Dodds said. "The only thing I know about it is that it's big and has a lot of guns."

"I've seen it," Kelly piped up, trotting up alongside the pair in an attempt to keep up with the long strides the two men were making to match speed with the officer leading the way. "And yes, it's big. My father arranged for me to be given a flyby before I joined up."

"Yes, we know, Kelly," Dodds said, putting a hand up to his temple. "You've told us about a million and one times."

"Mate, don't bite her head off," Enrique jumped in.

Dodds looked at Kelly, seeing her a little incensed by his comment. "Sorry, Kelly. My bloody head is killing me. That shuttle ride didn't help at all."

"It's your own fault," Kelly said.

"Yes, I know," Dodds said. "Okay, so, anything else you can tell us about *Dragon*?"

"No," Kelly shook her head. "Nothing that you don't already know."

"I hope we'll be given a bit more information other than "it's big" before we get to Aster and have to face off against it," Estelle complained. "A basic strategy would be a good start."

"If you're talking basics, then how about that *Dragon* has a maximum crew complement of just under fifty thousand, including starfighter pilots," a man's voice stated. "And that it can also comfortably accommodate over a thousand fighters in its hangers, without any concessions for type."

Heads spun around, stunned to discover that Chaz was the one offering up the information.

Dodds caught Estelle's eye, before she looked back at the big man. "What about its weaponry? Defences?" she asked.

"Numerous enhanced plasma and laser turrets and batteries," Chaz said. "And the entire ship is protected by multiple high powered shield generators; far more efficient than a carrier's or a frigate's."

"Still wishing you'd asked?" Kelly said to Estelle.

Estelle ignored Kelly and pressed for more information. "What else?"

"It's secondary offensive armament consists of eight plasma accelerators," Chaz said.

Estelle almost stopped walking. "*Eight* accelerators?"

Chaz nodded. "Three on the aft and starboard, two on the bow."

Dodds and Enrique swore simultaneously.

Chaz added, "I'd suggest that if you're going to attack that thing you should aim to do it from the maximum possible distance to counter its defensive capabilities; and unless you can apply sheer strength of numbers, attempting to take it on with starfighters alone would prove next to impossible."

The other four *Knights* exchanged disquieted looks.

"How many fighters are we talking?" Enrique wanted to know.

"More than we're taking," Chaz answered, almost inaudibly.

They had arrived at the quarters where they would be spending the next few hours, whilst *Griffin* made the jump to Aster.

"How do you know all this?" Estelle asked.

"Let's just say a little knowledge is a dangerous thing, Lieutenant," Chaz said, pulling himself up on to a nearby bunk and lying back.

Dodds spied one of quarters' beds past the others and made for it, slumping down onto the mattress. It was far from the most comfortable thing he had ever sat on – even the beds at Spirit offered more – but right now it met his needs. He sat for a moment before stretching out across its length and closing his eyes, grateful that he could start on recuperating. What he really needed now was to get his hands on some painkillers.

"I can see why it would be best to disable it before we attempt to retake it now," Kelly commented, settling down at the foot of a bed that Enrique had also taken to.

"Wait," Estelle said. "You said the accelerators were it's *secondary* defence system."

"I did," Chaz said.

"So, what's its first?"

"An anti-matter cannon. Only vessel in existence to be kitted out with one."

"Oh. I'd forgotten about that," Kelly said.

"It's got a *what?*" Enrique said.

"*Dragon*'s main offensive weapon is a high-powered cannon that is capable of directing a concentration of anti-matter at any frontal target," Chaz said.

"What exactly does that mean?" Estelle asked.

Though Dodds had his eyes closed, he could tell that for all Estelle's knowledge of the ins and outs of Naval protocol, Chaz was now speaking a language that even she did not understand.

"It means it can destroy anything in its path," Kelly explained. "It is powerful enough to even take down Spirit Orbital with a single shot. We don't want to be in the way of that if it happens to get a chance to use it."

A handful of other pilots had been assigned to the same quarters as the *Knights* and people began to chatter, discussing what Chaz had said.

"So whilst we're all telling stories, does someone want to tell me what's so special about this Zackaria guy that Parks wants so badly?" a man's voice said.

"He's the current Fleet Admiral of the Imperial Senate's naval forces," a voice spoke up.

Dodds thought he recognised it, and tilted his head to look over to see if it was the same fountain of knowledge from the previous night; the one that had been spreading rumours and speculation at their card game. It turned out it wasn't, but the conversation did perk Dodds' interest somewhat. Even so, whilst the others, with the usual exception of Chaz, turned to give their attention to the speaker, Dodds was happy to lay back and listen where he was.

"Yes, I know he's the admiral of the fleet," the first man said. "I was awake for that part of the briefing."

"Right, so how much do you know about the civil war?"

"Well, there's a lot of a dead people as a result. As well as a huge influx of asylum seekers and illegal immigrants that I'm having to prop up with my taxes."

"Apart from that."

"Nothing."

"Not how it started or who's involved or anything?"

"The Senate and the Emperor, wasn't it? Actually no, nothing," the first man said.

A few other answers of *no* followed there after.

"All right, well, basically there are two main sides in the Imperial civil war: those fighting for the Imperial Senate and those fighting for Emperor Lorenzo III," the story teller started. "The civil war began when the Senate disagreed with the Emperor's decision to grant independence to two Imperial star systems, and having another three under consideration. The Emperor was extremely popular with his people for things like that, as well as improving relationships with other Independent worlds and the Confederation. You probably already know that until recently the Imperium was very prosperous and actually envied throughout the galaxy."

"No," the first man scoffed. "Can't say I've really ever cared. What happens over there is their problem, not mine."

"Stop interrupting and let him finish. No, really, shut up! That's an order," Estelle said. There was a pause. Dodds glanced over to see Estelle glaring at a man. For once he was glad to hear Estelle pulling rank. Political yarns tended to bore him, but this one was intriguing enough to make him want to hear what had happened.

Estelle looked back to the story teller, a thin, lanky looking man with a bowl hair cut. He closed his eyes as she said, "Go on, what happened? Who was the instigator?"

"Most believe it was the Senate," the story teller resumed. "One day the Senate, led by the senior magistrate, upped and left, setting up house in an Imperial star system that held a majority interest in the Senate's position, and was as far away from the Emperor's Seat as they could get. They felt that the Emperor's actions were a threat to the continued prosperity of the Imperium and that the Emperor could one day bring about the collapse of the Empire. They said it was becoming too diluted and the constant undermining of the core strength would make it appear to be growing weak to the Independent worlds and the Confederacy. At the time the Senate was backed by something like ten percent of the Imperium."

"Ten percent? That's not a lot," a woman interrupted the speaker. "That's like those minority parties you get, the fascists and the ones obsessed with trivial matters. I mean what exactly did they plan to do?"

"Hold on, I'm getting there," the story teller said. "Ten percent is still quite a lot when you think about it: it's several hundred million people at least. And with those behind them they attacked all the worlds that had split from the Empire and then attempted to assassinate the Emperor himself."

"Wow."

"Yeah, but they failed. And the Emperor, as was his nature, invited them to an open dialogue to resolve the issues between the two. The Senate refused and then attempted to assassinate him again. The second time they were a little more successful, although they didn't actually manage to kill him. The assassin ended up killing the Emperor's wife and injuring the Emperor very badly, before he himself was killed."

Dodds opened his eyes to see all attention was on the speaker, listening to what he had to say. Although the information he was providing to them could have been garnered by anyone who had taken the time to follow the news over the last few years, to many in the room this was new information; hot off the presses. Some others, outside the quarters, had stopped on their way past, hovering in the doorway to listen in to what the man had to say.

The story teller continued, "Following that attempt on his life the Emperor didn't hold back and launched a full scale assault on the Senate, deploying a massive strike force to the systems they had moved to. They completely overwhelmed the forces the Senate had mustered to defend themselves, but the Emperor fell short of wiping them out completely. He gave them one last chance to yield, rejoin the Empire and accept his rule, rather than completely destroying them. And for a time it appeared that they were preparing to do so, but then one day..."

"Sorry," the first man cut in, sounded already bored with the history lesson. "But what exactly does this have to do with this Admiral Zackaria?"

"Admiral Zackaria was the fleet admiral for the Imperial Naval Forces; he worked for the Emperor. But he defected to side with the Imperial Senate, and around five years ago they fought back harder than ever before and started to win the war."

"How?" Estelle asked. "You said that only a small fraction of the Imperium supported the Senate. How could they be winning? They were outnumbered to begin with, and after what you said about the Senate's supporting systems being almost destroyed I don't see how that's possible?"

"Well, I don't know either," the story teller said. "But that's why the Confederacy want him. Because whatever he's up to is starting to affect the Confederation's own interests. He's apparently already orchestrated the theft of a Python-class battleship, and I don't think anyone really wants to stand around and watch to see what he does next."

"I don't see the point," the man whom Estelle had shouted at said. "Why even bother bringing him in? What they should just do is put a bullet in his head the minute they find him. That's what I'd do. Bang! Would solve the problem straight away."

"He'll probably already be dead by the time they get to him," a woman chipped in. "Since they're planning on flooding *Dragon* with nerve agent or whatever it is."

"The whole place'll look like Hentose back in 2612 after they're done with it," another commented.

"Hentose?"

"Yeah, that underground station that had the accident with the bio-engineered stuff. Everyone's skin was practically melted off when they found 'em. I think one poor guy was still alive. He was a right mess."

"Good luck identifying Zackaria if that happens."

"Whatever they want that guy for, I hope it's worth it."

The quarter's musings were put on hold as Parks' voice came over *Griffin*'s intercoms.

"All crew, this is your captain speaking. Prepare for jump."

Parks strode down the long, central aisle of *Griffin*'s bridge, and up to the front to check on how the departure preparations were progressing. Around him crew busied themselves performing last minute checks to ensure that their route was clear and all essential safety measures had been followed.

Just ahead of him, seen out the frontal viewport, the last few transport craft could be seen departing *Ifrit* and *Leviathan* and making their way either back to Spirit Orbital or returning to the planet surface. Many other supply craft were leaving the carriers with each passing second, their cargo of essential equipment and armaments having been offloaded. *Ifrit* and *Leviathan* rested on either side of the lead carrier, *Griffin* being granted flag ship status if only due to its larger size, armaments, and crew complement.

This is it, Parks thought to himself. *This is where I find out whether I'm ready.* He held back on thinking the next few hours would be a case of easy in, easy out. He was sure that such assumptions had been made before, and the consequences had been disastrous. *You can do this, Elliott,* he told himself.

"All safety checks completed and route confirmed clear, Captain," his ensign said, yanking him from his thoughts and back to the bridge of the carrier.

"Thank you," Parks said, and watched as the final few preparation craft cleared the way, leaving the Confederation's three most well known carriers alone. "Open communications with *Ifrit* and *Leviathan.*"

Above him two two-dimensional holographic images sprang into existence, each bearing the simple combination of black and white shapes that were the CSN's insignia, against a smooth black and white gradient background. The symbols were soon replaced with images projected from their respective sources: one displaying an image of Hawke, standing on the bridge of *Ifrit,* the other with Meyers and *Leviathan.*

"Hello, gentlemen," Parks said. "Preparations aboard *Griffin* are complete."

"*Ifrit* has also completed preparations," Hawke confirmed.

"As has *Leviathan,* Commodore," Meyers said. "Ready to jump on your order."

"Very well," Parks nodded and looked to the ship's helmsman and navigator. "Mr Liu, open a jump point to Aster."

"Yes, sir," the man tapped away at the multicoloured display of the console he sat at.

Parks watched the space in front of the trio of huge carriers as it began to twist and distort. The distortions subsided quickly, leaving behind a blue tinged swirling mass, that turned like a lazy whirl pool.

"Jump point opened, sir," Liu confirmed.

"Ready, gentlemen?" Parks asked one last time.

"With your lead, Commodore," Meyers confirmed.

"Ready," Hawke nodded his agreement.

Are you ready, Commodore? a voice within Parks asked.

Yes, he said.

"Take us forward, Mr Liu."

Those observing from Spirit Orbital watched as the carrier started forward, *Ifrit*'s and *Leviathan*'s engines engaging and propelling them just behind *Griffin*. The three ships slipped gracefully into the vicinity of the jump point and then, one after the other, appeared to accelerate at terrific speed.

A few seconds later the point closed behind them, and they were gone.

XII

— The Sleeping Dragon —

M any hours passed as the three Confederation carriers made the journey from Spirit to Aster, to meet with their appointment. During that time preparations were made for their arrival and the start of the operation – Boarding parties suited up, checked their equipment, and were once again briefed as to how they were to invade *Dragon* and what their objectives were once they were inside; teams across flight decks loaded armaments onto fighters and bombers and performed a variety of safety checks to ensure the craft could be deployed in a timely fashion; others tucked into a piping hot cooked breakfast, as well as a plentiful supply of caffeine.

After struggling to swallow a few mouthfuls, Dodds pushed much of the rest around, his stomach warning him that he might come to regret consuming any more of the fried food. In the end he scraped what remained onto the plate of a man sat opposite him, who was more than grateful of the second helping. Much of the conversation at the table was focused on the upcoming operation, mixed in with varied opinions of the fate of *Dragon* and the political strife within the Empire.

A mug of tea and a visit to the ship's doctor was enough to see Dodds through the lengthy mission profile that proceeded breakfast. A round of questions concluded the brief, and then it was back to the quarters again.

A short while later the call came in – they were approaching Aster; all participants of the Initial Run were to prep for deployment. The flyers jumped up from seats and off bunks, filling corridors and lifts as they made towards the flight decks to answer the request.

Dodds watched them go, feeling Estelle's anguish at having to stay put until they were required; if at all. Though he regretted the previous night's activities, he hoped that his services would not be called upon. In his groggy state he was certain that to do so would only invite yet more disaster, and he'd had enough of that for one lifetime. He was determined to see the morning's wakeup call as the last he needed.

Parks watched from the bridge as the blue haze of jump space peeled away and the nearby stars came rushing forward. The Aster system lay in close proximity to a number of nebula: red, blue and green hues hanging like fine silk curtains amongst the distant stars. There were few who failed to be impressed by such a sight, many of the inhabited star systems throughout the known galaxy lacking any such splendour. The magnificence of the scene was not wasted on Parks either, despite the reasons for their being in the system. He remained motionless for a moment to gaze upon it and felt some of his stress slip away. *Griffin* decelerated quickly, the stars around the carrier slowing.

"Jump completed, sir," he heard Liu say as *Ifrit* and *Leviathan* came alongside. Though it was rare for accidents to occur during jumps, it was good to see the other carriers were still with them. So far so good.

"Excellent. Open communications," Parks said. The holographic screens sprang up once again, and Hawke and Meyers appeared. "Commodore, Captain. Any issues to report?"

"None here," said Meyers. "Fighters and transports are prepped and ready to be deployed on your command."

"No reported issues," Hawke added. "Also ready for deployment."

There was a flash by *Griffin*'s starboard side. A jump point was forming. From it emerged two carriers of similar design to that of *Griffin* and her two companions.

"Sir, *Grendel* and *Grendel's Mother* have just arrived in the system," a man by the name of O'Donnell, *Griffin*'s head of communications, said.

"Perfect timing," Parks said. He turned back to Meyers and Hawke. "Commodore, Captain, deploy your teams. I want to ensure that we are able to execute our strike not only the very second enemy forces appear, but also if *Dragon* arrives earlier than was originally anticipated. The element of surprise should give them little chance to plot an escape and could well be key to our success here today."

"Yes, sir. I will begin fighter defence deployment immediately," Meyers said before closing the communication link.

"And I will begin preparation for rear guard, Commodore," Hawke said.

Parks opened his mouth to speak, then hesitated. Hawke had volunteered to operate *Ifrit* and its full complement alone as rear guard to the mission, defending *Griffin*, *Leviathan*, *Grendel*, and *Grendel's Mother*. Should enemy forces manage to attack the main strike force from behind, Hawke would move *Ifrit* in to offer support. Parks had raised doubts about the validity about such a tactic, suggesting it would be better for Hawke to concentrate *Ifrit*'s strength up front, rather than reduce their offensive power. Even so Hawke had argued that whilst this would indeed allow them to take down the enemy faster, they should not assume that enemy support would not be forthcoming. To do so could risk the allied forces being flanked or otherwise surrounded by hostile forces, meaning that retreating from the system could prove difficult.

After much deliberation Parks had begrudgingly agreed to Hawke's tactical proposals. But having now arrived at Aster he was once again considering ordering Hawke to remain up front. He pushed aside the urge to enter into another debate with the man, not wanting to stall the operation for even a second.

"Very well," Parks said to Hawke. "I will be in contact as soon as we are ready to begin manoeuvres."

He ended the communication as another request came in. He acknowledged that it should be received, and was greeted by the holographic projection of a deceptively young looking woman. She was graced with near flawless olive skin, bright hazel eyes, and black hair tied into a neat bob on the top of her head.

Parks had met Commodore Sima Mandeep on a number of occasions before and each time had forgotten just how beautiful he found her. He had always been disappointed that he had never found the time to get to know her better. Today was very unlikely to offer any such opportunity either.

Mandeep presented a warm smile. "Hello, Elliott. Good to see you again. I hope we didn't keep you waiting long."

"Your timing was perfect, Sima. We just arrived ourselves," Parks said, finding it difficult not to return the woman's smile, something about it feeling a whole lot more personal than professional. Even her teeth looked perfect.

"Nice setting for it," she said, her eyes shifting to gaze upon the generous backdrop they had been granted.

"I will be sure to send you a copy of our footage after everything is wrapped up."

"Much appreciated, Commodore," she smiled again.

Parks shifted the conversation back to the operation. Now was not the time to be drawn in. "We are beginning fighter defence preparations and will shortly be executing tactical formation manoeuvres. As agreed *Grendel* and *Leviathan* will lead the assault run. If you could have Captain Silverthorne liaise with Captain Meyers to ensure that everything is in place, then I will give the go ahead for us to begin. *Griffin* and *Grendel's Mother* will cover the midfield, with *Ifrit* acting as rear guard."

He knew that Mandeep had already been fully briefed on every aspect of the operation, but reiterated it once more to ensure that all bases had been covered.

"Understood. I will be in touch. *Grendel's Mother* out," Mandeep said, before her face disappeared from the holographic screen.

Parks watched from the bridge as a variety of craft streamed from each of the assembled carriers and took up positions ahead of the group. A number of fighters turned about and came to rest next to the capital ships.

"All of *Griffin's* Initial Run fighters and transports deployed and ready, sir," Parks was told.

"Excellent, send word that we are ready to move into position," Parks ordered.

The word was sent and *Leviathan* and *Grendel* started forward, their starfighters following them like obedient puppies. *Griffin* and *Grendel's Mother* in turn followed at a distance, the four carriers all moving closer to the expected arrival point of *Dragon* and her escorts. If they were too far from *Dragon's* arrival point it would give the battleship ample time to escape the ambush. They slowed as they approached their designated positions and Parks addressed all four carriers for one last time before they adopted radio silence and awaited their quarry.

"Manoeuvres complete, Commodore. In position," Meyers reported.

"As we are," Silverthorne added. "We have boarding parties on standby."

"In position," Mandeep said.

"Rear guard ready," Hawke said.

Parks noted that *Ifrit* had barely moved since arriving at their destination. Though it irritated him he chose to ignore it. Hawke did have a somewhat persuasive argument, but Parks still felt that his command and fire power would be more appreciated up front. He once again buried his feelings.

"Good," he said. "You should each be aware of your role in this operation, which we will begin the moment *Dragon* is sighted. Should anything unexpected occur, that we cannot quickly and effectively handle, then we will form a tactical retreat. Commodore Hawke, I expect, will cover us in such an event."

"You will have my full support if such an event does arise," Hawke replied.

"Excellent," Parks said. "Excellent. Now we wait."

Although, from the way his hands had started to perspire, he got the feeling that they wouldn't be waiting for very long.

Dodds sat up as the red alert rang throughout the carrier, various orders and requests sounding from the PA system and echoing down the ship's corridors. He felt a sudden overwhelming compulsion come over him and he sprang off the bed and made for the quarters' exit.

"Hey, come," he said to the others.

"Where are you going?" Estelle said.

"To find somewhere to get a look," Dodds said. "I've never seen *Dragon* before, and I might never get a chance like this again. I want to see this thing with my own two eyes." He was surprised that Estelle was not keen to do the same.

"Wait for me," Enrique said, as he clambered off his own bed. Kelly followed suit, stretching as she did so. Chaz tailed the two out the door, heading off down the corridor, silent as ever. Dodds lingered by the quarters' doorway.

"Hey, Dodds, what's the hold up?" Enrique called back.

"Just a second," he said.

"Okay," Enrique nodded and continued walking with Kelly and Chaz.

Dodds looked back to Estelle who was still perched on the end of the bed he had once occupied. "You not coming?"

"No, I'll wait here," Estelle said, shaking her head. "If they need us they'll look for us here first."

"Sure?"

"Positive."

Dodds studied her. She looked pensive. He made to head off, then hesitated and came back to the doorway. "Are you okay?"

"Yeah. Like I said I just want to make sure we can be contacted."

"Hmmmm, okay." Dodds was certain that Estelle, as he, knew that it was a not a well tailored excuse. The ship's PA system could be used to contact anyone aboard the ship no matter where they were.

As he jogged down the corridors to catch up with the others, he wondered if there was something else playing on Estelle's mind. Had she suffered a sudden attack of nerves the moment that the alarm had started, the reality of the situation having only now sunk in? Perhaps Estelle was now feeling some of the concern that had gripped Kelly back on Spirit: realising that they wouldn't be fighting against a bunch of pirates or supporting an assault on a small, little defended insurgent installation, but instead be facing up against seasoned starfighter pilots and battleships.

No, he thought to himself, catching up with the others who were holding the door to the deck lift. *Estelle just needs time to prepare.*

With the quarters empty, Estelle lay back on the bed Dodds had vacated and began taking slow, measured breaths, her heart threatening to burst out of her rib cage.

"Please stop ringing," she whispered to the alarm. "Just stop."

Emerging from the deck lift, Dodds found himself in the one part of the ship that he would have preferred to avoid, his arrival here a result of following others who also wished to observe the operation.

Griffin's bar, located on the port side of the main elevated portion of the carrier, offered a panoramic view of the surrounding space. The intention was to provide a pleasant backdrop for those relaxing and enjoying drink. Due to its position the bar was - aside from the bridge - the best place on the carrier to get a feel for what was happening outside.

Many other crew members were already clustered by the windows towards the bow and the four *Knights* hurried over to see what was happening, Dodds thankful that he was spared the sight of any alcohol with the way that he was feeling. Even before he had made it to the windows Dodds could hear people cursing under their breath.

"*That* is a big ship," Chaz said. Taller than his companions, he did not have to try and see between people's heads, being able to look over them instead.

Dodds managed to find himself a spot and felt an equal sense of pure ambivalence. Unmissable, even at its distance ahead of *Griffin*, was *Dragon;* the massive battleship lying side on to their carrier, looking graceful yet menacing in every aspect. Ahead of them, *Grendel* and *Leviathan* could be seen approaching, the tiny blue specks of starfighter engines leading the way.

"Where are the frigates?" Kelly asked, searching in all directions. She was standing on a chair.

"Don't know. Can't see any," Dodds said, though he took little time to look. He found he was unable to tear his eyes away from the battleship that was their target.

"Intelligence may have got it wrong," Enrique said. "Wouldn't be the first time."

Parks had been bemused by the appearance of the stolen Confederation battleship without its escorts. Not that it needed any.

Dragon had arrived in the system not long after the allied forces had completed their tactical manoeuvres. A jump point had formed within their vicinity and Parks had ordered the immediate commencement of the operation. Bombers, alongside their support fighters, had surged forward to greet the newest arrival to the Aster system. Troop transports had joined just behind them, ready to attach themselves to *Dragon*'s hull and deploy their deadly cargo of toxic gases and boarding parties the moment the battleship was disabled.

"Prepare to transmit the override, Mr O'Donnell," Parks said.

"Ready on your order, sir," O'Donnell said after verification at his console.

With the glow of starfighter engines growing ever smaller, Parks turned to the four holographic camera feeds he had earlier requested to monitor the operation. Each was sourced from a different target: one traced the starfighter and troop transports, another focused in on *Dragon* herself. Yet another followed *Leviathan* and *Grendel*, and the last, the cockpit view of the leader of the Initial Run flight group.

Even from where he stood, watching the holographic relays, Parks found the sight of the massive Confederation battleship staggering. The fact that it was also in the hands of the Enemy was causing him considerable apprehension. He could not begin to imagine what the pilots seated within the front line might be feeling at this time; though with the battleship having begun to turn to face its attackers, it could well be a sense of utter foreboding.

"Approaching *Dragon*," the flight group leader communicated to *Griffin*. "Will be within weapons range in thirty seconds."

Parks noted that some of the fighters were lowering their speed so as not expose themselves to the battleship's weapon systems too soon, their wingmates passing them by. Although both *Dragon*, and the carriers that had come to meet it, had been outfitted with similar weaponry, the turrets of *Dragon* had been upgraded to compliment the ship, granting them an increased range and thereby allowing them to be fired from a greater distance. That distance would soon be met by the flight group.

The closer the flight group drew towards it, the sharper their target's details came into relief. A graphic of a magnificent, blue scaled Chinese dragon clung to the battleship's hull, its claws appearing to be latched deep into the metal. Dozens of tall yellow and red ridges covered the creature's back, whilst a pair of long, curved, white horns rose from the top of its head. Its mouth was open, drawn back into a ferocious snarl, displaying row upon row of sharp, pointed teeth. Two red eyes seemed to project a furious warning, warding off would be attackers.

But now Parks was satisfied that the flight group were as close as they needed to be. He turned to his chief communications officer. "Mr O'Donnell, send the code."

"Sending code," O'Donnell acknowledged both the commodore and the flight group. He made two brief strokes at his console. "Code sent."

Parks further relayed the update to all on the battlefield. The confirmation came back. He then looked back to the holographic screens and waited. But after only a few seconds great trepidations overcame him, and his eyes flickered from one display to the next, seeing the same thing in each: lights continued to illuminate the surface of *Dragon*; windows, port holes, and exterior components all visual indications that the ship was still operational. He looked past the displays to the scene beyond the carrier's frontal viewport, considering that the feeds might not be running in real time, perhaps delayed by a few seconds. *Dragon* still glittered with light.

"Mr O'Donnell? What's happening?" Parks said, not taking his eyes off the massive battleship. *Have I just done the unthinkable and underestimated the Enemy upon my very first engagement?*

"Code was transmitted successfully, sir," O'Donnell replied, fingers darting across the console to confirm what he had just done. "Do you want me to try again?"

"Will be within weapons range in thirty seconds. Please advise," came the voice of the flight group leader, calm but with a notable trace of urgency.

Parks' mind raced to consider the possibilities and available options. There remained but two: he could request that the code be sent again or he could immediately fall back to their other approach. If he requested the code to be retried it would mean that the fighters, bombers, and landing parties would be vulnerable to *Dragon*'s attack upon subsequent failure. On the other hand the lack of frigates in the system could mean it would be easier to secure a forceful victory...

"Target disabled, sir," O'Donnell interrupted his thoughts.

Parks looked up from his musings and saw that *Dragon* had ceased turning and now lay in darkness.

"All systems terminated. Shielding, weapon systems and mechanics have been shut down," O'Donnell continued. "Life support is the only detectable working component. There must have been a delay in the transmission or reception of the code."

"Gravitation systems?" Parks asked, looking to the various feeds to gain a better indication of *Dragon*'s impairment.

"Down, sir," O'Donnell said.

"Good. Relay that information to the boarding teams."

"Yes, sir."

So far, so good, Parks thought. Aside from the minor delay, it looked as though everything was going according to plan. There now only remained the matter of flooding the interior of *Dragon* with toxins as arranged, picking off any adversaries that may have managed to survive, and apprehending Admiral Zackaria before rushing medical assistance to him.

A pity we could not have shut down life support too, Parks mused. *There would be no need to board the ship. We could have simply towed it back to Spirit and pulled the bodies out at the other end.*

"Phase one of the operation is complete," Parks said to the holographic images of his fellow command. "*Grendel* and *Leviathan* will continue as planned. *Griffin* and *Grendel's Mother* will stand their ground. Should *Dragon's* escorts arrive then we will be in a better position to engage them."

"Agreed," came the resounding answer.

"Passing weapons range," the voice of the Initial Run's flight leader came again. Parks looked back to the feed streaming from the Rook. Tension eased away as it and the rest of the flight group passed the danger threshold of *Dragon's* armaments unchallenged.

The group were bearing broadside to the battleship, the proximity now meaning that the flight leader's cockpit view could no longer fully accommodate the entire length of the colossal vessel. The words "C.S.N. Dragon" inscribed in tall, bold red lettering were now so close that Parks could start to make out where the paintwork was in need of touching up.

He beckoned to a member of the bridge's security team who approached him. "Please locate Andrea Kennedy and the other *Red Devils* and ask them to join me on the bridge." The man saluted and made his way to the bridge's lift, heading to the lower decks. Parks returned back to the mission still in progress, preparing to co-ordinate and delegate duties further when the time came.

"Beginning final approach," the flight leader said.

Perhaps I've overestimated *the Enemy*, Parks thought, feeling his spirits lift. *Maybe I can do this after all...*

"Target is live! Target is live!" the voice of the flight leader suddenly cried over the bridge's comms system, shattering Parks' illusions and bringing him back down with a crash. The stunned man strode to the very front of *Griffin's* bridge for a clearer view, feeling the need to look upon the battleship with his own two eyes rather than rely on the carrier's cameras. The flight leader was not wrong. As lights on *Dragon* sprang back into existence, disbelief hit him full on.

"What the hell just happened?" Parks spun back around.

"Power has just returned to *Dragon*! All systems are fully active!" O'Donnell said, poring over his console's readouts. "Shields are returning... Weapons and engine systems are powering up!"

"Resend the code!" Parks said, fighting to keep the shock out of his voice.

O'Donnell's fingers raced across the console. "*Dragon* is rejecting it, sir!" he said after multiple attempts.

Parks flew to the man's side, leaning over the console display and seeing the multitude of errors that were greeting O'Donnell upon each unsuccessful attempt,

```
           Authentication Failure
              Permission Denied
              PAM Error #80401
             Connection Refused
                Not Permitted
             Invalid Security Code
   Clearance Violation — This incident has been reported
```

"Abort! Abort!" the cries of the flight leader came once more over the bridge's comms system, accompanied by the noise of screaming computer systems, warning him of multiple weapon locks.

Parks watched as the man pulled out of his approach to *Dragon*, trying with all his might to shake off the battleship's targeting systems. All around him other craft could be seen attempting the same. Parks caught sight of a massive turret swinging around to face the flight leader. His eyes shifted to another of the feeds, seeing moments later bright green bolts of plasma belch forth, striking those behind him, scoring critical hits on some, whilst obliterating others.

The half dozen bolts become a veritable hail of fire, luminous bright green light flying in every direction, lighting dozens of surfaces on both *Dragon* herself and the allied forces.

"Pulling ba-" the flight leader began, before the audio became an ear splitting screech of static. The video tore, froze, and then shut off altogether. In another feed Parks saw the damaged Rook wheel for a brief second before it exploded, unable to evade *Dragon*'s cannons any longer.

The sound of loud voices spilled from the holographic links of the three other frontal carriers as they became a hive of noise, the captains barking new orders to their teams, instructing them to fall back and move out of weapons range. They, as he, all appeared stunned by the battleship's miraculous recovery.

Parks swallowed. This dragon had been watching them the whole time; it had just been pretending to sleep. And unless he was able to take back control of the operation that seemed to be falling apart in front of him, there was little doubt that the Enemy would not hesitate to turn the full power of the battleship against them.

He fought to realign himself and concentrate on falling back to attempting a forceful victory. With the absence of the frigates it might just be possible. Just as he prepared to do so, his eyes were grabbed by one of the remaining three feeds... and his blood froze.

With the allied fighter squadron all but destroyed and its power restored, *Dragon* continued to turn, bringing its bow around to face *Grendel*, the closest of the allied vessels to it. All along *Dragon*'s bow, locks and components began to release, shifting and docking into new positions. Gears engaged. A vertical seam appeared, running the length of the bow. The seam split, both sides moving aside, as if a great mouth were opening; the throat a cold, dark tunnel leading to oblivion. Parks felt his own throat close up, as the implications of the move became all too clear: the Enemy were preparing to use the battleship's main gun.

Grendel had made little progress in its attempt to evade *Dragon*'s attention, and as the enormous battleship brought itself around to face, Parks wished for nothing more than to be able to leap through the screen and pull them out of harm's way. But instead he stood rooted to the spot. There was nothing he could do. Silverthorne was shouting orders, his image turned away in the projection. He then looked back and Parks saw terror eyes.

Had it not been for the fact that the man had turned grey during his early twenties, Parks may have thought that the predicament Silverthorne now faced was wholly responsible for his appearance. Parks stared at him, as he looked back in silence. The somewhat stone faced man paled as he lowered his eyes to looked out of *Grendel*'s frontal viewport.

"Edward..." Parks started, before his own eyes fell to *Dragon*'s holographic feed. For a few seconds the battleship's "throat" was lit by an intense violet hue. Then *Dragon* fired.

What looked like an enormous bright white ball leapt from the front of the Confederation battleship and hurtled towards *Grendel* at a staggering velocity, taking mere seconds to traverse the distance between the two vessels, where it struck it broadside on. A tremendous explosion followed, for an instant appearing brighter than the Sun and causing Parks to shield his eyes.

Silverthorne's feed died, the CSN insignia replacing it as it had done with the flight leader's. Parks blinked, staring out the front of his ship to where *Grendel* had once stood. One moment it was there and the next... nothing. Not a single piece of *Grendel* remained. All that could be seen was a shower of particles that began to spread out and diminish, rippling as an invisible wave expanded behind them. The sea of debris that often followed the destruction of such a large vessel was nowhere to be seen.

"Oh dear God," a shocked voice came. Parks saw that Mandeep was covering her mouth, her breathing coming short, her eyes wide with disbelief.

"Commodore." It was Meyers. "We need to begin our counter offensive as soon as possible. If we do... could... t... Spirit." The signal broke up like a television signal in a thunderstorm. On one of the remaining feeds Parks saw *Leviathan* buffeted by the expanding shock wave. "We cannot risk losing any more vessels to that cannon," Meyers concluded.

Although Parks knew that it would be quite some time before *Dragon* was able to muster the energy required to use such a weapon again, whilst it remained the cannon was a formidable threat. He found himself in agreement with but one of Meyers' statements.

"Abort the mission!" he barked. "All ships, prepare to jump out of the system! Mr Davies, order the launch of all available fighters to cover our retreat!" There was an unpleasant awareness that he was almost certainly condemning those men and women to death. But at this very moment he had to follow protocol - and that meant that *Griffin*, *Ifrit*, and *Leviathan* came first.

He heard a console began a frenzied jingle. "What's that?"

"Sir, jump point forming!" the operator responded.

Parks felt his stress level spike. "Where?"

"Stern, port side!"

Dodds halted in his departure of the bar, running to meet the call for pilots, as a brilliant flash lit the room, light reflecting off the windows and wooden furnishings. Many of the other occupants had already left but he, as his fellow *Knights*, had found it hard to tear his eyes off the scene beyond.

There had been applause when *Dragon* had been shut down, gasps upon its recovery, and then cries as it opened fire. Dodds had looked on in horror as the hail of green bolts, clear even from where *Griffin* stood, flew around in every direction, striking targets and triggering explosions as they fell. He saw then, as Chaz had said, the fighter's attempts at returning fire was but a token gesture at best, their weapons no match for the tough defences of the Confederation flagship.

"What's that?" Enrique stopped beside him, staring out the tall port side windows.

"Jump point!" Chaz said.

Dodds swore as he saw the bow of a large vessel come into view, accelerating out from the point and coming to bear right alongside them. An arrangement of four red triangles came into view; the insignia of the Imperial naval forces.

"It's one of the frigates!" Chaz added.

"Dear God, that thing's close!" Dodds staggered back. He was able to read the vessel's designation along the side with no trouble whatsoever. Never in his life had he seen a manoeuvre such as this. The frigate was so close to them that it was - in astronavigational terms - within spitting distance. It could not have been four hundred meters from them, if that. One tiny error in its heading and the sides of both ships would have been touching.

But the frigate's heading was precise and its course put it perfectly in line with *Griffin*.

"No, no, no, no!" Dodds cried as the he saw cannons turn to face the carrier.

The words had not even left his mouth when the frigate opened fire, engaging its entire starboard battery at once and strafing the carrier's broadside. The first volley of fire was quick to cut down *Griffin*'s shielding, leaving the salvo that followed free to slam into the unprotected hull of the ship and tear a gaping hole in the armour. There were cries from the crew as fires and explosions engulfed them, before several interconnecting corridors were then exposed to the vacuum of space. Emergency systems sprung into action and sealed off the affected areas, but not before several unfortunate personnel were jettisoned through the gap.

Griffin lurched violently and Dodds crashed to the floor, the air being forced out of his lungs. Kelly and Enrique fell down beside him. Of the few that remained in the bar, Chaz was the only one who managed to steady himself against the jolt. Dodds rolled onto his side to watch the frigate pass by. Its fat, cylindrical body reminded him of an assault rifle, the long shaft of a cannon affixed to the underside of the bow making suggestion of a bayonet.

Seconds later a slew of starfighters joined it, streaking past the bar's windows. Dodds could only assume they had all entered into the system together and hoped that there were not more jump points surrounding the carrier. He had no time to find out - the view became obscured by the closing blast screens, sealing off the vulnerable glass windows in case they should shatter and expose the ship.

"You all right?" Enrique said, helping Kelly to her feet.

"Yeah," Kelly said.

Dodds got up, seeing Chaz attending to another of the bar's occupants who appeared to have suffered a more serious fall.

"Chaz," he said, making his way over towards the body that was sprawled out across the floor.

"He's okay," the big man looked around at him. "Just unconscious."

"Simon - Estelle," Kelly said.

"Yeah, we need to find her," Dodds said and started towards the deck lift. "She may have been hurt."

From the bridge of *Dragon*, Admiral Zackaria watched the ensuing carnage with no emotion. He was neither pleased nor displeased with what had occurred, only satisfied that the enemy were being destroyed.

To his second in command, Commodore Rissard, he ordered that *Dragon* should deploy her own fighters to join the others that had just arrived with the frigate. Rissard acknowledged the request and followed the orders through.

All about *Dragon*'s flight deck feet ran to board waiting Imperial starfighters, the pilots dressed head to toe in black suits. Upon their heads they wore dark helmets, piercing ruby-red eyes shining like those of a vicious predator. Their movements were regimented, almost machine-like, and they all acted without question, nor hesitation, as they prepared for launch.

Parks pulled himself to his feet as others returned to their positions. He looked to the main viewport at the front of the bridge, to reassess the standings following the assault on his ship. He saw that the frigate was past them now, accelerating away to come to rest in between the three front line carriers. The request for pilots was still ringing.

"Give me a damage report," Parks said, glancing from the frigate to *Dragon*. Some information he did not need: he could see parts of his ship drifting away, bodies floating in amongst the wreckage, already dead and rigid in the cold. "Poor bastards."

"Shields returning, some structural damage to the midsection. Weapons and other major systems have not been affected," he was told.

"*Grendel's Mother* and *Leviathan* are deploying cover teams," Liu said.

"The fighters that arrived with the frigate are looping back around on attack vectors," O'Donnell added.

There was very little for Parks to consider now. His number one priority was to ensure that the allied forces could exit the combat zone and minimise losses.

"Target those incoming fighters and make ready to bring the jump engines on-line," Parks ordered. "Get every spare pilot we have out there to cover our retreat. And get me Commodore Hawke!" He was determined to see the man fulfil his role in this battle.

Anthony Hawke continued to observe the scene from the safety of *Ifrit*, the carrier far detached from the battle that had erupted around the allied forces. From where he stood he could see *Griffin*'s guns blazing, firing at attacking enemy targets. He felt no sense of shame in watching.

"Captain, fighter support are asking whether or not they should engage the enemy forces," a young man seated close to where Hawke stood asked of him.

"Tell them to hold position," Hawke said in a flat tone.

"Sir, begging your pardon but I think we should offer our assistance," the man protested. "*Griffin* just suffered a major attack and I don't think we should be just sitting here doing nothing."

"We *wait*, Lieutenant. Only one frigate has jumped into the system and we were expecting two. If we move forward now then we could be playing straight into the enemy's hands. We have already been tricked once by *Dragon* and we don't want to walk into another one of their traps."

"But, sir, if we remain here and wait for a frigate that might not even show up, then *Griffin* could be destroyed. I really think we should assist."

Hawke looked at him through cold eyes. "If you question by command one more time, Mr Parsons, I will find you guilty of mutiny and have you locked in the brig. Now follow my orders and tell those fighters to remain where they are."

"Yes, sir," Parsons said, lowering his own eyes to his screen.

"Sir, *Griffin* is requesting communications," Hawke heard.

"Put them on," Hawke said, folding his arms and carrying a look of impatience. A holographic screen sprang up on front of him, Parks appearing on the display.

"We could use your help up here, Anthony," Parks said earnestly. "The additional fire power will help us to withdraw all the sooner. We will need to ensure that as many vessels as possible can be accounted for, including *Grendel's Mother*."

"I don't think that's such a good idea," Hawke said. "Moving all our forces up front could leave us even more vulnerable. As already agreed *Ifrit* will hold position here to prevent enemy forces from being able to surround us."

"But... Are you serious?!" Parks spluttered.

"My position is clear," Hawke said. Ahead of him he could see small explosions dotted around *Griffin* were starfighter fell and missiles connected.

Parks' face became stern. "Commodore Hawke, your commitment to this operation has been nothing short of disgraceful! You leave me with no choice but to force the chain of command - and as the senior officer in charge of this operation, I order you..."

Parks stopped talking, his holographic image turning away as someone interrupted him. The communication came to an abrupt end.

"They seem to have things under control," Hawke said quietly, his face impassive. "Hold position," he called to the bridge, not taking his eyes off the scene outside.

An explosion appeared towards *Griffin*'s bow and the carrier's once stable course began to deteriorate, many of the lights all about the ship flickering before they extinguished altogether.

Hawke's nose was bleeding once again, but this time he did nothing about it, letting the blood trickle from his nose and drip down onto the floor of the bridge.

"Hold position," he whispered.

XIII

— A Light in the Dark —

P arks opened his eyes to find that the bridge lay in almost complete darkness, and was filled with smoke. The events that had led him to finding himself sprawled out on the floor escaped him, and he realised that he must have blacked out for a few seconds. He noticed a man on the floor next to him, with a glazed look in his eyes. A trail of blood glistened as it trickled from his head. Parks became aware that he was staring into the face of O'Donnell, his CCMO. The man was dead. The commodore pulled himself to his feet and looked to the frontal viewport, to the continuing scenes of battle outside. He then remembered what had happened.

As Parks had spoken to Hawke, a member of the bridge crew had alerted him to a damaged Imperial fighter streaking towards them. Even in its damaged state the pilot had been a master of his craft and had managed to guide it straight towards *Griffin*'s launch bay, whilst evading all the carrier's attempts to bring it down. As it had disappeared from view security cameras all about the flight deck had relayed the short, but terrible seconds that followed.

Deck hands had watched horrified as the last bursts of the fighter's cannons had eliminated what remained of the bay quadrant's already weak shielding and sped down the launch tunnel towards them. There were cries of panic from the crew and awaiting pilots before people had fled in all directions, some attempting to take cover behind cargo containers, whose contents would offer nothing but a much swifter death. A missile had detached from the bottom of the fighter, slamming into the forcefield that lay ahead. With its last obstacle overcome, and with nothing left to stop it, the Imperial fighter had slammed straight in a row of waiting TAFs, all in the process of being rearmed, where it had gone on to do the most damage.

Its unspent payload of missiles had exploded, along with its reactor. Unopposed, the blast had ripped its way across the entire deck, which - as was its nature - was stocked full of volatile equipment. The resulting chain reaction had impacted almost every area of the ship, including the bridge, the total damage being nothing short of astronomical.

Parks felt a warm flow on the side of his head. He placed his hand against his temple and, even in the half light of the bridge, could see the blood covering his fingers. His left arm was also aching from where he had fallen on it. From the bridge's frontal viewport he could see that the carrier was no longer aligned with the on-going battle and that the blast must have thrown them off course. The view was skewed, no longer aligned at an angle appropriate to the task.

He turned back to the bridge itself, trying to see down its length, but finding that the smoke and haze was making it almost impossible to see what was happening around him. There was a sudden loud clunking noise, the sound of emergency systems engaging, and the bridge was filled with dim lighting allowing Parks to see the true extent of the damage: consoles sparked and smoked; people lay slumped forward in their chairs, burns all about their bodies where equipment had exploded in front of them. Parks hoped that for their sakes they were already dead. Others were struggling to their feet, some trying to wake the unconscious and checking them for injuries.

"Talk to me, people!" Parks called, his voice a distant sound even in his own head, as he struggled to regain all his senses.

"Here, Captain," a voice answered. It was Liu. Aside from the bruising on his face and an injured left arm he looked none the worse for wear, more shocked than anything; though the inability to take his eyes off the dead, still form of O'Donnell was not helping.

"Stay calm, Lieutenant," Parks urged the man, drawing his focus away from the corpse. "Are you hurt?"

"No, sir. Well, I am a little, but nothing I can't cope with, sir," Liu managed, his eyes dropping once again to the corpse splayed out on the floor.

Parks reached out and put a hand on the man's shoulder. "I need you to stay focused and maintain order here, Ali. Can you do that?"

"Yes, sir."

"Good, you have the bridge," Parks said. "I have to get to the flight deck and find out what the hell's happened."

"Yes, sir," Liu said, managing to tear his eyes off O'Donnell.

Leaving Liu to focus on getting the bridge back to order, Parks hurried to the stairwell, limping as he went.

Estelle stumbled down the poorly-lit corridors of the carrier's lower deck, trying desperately to locate the other *Knights*. She had been making her way towards the flight deck when the Imperial fighter had crashed on to it, plunging the entire ship into darkness.

She had been lying on the bed vacated by Dodds when the call for pilots had come in. She started towards the quarters door when a loud explosion and the rocking of the carrier knocked her off her feet and sent her tumbling backwards, causing her to strike her head against one of the metal beds. The blow had not caused any serious damage, but had left her with a headache. She was now experiencing a dull ache that smarted with each step she took.

She had to find Dodds, Kelly, Enrique and Chaz. She had decided to head straight to the flight deck in anticipation of finding them there. Other crew members were running and pushing past her, hurrying to deal with their own problems. As she continued her journey she discovered an emergency door was cutting off her most direct route. She doubled back, attempting to find another way around.

"Estelle!" a desperate voice cried out to her. Along a smoky corridor, just off from the one she walked down, a woman lay on her back buried beneath wreckage that had fallen from the ceiling. From where Estelle stood the wreckage appeared to have trapped the woman's legs and one of her arms.

Estelle started forward to try to help.

"Be careful!" the woman shouted to Estelle as she approached.

"Andrea?!" Estelle asked, startled as she saw who it was trapped beneath the collapsed steel. She gingerly walked forward, wary of any loose sections of the roof that may not yet have fallen, as well as dangling electricals.

"Estelle, help me... No one will stop to help me... Please," Andrea pleaded.

Estelle looked around herself for a way to help her remove the wreckage, but could see nothing that could be of any assistance. "What happened?" she asked, kneeling down next to Andrea.

"We were heading for the bridge, the others were... walking just in front of me... The wall ahead of us exploded. I managed to grab on to something, but the others..." she started to weep.

"What happened?"

"They were spaced! I couldn't save them, Estelle! Their faces... I watched them die," she said through the sobs. "I tried to find another way to the bridge... and then the ceiling came down on top of me... Estelle, I can't move my legs... It hurts so much..."

It had become apparent to Estelle that Andrea's legs had been crushed by the collapsed roof, and that the same fate had befallen the woman's trapped arm. She grabbed at some of the steel, trying to find a way to pry it loose. When it became clear that it was not going to budge she moved around to try another section. She only managed to move a handful of light parts before the heavier portions of the wreckage defeated her. Andrea watched her the whole time, coughing and sobbing. Estelle ducked down next to the woman, trying to see if there was a way to pull her out from under the mess. There was none.

"I'm going to find help," Estelle said, standing up. "I won't be long, I promise."

"Okay," Andrea managed, gravely.

Estelle hurried away, darting down the corridors looking for someone to assist her. Few paid her any attention, Estelle unable to get the words out before the person she tried to stop pushed past her, and those that did listen already had higher priorities. She wished that the others were here now. The five of them would have little trouble freeing the trapped woman. Even Enrique and Chaz would have had enough strength between them. Eventually, a man and woman followed her back to the scene.

"Andrea," she called, returning to the trapped woman's side. "I've got help. Don't worry, we'll have you free..." She stopped talking and knelt by the curly, haired blonde, seeing her eyes open, staring straight upward, a trickle of blood running from her mouth. "Andrea?"

The woman who had followed Estelle knelt by her side and felt Andrea's neck. She then shook her head. "She's dead."

"Help me!" a hysterical cry came from behind. Estelle saw the woman next to her turn around, and then spring up to assist the owner of the voice. She heard those that had accompanied her to where Andrea lay urging someone to keep calm, before all three hurried from the scene, their voices fading away down the corridor as they went.

Estelle saw none of it, her eyes focused on Andrea's face, racked with the guilt of the jealousy she had felt only hours earlier. She reached down and closed the dead woman's eyes, no longer wishing she could be in her place.

An out of breath Parks arrived at one of the flight deck's observation galleries; or at least, what remained of it. All access to the deck had been sealed off, blast doors preventing anyone from getting any closer to the source of the devastation that had crippled the carrier. Even the gallery refused to permit its occupants any idea of the destruction that lay beyond: thick blast screens covered the windows, allowing them to see no further than the inside of the room.

The smouldering remains of terminals and computer screens, as well as shattered glass covering the ground, was all that remained to suggest what the gallery's purpose may have been. Everything around Parks was charred black, the damage spreading down the approaching corridor. The doors, which usually slid open automatically as they were approached, had to be pushed apart by hand. As on the bridge, people were attending to the wounded and trying to revive others.

Kneeling down on the floor, just inside the doorway, was a woman attending to the injuries of a man propped up against a wall. His face was quite bloody, the result of a wound somewhere on the top of his head.

"Captain," he said upon seeing Parks enter. He pushed aside the woman's hand and attempted to get to his feet.

"As you were," Parks said, waving him back down. Though they were injured Parks had found that some of the carrier's crew still attempted to adhere to a certain standard of correctness. Right now he did not want either of these two to stand and salute.

"What's the status of the flight deck?" he asked, though by the state of the observation deck he believed he already knew the answer.

"Badly damaged," answered the man on the floor, wincing as the woman tended to his wounded head. She was now making a clumsy effort to wrap a bandage around the affected area. "There is no hope of launching fighters until it receives some extensive repairs, and that won't be before we re-establish the force fields. The whole deck has been exposed to space. If we open it up then we risk depressurising the entire ship."

"Survivors? Anyone still alive down there?"

"Not a chance. If they weren't killed when that damn fighter hit, then they would have been spaced straight after. We'll have lost everyone: pilots, attendants, the OOD and the junior, technicians and munitions handlers..."

"Stay calm, man!"

"Captain!" another voice came.

Parks looked around as a man came bounding up the stairs to the remains of the observation room; it was the security officer who he had sent to fetch Andrea.

"The *Red Devils* are dead, sir. They were spaced during the frigate's initial attack."

Though he knew the shock on his face was clear for all to see, Parks made no attempt to conceal it. This was news that he had not been prepared for. As it stood the entire plan to attack and retake *Dragon* had been nothing short of a total disaster. Even retreating would not be possible until the engines were brought back on-line, and abandoning the ship was not an option. The evacuees would be sitting ducks in their escape pods. Prisoners would not be taken, lives would not be spared. Even without full shielding or weapon systems they stood a much better chance of survival by remaining on the carrier and attempting to restore power, than floating around in escape pods in the middle of the battlefield.

And minutes from destruction or not, Parks would *never* abandon *Griffin*.

Regaining some of his composure, the commodore felt his shock turn to anger at his own stupidity. He turned to the man and woman on the floor next to him, "You two, once you are able, start organising an assessment of repairs needed to the flight deck. We must find a way to launch fighters. If we cannot get weapons systems or shielding back on-line then we will be totally defenceless."

"At once, sir," the man said.

"Come with me," Parks said, looking at the bridge security officer. They started back to the stairways interconnecting the carrier's decks. "I want you to get as many crew members as possible to help with repairs, skilled in that field or not. The restoration of power to the engines, shields and weapon systems should be our number one priority."

"Yes, sir."

"In the meantime we must find a way to defend ourselves," Parks continued. "*Leviathan* and *Grendel's Mother* will only be able to provide cover for so long against a dedicated attack on us. The ATAFs weren't on the flight deck and can still be deployed, but with the *Red Devils* dead we have no one to fly them..."

"We can fly them, sir!"

Parks spun around at the sound of the familiar voice, to see Estelle, Dodds, Enrique, Kelly, and Chaz all standing behind him; the five *White Knights* shining like a beacon before his eyes against the dark of the corridor. He looked to the security guard and gave his next order without even one second's hesitation,

"Get them to the rear cargo hold."

XIV

— The Knights' Charge —

As he stood in *Griffin*'s rear cargo hold, Dodds was at a loss for words. The footage that he had viewed of the ATAF back on Xalan had failed to fully convey the magnificence that he now felt radiating from the craft. Even in the dim ambience of the emergency lighting, the sleek black armour of the fighters seemed to gleam with elegance.

He found himself drawn towards it, and approached to run his hand over the smooth curvature of the nose, his eyes wandering across every surface, absorbing every detail. He found it beautiful, but knew that that beauty concealed the fighter's nature. As he continued to gaze upon the craft, he began to understand how Estelle sometimes felt, striving always for moments like this. He caught the dim reflection of Enrique in the fighter's armour. The man was standing beside him, his face frozen with an equal look of reverence.

The spacious cargo hold had been quite empty when the five starfighter pilots had entered it, containing only the ATAFs and equipment necessary to handle them. It was now beginning to fill with other personnel who had come streaming in to aid with the launch of the fighters. They buzzed around, for a time ignoring the *White Knights* and concentrating on what had to be done.

Dodds took little notice of them, hearing only their dim voices in the background. One was speaking to Estelle.

"Yep! Fully prepped and ready to go, Lieutenant."

"Right, right... Dodds, Enrique, get over here," she called to the men who was still lost in their admiration of the craft before them. There was the sound of running feet, and she looked around to see an out of breath, red faced man come sprinting into the cargo bay, almost knocking down several others in his haste.

"Commodore Parks wants you to get these guys out there ASAP!" he gasped to the conning officer. "*Dragon* just deployed fighters and unless we get these guys out there now... What the hell are those?" He was staring at the ATAFs lining the walls.

There was a loud clunking sound and the occupants of the cargo hold found themselves squinting against the glow of the carrier's restored lighting. Silence gave way to the sound of various pieces of machinery and computer system starting back up. *Griffin* had come alive once more.

"Okay, here's the plan," Estelle said as her wingmates drew around her. "I will takeoff first to get an overview of the standings and liaise with Commodore Parks. Dodds, I want you out next, followed by Kelly, Enrique, and then Chaz. Once we are out there I will issue you all with objectives." She looked to the ATAFs. "Just... just remember – it's like flying a TAF."

She could hear her voice quivering ever so slightly; the anticipation of what was to come was causing her to draw breath much faster than usual. She turned to the conning officer. "Ready?"

"Ready," she replied, signalling to others in the bay who wheeled over a ladder so she could enter the cockpit. "Those special considerations I mentioned: we're not able to set up any sort of launch catapult down here, so you're going to have to maintain a hover whilst we rotate the inner and outer force fields. You okay with that?"

"No problem," said Estelle.

The conning officer looked to the other four, who nodded their understanding. Then, to Estelle, she said, "Don't boost until you're fully clear, otherwise you could cause major damage to the hold. Clear?"

"Understood," Estelle said. She leapt up the ladder, scooped up the helmet that was nestled into the seat and slipped it over her head. Despite the ATAF evaluation program being concluded several weeks ago, the cockpit layout was still fresh in her mind. Her fingers pressed buttons and flipped switches as they had done many times before, the starfighter's systems coming on-line just as she expected. As the last notification appeared Estelle informed the flight crew she was ready to go. She then took up the position the conning officer had requested.

She could feel her heart beating hard, threatening once more to burst out of her chest, though now out of sheer exhilaration, rather than fear and uncertainty.

This is it, girl. This is what it has all been about, she thought to herself. *Do yourself proud. Do us all proud.* Looking to her side she gave a thumbs-up to her wingmates and then faced forward as the cargo bay doors slid apart. Moments later the force field rotated, the all clear was given, and she accelerated out.

Beyond *Griffin* the battle raged on. Though *Grendel's Mother* and *Leviathan* were struggling against the increased enemy presence, they had still managed to earn *Griffin* a reprieve. After seeing the damage their allied carrier had sustained, and the loss of stability, Meyers and Mandeep had ordered all their crew and starfighters to divide themselves between protecting all three carriers. Against the odds their efforts were admirable, but cracks were beginning to show in their defence, the increasing swarm of enemy fighters on the verge of overcoming the allied forces. *Grendel's Mother* had held her position next to *Griffin*, Meyers taking *Leviathan* to stand some way in front of them.

"You're going to have to work harder to keep those fighters off us," Meyers told the allied squadrons. "If they put either *Leviathan* or *Grendel's Mother* out of commission then it's all over."

"Doing our best, captain," one of the pilots responded. "But these guys are proving tougher than expected. I've never seen Imperial pilots fly like this before!"

"That's because Imperial pilots *don't* fly like that!" another pilot broadcast his feelings to the entire field, the anxiety unmistakable in his voice. "I've flown against them before and these guys... these guys are something else! Those are *not* Imperial pilots in those fighters!"

They were the same concerns that Meyers had heard levied by many others about the field. The skills possessed by those commanding the Imperial starfighters was truly something to behold: it was as though they were more than capable of exploiting every weakness of their opponents, whilst at the same time able to anticipate and compensate for every return attack. Their reactions were unparalleled, as if they had minutes to deal with situations that others were required to handle in seconds.

"Captain, power has been restored to *Griffin*," came a voice from the bridge.

Meyers turned from where he had been watching a pair of TAFs' luckless attempts at taking down an Imperial fighter, to see *Griffin* was once again back on-line. He was relieved to see that the enemy fighter that had crashed into its flight deck had not left the carrier permanently dead in the water.

"Thank God for that." He turned to his communications officer. "Have you managed to establish contact with Commodore Parks yet?"

"Negative, sir," the woman answered. "There is too much signal corruption to maintain a stable connection. The link keeps dropping out every few seconds. Their comms system must still be down."

"Keep trying," Meyers said, staring at the swarm of Imperial starfighters that had just issued from *Dragon*. Against such odds they would need some sort of miracle to see them through to the end of the day.

The *Knights* were clear of *Griffin*, and the ATAFs looped around the rear of the carrier to face the incoming threat. Dodds realised that the situation they now faced mirrored one from the many hours they had all put into the simulators. It reminded him of the team's very first failure and of how the training manager had assured them it had been designed to be unfair, unrealistic, and not ever likely to occur in real life. With all that in mind he approached the battle with added caution.

Estelle's orders - derived from what she had managed to understand from Parks between the static and regular loss of signal – further compounded it. They were to lend support to the three carriers that were attempting to escape the system, providing extra support to *Griffin* in its crippled state. Parks had also requested that they attempt to take down the frigate at the earliest opportunity.

"... though it looks like we're going to have to fight our way through this lot first," Estelle concluded.

Dodds noted that whilst some of the fighters that had departed *Dragon* had peeled off from the main group and were headed in the direction of *Leviathan*, the majority were headed straight towards *Griffin* and *Grendel's Mother*; and with them, the *Knights*. Dodds swallowed and then braced himself. Along with his wingmates, he put himself on an intercept course with the approaching squadron and sped towards them.

As they drew within range of one another, both sides spread out to gain more fighting room, three of the Imperial fighters aligning themselves with Dodds. He eyed his opponents. Though he had never seen them outside of a simulated environment, there was no mistaking the form of an Imperial Mantis: a Y shaped frame and egg-like body, where the cockpit and single large engine resided. Three struts jutted out of the body, a single cannon affixed to the tips of the frame's top two; the lower, central one, home to a number of missiles set into a rack. Though not visible from the distance, Dodds recalled that the fighter's designers had also seen fit to squeeze on another pair of guns, just beneath the main body. The appendages appeared almost as if they were claws and mandibles, poised to rip their opponent apart; the maroon hues of the Imperial colour schemes that decorated the armour looking like the blood of its previous victims.

The three fighters continued to close in on him and Dodds held his course unwavering, making no indication that he intended to deviate from his present course. He kept in mind his experiences of the ATAF back on Xalan, confident that the fighter he occupied was in every way superior to those he faced, no matter the odds.

Weapons ranges were met, and at once the three Mantises' guns opened up, a torrent of green and purple bolts streaking towards him. At the sight he felt his heart leap into his throat, panic deriding the pride he had felt only moments earlier. He banked hard to evade the shower, though not as fast as he would have liked. Much of the enemy fire hit home, his fighter's encasing shields bathing the entire cockpit in rippling blue hues as they absorbed the hits.

As the Mantises streaked past, Dodds' hand flew to the ejection handle, preparing to blow the canopy and jettison himself out of the doomed craft the moment he heard the blare of the warning siren. It never came, and all was silent, save for the jumble of noise from his comms.

Relief washed over him as he glanced to the instrument panel. The attack he had feared had barely even registered. It was like the first day with the simulators all over again, where he found it difficult to get used to the fact that the ATAF could handle itself far better in combat than anything else he had ever flown.

He exhaled, though his heart was still beating hard. He then wheeled the

ATAF around and gave chase to the three Imperial fighters that had just passed him.

With the realisation that their target had been spared destruction and was now tailing them, the Mantis group dived. Dodds stayed behind them during the manoeuvre and the ones that they followed up with, utilizing all the skills he had been taught. He then shifted his heading over, so that his crosshairs met with the HUD's predictive targeting receptacle, before returning fire.

It was far from the first time he had seen it, but the resulting hail of fire from the ATAF's cannons still floored him; even more so when his target connected with the thick stream of plasma bolts. The Mantis exploded, scattering metals, alloys, and sparking components in every direction. Dodds was quick to react to its allies who were pulling away, repeating the same tried and tested technique against them.

Thirty seconds later Dodds found himself victorious, staring at the tumbling remnants of an enemy that had at first outnumbered and out gunned him. A small chuckle of disbelief escaped him, and he turned about to face the ongoing struggle he had lost sight of during his fight.

His eyes swept across the scene: cannon fire, lasers, missiles, and fighters of various different configurations flew in every direction. *Leviathan*'s and *Grendel's Mother*'s cannons were hunting targets within the hordes of Imperial fighters that were swarming all about them. At one time a sight such as this might have terrified him; made him wish that he was some place else. Not now.

He looked for the W shaped forms of the other four ATAFs in amongst the swashes of other fighters, then gave up. He would find him them later. For now there were bigger issues to address. He could see more Imperial fighters turning his way. He suspended his disbelief, buried his sense of glory, and took a good grip on the stick.

"Okay, let's see what this thing can really do." He raised his velocity to maximum and dove headlong into the chaos.

With power restored to *Griffin*, Parks was once again able to immerse himself back into the battle. For all the damage the carrier had incurred, he was surprised – and grateful – to discover that the on-board camera systems and audio transmissions had been least affected. As the feeds tracked the ATAFs speeding around the conflict zone, he caught snatches of reaction from other allied fighters whilst the bridge crew attempted to establish a more stable comm system.

"Who the hell are *they*?!"

"I don't know, I've never seen them before!"

"Are they on our side?!"

"I don't know - there's no markings on them!"

"Should we attack?"

"No! They're not shoot at *us*; they're shooting at *them*!"

From what Parks could tell the Enemy forces had ceased many of their attacks on the allies present, concentrating all their efforts on attempting to bring down the five unknown starfighters that were tearing their way through their forces. Although for all their might they may as well have been trying to hold back the tide.

"Captain, we've managed to establish a stable connection with *Leviathan*," Parks heard.

"Audio?" he asked.

"Both audio and visual, sir."

"Finally," he said and turned away from where he had been watching one of the ATAF's astral acrobatics. "Bring it up."

The holographic image of *Leviathan*'s captain was far from perfect. Even under normal operation the image and audio could suffer from breakup and distortions as the signal failed in places. It was now a permanent mess of discolouration and blocky pixels, the audio scratchy and accompanied by white noise. But it represented the best efforts of the crew in the time given to them and, for now, fulfilled its purpose.

"How are you holding up, Aiden?" Parks said.

"Better than you by the looks of things, Elliott."

Parks picked at some of the blood caked to his face. Aside from a handful of pain killers, he had refused any proper medical attention once he learned he was suffering from nothing more than a superficial head wound.

Meyer said, "I requested that Commodore Hawke bring *Ifrit* up front to lend their support for our withdrawal, but I'm sorry to say that he point blank refused. I did my best, sir."

Parks waved away the man's apology. He had long since given up attempting to involve Hawke in the battle, communication problems notwithstanding. Should they both survive the day he would be bringing his actions - or lack therefore of - to the attention of Turner and Jenkins, as well as other top brass. He could not believe that someone whom he had once seen as a good friend and mentor would desert him in his hour of need. But for the moment there were more important things to deal with.

Meyers' attention turned for a moment and he looked back at Parks. "I see you managed to deploy the ATAFs."

"Eventually. And by all accounts they are exceeding expectations."

"As are the *Red Devils*."

Parks shook his head. "The *Red Devils* aren't piloting the ATAFs, Captain, the *White Knights* are. Unfortunately the *Red Devils* lost their lives when the frigate attacks us."

"Hell, that's... regrettable," Meyers said.

Although Parks felt the same way, there was no time for anyone to grieve. "Captain, I want *Leviathan* to fall back to my position so that we can complete our withdrawal. I have ordered the *White Knights* to engage the frigate and *Dragon*'s fighter wing to provide you with cover."

"The frigate *and* the fighters?" Meyers said, looking stunned.

Parks raised a hand. "Don't worry, Captain, they can cope. This is an ideal opportunity to collect combat data on the fighter. I shouldn't worry too much about the threat of attacks from the Enemy for now - they have enough to contend with as it is."

"Very well, Commodore," Meyers said. "I will prep torpedoes in case things turn ugly."

Hawke had watched the battle from the bridge of *Ifrit* without a flicker of emotion, despite the numerous calls from his crew that they should move in to assist. They challenged him no longer, the threat of a stay in the brig and a disciplinary hearing should they continue to question his command being enough to silence them. Even after the damage that *Griffin* had sustained he had refused to acknowledge the calls for assistance by Meyers, who could do nothing but ask, unable to order the higher ranking officer to take action.

But now Hawke was almost ready to make his move. He turned to the carrier's helmsman. "Prepare to take us forward on my command, Mr Cox."

"Yes, sir," Cox said, without raising his eyes from his console.

Dodds continued to strike down the Imperial starfighters that darted about him. His adversaries, for all their impressive flying skills, were able to do little to protect themselves from the advantages the ATAF granted him. They could only weave and dive for so long to throw off the targeting systems before they succumbed to the hail of fire that chased them, or were downed by another of the *White Knights*.

He had long ago lost count of the number he had taken down; though judging by the sheer amount of debris that now floated around, littering the area between the two sides, it must have been a lot. He was certain that at one time the bulk of the wreckage had been made up of the remains of allied Confederation and Independent craft. But in only a short space of time the *Knights* had managed to drive the enemy away from the four carriers and were now on the offensive, plunging deeper into the cluster of *Dragon*'s support.

He had since caught up with his fellow wingmates and asked each in turn if they were in need of any assistance. None of them were, all confident that they stood a good chance of handling the battle all by themselves. Dodds agreed. The effect of the attacks brought against his fighter's defences were so minimal that he had taken to more or less ignoring them.

As he sort out his next target within the scrum, a group of Imperial fighters ahead of him slowed, flipped around and sped away. A wing further up field followed suit. Glancing around his canopy he saw others performing similar manoeuvres, a blur of Mantises, Jackals, and Sphinxes racing past him, their guns silent.

"Enemy fighters are pulling back," he heard Chaz's voice come over his comms.

Dodds held his own fire, watching as his enemies fell back to more defensive positions, drawing a line between the allied forces, *Dragon*, and the frigate. A pair of ATAFs came up alongside him and brought themselves to a halt.

In the brief calm that followed he considered the scene before him: they were five lone fighters pitted against a frigate, dozens of Imperial starfighters, and a monstrous forty-five-hundred-metre battleship. But they were also five fighters that had caused their opponents considerable upset. His hand tightened on the stick, readying himself for the anticipated push.

Estelle was quick to issue new instructions to the team, aiming to capitalize on the break in the enemy's attacks whilst they reorganised themselves, and ordering Kelly, Enrique, and Chaz forward to take down the frigate that was still exchanging long distance fire with *Leviathan*. She then ordered Dodds to follow her lead, and the two swung about, the pilot becoming aware of the reasons for splitting the team – Emerging from a jump point, just behind where the three allied carriers had gathered themselves, was the expected second and final frigate.

An eager Estelle raced ahead of him and he shot after her, surging through their own ranks to tackle the approaching warship.

As Estelle and Dodds headed toward the second frigate, Kelly, Enrique, and Chaz made for the first. Missiles, plasma bolts, and laser sprayed towards the three as the frigate's cannons focused on them. They avoided much of the barrage, the missiles that sought them falling to the starfighter's countermeasures. What remained of the frigate's attack was easily fended off by their shielding.

With Kelly's lead, the three tackled their target in a similar manner to the way they had done time and time again on Xalan: starting with their lasers, they circled the vessel until the biting red beams had made significant impacts on its defences. Next, they flew up and around, racing lengthways across it, bombarding the topside with their own missiles. Finally they looped back around, skimming over the surfaces and concentrating their cannons on the weakest structural points.

All the while the frigate returned fire, bolts, beams, and missiles chasing the three starfighters, all failing to stave off the attack. It was not long before the midsection began to come apart, explosions haemorrhaging the hull and bulk heads, and began to tear the frigate apart.

Soon after the three *Knights* pulled out of their assault and re-focused on the Imperial fighters, who had been able to do little else except standby helpless as the ATAFs dispatched the ship they had escorted in.

* * *

Dodds and Estelle plunged into the second frigate's fighter escort as they streaked past *Griffin*, lending support to the carrier's defences that had been caught on the backfoot.

"The first frigate has been taken down," Estelle said, not a few minutes into their engagement.

"Already?" Dodds said in disbelief. He could have put full trust in his radar, but instead he wheeled around to witness the final moments of the frigate, as it was torn asunder by the explosions that continued to issue forth. He lingered for a while, aware of the fire striking him, but paying it no more attention than he had before.

The questions returned: just what *was* this thing that he sat in? Had the Confederation really built this alone? And if they had, for what purpose? This was not just the next step up, it was a leap; and giant one at that.

Estelle's voice dragged him back. "We need to hurry up, Dodds. These guys won't be able to handle the fighters themselves and *Griffin* is in trouble if that frigate gets any closer."

He adjusted his heading to pass over *Griffin* and onward to meet the approaching frigate. As he drew closer he concluded that the quickest solution to the problem of the frigate was to employ the use of his fighter's plasma accelerator. Having only used the weapon during the first few days of the ATAF's simulated courses, a real world test was long overdue.

Traversing the craft's system menus he located the screen he needed to activate the weapon, only to be confronted with an access denial. He nevertheless tapped the screen a few times in defiance. The console did nothing save for emit a dull bleep, further enforcing its rejection.

"My accelerator has been locked," Dodds said. "If yours isn't working either, then we'll have to do this the old fashioned way." Estelle said nothing and Dodds returned his full attention back towards their target, discovering the reasons for her sudden silence.

A large explosion appeared at the stern of the Imperial frigate, followed by another. The vessel began to come apart, venting gases and chemicals, and trailing chunks of hull and bulkhead in its wake. An enormous hail of cannon fire came from somewhere behind, slamming into the stricken vessel and putting an end to its involvement in the battle.

"Hawke," Estelle said, as *Ifrit* came into view.

With Rissard next to him, Zackaria watched the destruction of the two frigates in silence, their short lived victory coming to a swift end. He turned and signalled to the crew that they were to leave at once. He felt no disappointment over their loss, nor in the direction the battle had turned. He had gained considerable knowledge and insight into his enemy, experience that would prove invaluable in the future.

Parks glowered, observing a feed of the spinning remains of the second frigate. True to his word, Hawke had engaged the enemy vessel as it had jumped into position behind the three carriers, effecting a flank. Hawke's belief that the enemy might attempt such a manoeuvre had come to a head, and he had made good on his own proposal to await such a move and step in to undo it. Parks could fault him for that.

He looked back to another feed of two ATAFs chasing after the wing of fighters that had arrived with the frigate. The fighters were pulling away the battle, heading back towards *Dragon*. Likewise another group were retreating from the three ATAFs that had taken down the first frigate.

"*Griffin*, this is de Winter. Enemy forces appear to be withdrawing. Should we pursue?"

"Stand down," Parks said. "Let them go. I don't want anyone to throw their lives away needlessly."

They did so, and as he watched *Dragon* turned away from the allied forces. A jump point formed beyond and the battleship, along with the enormous squadrons of Imperial starfighters, accelerated in, disappearing from sight. Though chatter and noise still filled the bridge, Parks felt an ominous silence descend upon him. It appeared that the danger had passed, yet he continued to stare at the feed, expecting at any moment the mighty vessel to reappear. It did not.

"*Dragon* has departed the system," he heard from somewhere up the bridge.

It's over, Parks thought to himself. *Thank God.*

"Yeah, but it looks like it left some of its babies behind," a voice came. It sounded like Enrique's.

Parks noted that some of the Imperial fighters had not made it into the vicinity of *Dragon* before it had departed the system. Unable to jump out of Aster, the orphaned craft now looked to be stranded, and for a time they milled around in the area once occupied by their allies. All of a sudden they changed their heading and began back towards the allied forces.

"Hey, they're coming back," Enrique said.

The cameras tracking the group began to pan faster.

"They're coming back bloody quickly!" the pilot then added.

The fighters were accelerating at an alarming rate, putting themselves on a collision course with the three ATAFs that remained the furtherest out from the allied forces.

"They're going to ram us!" That was Chaz. "Get out the way!"

Two of the ATAFs moved, the remaining enemy forces shooting past them, several making last ditch attempts to collide. For a moment it looked as though their efforts had been in vain. Then came an explosion.

Parks spun from the video relay to the frontal viewport, where even without the feeds, the fading burst was quite visible. A ripple of shock ran the length of the bridge, gasps and curses filling the air. Shouts and cries exploded from the various feeds and the other bridges, all intermixed and indistinguishable, and none providing the one answer Parks needed.

"What happened?" Parks demanded, above the cries. "Someone tell me what the hell just happened?"

"Collision, sir," Liu answered him.

"Between?"

"One of ours and one of theirs. It looks like both vessels have been destroyed."

Parks paled. It had been just as he had thought: the pilot had faltered, lingering too long as they tried to decide the best direction to take to best avoid the dozen or so Imperial fighters that were speeding towards them. In the end, one of the craft had ploughed straight into them. For everything that had happened that day, this was by far the worst. With the destruction of the ATAF, their one hope against the Enemy had been dashed. Everything now seemed hopeless.

He stood staring out of viewport. Seconds later he shook the shock from his system, remembering that several suicidal Imperial starfighters were still racing toward the allied group.

"Shoot them down!" he shouted.

It did not prove difficult to do so, the craft making no effort to deviate from their course. Cannons from the line of allied vessels blazed, finally putting an end to the battle.

Parks looked back to the two ATAFs that the cameras were still tracking, not far from where the fateful collision had taken place. He caught a glimmer of something as it emitted a faint glow. It appeared to be spinning over and over. It took him a while to realise what it was he was looking at.

Kelly blinked her eyes open and tried to clear her blurred vision. There was a jumble of noise in her head. It sounded like voices calling out to her and demanding attention. After some time she realised it was her craft that was spinning and not her head, and with considerable effort she managed to slow and halt the spin of the fighter, bringing it to a complete stop.

Closing her eyes, she concentrated on her breathing, calming herself so that she did not do the unthinkable and vomit inside her helmet. What was going on? Where was she? In a cockpit to be sure. The act of slowing the fighter had been somewhat instinctual.

She opened her eyes once more and looked all about the cockpit, then to the nebulas that hung nearby. A forest of spinning metals floated in every direction the eye could see. What looked like the broken, burnt, and scorched hull of some unknown large vessel tumbled.

"Kelly, are you okay?" a dim voice asked.

It seemed to come from all around her. She winced against a dull ache on the left side of her head.

"Kelly?"

"Where are you? What's going on?" she said to the voice.

"You hit an Imperial fighter," the voice said. "It flew straight into you."

"It did?" Kelly said. She found that hard to believe. If the voice was telling the truth, shouldn't she be dead? Maybe she was?

"Kelly, are you okay?" the voice said again. "Is anything broken? Are you bleeding anywhere?"

"Enrique, give her a moment," another voice cut in. "It's obvious she doesn't remember what just happened. Kelly, it's Chaz. You've just had a crash. Don't panic, just stay calm; ignore everyone and take your time. We're right here."

For a time the voices stopped and Kelly's memory gradually began to rebuild itself as she looked about the cockpit and at the scene outside. She started to recall the events that had led up to her current situation.

"Yes... yes... I'm okay," she said, several minutes later. "I just can't remember very much about what happened."

"Sounds like you might be suffering from a concussion," Chaz said.

Kelly reached up to touch the side of her head, before her hand encountered the helmet she wore. Even so, she rubbed around the area where her head was aching. She must have struck her head hard against the canopy. That would explain the blackout. She still felt quite dizzy, but at least the sick feeling was passing.

"How's the ATAF?" Enrique said. "Are you good to fly it?"

"Yeah, I think so."

"How badly is it damaged?"

She pulled herself together and looked at her read-outs. She squinted at the displays, sceptical of the numbers she was reading and the images she was looking at, thinking the blow to her head might be causing her to see things.

"It's not."

"*At all?*" Enrique said, sounding surprised.

"No." she said. She might have been surprised if she had not been feeling so groggy.

The report was relayed to Parks who started to wonder how many other surprises the day had in store for them.

"She's *alive?*" Liu said. "After *that?*"

Parks nodded to the helmsman.

"By all rights that fighter should have been destroyed and she should be dead! That's incredible!"

It's more than that, Parks thought. *It may well represent our only hope.*

With the departure of the enemy forces and the silence of weaponry, the scene beyond the bridge had become still once more. But amongst the multicoloured splendour of their surroundings lay the remnants of a battle that had not been easily won. With the operation over Parks found himself able to slow down and take in everything about him. He turned around.

The bridge had been laid to waste; and whilst his crew were coping with the damage that had been dealt it, *Griffin* would without doubt be out of service for several weeks, if not months. It was not time they could spare.

Idiot, he thought to himself, looking over how much the carrier had suffered at the hands of an enemy he had been foolish enough to believe he was ready to tackle. *We're not ready yet!* You *are not ready!*

Leviathan's condition was not much better, the damage to the exterior quite clear from where Parks stood. The emblems of the mythical creature that graced the hull were torn and burnt from where missiles, plasma bolts, and lasers had scorched the armour. Small glistening crystalline shapes could be seen emanating from damaged areas, where leaking gases and chemicals froze in the cold. Loose metals and alloys threatened to break off at the merest brush with solar winds. *Grendel's Mother* told a similar story, the carrier in no better condition for her part in the battle.

And then there was the loss of *Grendel*. The destruction of one of their carriers would not please the United Naval Forces who had agreed to support the Confederation in their endeavour, on the condition that the safety of their forces would be made a top priority. Parks had a lot to answer for, though he realised it could have been a lot worse.

"Good job, everyone," Parks said to the bridge crew, although the congratulatory offering felt decidedly hollow. "Now that we have time to breathe, please prioritise yourselves with seeing to the wounded and dealing with repairs."

He would call a meeting of his senior staff after he'd had time to see to other matters.

"Mr Liu, please put me in touch with *Leviathan, Grendel's Mother,* and..." he started, before a sudden anger gripped him. "No, wait, disregard that. Put me in touch with *Ifrit* alone."

As he waited for the link to establish he tried to cool his anger by counting slowly to ten. He made it to three.

XV

— The Journey Home —

"Thank you so much for your assistance, Commodore," Parks began. "We certainly would not have been able to cope without your timely intervention." Parks made no attempt to conceal the sarcasm in his voice, the man sure that, even if *Ifrit*'s captain had somehow failed to detect it, his expression would do an adequate job of conveying his dissatisfaction.

Hawke's expression in the holographic screen remained quite neutral as he composed himself before replying. "As we had both agreed prior to the commencement of the operation, Commodore, I took up the position of rear guard and moved in to fulfil my role as needed. I stand by my belief that had I acted sooner than was necessary we would, without a shadow of a doubt, have been surrounded by enemy forces and certainly not be having this conversation now."

"That is besides the point, Commodore!" Parks glared. "I gave you a very specific request that our forces were being overrun and we needed your support. You chose to ignore that request."

"I did no such thing. Your communication was cut short and I took it upon myself to hold position until I could make a better assessment of the situation," Hawke replied with the same air of infallibility.

Your stubbornness and downright arrogance is staggering, Parks thought. *What the hell happened to you?* It was almost as if the man didn't *want* to help. Had Hawke panicked in the face of the Enemy? Had a repressed memory of his experience aboard *Dragon* during the time of its theft reared its ugly head? Whatever it was it was still unacceptable to stand idly by as hostile forces tore the allies apart, and for that Parks was infuriated. With all that had happened that day he felt the rage building within him and decided to end the discussion rather than make his feelings known to the entire bridge crew.

"We will continue this later during debriefing," Parks said, fully intent on bringing the man's almost total lack of participation in the operation to the attention of Fleet Admiral Turner and other members of naval high command.

He signalled to the bridge crew to open communications to *Grendel's Mother* and *Leviathan*. The holographic images of Mandeep and Meyers appeared alongside the already present image of Hawke, the quality of the images as poor as ever.

"Commodore, Captain," Parks greeted them. "Are you in any need of assistance?"

"We will be fine for the return journey, thank you, Commodore," Mandeep replied, the smile that Parks had grown so accustomed to and fond of no longer gracing her face. "Much of the damage we received was superficial, a miracle given what we just faced." Mandeep looked sad and disappointed, the tremendous losses they had suffered and the deaths of her colleagues undoubtedly an enormous weight on her mind.

"Likewise with *Leviathan*," Meyers said. "We did take some considerable damage, but it's nothing that we cannot cope with prior to our return to Spirit."

Parks nodded in understanding. "Very well. Whilst going about the repairs we should perform a brief sweep of the area and pick up any bodies we can find. Obviously there is nothing we can do for those poor individuals, but we can at least return their bodies home for a decent burial."

His eyes flickered past the holographic images to the debris that floated about beyond the carrier. Many of the starfighter pilots that had lost their lives would have been all but vaporised in the explosions of their craft. This he was glad for. After everything that had happened too many questions would be asked if they pulled in the body of one of the Enemy. Such an occurrence would only act as a catalyst and foundation for increasing rumour and speculation. A count and name-check of those returning on the carriers would be performed at Spirit, with those unaccounted for being marked as killed in action.

With that in mind he looked to Meyers. "Captain, can *Leviathan* carry some of our fighters? Our flight deck is too badly damaged to land any and we can only accommodate so many in our cargo holds. I don't expect *Ifrit* will have room to spare," he added dryly.

Meyers nodded. "That shouldn't be an issue since, regrettably, we have many empty bays."

"Thank you, Captain," Parks said, before he turned once again to Mandeep. "Please convey my sincere condolences to the families of those who were aboard *Grendel*. A lot of brave men and women lost their lives on that ship today." To lose an entire carrier was disastrous to any naval force. Matters were made worse by the fact that the crew were made up of military personnel volunteered by a number of Independent World naval forces. Parks could almost hear the cracks widening in the already strained relationships between some of the worlds.

"I will make sure your sympathies are known, Commodore," Mandeep said, the sadness clear in her eyes even through the distortion. "Please contact us when you are ready to leave. We will wait with you here in case we can provide any further assistance."

"Thank you again, Sima," Parks said.

"Excuse me, Commodore, but how do you suppose the enemy forces were able to override the shut down code that was sent to *Dragon*?" Meyers asked. It was a question that had played on Parks' mind - and he suspected very many others - throughout the course of the battle. The sudden restoration of power to *Dragon* had tipped the scales well in the enemy's favour during the opening part of the operation.

"I don't believe they did, Captain," Parks answered. "Our initial attempt at transmitting the code was not immediately successful and it took a lot longer for *Dragon*'s systems to be deactivated than I was led to believe. I was informed that the shutdown procedure would take place upon receipt of the code. The fact that it did not do so should have been our first warning. It is my belief that the Enemy became aware our intentions and purposely shut down all systems themselves in compliance. Once we were lured into a false sense of security they sprung their trap."

"How could they have known about something like that?" Mandeep asked.

Parks had a hunch that she was asking a rhetorical question, implying that the Enemy had either been tipped off ahead of their encounter or that *Dragon*'s previous crew were now working alongside its new owners.

"I'm afraid I don't know the answer to that, Commodore," he said. "Until we can collate a battle report and analyse all the data, then my guess would be as good as yours. Once we have further information I will ensure that it is shared with the IWC.

"Now, if there is no other business that anyone wishes to discuss?"

Even with the interference caused by the damage to the holographic projection systems, Parks had no trouble making out the subtle confrontational look that Hawke was giving him. There were shakes of heads and answers of no.

"Then we will make preparations to leave. I will be in contact shortly."

For the next hour the allied forces continued with repairs, most of *Griffin*'s surviving starfighters docking with *Leviathan*. A sweep for bodies resulted in only a handful of recognisable pick ups, a mixture of both Confederation and Independent uniforms in the group. The four remaining *Red Devils* were found and taken aboard *Leviathan*, the women identifiable by the colourful emblem of a cartoon devil clutching a pitchfork, on the left breast of their flight suits.

Dodds watched the shuttles do their work. He was happy to do nothing now but take a well earned breather. He listened to Estelle conversing with *Griffin*.

"Do you wish for us to return to *Griffin*'s cargo bay or should we dock with *Leviathan*?" she asked.

"Negative, Lieutenant. I want you and your team to return to *Griffin*," Parks answered her. "Land via the rear cargo bay and then await further instructions."

"Acknowledged."

Estelle was the first to return to the rear cargo bay, the awaiting crew taxiing the sleek, black starfighter back to its original position so that the others could land uninhibited. Dodds saw her waiting at the rear of the bay, stood next to Enrique as he landed. Even before he stepped out of the fighter, he could make out the grin on the man's face.

"Good shooting out there, mate," Dodds said to Enrique, as he walked over to join them. "Think I might have gotten one or two more than you though!"

"I think you'll find I was ahead of you the whole the time," Enrique said, with a chuckle. He shook Dodds' hand and they gave each other a hearty slap on the back.

"That frigate still only counts as one," Dodds grinned.

"I am glad to be out there, though," Enrique said, nodding towards the ATAFs.

"Definitely. After all of that I could do with a nap," Dodds admitted.

They looked to Chaz who was making his way over to them. He appeared quite upbeat for a change, a smile on his face. With Kelly the last to land and now out of her ATAF, the *Knights* gathered around Estelle.

"Good work out there, everyone," she beamed, looking happier than she had done in weeks.

"I don't think those Imperial pilots knew what hit them," Dodds said.

"I'm not sure anyone out there did either to tell the truth," Enrique said. "Those fighters are still supposed to be a military secret."

"Test run," Chaz said, glancing back around at the fighters, which still looked as fresh and new as the day they had completed construction. There didn't appear to be one dent or scratch on any other them. Not even on the ATAF that Kelly had been piloting, having been hit head-on by the suicidal Sphinx fighter pilot.

"We should meet with Commodore Parks for debriefing and then get you some medical attention, Kelly," Estelle said.

Together the *Knights* started out the cargo bay. But as they approached a number of security personnel, standing by the hold's exit, gathered themselves across the already thin gap of the tall doors, blocking the five pilots from exiting. At first Dodds thought their presence was to ensure the security of the bay and to escort the ATAF pilots to Parks. Estelle attempted to pass. A halting hand was raised.

"Something wrong?" she asked.

"Sorry, but I can't allow you to leave," Omar Wyatt, *Griffin*'s head of security, explained. "I have orders from Commodore Parks that you are to remain here until further notice." The man stood ahead of the other members of his team who were each brandishing a rifle.

"But we must attend our debriefing," Estelle protested.

"I have my orders," Wyatt said. "Commodore Parks feels that in the ship's current state it would be best for you all to remain here."

"Couldn't you at least escort us to our quarters instead?" Dodds said.

"There is a member of my team who requires some medical attention," Estelle interjected, nodding in Kelly's direction, not waiting for the head of security to answer Dodds. The man looked over at Kelly who, other than appearing to be a little tired, displayed no signs of trauma or physical injury that required any kind of urgent attention.

He shook his head. "No, sorry. No one is allowed in or out of the hold. And all our medical teams are also busy dealing with those suffering from more severe injuries."

Estelle fumed and was about to say something before Kelly stopped her, shaking her head. Chaz did not seem in the least bit surprised by what was happening. He swore, let out an audible sigh and then stalked off from the rest of the group, settling down on the floor and propping himself up against a rack of maintenance equipment. Dodds watched him for a bit, but the big man did not acknowledge him or the gathering of people by the exit. It was clear his short lived upbeat demeanour had now been pushed to the wayside and he would only sink back into silence.

"All crew, this is your captain speaking," Parks' voice came over the ship's PA. "We are ready to make the return jump to Spirit. Please finalise jump preparations."

Estelle, Kelly and Enrique wandered off to join Chaz, whilst Dodds made one last ditch attempt to leave the hold. "I need to take a leak," he threatened.

"Then you'll just have to go in your suit," Wyatt answered with a shrug.

Parks bid farewell to Mandeep and watched as *Grendel's Mother* opened a jump point and exited the system, the swirling jump point closing with the departure of the carrier.

"Open a jump point to Spirit," Parks said to Liu.

"Yes, sir." Liu punched the required data into his console. Ahead of them the jump point formed and, as before, when they had originally departed Spirit, *Griffin* started forward, followed by *Ifrit* and *Leviathan*. This time, however, Meyers and Hawke allowed a greater distance between their carriers and Parks'. If *Griffin* suffered a power failure they would have ample stopping distance.

Parks, sat in the captain's chair, just behind the navigator and comms officer at the front, was drawn from his deep thoughts by the flicker of something out of the frontal viewport. Had something happened around the jump point? Something that wasn't normal? Just as he thought he had imagined it, it happened again.

A streak of what appeared to be lightning coursed its way right around the portal, closely following its rotation. In its wake it left a jagged tear that ripped open, revealing the colourful space behind it. The tear then appeared to heal itself, leaving behind no evidence of the abnormality that had grabbed Parks' attention. He rose from his chair and wandered to the front of the bridge.

"What was that?" he asked.

"Captain?" Liu asked.

"That... thing around the jump point? It looked like lightning."

"I'm sorry, sir, I must have missed it." Liu tapped at his console. "Systems are not reporting any issues."

Parks began to wonder if the injury to his head was preventing him from thinking and seeing straight; though the stars were usually never that big or that shape. He began to return to his seat, seeing that the portal had returned to its normal state.

The portal, however, did so for but only for a few seconds, before two smaller streaks ripped through it just as the first, rupturing it in the same way. Yet another and another appeared, tearing the pool in a similar fashion, like a knife slashing a canvas. Pockets of intense white light started to build in the region of the slashes, giving the impression that the jump point was bleeding.

None of it was sitting right with Parks and the sight was now grabbing the attentions of most of the bridge crew, their concern for the anomaly causing them to leave their systems unattended.

Liu's console began to whine.

"What's that?" Parks said.

"Sir, the jump point appears to be collapsing!" Liu said, his hands darting across his console. "I would strongly suggest we pull back."

"Bring us to a halt, Mr Liu! Cancel the jump request!" Parks ordered as *Griffin* began to cross the threshold.

Liu attempted to prevent the carrier's further descent into the unstable jump point, but his efforts served only to slow their advance rather than stop it. Moments later the frontal viewport was swallowed by the swirling mass and *Griffin* hurtled forward.

Griffin started to tumble, slow at first before it started to build up speed. As the carrier began to shudder Parks ordered his crew to brace themselves, before finding his own seat. He held on tight to the arm rests, staring out at the usual sight before him.

Whilst what the carrier now travelled through bore many the hallmarks of jump space, the familiar blue haze was nowhere to be seen. Instead, *Griffin* appeared to be surrounded by what looked like thick, blood red clouds. Angry streaks of electricity danced and crashed within them, as *Griffin* continued its journey into the unknown. The intensity of the shuddering grew the further they seemed to plunge.

Time appeared to slow. Parks turned his head to look around the ship, his surroundings somehow blurred. Everything appeared to be leaving translucent, multicoloured trails behind them as they moved. It was like he was drunk, stumbling down the neon jungle of one of Shai-Jin's tourist traps, the bright lights of the city blinding and confusing his vision.

Just as Parks thought that the already damaged carrier would be torn apart the shuddering came to an abrupt end and, just like the blue haze of jump space, the thundering red clouds parted gracefully to give way to normal space. Stars came rushing towards them. Time returned to normal. The trails faded.

"Everyone okay?" Parks asked after Liu managed to bring the carrier under control, following a bout of rapid tapping at his console's controls. Parks did not hear the answers as he looked out into the featureless void that lay all around them. It was in stark contrast to the nebulas that had played host to the conflict zone they had just departed, and Parks walked to the front of his ship to take stock. There was not a single thing he recognised: no Temper, no Spirit, no Aster, and no *Ifrit* or *Leviathan*.

He looked around at the bridge crew who had been following his gaze out the front of the ship. "Where the hell are we?"

XVI

— A Grand Opportunity —

Friday, June 13ᵗʰ 2617

I'm sitting in the rear cargo hold of Griffin, *waiting for someone to tell me when I can get my head seen to, get a shower and get some food. We (that's me and the usual guys) are returning to* Spirit *after a failed operation. It was sprung on us early this morning by Commodore Parks and together with a bunch of others from the United Naval Forces we engaged Imperial forces in the Aster system. The mission was unsuccessful and we suffered heavy losses, but at least we didn't lose our lives too; the Imperials retreated when we managed to fight back.*

I knocked my head against the canopy whilst in combat and that really hurt, even with the helmet on. I think I blacked out for a bit and I still feel a bit groggy and dizzy. Chaz and Enrique seem to think I'm suffering from a mild concussion, though I'm sure that I wouldn't be able to think straight if I were.

Or at least that is what I'd be writing if I had my journal with me, Kelly thought to herself, waking from her daydream and finding herself sat back on the floor of the rear cargo hold.

"What's going on?" Enrique asked Dodds as he returned from talking to one of the security team.

"He doesn't know," Dodds said, settling back down on the floor next to the others. "He assumes it's just a result of the damage that *Griffin* sustained during the battle."

"I've never felt a ship shake like that before."

"It's probably nothing to be concerned about," Estelle muttered. Dodds guessed that since being ordered to remain in the cargo hold, Estelle was feeling as though she had once again been shot down in her prime. With that in mind the others, with the exception of Kelly, were largely ignoring her.

"I just want to get out of here and get a shower," Enrique started again.

"And some food," Dodds added. "I can't believe he wouldn't even let me go out for a pi..."

"Stop moaning you two!" Estelle snapped. "We'll get out of here in good time, so stop your griping. At least there's nothing wrong with you. Oh, how are you feeling, Kelly?"

"Better now. The dizziness has just about cleared," Kelly said, still rubbing the side of her head.

"We'll get you some attention as soon as we get back to Spirit," Estelle said.

"What did you think of those Imperial pilots?" Enrique asked Dodds.

"They were good. I don't think we would have stood much chance without the ATAFs, to tell you the truth." Both men turned to the innocent looking starfighters that sat along the walls of the cargo bay.

The crew that had helped taxi the craft around and assisted the *Knights* in departing their fighters were also sitting on the floor, looking bored and frustrated. Some had wandered over to talk to the *Knights*, but the security team had soon put a stop to their attempt at socialising, fuelling Dodds' suspicions that Parks wished to keep them apart from the rest of the ship.

"You're right there," Enrique said. "If that civil war does boil over and they're all as good as that..."

"No, something wasn't right there. They were *too* good. You saw what they did to those other fighter pilots. Their reactions were too fast and they were too accurate. They were tearing those guys apart before we arrived."

"Maybe they've all got some kind of computer assistance?" Enrique offered. "Something that was helping them to get the edge?"

Dodds noticed that Chaz's head was tilted in their direction, subtly eavesdropping in on their conversation. "Yeah, something like that."

In one of *Griffin*'s conference rooms Parks sat down at an oval glass table with a number of his senior staff. The wound on his head had been bandaged and he'd given himself a general clean up while he charged Liu with finding out where the carrier had emerged. Many of those present in the conference room also wore reminders of the earlier conflict, everything ranging from cuts and bruises to arms in slings.

Following their arrival into the unknown, Parks had requested they gather as much information as possible pertaining to the unexpected events. He had then called a meeting of the carrier's heads of section.

"Right, now that we're all here; Mr Liu, could you please start by giving us an overview of our current situation," Parks requested of the man sitting across the table from him.

"Yes, captain," Liu nodded. He picked up a small hand-held device and tapped away at the screen, prompting a large holographic projection to spring up in the centre of the table, displaying a galactic map. It was cluttered with somewhat excessive amounts of detail, highlighting trade routes, jump gates and points, as well as marking entire regions of space that were a part of the Confederacy, and those that were declared Independent. At one end of the map the Confederation star system of Temper was highlighted and, at the other, the Independent system of Aster.

Liu continued to tap away at the device he held, dimming star systems and removing trade routes, jump gates and other pieces of data that were of no relevance. Eventually the Aster and Temper systems were left as the main focal points of Liu's presentation. He made some final adjustments, centring in on *Griffin*'s position on the map, located within the Aster system, and then began to recount.

"Following the previous operation we prepared to make the jump back to Spirit."

A dotted line made its way across the galactic map from Aster back towards the Temper system, illustrating his point.

"As we witnessed the jump point became unstable and we were unable to prevent our descent within. The 'jump' we experienced threw *Griffin*'s navicoms out of sync and it took them quite some time before they were able to establish a link with the nearest navigation buoy. If we assume the data it has transmitted is accurate then it appears we arrived not back at Temper, but..."

He tapped at the device in hand. The galactic map zoomed out a long way, revealing yet more star systems. The dotted line traced its way, not towards Temper, but to a star system in the opposite direction to that which the carrier had intended to travel.

"... here," Liu concluded.

The section heads gathered around the table gaped at the holographic display and the highlighted star system that the line had traced itself toward. The system was named Phylent.

"Phylent?" Parks asked in total surprise.

"Yes, sir," Liu said.

"We're in Imperial space?!"

"I'm afraid so, sir."

Parks' gaze shot to the many windows of the conference room and to the space outside that, thankfully, remained calm and uneventful. Even so, there were mutterings and mumblings from the others at the table as they stared in disbelief at the map. Parks' mind raced. At this very moment in time he and his ship were in the one place that they did not want to be. He looked around those seated at the table knowing that, whilst they were aware of the danger that they faced, being in a part of space that was said to be embroiled in civil war, none could confess to appreciating the danger more than he. The failed operation to retake *Dragon* had merely hinted at what the Confederacy and her allies were up against, and had it not been for the ATAFs no one would have returned home after the battle. They had to get away from Imperial space as soon as possible.

After a moment Parks regained his composure and turned his attention back to the meeting. At this time, more than ever, he must maintain a cool, calm and collected conduct.

He called for silence. "How is that possible, Mr Liu?"

"I think that perhaps Mr Marsh could explain in more detail?" Liu said.

Heads turned to a rather thickset man seated next to Liu, who straightened up. As *Griffin's* chief engineer, Matthew Marsh was in a far better position to answer Parks' question.

"It seems that there was a malfunction in the jump engines, most likely caused by the damage we sustained during the battle," Marsh began. "Unfortunately, due to the nature of the issue it was not something that we could have pin pointed until we attempted to use them."

Parks scowled. It sounded like a very weak excuse for such a serious issue.

Marsh added, "Our pre-jump safety checks and individual unit tests reported no faults and everything seemed to be working as expected."

"But it *didn't* work, did it, Mr Marsh?" Parks said, irritably.

"No, sir."

"When we get back to Spirit I want a full review of all jump safety checks. This could have destroyed the ship and killed everyone aboard." This was directed at everyone within the room, though Marsh fidgeted as Parks' eyes fell upon him. "How is it that we managed to get from here to here so easily?" Parks asked after studying the galactic map for a few moments, pointing from Aster to the Phylent system, that lay close to the Imperial-Independent border.

"Well, that is actually quite interesting," Marsh started, before back-pedalling upon seeing Parks' stony face. "Er... I think that the malfunction in the jump engines must have thrown some of the astral calculations out. However, owing to some other factors we have successfully compensated for those miscalculations. The jump computers selected a cached version of one of Phylent's navigation buoys as their destination and dropped us in a random part of the system."

"That actually fits in with what I was thinking," Liu said. "Phylent and Aster are more or less equidistant from Spirit. Basically we just went the wrong way; albeit exceptionally fast."

Parks considered the explanation for a moment. "Fine," he said.

"A shame we don't know what the secret speed ingredient is," Marsh started to babble. "I have to say that I am actually amazed at the distance we managed to cover in such a short space of time. I'm planning on holding on to the data from the jump so we can analyse it once we return to Spirit. The findings could help to revolutionize space travel and..."

"Put it in a report," Parks said, waving away the rest of the comment. Right now he was not prepared to allow the man to indulge his knowledge and enthusiasm for the inner workings of interstellar transportation. "And I think you'll also find that the secret ingredient you are searching for is just plain dumb luck, Mr Marsh. By all rights this carrier should have been ripped apart." He looked back to *Griffin*'s navigator. "Mr Liu, from here how long would it take for us to return to Spirit?"

Liu frowned. "Under ideal circumstances? Roughly twelve, thirteen hours."

"And with the engines in their current state?" Parks once again addressed the chief engineer.

"I would say we are looking at sixteen to twenty hours, if not a little longer," Marsh said. "However, the engines aren't in a state where we could safely make another jump."

"And how long before we can?"

"I've not had enough time to estimate the cost of the damage to all the dependent systems, sir."

Parks sighed. "I realise that Mr Marsh, but I need the best answer you can give me."

"I would reckon around nine hours."

Parks nodded as he digested the information. They were looking at a time frame of more than a day before they were back at Spirit. If the ATAFs had not been aboard he could have ordered they jump back to an Independent system. But he knew that such a move was not an option since that could result in the discovery of the advanced starfighters by an Independent World state. The Confederation were already hard pressed to keep the fighters under wraps, without dumping them in the middle of a random system for anyone to gawk at. They would just have to take their chances here.

"Okay," Parks said to Marsh. "Begin the work as soon as this meeting is over. Now, I need the rest of you to find members of your respective teams who may be able to lend their skills to repairs and maintenance. I shouldn't need to reiterate to any of you that in its current state *Griffin* is a sitting duck. Most of her major systems are operational, but shielding is minimal and we have little in the way of offensive measures. We are also unable to deploy what remains of our starfighter complement easily; the cargo holds are simply not equipped to launch fighters at the rate we'd need to fend off attackers."

He thought of the cargo holds. Whilst those holding the ATAFs contained nothing more than the five fighters themselves, the others were crammed full of *Griffin*'s starfighters. Deploying them in an emergency would be next to impossible.

Those around the table appeared to all be in agreement with his plan, their eyes drifting from the holographic display to the quiet space outside. The words "Imperial Space", "Phylent" and "Griffin" were far too close together on the galactic map for anyone's liking; especially his own.

Parks continued his delegation. "I need a seventy-thirty split in duties for repairs to the jump engines and repairs to the flight deck. It is vital that we get out of this system and away from Imperial space as soon as possible; but it is just as important that, in the highly likely event that we are discovered by enemy forces, we are able to defend ourselves."

"Yes, sir," came the resounding answer from those assembled.

"Lieutenant Weathers, have you managed to contact either *Ifrit* or *Leviathan*?" he asked of a woman who was sitting further down the table.

Weathers, now working as communications officer in place of O'Donnell, flipped through some papers as she spoke. "We don't believe that *Ifrit* and *Leviathan* are within range. It does not appear that they followed us into the jump point and may not be aware of our current position. It is unlikely that they were able to follow us either given the unstable nature of the jump point."

It was as Parks had suspected; they were on their own. "Very well. Is there anything else?" Parks' query was met by head shakes and silence. "Then let's get to work immediately. We have a lot to do and very little time to spare. Get moving, people."

As the staff officers left, Parks noticed that Weathers was hovering, waiting for everyone else to vacate the room.

"Yes, Lieutenant?" he asked once they were alone.

"An encrypted communication has come in from CSN HQ, sir."

"From HQ? Are you sure?"

"Yes, sir. It arrived just before the meeting." Weathers seemed as surprised as he was.

"Thank you, Lieutenant. I'll take it in my private office."

Weathers nodded and left Parks to ponder the speed at which the Confederation Stellar Navy had succeeded in pin pointing his location so soon after their recent accident.

• • •

Compared to the rest of the ship, Parks' private office was far more lavishly decorated. Wood panelling covered much of the cold, grey steel and a number of colourful ornaments were scattered here and there. A handful of small paintings hung on the walls, depicting *Griffin* and other vessels. Parks' eyes strayed to the painting of *Dragon* as he made his way to his desk and the commodore caught himself wondering of how different things might have been had their mission been a success.

Activating the computer screen at his desk he saw the CSN message. The screen read,

Encrypted Message Received
FTAO: Commodore Elliott F. Parks

On either side of the greeting resided an image of a padlock, further emphasising that the message was secured. Parks tapped "Read" with his finger tip and was duly challenged to authentic his identity to the system, prompting him for a password, iris scan, and voice recognition. Both the iris scan and voice recognition took a number of attempts to verify. It appeared the system was still suffering. After a time the message playback started.

"I hope this message finds you well, Elliott," a grating voice began.

Parks was stunned to see that he was looking at a video recorded by Admiral Turner. The picture and audio were suffering; he guessed it was a result of the damage to *Griffin* rather than the message itself. He moved closer to the display, to listen carefully to what the Fleet Admiral had to say: right now he could do with all the advice he could get.

Turner went on. "After you failed to return to Spirit with Commodore Hawke or Captain Meyers, we immediately began a galaxy-wide sweep. Lucky for us it did not take us very long to locate you. Since you arrived within a formerly inhabited Imperial system we were able to detect *Griffin* quite quickly. In case you do not already know, you are in the Phylent system, close to the Imperial-Independent border.

"First of all, do not concern yourself with the outcome of your mission to retake *Dragon*. We both knew that this was never going to be an easy task to accomplish, and once again we have both been given a truly unpleasant reminder of the kind of enemy we are up against."

Parks was in total agreement. He recalled how, when he had mentioned the appearance of *Dragon* within Independent World space and his plans to ambush and retake the massive battleship, the admiral had warned him of the risks. Though the admiral had given him his full backing at the time, Parks wished he hadn't been so hasty.

"Secondly I understand that *Griffin* has been heavily damaged in battle," the video message continued. "I have dispatched Meyers to your position, along with a number of repair and medical vessels. They will not be with you for several hours yet so I need you and your boys to sit tight. Imperial space is certainly not a place you wish to find yourself adrift and defenceless.

"I shouldn't have to remind you either that whilst you are close to Independent World space, there will be no help coming from those frontier systems, since you should be more than aware that they have already been evacuated. Even if they could help, there would be great reluctance to do so, given the tremendous loss of life resulting from the destruction of the carrier support they laid on for us. I advise that we not seek to involve the UNF any further at this point. So until Meyers arrives you're on your own out there and will just have to wait it out."

Parks nodded once more, relieved to hear that Meyers would soon be there to assist them. He then noticed Turner sit more upright, leaning forward in his chair. Parks had seen that look on the man's face before; he swallowed.

"But having said that your current location could not be more convenient. Regarding matters within the Temper system some seventy-two hours ago: intelligence have managed to locate the raider who fled the *Cardinal* just before its destruction and discovered him to be travelling around the Imperial frontier systems. He arrived in Phylent some time ago, so it's likely he won't be hanging around too much longer.

"Special agent Barber has followed the man to Arlos starport where he has been attempting to offload various items of his *stock*. This whole thing could have ended up as a wild goose chase, which would have been all the better for us, but unfortunately Barber has confirmed to me that the man does indeed have the entire dump of *Cardinal's* databanks in his possession.

And that means he has the ATAF plans.

"At least we now know he has them and they haven't already fallen into unwanted hands. Right now he is struggling to find a buyer and Barber is currently attempting to verify whether he has them about his person or has stowed them some place else.

"She planned to make her own way back to Confederation space once she has secured the data, but I imagine this could prove a lot trickier than she thinks. And that's not a gamble I'm willing to take. I don't know whether to call your accidental winding up in the Phylent system luck or fate, but I know that we need to get those plans back, ASAP."

Parks was getting a bad feeling about what the admiral was about to suggest. He began scratching at the stubble on his chin as Turner's request continued to unfold.

"Therefore I will need you to bring her home with you or, at the very least, the data. If you cannot bring her, don't worry. You and I both know she is more than capable of getting out of there herself. I would rather this is done whilst you await the arrival of Meyers, so you can depart the Phylent system as quickly as possible. We cannot risk losing yet another of our most powerful weapons to the Enemy and as such this should now be your number one priority. I'm sure that I shouldn't have to remind you that those plans are worth far more than every life on that ship."

Parks groaned as the admiral's request set him on very awkward footing.

"This may be an opportunity to kill two birds with one stone, Elliott. We can gain twice from this situation. With the *Red Devils* dead we have to play catch up and an opportunity like this may not come by again any time soon, if ever. I have taken the liberty of transmitting the coordinates of Arlos starport to you as well as extended intelligence concerning the Phylent system. I'm hoping you have all the information you need since I do not recommend that you respond to this message. Although we still have a handful of comm relay points secreted around Imperial frontier systems, communications fed through sub-space are minimal. Any increase in the tachyon streams could expose you to hostile tracking systems."

Just as Parks began to wonder what had happened to Hawke in all of this Turner answered his question.

"As for Commodore Hawke, he is much closer to your location than

Meyers is. When he saw *Griffin* disappear into the jump point with no clue as to your destination, Hawke took it upon himself to assume command. He ordered Meyers to return to Spirit to search for you there whilst he took *Ifrit* to search all the star systems adjacent to Aster. He, like Meyers, is aware of your situation and that I have requested you perform a little errand for us before you are ready to return home. Neither of them, however, are privy to the full details of that errand, as I'm sure you can appreciate. Unless he runs into difficulties, or delivery of my instructions are delayed, you should expect Hawke to arrive at your location sooner than Meyers. If you are able, you should return to Spirit with him. Don't wait for Meyers, he will understand that you had to leave as soon as you were able. In such an event we will let him know that you have been found and are returning home.

"There is more information attached in the brief I have included with this message. You will need to relay this information to the *Knights*. I realise that it does not paint the rosiest of pictures, but we need to make sure our bases are covered for all eventualities.

"Take care of yourself, Elliott. We'll see you soon," Turner concluded. The message playback ended, and the screen displayed a number of icons, detailing the additional information that Turner had transmitted.

Parks sighed. At least one of his questions had been answered: the Confederation's comm points had sent information about *Griffin*'s arrival in the system back to CSN HQ via sub-space channels - Turner had sent a message to the carrier in the same way. Though messages travelled far quicker through jump space than ships themselves, Parks was willing to bet that *Griffin*'s most recent jump would give them a run for their money.

He stood up and paced beside the window. He knew what he had to do and didn't like it one bit. As the admiral had said, the ATAF plans were far more important than all of the lives aboard *Griffin* - in fact, more so than *Griffin*, *Ifrit* and *Leviathan* combined - and that fact terrified him.

He stared out the window at the endless void of space. Now that the blast screens had come down from the carrier's windows, Parks was able to make out a dull grey planet hanging all alone, not too far off. He did not need to consult a system map to know that was where Turner needed him to go.

"Dammit," he said in a low voice, placing a fist on the window and leaning against the glass. "There *must* be another way; there has to be a way for Barber to come to me instead of *us* having to go to *her*."

He racked his brains, giving full consideration to every possibility that he could think of, all the while staring towards the dull grey planet. But his attempts to find a workable solution all hit dead ends. Turner was right: he had little choice in the matter, and whether he liked it or not he was going to have to send the *ATAFs* and the *Knights* to Arlos alone, and leave *Griffin* all but defenceless. And the sooner that was done the sooner they could all get home.

With his mind made up he turned back to the console and closed the message, before rounding his desk and striding out the door to make for the bridge.

XVII

— Of Cloaks —

C haz continued watching the security team that guarded the entrance to the cargo bay. He had noticed a new face arrive earlier. The head of the security team had exchanged some brief words with the man before the pair had departed together. It did not seem to Chaz that anyone else had noticed; little details such as that were apparently lost on them.

Estelle was staring at the floor looking quite glum, though he suspected that her current state owed more to sorrow than to being restricted to the hold.

"... gonna be a lot of weeping mothers after this one, I can tell ya," one of the team's conversations had carried to the hold's current occupants.

"Tell me about it. They pulled out this one girl who had been buried under a collapsed ceiling. Legs were a complete mess. Even if she'd lived through that she certainly wouldn't be using those again."

"Not sure I'd take that over being spaced, myself."

"Nice looking thing too."

"Yeah?"

"Yeah."

"That's a shame."

Chaz had noticed Estelle's expression change as the two men had spoken, the woman lowering her gaze to the floor.

"You all right, Estelle?" Dodds had asked sometime later.

"Just thinking."

"Sure?"

"Yeah."

"Okay."

"Thanks, Simon."

Simon. That was a name he didn't hear used all too often.

The head of security was now back, and speaking with the rest of his team. As he did so he looked around the groups of people sat in the cargo hold, but mostly at the *Knights*. The other members of the security team were doing likewise. It was clear to Chaz that the man was discussing the *Knights* and he'd guessed what was going on well before Wyatt strode over to the five pilots.

"Lieutenant de Winter?" Wyatt asked as he stood over them, flanked by two others from him team.

"Yes," Estelle said, getting to her feet.

"Commodore Parks wishes to speak to you immediately in his private office. Please come with me."

The *Knights* were escorted from the cargo hold by the head of the security team. As they walked through *Griffin*'s decks towards Parks' office they were at last able to see the true extent of the damage. There were still many safety and fire doors closed across every deck and as a result their journey was not straightforward. Parks had insisted that the security team avoid the use of elevators in case they became stuck and delayed the meeting.

Parks turned back from where he was gazing out the window, in the direction of Arlos, as the six people entered his office.

"Thank you for being so prompt, Omar," he said. "Please wait outside. I have a confidential matter I need to discuss with the *White Knights*."

"Yes, sir," Wyatt nodded and departed the office.

"*White Knights* reporting as..." Estelle began, before Parks waved her down.

"At ease. Please excuse me for restricting you to the cargo hold. I intended to explain the reasons behind the move back at Spirit, but that is going to have to wait. You may have noticed that we are currently not in jump." He indicated to the inky blackness of the world outside the carrier, the scene punctuated by tiny pin-pricks of greys and whites from distant stars. "When we departed Aster, *Griffin* suffered a miss-jump, and as a result we did not make it to our intended destination. Instead, we have become temporarily stranded in the Phylent system."

"Phylent?" Estelle and Kelly both said.

"We're in Imperial space?" Chaz asked, mimicking Parks' own reaction to the news the first time that he had heard it.

Parks nodded. "That's correct, and we will be remaining here until we either repair our jump engines, Captain Meyers or Commodore Hawke arrive to assist us, or we are discovered by hostile forces. The situation is not in the least favourable to *Griffin* from whatever angle you look at it. Whilst rescue is on the way, we cannot count on its arrival for at least several more hours.

"*Griffin* has sustained a considerable amount of damage and in the face of an attack would be almost totally defenceless. Our weapon systems are unreliable, our shielding is barely adequate, and we have no means of launching fighters."

"Excuse me, sir, but we could launch the ATAFs from the cargo hold," Estelle chipped in.

"Thank you for letting me know that, Lieutenant," Parks answered with a hint of sarcasm. "But the situation is no longer as straightforward as that, and I have just received a communication from Fleet Admiral Turner that has further complicated matters. I believe you were all present when *CSN Cardinal* was boarded and destroyed by a raiding party?"

"Yes, sir," Estelle said, the others nodding.

"We believe that the raider who escaped stole some highly classified and sensitive data that, if it were to fall into enemy hands, could spell utter disaster for the Confederation and all her interests."

"What was it?" Enrique asked.

"As already stated, Mr Todd, that is classified," Parks shot. "Now keep that big mouth of yours shut. This is very important and I need you all to listen very carefully."

Enrique did so.

Parks pressed on. "All you need to know is that we have to get it back. As it happens a government service agent has tracked the raider to this very system and is in the process of reacquiring the data. She planned to immediately return to Confederation space once she had done so, but the instability of this entire region could make that considerably more difficult than she first expected. And it is that which has made my next decision so very difficult, because I need you five to go and get it from her."

He scanned the group as he finished speaking, noticing, as he had expected, Chaz's narrowed eyes upon him. The others said nothing, turning to look at one another. Parks pressed on, looking to head off the two dozen questions he could see coming. "So, I will be requiring you to travel, in the ATAFs, to Arlos starport where you will meet the agent, retrieve the stolen data card that was her mission target and return to *Griffin*."

It sounded very simple when Parks put it that way. He only wished that it was.

He tapped the keyboard in front him. "This is who you will be looking for." Parks turned the monitor of his desk around to face the *Knights*, keeping a close eye on Chaz as he did so. Unlike the others, whose attention was focused on the screen, studying the profile of the woman they were to meet, Chaz's eyes flickered to the monitor for only a couple of seconds before darting back to meet Parks'. For a while the two men locked eyes, Parks maintaining a serious and unwavering expression, Chaz keeping his own just as steady.

Parks said, "This is Clare Barber, an agent working for the Confederate Secret Service. She has a long standing history of providing her government with outstanding results." He continued to lock looks with Chaz. None of the others had picked up on the exchange, their eyes remaining focused on the screen, which detailed Barber as being light skinned, thirty-nine years old, five foot nine inches tall, and with shoulder length, straight black hair.

"She's likely to be maintaining a low profile, so you will need to put in a little extra effort to find her when arriving at the starport. She is obviously not aware of your coming to meet her, so do not expect her to come running and waving her arms in the air the second you arrive. We are aware that the Imperium has extensive information on some of our operatives so she will undoubtedly be on their watch list, due to her persisted presence within their space."

He had still not broken eye contact with Chaz.

"I shouldn't need to remind you all of the very hazardous predicament that we all find ourselves in right now," Parks said, before he swivelled the screen back around. "And as such it is necessary that upon leaving *Griffin* and travelling to the starport you take maximum precautions. That means avoiding detection by hostile forces at all times."

Estelle cleared her throat, then said, "Pardon my ignorance, sir, but whilst they are black, the ATAFs are not invisible."

"You're half right, Lieutenant. They are indeed black, and the cloaking device fitted into each of the fighters is a feature we wished to keep under wraps for as long as possible. However, circumstances like these often force matters forward." He paused for a moment to watch their expressions, the look of total surprise clear on all of their faces; his own deadly serious.

"Sorry, sir. Did you say a cloaking device?" Dodds said.

"Yes, Lieutenant, I did. And it is exactly what you likely believe it to be: a system designed to render the fighter totally undetectable by almost any means," Parks said. Now that he had their total and undivided attention he went on to explain the activation and features of the device. The system would render the ATAF completely invisible to both the naked eye and all radar systems, with the exception of those on-board the ATAFs themselves. Even the glow of the engines would be effectively masked by the device.

"The invisibility effect of the cloak itself is linked to the ATAFs' shields so they must be enabled at all times, even when you disembark upon entering the port. I want to make it absolutely clear right now that if you disengage the cloak or the shields then you will expose yourselves and blow your cover. You will therefore have to push yourselves back through the shield when you wish to re-enter the fighters, a tedious but elementary exercise as you all should know.

"You should also know that although you can use your weapons whilst the system is activated, it is not recommended as it will have detrimental effects on your cloak. Should you do so then your shielding will react for a few seconds and light you up like a Christmas tree. Similar effects will be caused by anything that tests your shields to any degree.

"Unfortunately I'm not a scientist, so I cannot list every conceivable failing of the device. But since you are not to engage any hostile forces at all, I would strongly advise against using any of your weapons whilst cloaked. The technology is something that we do not wish anyone to become aware of – whether allied or enemy - and that means not de-activating the cloak for any reason whilst you are proceeding with this mission.

"Now: do you all fully understand me?"

"Yes, sir," the five mumbled.

"*What?*" Parks said. It had been a lengthy brief, but he needed to ensure they were all still very much awake.

"Sir, yes, sir!" they repeated much louder, though with the exception of Chaz.

"Excellent." Parks tapped at the screen before him and Omar Wyatt re-entered his office, coming to stand by the *Knights*. "de Winter, Dodds, I want you two to remain here for a moment whilst I discuss some extra details with you. The rest of you head back down to the cargo hold. I have already made the flight team down there aware of my plans and they should have almost completed preparations by the time you return. Dismissed."

The head of security led the other three out. Parks watched them go, Chaz meeting his eyes for one last time before he left the office.

Dodds watched as the commodore rose from his chair and paced back and forth in front of his office window for a moment, the grey and uninviting form of Arlos just visible to one side of his view. He began contemplating why Parks may have requested he and Estelle remain behind. Parks did not take his eyes of either of them, studying them as if they were a pair of wanted criminals he had chased for years, having at last been brought before him.

Parks stopped his pacing and fixed him with a stern look. "I don't suppose I need to ask if you're sober now, Dodds?"

"Totally, sir," he said in earnest.

"And I should damn well think so, Lieutenant!" Parks snapped, his eyes narrow.

Despite his earlier actions it was very clear to Dodds that Parks did not feel he had redeemed himself. Dodds detected that he was struggling with second thoughts about sending the team away, unsupervised.

"When you get to the starport I don't want any performances from you, Dodds. You and Todd will fall in line behind de Winter and follow the chain of command. You will do *exactly* as you are ordered, without letting either your over-inflated ego or have-a-go-hero attitude interfere with your assignment. Got that?" He stabbed a finger onto his desk with each point he made.

"Yes, sir," Dodds said.

"I want you to understand that this is the most difficult decision I have ever had to make in all of my career, if not my whole life," Parks continued, now looking to both Dodds and Estelle. "I am leaving my ship and its entire crew defenceless whilst I send you off on a mission you were never trained for. I don't want any of you to take unnecessary risks. Get into the starport, identify yourselves to Barber, get the data card and return to *Griffin*. Nothing more. Am I making myself clear?"

"Yes, sir," they both said.

"de Winter," Parks said, his voice still lined with traces of anger. "Upon leaving *Griffin* I want you and your team to position yourselves as close to the underside of the carrier as you can before activating the cloak. This will ensure that you are not seen by any of the crew and your close proximity to the carrier will ensure you cannot be detected by the radars. Do not move away from the carrier until you are all fully cloaked. As I already stated, it is vital that we maintain secrecy regarding the device - from both enemy and allied forces. Is that understood?"

"Yes, sir," Estelle answered.

"On top of that, Lieutenant, I am expecting you to keep this group together. I am charging you with no less than the full responsibility of bringing back not only that data card, but five ATAFs and five starfighter pilots as well. I want to make it absolutely clear that you are not to return to *Griffin* until you have the data card in your possession, or you can at least reliably determine what has happened to it. If, after successfully completing your mission, you return here only to discover that *Griffin* has been blown to pieces by hostile forces, you are to do nothing but wait for Captain Meyers or Commodore Hawke to arrive in the system. Even if *Griffin* is nothing more than a burnt-out hulk you will not disengage your cloak, engage hostile forces, or attempt to establish any contact with non-Confederation vessels. You will hold position even if it means waiting for your air to run out. Do not even make for any of the jump gates since they will likely be swarming with hostile forces. Am I making myself fully understood?"

"Yes, sir," Estelle said again.

Dodds shifted his eyes in Estelle's direction. He could hear in her voice that she was starting to get frustrated. It was only some time ago that she had led her team to victory against Imperial forces, saving a great deal of not only Confederation lives, but also those of the allied United Naval Forces. Even so she had not been allowed to be debriefed and receive the congratulations and thanks she merited. Instead she had been stuffed into a cargo hold and been made to sit and wait. And now she was being shouted at. Dodds felt for her; she deserved the praise.

Parks, however, seemed satisfied that he was being taken seriously and that he could trust the *Knights*. He relaxed his tone somewhat and asked the pair if they were clear on what they were looking for and what they had to do.

After he had finalized all the details, Parks said, "I should also let you know that neither Commodore Hawke or Captain Meyers are aware that the ATAFs have cloaking abilities and, circumstances notwithstanding, I'd like it to remain that way. The details of your 'errand' are also classified and you should refer either the commodore or the captain to Admiral Turner if they need to know what you have been doing. Now, do you have any other questions?"

"Sir," Dodds began, before pausing to consider his question. "Er... some of the ATAF's weaponry is not active. Are there any other systems that may not be operational that we may need to know about ahead of our task?" He was aware that the question might be just the sort that could enrage the commodore.

"If you're referring to the plasma accelerators, Dodds, then this is intentional. There was an agreement made prior to the beginning of *Operation Menelaus* that no beam weapons or torpedoes would be directed at *Dragon*. This agreement was in place to ensure that we could retake the battleship without causing it critical or irrecoverable damage. But, no, there are no other features of the fighter that you need to be aware of. Now, if that is all?"

"Yes, sir," Estelle said, whilst Dodds nodded.

"Good. Now get down to the cargo hold and get going. There is not much time to spare. Security will escort you back down. Dismissed."

Dodds and Estelle started out of Parks' office and caught his last words to them as the doors opened.

"Good luck, *Knights*. I'll meet you upon your return to *Griffin*."

A little way from where Dodds and Enrique stood, Estelle ascended the ladder into her ATAF, just as they had all done only a few hours earlier, crew milling around to make preparations for her departure. As Kelly was beckoned forward to board her fighter and perform safety checks, Enrique sensed Dodds lean over in his direction.

"Doesn't this strike you as weird?"

"How do you mean?" Enrique asked, keeping his voice low as Dodds had done.

"That starfighter is monstrously powerful compared to the anything else I have ever seen."

"Of course it is – it's the next generation of fighter."

Dodds shook his head and leaned closer. "Mate, listen: it took just *three* of these things to take down an Imperial frigate; Kelly had a head-on collision with a heavy class Imperial fighter. That thing was blown to pieces but there isn't one single, tiny little scratch on her ATAF; and now we're being told that these things can *cloak*? I mean, don't you see? You don't build something like this for no reason. This is a lot more significant than just the next generation of fighter. What the hell is going on?"

Enrique thought about it for a moment, then shrugged. "Dunno, man. We'll probably find out a little later on."

"I'd rather know sooner. There's something about all this that doesn't feel right."

The pair stood in silence for a while, watching as Kelly affixed her helmet and the ladder was wheeled away from the side of the craft. Dodds was then called forward to prepare for takeoff, leaving just Chaz and Enrique together on the cargo bay floor.

"You okay?" Enrique asked the big man, as Estelle taxied forward.

"Will be once this is all over," Chaz replied.

Enrique noted the usual enthusiastic tone in his voice. "Shouldn't be more than a few more hours," he said. "Let's say, four hours there, one hour to find that spy, four hours back. Then we can relax."

Chaz said nothing, the air about him somehow deader than ever.

"So, let me get this straight," Enrique was saying, his voice coming in through Dodds' intercom. "We have to go and rescue a spy? Shouldn't those guys be able to look after themselves?"

"Agent," Kelly corrected him.

As ordered by Parks the *Knights* had positioned themselves beneath *Griffin*, the starfighters not a few meters from the underbelly of the vessel. Just ahead of them hung the small, grey, uninspiring planet that was their destination.

Dodds felt an unwelcoming vibe coming from it and thought it not a place that would traditionally be home to a starport. As he had positioned himself underneath the carrier and awaited Enrique and Chaz to join the others already there, he had studied the overview of the Phylent system on his starfighter's computer, discovering it to be home to a number of asteroid belts and planets. For the most part the system was uninhabited, though it was rich in raw materials, minerals and other elements. It occurred to him that the port would be favoured by those seeking their fortunes, typically frequented by miners and entrepreneurs.

It made him think back to the time before he had joined the Navy, when he had entertained dreams of mining asteroids for their raw content. He had been talked out of it by his father, who had told him horror stories of the incredible hard work, long hours and many terrific accidents that went hand in hand with such a life style. He still sometimes wondered if he may have managed to make enough money to retire after a couple of decades of hard labour. It didn't have to be anywhere fancy, but so long as he had enough cash to buy a bar on a laid back planet and become the proprietor, he would be happy.

"Preparing to engage cloak," Estelle said, returning Dodds to reality.

"Think it'll work?" Enrique asked before their wing leader activated the system; it was obvious he was leaving Estelle out of this particular conversation.

"I heard about the last time they tried something like this and how it all went horribly wrong," Kelly answered.

"It did?" said Dodds.

"If it does then she'll either end up several hundred miles away from here or she'll travel into the future."

"That doesn't sound too bad," Enrique said.

"Before coming back a few minutes later having either gone mad or become one with the ship."

Dodds said nothing and just swallowed hard as Estelle activated the cloak. He found, however, that there was nothing for any of them to fear: the cloak worked just as Parks had described, and Estelle's fighter faded gracefully from view. Whilst his ATAF's radar could still detect and report the presence of an object in place of where Estelle once appeared, he could see nothing else.

After each of them had tested the system for themselves, Estelle confirmed to Parks that they had blanketed themselves from detection. Then, as one, the five invisible ATAFs slipped out from beneath the carrier and set off towards Arlos.

XVIII

— Of Daggers —

S itting amongst a huddled group of blanket-wrapped men and women, Daniel Sullivan's suspicions that he was being watched and followed had been confirmed. A woman - he assumed it was, by the way she carried herself - also wrapped in a blanket against the small chill of the starport, had been hovering just out of sight for the last hour or so. The blanket rested on the top of her head, the folds enclosing her and hiding her face from sight. He was now aware that she had been tailing him as he walked around the port, whilst he had been attempting to find someone who was interested in his wares; his efforts so far having been met with disinterest and the occasional outburst of anger from those wishing to be left alone.

Usually the massive central hall of the starport was bustling, filled with all kinds of people: miners, resting from their labour; traders and couriers seeking work and contracts; and many, many travellers. Bright, animated signs, and warm inviting lights from coffee shops, pubs, various food bars and trading posts lining the walls created a welcoming ambience. Even in the most backwater star systems the familiar branding of intergalactic corporations provided the port's guests with a sense of home and comfort.

Laugher and chatter no longer filled the port, the signs of the shops were inanimate, and the doors were locked, never to be reopened. Many of the windows of the stores had been smashed and the contents looted. The central hall had been transformed into a sea of people, settled on the floor, bags and other personal belongings surrounding them. Young children lay asleep, cuddled up to their parents.

Sullivan found that, though the port was not bitterly cold, it could have been warmer. Keeping warm could be achieved either by wrapping up, consuming hot food and drink or by moving around. The scarred man opted for latter.

Standing up, he began to stride away from his stalker, partly to put distance between the two of them and partly to get away from the place. Though he had only arrived at the port hours earlier he'd already had enough of Arlos starport. It was time to move on and find another place to sell his spoils. Perhaps he'd have better luck in the inner systems of the Imperium; the frontier systems that he had visited so far had been almost devoid of life.

In the grand scheme of his chosen career, he could be considered a petty thief. He found smuggling, weapons trading and gang associations too much like hard work, and there were too many risks involved. The boarding of the vessel within Confederation space had been one of his biggest jobs in recent years, working alongside an ad-hoc group of others he had met in a dingy bar sometime ago. They had been useless, some succeeding in getting themselves killed even before boarding the ship. He had decided to cut his losses there and then, putting a round into the back of the heads of the survivors, before rigging up booby traps and fleeing with what he could.

That had not been a venture he had enjoyed; not something he was used to. Instead he preferred to focus on the things that were easiest to carry and dispose of, mostly stealing to order. The trades were quick, for the most part effortless, and low-key. Starports were his greatest outlet, travellers and entrepreneurs being his best customers. Today, however, Arlos had been a waste of time.

He started back toward the docking port he had left his ship in, with the intention of heading to the nearest jump gate and departing the system for greener and more lucrative pastures. Although for some reason he was having difficulty making headway deeper into Imperial space. The navigation buoys were oddly reluctant to provide him with the necessary data. He would dig through his ship's databanks and see if the previous owner, from whom he had so violently separated it, could be of any more help.

Glancing over his shoulder he noticed that his pursuer had also risen and was once again tailing him, although not as subtly this time as before. It was not the first time he had been followed when he was trading, but judging from the way the woman had kept her distance and her profile low she was not one of the usual suspects. At first he had thought her to be in the same line of work as he was himself: some found it easier to let someone like him do all the hard work, and then pounce on them in the middle of a transaction, relieving them of their hard-earned goods. Parasites; he hated them.

But this woman was far too cautious for that. He had dismissed the possibility that she was a bounty hunter, chasing the reward money for either his head or something he had stolen from the wrong person. If she had been then the pursuit would not have been such a slow, quiet affair - more noisy, violent and very quick. No, this was a new one to him and he could make few assumptions; though one thing he knew he could be certain of was that the woman had decided it was time to come out of hiding and was about to move in for the kill.

Clare Barber swept between the groups of people, settled on the floor around her. She watched her step as she did so, though she did not take her eyes off her target, who walked now with a greater purpose than just the wish to sell his haul and leave.

He still had the card, though. She had heard him enquire a couple of times in the past hour as to whether anyone would be interested in *buying information*. They weren't, of course; these people only wanted to get away.

It seemed to her that the man was either far too ignorant or far too arrogant to appreciate the terrible fate that had befallen the Imperium, and so it had come as little surprise to her that he was having difficulties in offloading his stock here. She thought it likely that he had, until some time ago, only operated in Confederation and Independent World star systems, returning to Imperial space now after attracting too much attention and needing to disappear for a while. If that was the case, he was not having much luck escaping unwanted attention here either.

He stopped walking and Barber, anticipating his next move, calmly reached inside the jacket she wore beneath the blanket and removed a pistol from within. Her finger clicked the safety off.

The man turned around, his and Barber's eyes meeting for the first time, his scowl telling her that he was not happy with being followed. Many scars covered his face, showing many permanent reminders of the cost of his chosen life style. His eyes seemed to tell terrible stories of all he had butchered whilst in the pursuit of that path. He presented a look that would have had many hastily reaching for their valuables, rather than incurring the pain and violence promised. Barber was immune: she had seen many more terrible things.

He sighed audibly before speaking. "<You've been following me all day. Did you want to buy anything or is there something else I can do for you?>" His voice was calm and smooth, his eyes still locked on Barber's. He was playing with her, trying to throw her into a false sense of security, pretending that he was not as threatening and dangerous as his looks might suggest, giving her the chance to walk away.

Though the man spoke in an Imperial dialect, Barber knew that he would understand everything she had to say to him. "You are carrying something I want," she said, with equal calm. The pistol she gripped emerged from between the folds of the blanket that still enclosed her and she pointed it casually at the man's chest. "Hand over the data card. Nothing else, just the card. And do it slowly." Her other hand slipped the blanket from her shoulders, letting it fall to the floor behind her.

Though she had her pistol in her hand, she was not about to approach and frisk the man herself. Her experience with people such as this raider had taught her that they could be slippery characters, unpredictable and desperate, and either very cunning or very stupid. It mattered little to Barber which of those he might be since, no matter what, she could be certain he would be very dangerous.

At the sight of the pistol people close to the pair started shifting, shuffling backward and clamouring to stand and escape the scene that was unfolding before them. Despite the sudden goings-on about her, Barber did not take her eyes off her target.

The man sneered, watching the people gathering up their belongings and trying to get loved ones to move out of the immediate area.

Barber's face remained stern. "I won't ask you again," she warned. She could have shot him hours ago, but had refrained from doing so in case of a defensive knee-jerk reaction from one of those assembled in the immediate area, leading to her own death. She could no longer risk that the man might get away, though, and had taken the decision to confront him now.

The raider's eyes widened, but his sneer remained. "Well, if you want it so badly why don't you just come over here and take it?" he replied, reverting his dialect.

Barber straightened her arm, training the gun on the man's head, emphasising her point. The man's sneer disappeared, his face becoming serious. He reached into the coat he wore, his hand fumbling around in an inside pocket.

Barber tensed, anticipating the glint of a firearm and the need for her to react. The raider removed something and threw it at her feet, though it did not make the noise she was expecting: much louder and clunkier, and with a metallic clasping sound. The gasps and sudden cries about her confirmed her worries. She took her eyes off the man for just a moment to see, resting a little way in front of her, a tiny, flat octagonal device. A red light winked on the top of its dark grey surface, steadily growing faster and faster. It was a mini-mine, and it was about to explode.

Barber ran back, trying to keep an eye on the man as the device went off, fire, flames and smoke obscuring her vision. Through the haze she sighted him sprinting between the packs of people crowded together on the floor. Ignoring the screams of terror around her, Barber began a much more urgent pursuit of her target. The raider was fast, darting between groups and huddles, and hopping over bags, but Barber had few problems in keeping up. She kept a tight grip on her pistol as she ran, stopping every now and again to loose off a shot, none of which found their mark. The long coat the man wore flapped around as he zig-zagged, ducked and leapt about, concealing his form from her and making it much harder to know where to shoot.

She chased him for some time and soon had him cornered, the exit he had been making for unexpectedly closed. Barber had seen to that when she had followed him in, intending on minimising possible escape routes. He hammered at the button next to the exit, but it refused to open. She levelled her gun at his torso as he tried in vain to prise the door open where it met the wall, his fingers struggling to find anything to latch on to.

Barber had chosen a non-energy weapon for this assignment. Though an energy weapon was more effective, within the context of this fight it could destroy the data card she was after. Whilst she was aware that the impact of a bullet could also damage or destroy the card, the high amounts of energy dissipated by the impact of a plasma or other energy shot could cause destruction by proximity. And bullets served Barber's requirements just as well.

At the last second, just as Barber squeezed the trigger, the raider ducked along the side of the adjoining wall, and the shot that had been intended for his heart slammed instead into his left shoulder. Barber fired once again, but with the raider still ducking the shot missed altogether, ripping through his coat and ricochetting off against the wall behind him. The third squeeze clicked on an empty chamber, the tiny digital counter on the top of the weapon flashing two zeroes.

"Bitch! I'll kill you!" her quarry cried out with a mixture of pain and anger, his right hand clasped around his bleeding shoulder. Barber saw him swing around and aim his own weapon. It looked like a laser pistol.

Barber ducked down close to an assembled family who panicked at the sudden realisation they were now in the line of fire. The raider appeared to be left handed, or at least held the weapon with his left, and with his shoulder wounded his aim was far from true. The first shot cleanly missed its intended target, as well as everything else, the thin red beam striking the floor behind Barber, letting off sparks and leaving a scorch mark at the point of impact. The second and third shots found targets, neither of which were Barber. The first felled a man, hitting him square in the forehead. The beam passed straight through his skull, leaving a small hole in the front and back of his head before striking the ground behind. The second struck a mother in the hand as she reached across to grab her daughter, and the little girl screamed in horror as three severed fingers fell into her lap.

Following his unsuccessful attempts to down his target, the raider lunged forward with his outstretched right hand, and yanked a young woman up off the floor by her long hair, just as Barber prepared to raise her gun once more. The man held the screaming woman in front of himself, shaking her head and shouting at her in the Imperial dialect he had spoken to Barber in. At first he placed his gun against the woman's temple, before he lowered his quivering arm and rested it across her shoulder for support.

Barber felt no pity for the dead man or maimed woman, they were nothing more to her than collateral damage. However, to shoot the innocent woman held by the raider as a human shield went against her code of conduct and her own moral values. Even though the Confederacy had pressed upon her the tremendous importance of the data card she was after, there were some things she refused to do.

The raider began walking away, keeping parallel with the wall behind him as the girl continued to sob with fear and plead with her captor. He kept an eye on Barber the whole time, his laser pistol pointed over the shoulder of his hostage. Barber sidestepped in his direction, keeping up with his pace, her own gun trained on him the whole time.

Why isn't he firing? Barber wondered. *Is he low on ammo? Has his laser pistol overheated?* The man was in a far better position to attack than she was.

The three continued with their steady stepping dance for a while, the raider seeking to move himself into a more strategic position from where he could flee to the next docking port exit. He made occasional snap glances around to ensure he was not going to trip over items that were scattered about. But as Barber already knew his current location was not going to permit him an easy escape route and it could be seen that he was losing patience with the girl he was dragging along. His wounded shoulder was also making it more difficult for him to keep his arm straight, despite being able to rest it across the terrified woman's shoulder. Barber maintained a relaxed demeanour, following his every step.

The raider suddenly cast aside his hostage and began to run, making no attempt to shoot. Barber swore as she started after him. His gun had been empty the whole time; he had been bluffing. And Barber had been doing just the same thing. Neither of them had found the time to reload their weapons and neither wanted to give the other the advantage.

Barber broke into a run to catch up with the raider who was once again darting and skipping over people. He was not heading in any specific direction, but zig-zagging once more. Barber saw him fumbling around in his coat and assumed he was trying to buy himself some time as he searched for an energy capsule to recharge his laser pistol. With the huge scatters of people and baggage, coupled with the urgency of the raider to reload his gun, Barber could see it would not be long before he came undone.

As Sullivan leapt over a bag his foot became caught within an exposed, unturned strap, the sudden and unexpected additional weight caused him to topple forward and crash to the ground. His laser pistol and the energy cap he had only just managed to pull from his coat clattered and skidded along the floor ahead of him, far out of reach. He thrashed his foot around in a vain attempt to free himself, not wanting to take his eyes off his gun, though the struggling did him no good. He looked around at the problem, and his hands flew towards the straps that were curled around his ankle. His coat was equipped with a knife, built into one sleeve, and with a quick flick of his wrist it shot free and into his hand. It was exceptionally sharp, and with just a few slashes he managed to cut away the straps.

Free once more he leapt to his feet, just in time to see his pursuer descending upon him. There was a bang; she had wasted no time in shooting him square in the chest. Sullivan grunted as the bullet slammed into him, but despite the searing pain he still had a lot of fight left in him. He responded to her attack by driving his knife into her own chest.

"Yeah?! See how you like it, bitch!" he spat. The woman cried out in pain, but even before she had time to act Sullivan gripped her tight about the shoulder, withdrew the knife and plunged it twice more into her. Just as he prepared to strike for the third time, he heard several bangs and the remainder of his attacker's clip tore into his belly. He struggled to breathe, but could draw no air into his lungs. He held fast to his knife even as his vision blurred.

The raider sagged, his grip on Barber loosening as he fell to the floor. Barber could feel her own legs beginning to give way and she fought to control herself. As the raider lay dead on the floor before her she rummaged through his clothes. She prayed that he had the data card with him, rather than having left it in his craft. In her current state she wouldn't even be able to make it to the docking ports, let alone break into his ship. She coughed as she continued her hasty search, tasting blood in her mouth, seeing it splatter over the man and feeling it run down her chin.

Relief washed over her as her fingers encountered a thin piece of plastic which, once removed, revealed itself to be just what she had been looking for: a tiny, thin blue card bearing the Confederation insignia. Her head began to feel light and she sat down on the floor with a heavy thump, using one hand to prop herself up and keep from tipping over completely. There was very little time to act. She knew what she had to do and, reaching into her jacket, she removed a packet containing a tiny capsule and a small bottle of liquid. Breaking open the packet she placed the data card into the capsule and sealed it tight. She coughed some more, feeling the blood fill her mouth again, and the taste of iron with it. She spat it from her mouth, as well as the rest that wanted to follow.

It took her some time and considerable effort for her to achieve what she had planned for the card, but eventually she succeeded. Drawing heavy, staggered breaths, but confident that the plans were now in a safe place, she lay back. She was going to die. She found her breath coming shorter with each passing moment. The raider's knife must have punctured a lung.

She noticed that some of the more inquisitive witnesses to the scene were inching forward to investigate the man and woman who had fallen down together in a pool of blood, following their very violent encounter. She met another woman's eyes and saw them filled with pity.

"I hope you're luckier than I was," she whispered. But in her heart she doubted that. There was a good chance that she was the lucky one here. Running would not save these people any more than fighting would. They were only prolonging the inevitable. Eventually they would not be able to run any further; although she could not blame them for trying. And when they were caught, that would be it. Prisoners would not be taken, lives would not be spared.

Barber's vision became cloudy and the woman closed her eyes, letting the darkness take her.

XIX

— An Uncomfortable Revelation —

O ver time the grey form of Arlos loomed steadily larger as the ATAFs hurtled towards it, hidden from all but the most diligent observer beneath the veil of the starfighter's cloaking device. Owing to the direction of their approach the starport was obscured from the *White Knights*, behind the far side of Arlos; and as he rounded the dull planet Dodds expected to see a flurry of activity from their dodecahedral shaped destination.

Contrary to his expectation the starport was quiet, and appeared to be all but abandoned. The normal glow of lights and other illuminations that would have welcomed travels were absent, the port's lifelessness echoing that of the rest of the star system. He got the feeling that the port wished to convey the impression that it had been out of use for quite some time, its previous residents having upped and left many years ago.

It was the second time in almost as many days that Dodds' destination had presented him with a cold and dead demeanour, and it was a theme that was starting to become all too common. The only indication that the port was not as dead and lifeless as it would have had one believe was the presence of a solitary cargo vessel, resting near by; though it too was shrouded in darkness.

"Think anyone's home?" Dodds asked of his companions as they came closer to their destination.

"Looks abandoned," Enrique said. "Either that or our friend has been busy here too."

"Estelle, are we in the right place?" Dodds said, with genuine uncertainty.

"These are the coordinates that Commodore Parks gave us," Estelle said.

Dodds' eyes flickered over the surface of the port. Under normal circumstances a starport would be a hive of activity, its presence advertised far and wide by the constant flow of traffic to and from it. Mining vessels, transport ships of various shapes and sizes would be docked in and around the port, dropping off passengers, cargo and spoils. Even without the heavy flow of traffic the port could be spotted from a long way off, the bright multicoloured lights guiding people home. All that was gone now, cold uninviting grey steel the only thing remaining to greet visitors.

"I've just scanned for a possible means of entry," came Chaz's voice. "But it appears all docking ports have been sealed. Looks like we're going to have to find another way inside."

"We'll have to use an airlock," Estelle said. "Which means we'll have to leave the ATAFs outside the port."

"We're just going to leave them floating here?" Dodds said.

"We don't have much choice in the matter. As Commodore Parks instructed we'll keep them cloaked whilst we retrieve the data from the agent."

"Sure. And then we'll just fumble about in empty space looking for them when we come back out," Dodds said sarcastically. He could see no clear avenue to how they were supposed to get back into the ATAFs once they had left them. Since they were invisible the *White Knights* would have to grasp around in the starfighter's general area and try and feel their way back in the cockpit. But that could take hours, maybe even days. Maybe even longer. Dodds hoped that they would not be in a hurry. Taking any sort of mobile sensor device with them was not an option either. Whilst the ATAFs' radars themselves displayed the positions of the other fighters, cloaked or not, they were not removable from the craft.

"We'll have to turn the cloak off..." Dodds began.

"*No*, Dodds," Estelle said. "We were given very specific orders by Commodore Parks not to deactivate the cloak for any reason."

Dodds said nothing else on the subject, sensing that Estelle was still upset after being chewed out by the commodore, despite averting *Operation Menelaus* from becoming one of the greatest naval catastrophes in recent history.

"One of us will have to remain out here then," Enrique said.

"No one is staying out here alone," Estelle said. "I want everyone to be where I can see them."

"We'll have to find some way of returning to the ATAFs once we leave them, then," Enrique responded. "Otherwise we might never find them again."

"If we leave them next to that freighter it'll be a lot easier to locate them," Kelly chirped up. "We'll have a better point of reference."

"That's a good idea, Kelly," Estelle said. "Okay people, let's form a line close to the freighter and disembark. Once you're out make your way over to me."

The others acknowledged her order and guided the ATAFs close to the freighter, watching their radars and HUD so as not to collide with one another.

Bringing his ATAF to a stop Dodds informed the others he was disembarking. He reached under the fighter's seat and pulled out a small propulsion pack that resided beneath. The pack was a standard feature of all the CSN's starfighters, though it was only of any real use to the pilot during events such as ejections. Dodds had received training in the usage and general application of the pack, but he had never found the need to use it himself. Ensuring his helmet and flight suit were securely set up and fastened, he opened the canopy. He unbuckled himself from his seat and, taking a good grip of his propulsion pack, let himself drift out into the vacuum.

His flight suit was well insulated against the cold of outer space and upon leaving the ATAF he experienced nothing more than the sensation of free movement within the vacuum. Dodds started slipping his propulsion pack on to his back and, looking around, saw Enrique making his way from his own ATAF. It was a bizarre sight to behold: from the middle of nowhere a helmet emerged, followed by shoulders, a body, legs, and then feet. It was as if a magical door had opened and his friend had just slipped out of it. His pack on he watched as the others left their ATAFs, before Estelle's voice sounded in his helmet's speaker.

"Over this way, people," she requested, raising her hand. She was waiting a little further up the side of the freighter and the *Knights* began to make their way over to her.

"We'll make our way to the port and look for an airlock so we can get inside," Estelle informed her team once everyone had made it over. "Follow my lead."

As she moved further away from the freighter Kelly took a look back. During their approach Kelly had stared at the vessel, very certain that she had seen it before; or perhaps the blow to her head was making her see things again. She had then scanned the ship with her ATAF's targeting systems and the resulting readouts had once again made her question her own sanity. Given the lack of comment from her wingmates, the others had not noticed what she had.

In large eroded and rusted orange letters along the central container was the name of the ship, "*La Brabena Bella*", and underneath it in much smaller lettering, "Gloucester Enterprises". The lettering was well worn, barely legible with little more than the outline remaining; but it was readable if one knew what they were looking for.

Gloucester Enterprises, one of the galaxy's most successful trading companies, was owned by Kelly's family. This was one of her father's ships. She had thought it looked familiar when the *Knights* had first approached it, and her fighter's computer had confirmed the ship's configuration. The vessel had been designated a new name ("*The Mayflower*") and universal identity signature, but there was no chance of disguising its distinctive appearance from Kelly. The body was segmented into three main parts, like a rigid snake that had swallowed three large rectangular boxes. The lick of dark red paint was also something of a give away.

What's it doing here, all the way out in the middle of nowhere? Kelly wondered. Despite its success and reputation throughout Confederate and Independent systems, the Imperium had never granted Gloucester Enterprises a trading permit; the Senate had seen to that. It was unlikely to have been stolen, and she knew the company removed all affiliated branding before selling off old ships. Something about its presence here did not add up.

She lingered for a while, staring at it, contemplating a number of explanations. She was about to say something to the others when her eye was caught by something else: port holes and windows dotted the length of the freighter at various points and from out of one of the windows a small face was staring back at her. As Kelly squinted it remained there, transfixed, gazing back at her in wrapped, abject horror. It was the grubby looking face of a little girl, long, unkempt dirty blonde hair dangling down around her head. Her mouth hung open, as if she had just made a great intake of breath and was now too scared to make any other noise or movement.

Kelly prepared to start forward to the window when a new face appeared alongside the child. It turned to glance at Kelly before it and the little girl vanished from sight. From what Kelly caught, it looked like an older woman, perhaps the girl's mother, who had come to move the child away from the window. From the looks of things they were trying to conceal their presence.

The surprise made her gasp.

"What's up, Kelly?" Estelle's voice came in her ear piece.

Kelly looked around to see the others, now quite some way from her, had stopped their journey towards the port. Had she just imagined it? No, she couldn't have. The knock on her head did not appear to be doing her as much harm as she thought; after all, she had been right about the freighter.

"I just saw someone," Kelly answered Estelle.

"Where?" Estelle asked, the three men next to her looking in all directions, as if expecting to see a body swimming through space.

"In the freighter. There was a girl, and a woman, in one of the windows."

Silence from the others.

"And?" It was Dodds.

"That's one of my father's ships," Kelly insisted. "And they don't carry passengers - it's a freighter." Kelly saw that all four of her team mates were staring in her direction. She guessed that they were peering past her at the window, scrutinizing it.

"I don't see anyone," Estelle said eventually. "Are you certain you saw something?"

She hesitated. "Pretty sure. They didn't stay there long."

"Hey, wait. What's one of your Dad's ships doing out here?" Enrique asked. "That doesn't sound right."

"That's what I've been saying," Kelly said.

Kelly heard Estelle let out a tetchy sigh, then, "Look, we don't have time for this. Kelly, did they look dangerous?"

"No, they just looked like civilians," Kelly said.

Estelle mumbled something offensive under her breath.

"Right, that's all we need to know. Now get a move on and try to keep up," Estelle said.

Kelly tore herself away from the window and started back towards the rest of the group.

"We need to find a way inside. A service hatch or an airlock," Estelle told the group as they arrived next to the port's outer surface. "Spread out and see what you can find. Call in if you get into any trouble."

Even up close and personal the port was nothing but a mass of grey steel plates, the occasional warning sign or instructional panel adding a tiny splash of colour to the otherwise dull surface. The group set about on a fruitless search for a while, discovering hatches and doors, none of which could be opened.

"Found one," Dodds eventually reported as he checked out a door close to the main docking entrance to the port. Unlike the others it was not security locked. He pulled it open as the rest of the *Knights* regrouped and joined him inside.

With the outer door sealed behind them, Dodds took a look at the control panel inside the chamber and managed to re-pressurise it. He gratefully removed his helmet and breathed in the air that now flowed into the small room. He then worked the control panel some more, looking for a way to grant them further access into the station. The inner door opened and, as it did so, the group found themselves standing in a narrow corridor. A number of men and women, sat along it, looked up.

The sudden appearance of the *Knights* sent a ripple of shock to down the line and a man close to the group shot to his feet, screaming in terror. He stumbled and ran down the corridor as fast as he could, pushing aside a woman who was also trying to escape.

"What the hell was his problem? Did we spook him or something?" Dodds said as they watched the man who had leapt to his feet round a corner on his continuing quest to escape whatever it was that had scared him. The remainder crawled backwards down the corridor, eyes fixed on the five people that had just entered the port, terror etched into all their faces. It was as if they had just seen their worst nightmare step through the airlock.

"Beats me. Maybe he thinks he owes Chaz money," Enrique said, looking around at the big man with amusement.

Chaz said nothing, his face stern and his eyes sweeping over the groups of people. "Let's go," he said, pushing the others gently aside and starting off down the corridor. "We've got to find Barber, get that data card, and get back to *Griffin*."

A stunned Dodds watched him go. He exchanged a confused look with Estelle, who was wearing her own muddled expression. The people on either sides of Chaz backed away as he passed them, the often silent man not giving them a second glance. Dodds, Estelle and Kelly looked around at Enrique, who shrugged.

"Hey, look: he might talk to me more than anyone else, but that doesn't mean that I know what goes on in that head of his," Enrique said almost inaudibly, not taking his eyes off the big man. "Don't go expecting me to provide all the answers."

"Come on," Estelle said, following Chaz down the corridor, passing by the people who were now trying to crush themselves into the walls.

"<Please don't hurt us,>" a woman pleaded as she tried to move further back than the wall would allow.

"What did she say?" Dodds asked Enrique.

"Sounds like she was speaking some sort of Imperial," Enrique said, looking at the woman.

"Either of you guys understand any Imperial dialects?" Dodds asked of Estelle and Kelly.

"Just ignore them," Estelle said, striding around the corner and through a set of doors. She stopped in the doorway, where Chaz had also stopped.

Dodds walked up behind the pair and peered around them. "Ah. We might be here a while." A sea of people lay before them, occupying almost every inch of floor that could be found.

The five pilots stepped into the central main hall of the starport, many heads snapping around to take note of the new arrivals. Dodds noticed that the *White Knights* received the same reaction from groups of people in the hall as they had done in the corridor, with many of those close by pushing themselves further back. Some sprang to their feet and moved away, appearing to not trust the new arrivals. It was obvious the man who had fled the corridor had passed through here already, putting everyone on edge.

"You're right, Dodds. Something's spooked these guys pretty bad," Kelly said as they began walking aimless between huddles, the search for Barber temporarily forgotten. The people gathered about did not take their fearful eyes off the *Knights* for one second.

"What's this all about?" Dodds asked, looking all about the huddles of people. "Are they all waiting for transit or something?"

"Yeah, and what's with all the bags? They look like refugees..." Enrique said. He stopped walking.

Dodds stopped and turned to him. "Just like that guy said last night..." The realisation of what he was looking at dawned on him. Links were beginning to form from the conversation he now remembered. Refugees, secret projects, genocide... "Didn't he say that the Empire had been completely wiped out?"

"What are you two talking about?" Kelly asked.

"Last night whilst we were playing poker, this guy said that the Empire had been destroyed, that the civil war actually ended years ago, and that all that were left were a load of refugees."

"But... we just went up against Imperial forces when we attempted to take back *Dragon*," Kelly said, appearing a little concerned.

Dodds shook his head. "Those weren't them."

Estelle's irate demeanour appeared to have all but abandoned her for the time being. She then scowled. "Wait, what are you talking about? Kelly's right. Pay no attention to him. The Empire hasn't been *wiped out*!"

"Estelle, you were *there*! What happened in that battle wasn't... well, it wasn't normal. I don't know who they were, but those were *not* Imperial pilots in those fighters. None of us would have survived that battle if we'd not been in the ATAFs."

Estelle folded her arms, but did not argue with him further.

Dodds couldn't shake the feeling that he had his head in the lion's mouth. He looked again at the groups of people on the ground, some meeting his eyes before turning away, even those who looked as though they could handle themselves. "We'd better get on with this and get out of here," he concluded.

"How?" Enrique said. "How are we going to be able to locate Barber amongst all these people. She doesn't know we're coming, and like Parks said she's hardly likely to be jumping up and down waving to us."

Dodds' eyes swept over the groups and huddles, then turned back to his team mates, seeing none of them looking very optimistic. Even Chaz, who had been the first to step forward, seemed taken aback and a little out of his depth. There must have been hundreds of people in the main hall alone and, to make matters worse, a few sets of stairs at one end led up to another floor above. How many more floors were there? How many pockets would they have to search?

"You know what? How about we just ask someone if they've seen her," Dodds suggested. He broke from his team mates, making his way over to a man he had singled out at random.

"Dodds..." Estelle started.

"Estelle, it's cool, I've got it," Dodds said. "I'm just going to ask if they've seen her."

"Be careful," Estelle called after him.

Dodds looked back over his shoulder with what he hoped was a confident smile. The man he walked towards was sat crossed legged on the floor, hunched over a bowl of noodles, two chopsticks clasped in his hand. He glanced up as Dodds approached him, a look of fear spreading across his features. He shuffled backward as Dodds drew closer and began shaking his head before turning his full attention back to his food, not wishing to make eye contact.

"Hi, how you doing?" Dodds began. "I'm looking for a woman... er... girl? You know... not a man?" He gestured towards men and women as he spoke, hoping to make it clear which gender he was after.

"<Don't talk to me! There's already been enough trouble today! Just leave me alone!>" the man spluttered back at him. His hands started to shake and he tried to continue eating, unable to manipulate the sticks enough to grasp the food in the bowl.

Dodds looked around at Estelle who shrugged with puzzlement, not understanding either. He tried again, "She's a bit shorter than me, long black hair..."

"<Go away! Leave me alone!>" the man spluttered again, before casting his bowl in Dodds' direction. He struggled to his feet, pushing aside those behind him in a bid to escape. His bowl of noodles clattering to the ground, spilling its warm contents across the white marble tiled floor. The *Knights* watched as he left, other refugees nearby moving closer to one another and a bit further back from the five pilots.

"This isn't going to be easy," Enrique said. Estelle was in agreement. They were going to have to apply a little more effort if they hoped to locate their contact amongst all these people.

"We'll just have to search for someone who is a little more cooperative," Estelle said. "Split up and see if you can find someone who is more willing to talk. We'll try this central area first and then move on into the other parts of the port. If any of you get into any sort of trouble, shout and we'll come get you. The moment you find out *anything* I want to know. Don't do anything without me, that's an order. Let's go, people. The sooner we find the agent, the sooner we can leave and get back to *Griffin*."

XX

— Hawke's Ambition —

O n the bridge of *Ifrit*, helmsman Alan Cox stood waiting patiently as an engineer took a look at his console. It was not behaving as it should: the touch sensitive surface seeming to be off by a few inches. Every time he tapped at the screen there was a chance that a different control to the one he wanted might be activated. He had started to become concerned when some of the more delicate operations he needed to perform while the carrier continued to search for the missing *Griffin* became more difficult to execute. For a time he had traded places with the controller across from him, so that he could continue his duty. But now the carrier was holding position, pausing in its search, he had taken the opportunity to have the problem dealt with.

"Looks like one of the calibration relay nodes has given out," the engineer said from beneath the console, pulling out a small circuit board.

"Do you have a spare?" Cox asked, toying with a screwdriver the engineer had used to remove the bottom panel of the console.

"Plenty. I can go and get one and be back up soon. Shouldn't take more than ten or fifteen minutes. Do you need it urgently?"

"So-so," the navigator replied. "The captain has ordered us to hold position here. According to him *Griffin* should be somewhere close by. But so far we haven't detected anything, not even on the long range scanners."

The way Hawke had been acting had set Cox on edge. He had voiced these concerns with some of the other crew once his captain had departed the bridge, on his way to his private office to receive a communication that had come in from CSN HQ. Though they did not talk for long, it became evident that the rest of the crew shared his feelings.

Upon his return, Hawke had ordered that they jump to an adjoining star system in which they would at last find *Griffin*. Within minutes of *Ifrit* arriving at its destination, the commodore had once again departed.

Following the allied forces' failed attempt to retake *Dragon,* and the unusual disappearance of *Griffin,* Hawke had ordered Meyers to return to Spirit alone. He had then taken *Ifrit* and begun a systematic sweep of the nearest adjacent star systems to Aster, in case *Griffin* had become stranded in one of those. But though they had hunted for many hours their search had turned up nothing, the likelihood of finding *Griffin* close by diminishing with each system they came too.

It was as they scanned their fifth system that Hawke had received the message from naval headquarters. It had informed him that *Griffin* had been located and, as luck would have it, was drifting in a star system alongside the one they were currently scanning. Hawke had ordered that *Ifrit* make that their destination. But upon arriving the crew had been greeted by nothing except another empty system, the only highlight of the region being the twisted hues of the nebulas that were so prominent in that part of the galaxy. Hawke had returned to his private office to watch the message again so as to, as he had put it, "ensure that he had not made a mistake".

After his lack of commitment to the previous battle, the crew were beginning to question his command. Cox was not about to challenge the man's authority, however; the thought of a stay in the brig and a court martial were not high on his list of priorities.

"Are you sure we're in the right place?" the engineer wanted to know, emerging from beneath and console and looking out the thick glass windows of *Ifrit's* main viewport to the empty space beyond. "You could have punched the wrong destination into the console? Wouldn't be surprising the way this thing is so out of whack."

"I was using that one," said Cox, indicating the console across from his own.

"Maybe I should check that one too?" the engineer suggested.

At that moment Cox heard the bridge lift doors open and looking around he saw Hawke come striding down the long aisle, people on either side turning in anticipation of what *Ifrit's* captain would say about the situation.

"Sir," Cox requested his captain's attention. "We've performed a full sweep of the system and we've not been able to detect *Griffin.* Either it's not here or we're in the wrong place."

"No, Lieutenant, we're exactly where we need to be," Hawke answered him, eyes focused on the space ahead of him, not shifting his head the slightest bit to acknowledge the man who had spoken.

"Sir..." Cox tried to engage Hawke once more.

"*Wait*, Lieutenant," was all that Hawke said.

Cox turned and looked at the engineer, who gave a slight shrug. It appeared to him that Hawke was watching for something. Cox heard confused whispers being exchanged across the length of the bridge, many seeking an explanation for Hawke's statement. The answer came in the form a number of consoles that all started to wail.

"Captain, jump points forming!" a woman's voice called out. "We've got incoming on the port, stern... All sides, sir!" She, as did many others, looked to Hawke for the course of action to take. But despite what he had just been told, the man did not so much as even flinch. Hawke stood still, watching ahead of him as a large jump point swirled into existence. From out of it slipped the dagger-like form of *Dragon*, the enormous Confederation battleship slowing as it drew itself up to *Ifrit*.

During the previous battle *Ifrit* had held back from the action, granting Cox only the merest of suggestions as to the tremendous size of the battleship. Now, with the hulking mass of *Dragon* bearing down upon them, Cox found himself wishing he could once again be much further away; the other side of the galaxy preferably.

"Captain, radars indicate a number of Imperial frigates have exited jump points and are on approach vectors," the same woman reported.

Hawke said nothing.

"Captain, I suggest we put full power to shields, arm weaponry and prepare to withdraw from the system," Lucas Short, Hawke's second in command, said.

"Stand down!" Hawke spun around, addressing the crew for the first time since returning to the bridge. Cox, stood the closest to the man, subconsciously backed up. Hawke's eyes were alight, almost daring anyone to challenge him. "We're completely surrounded! We make any sign of aggression and they will blow this ship to pieces!"

For a moment Cox did not know what they should be more afraid of: the arrival of *Dragon* and a host of Imperial warships, or Commodore Hawke.

He turned worried eyes in the direction of the engineer who had backed off a lot more himself.

"Sir, *Dragon* is requesting communication," the operative of the console adjacent to Cox's said.

"Grant it," Hawke said.

A holographic screen sprung up at the front of the bridge moments later. The screen showed a man whom none of the crew failed to recognise, having seen his face not hours earlier that morning during the mission briefing.

"This is Fleet Admiral Zackaria of the Imperial Senate battleship, *Dragon*," began the highly decorated man on the holographic projection. "You will surrender immediately. Drop your shields and prepare to be boarded." Zackaria's face was impassive throughout his brief speech.

"As you wish, Admiral," Hawke said. Zackaria's statement was short, but to the point, and Hawke made no attempt whatsoever to argue against it.

Cox felt his blood freeze as Hawke turned to look straight at him. There was something about the look in his eyes; as if all humanity had been stripped clean. Cox fought an urge to flee and escape the unwanted attention.

"Relay the order that we are to receive boarders. All crew are to stand down. We are to give Admiral Zackaria full, unchallenged access to the ship."

"Sir, my console..." Cox somehow managed.

Hawke's eyes lowered, seeing the panel beneath lying open on the floor. He looked to a man sat at the console across from Cox's.

"Mr Parsons..." Hawke said.

"Captain, might I suggest that we take immediate actions to..." Short interrupted.

"We are *surrounded*, Mr Short," Hawke flared. He looked again to the man he had addressed as Parsons. "Relay the order to stand down."

Parsons hesitated for a moment and then did as he was ordered, his voice issuing from speakers and echoing down the numerous corridors of the ship.

Cox began to wonder if this was some sort of ruse, designed to lure the Imperial admiral over to the carrier where he could be dealt with. If it was, it was a particularly dangerous one, with no apparent room for error.

"Lower shields," Hawke ordered.

"Bow quadrant?" came the reluctant answer.

"*All* shields," Hawke said.

The image of Zackaria remained patient and still in the hologram, waiting for the acknowledgement that the Confederation carrier had complied with his request.

"Shields lowered," Cox heard, his heart beat starting to increase. He fingered the screwdriver he still held, his grip tightening on it.

"You're free to come aboard, Admiral," Hawke prompted to Zackaria, who terminated the communication without another word.

Moments later, from out the frontal viewport, Cox saw transport craft begin to depart *Dragon*, swinging themselves around from the launch bays running along the side of the battleship, and heading towards *Ifrit*. At first it appeared that only three shuttles were making their way over. It then became apparent that the enemy forces intended to fill every last inch of the carrier with their ranks; the three becoming five, then seven, then ten as the numbers built up.

Out of the corners of the bridge's thick glass window Cox spied two Imperial frigates, hovering closed by. He looked to a display further up the bridge: *Ifrit*'s radar told the whole story, indicating that the carrier was surrounded by a total of six frigates; three on each side. Not that their presence was required. *Dragon* needed no assistance. He swallowed and felt a chill run down his spine.

Hawke turned his back on the crew, to instead follow the progress of the transports that were streaming from the former Confederation flagship. As he did so, Cox glanced down the aisle of the bridge. He noticed that Short had begun to whisper with two others sitting close to him, peeking at the commodore who was staring out at the enormous battleship that rested so close to them. He assumed they had come to the same conclusion as he: this was no ruse. Whatever the man was planning it did not appear to involve the capture of Zackaria. Whether he intended to bargain with him, whether it be with the crew or the carrier, matters could not be allowed to progress any further. He watched as they conferred for some time before they all nodded in agreement and prepared to make their move.

Short rose from his seat. "Commodore Hawke, it is my belief that you are no longer functioning with the best interests of *Ifrit*, her crew or the

Confederation at heart." He started towards the front. "It is also my belief that your judgement have been adversely affected by recent events and that you are no longer capable of making rational decisions. As second-in-command of *Ifrit*, I am exercising my authority to hereby relieve you of your post."

Hawke turned from his admiration of *Dragon*, wearing a tired expression, as though his crew had now become a bother unto him. The two others that Short had been speaking with stood up with him, flanking his sides, as they strode towards the carrier's captain.

Hawke's face darkened, his expression became quite grim, and in a cold voice he said, "Return to your seat, Commander."

Short continued as though not hearing the words. "Lieutenant Lee, Lieutenant Dawes, please escort Commodore Hawke from the bridge and confine him to quarters," he said to the man and woman who walked by his sides.

Hawke said nothing more. With lightning relaxes he reached into his jacket and produced a laser pistol. He trained the weapon on both Lee and Dawes and, before either of them could react, shot them both neatly in the foreheads. Their limp bodies slumped to the floor.

Cox jumped back. The need to escape the bridge was now very urgent. He saw that the rest of the bridge crew appeared to share his thoughts, many having left their seats and now standing. Cox was unable to comprehend what had just happened: the speed at which Hawke had not only produced the weapon, but then dispatched Lee and Dawes, had left him in a state of total shock and confusion.

As Lee and Dawes dropped down beside him, Lieutenant Short's eyes grew wide with fear and he started to back away from Hawke, looking behind him to two men stood by the bridge's lift doors. Hawke then trained the pistol on Short himself.

"Security..." Short started, before Hawke pulled the trigger and he too collapsed in a heap on the ground, blood from all three of the dead beginning to seep from the wounds in their heads.

Hawke's eyes darted over the others occupying the bridge, marking out all the men and women who, though standing, remained rooted in shock. Movement at the other end of the aisle grabbed his attention and he focused the pistol to meet the new threat. "Drop them!" he called to the two security guards who stood at the far end of the long bridge, next to the lift, who had just broken into a run towards him. "Drop them, now!"

The two men obeyed without question, throwing their guns aside and raising their hands in surrender. Even though they were a great deal further away than Short had been, the two security personnel were clearly not prepared to test just how fast or accurate Hawke could be.

"Everyone, down on your knees, hands on heads," Hawke spat to his entire bridge.

No one moved.

"KNEES! NOW!" Hawke shouted, waving the laser pistol about. It passed in Cox's direction and the man found himself dropping to the floor as his legs gave way, his hands flying to the top of his head. The tone in Hawke's voice told him that the man was in no mood trifled with. In the floor's dim reflection, Cox saw the engineer lower down next to him. A few moments later he gingerly raised his eyes from the floor to look at Hawke.

Behind him the transports continued to stream from *Dragon*, making their way towards the main launch bay of *Ifrit*. Hawke continued to mark the crew as they got down on the floor, watching each and every one of them for the slightest attempt at escape or attack. In the face of what had just happened however, none of them were about to dare, some preferring to stare down at the floor than at Hawke's rage-twisted expression.

It was not long before the first wing of transports started to enter *Ifrit*'s launch bay, setting themselves down inside. Even as they did so more could be seen departing *Dragon*, forming a huge caravan reminiscent of those departing Spirit earlier that day. The image of the transports streaming towards the Confederation carrier, no doubt carrying with them scores of Imperial soldiers, deadly weaponry and God only knew whatever else, did nothing but fill all its witnesses with a sense of dread and terrible unease.

What would happen when they arrived? Why was this happening? What did Hawke plan to do? The questions raced through Cox's mind. Though for some reason he felt fear starting to pass, being edged out by a new feeling: anger. He looked down the bridge along the rows of crew that were on their knees. He noted one young man who he could see was trembling. The man made a quick snap look at the lift. Cox wished he could tell the man to stay where he was, but he had already made up his mind. Cox saw him leap to his feet and start towards the lift, arm outstretched, reaching for the call button.

He managed but a few feet before Hawke felled him, the thin red beam of the laser cutting its way through the back of his head. The young man crashed forward across the floor, legs giving way beneath him, his arms splayed out as he went down. Like the others that had fallen to the shots, he gave no cry as he fell, but those who continued to comply with Hawke's command flinched at the sound of his body slamming down. Still they kept their hands on their heads, facing the floor, looking down at the dim reflections of their own worried faces staring back at them.

The occupants of *Ifrit*'s flight deck stood by powerless as the first of the transports opened up, the passengers like none they had ever seen before: they were clad almost entirely in black, save for a strange white emblem on their left breast and right arm, and a pair of scowling ruby-red eyes affixed into their helmets.

The soldiers spilled out of the craft, rifles raised to secure the area. They spoke no words, but gestured to the deck's occupants that they should, like those on the bridge, place their hands on their heads and get down on their knees. The various maintenance workers, pilots and other service personnel did as they were ordered, terrified by the sight before them.

It did not take long for the soldiers to secure the area, and before long they were beginning to permeate through into the other areas of the carrier.

"Sir, the admiral..." Cox heard a woman's voice come over the carrier's PA system.

"Escort him up to the bridge," Hawke said without waiting for her to finish.

After a time the bridge's lift doors opened, and Cox turned to see who was entering the bridge. Four figures stood within the elevator car as the doors parted, one of them a member of *Ifrit*'s security team. The woman was being held under the arms by two tall soldiers, who stepped out of the lift and tossed her body down on the floor, bringing the bridge's body count up to five. She had been shot in the back of the head, her blonde hair wet, sticky and matted with the blood that had poured from the wound. He guessed she had attempted to get to the man whom the two soldiers were escorting.

Now on the bridge, the two soldiers stood to attention either side of the lift doors, presenting their rifles and making way for the last person to depart.

Zackaria strode down the long aisle towards Hawke, the commodore returning the laser pistol to the inside of his jacket. He was clothed in formal Imperial naval dress, the condition of his uniform verging on perfection: crease free and decorated to great spender. A long, blood red cloak rippled gently behind him as he walked, falling about a foot clear of the floor and fastened about the shoulders by a gold chain that ran just under his neck. Though surrounded by his enemies, he walked with calm down the bridge's central aisle, the soles of his dark gleaming shoes clopping on the floor as he went. They seemed to perfectly punctuate his entrance, being now the only sound besides the tense breathing of the crew.

Hawke remained where he was, waiting for the admiral to approach, whereupon he saluted.

Cox was shocked; even more so when the two men began to speak. The language was strange and he could not understand a single word, yet Hawke's command of the dialect appeared perfect. It rolled off his tongue effortlessly, and sounded nothing like the Imperial dialects he was expecting, even with the admiral's accent. And there was something else there, something that did not quite sound like normal human speech.

The two men spoke at length, Hawke detailing much of what he knew and what his plans were: they would take *Ifrit* to Phylent, draw *Griffin* into a false sense of security and then destroy it. When the ATAFs returned from their errand they would be met by *Ifrit* and the remains of *Griffin*, the former having arrived too late to save the carrier from its fate. The *Knights* would then return to *Ifrit,* giving the admiral everything: the ATAFs, the pilots and the means to study, reverse engineer and construct more. They would then be unstoppable; and finally Zackaria would be able to complete his Mission.

The discussion over, Hawke readdressed the bridge crew. "I have negotiated the surrender *Ifrit*. From here on out I alone will fall under the command of

Fleet Admiral Zackaria. The Empire no longer has need for any of you; you are all now redundant."

Heads looked up in shock, eyes darting from the two men that stood at the front of the bridge to the two black clad soldiers that marked the lift doors. Cox met many eyes as he looked to those knelt on the floor, and they all said the same thing: their worst fear was upon them, they were going die. Even if they could escape the bridge and make it down to the flight deck, there was no telling just how many soldiers would be waiting for them down there.

But for Cox, that was the last straw. He had to do something about this. He might not be able to save *Ifrit* or guarantee that the crew could get away from the enemy forces that surrounded them, but he would make certain that Hawke did not celebrate his victory here today.

Grasping the screwdriver that he had secreted in his hands when Hawke had ordered them all down on the ground, he ensured the shaft was fully exposed. Just like Hawke's neck. He started to build himself up; preparing to drive the tool into the man's throat; to rip it apart so that the man suffocated or drowned in blood or whatever would happen when he drove the implement home. And after a few moments of mental preparation, he was ready.

He made no sound as he moved. No heroic cry or final comment as he went at the commodore. He moved fluidly, as only one might under such circumstances, in one final attempt to bring about justice. He did not falter nor stumble, his leap from his knelt position towards Hawke verging on perfection.

The next few seconds became a blur of pain and confusion. It started with a solid grasp of the arm in which he held the small weapon. It was followed by a loud snapping noise, a spinning of his world, and ending a tremendous amount of pain, the screwdriver flying from his hand, its task unfulfilled. He felt himself crash against both a wall of the bridge and then the floor.

For a time his world was black. The dizziness then cleared and he came to, feeling total agony. He lifted his head as best he could, trying to will the stars away that were filling his vision. He couldn't move his legs; they were unresponsive and useless. Even lifting his head felt like a monumental task.

He fought to piece together what had happened to him...

As he had leapt up, the handle of the tool held tight in his hand, his heroic intents had been thwarted by Zackaria. Without a word the admiral had caught his outstretched arm about the wrist, as he drew back in preparation to plunge the implement into Hawke's neck. With one quick and powerful twist, he had broken the helmsman's arm and the screwdriver had tumbled from Cox's grasp. Zackaria had then spun the man around and *thrown him* in the direction he had been heading.

He remembered feeling the sensation of travelling through the air, but it was something he struggled with; for he had not travelled just a few feet with the throw, but the remaining width of the bridge itself. He had flown a distance of well over ten meters, his feet leaving the floor by several themselves. The height baffled him. He may have travelled much further, if the wall on the opposite side of the bridge had not halted his advance.

He couldn't believe what had just happened: *the man was over sixty years old!* And yet he had, with precious little effort, disarmed and then thrown him across the bridge, as if he were nothing more than a small animal.

Cox could not stand, nor move his legs, no matter how hard it tried. He became aware of a pair of black shoes in front of him, and turned two pleading eyes up to face *Ifrit*'s captain, imploring him to find mercy.

But the pleas passed straight through the man.

"Thank you for all your hard work over the years, Mr Cox," Hawke said, his face pitiless. "But your services are no longer required." He once again drew the laser pistol, pointed it at Cox's head, and pulled the trigger.

With the carrier under his command Zackaria ordered that the crew be killed and their bodies dumped out in space. There were to be no exceptions: prisoners would not be taken, lives would not be spared.

They fought valiantly, but *Ifrit*'s crew were no match for the invaders. The black clad soldiers slaughtered each and every one of them, showing no mercy as they followed their leader's orders to the letter. For Zackaria's command was what they adhered to; what they believed in; and what they would obey until the day they died.

XXI

— A Hard Truth to Accept —

After much searching around within the starport, the *Knights* had made very little progress in finding Barber.

"Something's happened to her," Dodds said to Estelle, who walked by his side. "She would have found us by now, we're not exactly being inconspicuous." Despite Parks' statement that the woman wouldn't be jumping up and down and waving her arms, they had reached the conclusion that Barber would have made herself known to them by this time. They continued to walk through the ranks of refugees, once again trying to spot that which they may have missed. Most of the refugees had refused to speak to them, and those that had spoken had been unwilling to help, wanting nothing more than to be left alone. A few had even made violent responses to the enquiries, either shouting and throwing things, or leaping up and taking a swing at the Confederation pilots.

"I think you're right," Estelle said. "But we can't leave until we find her. Keep looking and let me know as soon as you find out anything."

"Nothing on the upper floors?"

"No, everyone is down here. I think they're waiting to get out of here. But having said that I'm going to check again."

"Right," said Dodds and left Estelle to start off on another round of searching.

Chaz continued his own walk amongst the ranks of refugees. Those he passed were still not used to his presence, and acted as though he was an executioner, seeking out the next prisoner for the gallows. Many turned their eyes away.

Unlike his fellow *Knights* he had not spoken to anyone since arriving, having instead taken his time to pace the huddles, searching for just the right person to make contact with. Now he believed he had found them and stopped in front of a little boy who had been watching him the whole time. Compared to the others, the boy did not seem in the least perturbed by Chaz's presence; more curious. Sitting alone, he must have only been about six or seven years old, maybe younger.

Chaz crouched down in front of the boy, who still had not taken his eyes off him. Unlike so many of the others in the port, the boy did not pull back or try to hide himself, though many of those near him did, shuffling back and crushing up against one another in Chaz's presence. No one came to assist the little boy or take him away.

Chaz had been correct in his assumption that the boy was all alone, a heavily stuffed bag containing a few items of clothing sat next to him was his only apparent possession. What had become of his family and friends Chaz did not need to guess at. Nevertheless, the boy in front of him appeared to be quite brave and one of the few people who may offer a helpful response. Before all that, however, there was one small hurdle that needed to be overcome. Chaz stole a glance over his shoulder to see if his team mates were anywhere close by before he started talking.

"<Hello there. My name's Chaz. What's yours?>" he asked with a warm smile. He spoke in a near fluent Imperial dialect, keeping his voice calm and relaxed.

"<Ben,>" the boy said.

"<Nice to meet you, Ben. I'm looking for a friend of mine. I was hoping you might have seen her.>"

"<What's her name?>" Ben asked.

Chaz smiled to himself. It amused him that the boy was assuming that was all the information he would need. His mind wandered for a scarce few seconds. *I bet you're just like that*, he thought, before returning to the job in hand. "<Her name's Clare.>"

"<No, I don't know her,>" Ben said, with a shake of his head.

Chaz decided to supply some more information. "<She's a tall woman, with straight black hair, very pretty. She's about my age. She wasn't born in the Empire, she comes from...>"

"<The Confederation lady who was chasing the man?>" Ben interrupted.

"<That's her,>" Chaz said, still smiling.

"<She's dead.>"

Chaz's smile slipped. The little boy did not seem to notice or, more likely, could no longer feel sympathetic towards those suffering from loss, it being an all too common occurrence for him.

"<They put her in the hospital with the other man she killed when they had a fight together. They were shooting each other a lot,>" Ben added.

"<Thank you, Ben.>" Chaz stood up; he had all the information he needed.

Still wandering about, trying to find someone who might be able to help him, Dodds saw Chaz striding in his direction. As he approached Dodds noted a look of anger on his face and took a step backward. It was the same expression Chaz had worn when Parks had reassigned the five *Knights* to the Temper system. The man's fists were balled, his eyes, though narrowed, blazing. If the security guards on Xalan Orbital had shown reluctance in tackling Chaz back then, Dodds knew that right now it would be like confronting a fifteen-hundred-pound grizzly bear.

"What's happened?" Dodds asked as the big man strode up.

"Barber's dead," Chaz growled, not bothering to stop and causing Dodds to hurry along after him. "She's been taken to the infirmary."

"We should let the others know."

"Yes, you should," was the blunt reply.

Dodds stopped walking at the comment. For the few months Dodds had known him, he had found that Chaz was generally a very quiet character. Every now and again he was moody, but easy to get along with when you got on the right side of him, even if he did have almost nothing to say. Watching the man's back retreating past him Dodds figured that at this very moment there was no right side of Chaz to be on.

Under the circumstances he decided it would be best to do as Chaz had suggested and soon rounded up the other *Knights,* who then, after consulting a floor plan, made their way towards the port's medical unit.

"Sound proof," Dodds said as the doors to the infirmary swung closed behind the four men and women, dampening the sounds from the rest of the port.

"Probably to help the staff and the patients relax," Enrique said.

"You're sure he came in here?" Estelle said. She had almost lost her mind when Dodds had informed her that Chaz had headed off to the infirmary alone and without consulting her. Not that there had been very much to discuss.

"Like I said, he seemed rather keen to get here," Dodds said.

"See if you can lock the door," Estelle ordered. Dodds did as he was told and after studying a panel next to the door he succeeded in securing it. The little clicking sound told him that it was not a very sturdy lock, more of a deterrent than anything else.

The *Knights* moved down various corridors in their search for Chaz and Barber, the whole place looking like a small hospital. They searched every waiting and examination room they came to, but found them empty, without any sign of their missing wingmate or the woman they had arrived at the station to meet. They then came to the mortuary.

"Are you okay?" Enrique said to Kelly as they approached the mortuary. Dodds too, had noticed that she had not spoken to anyone whilst looking for Barber, and seemed to be in a world of her own.

"I'm fine, just a bit distracted," Kelly said.

"Sure?"

"Yes. It's nothing," she said after a moment's hesitation.

"You don't have to come in if you don't want to," Dodds said, aware that Kelly was not good with dead bodies. No matter how many she saw she could never get used to them, absurd visions and fears filling her head. The thought of walking into a morgue, knowing it to contain at least one body already, couldn't have been sitting too comfortably with her.

"No, we stay together," Estelle interjected, before she heaved the heavy door of the mortuary open, revealing the scene within to all. There, standing over a gurney with his back to them, was Chaz. A sheet, stained with blood, lay on the floor at the foot of the table.

Estelle stopped just inside the doorway, her arms folded across her chest, displeasure written all over her face. Dodds took in the scene. Estelle was used to having Dodds and Enrique challenging her authority from time to time, but they did at least either fall back into line or back down. Chaz on the other hand had completely ignored her order to inform her of any developments in the search for Barber and not to take any action without

THE HONOUR OF THE KNIGHTS

first consulting her. She would not stand for his insubordination.

"Lieutenant Koonan, what the hell think you're doing?" Estelle asked, scowling at his back. Chaz did not turn around or react at all. Estelle glowered; now the man was ignoring her. "Lieutenant?" she said again. Chaz neither moved from where he stood, nor made any other sign to acknowledge her presence.

Dodds walked forward and came to stand next to Chaz, Estelle and Enrique following behind him. He looked down at the woman lying on the gurney, her eyes still open, dried blood staining her mouth and chin, her face very pale. Chaz's eyes were filled with a mixture of anger and sadness as he continued to stare down at the woman, his fists still clenched into tight balls by his sides.

Dodds looked around and saw that Kelly had taken few steps forward, making little effort to cross the threshold of the mortuary doorway. She gave him a look of deep concern as her eyes shifted from Barber to Chaz.

After a few moments one of Chaz's hands left his side. Two fingers found their way to the woman's eyes and gently closed her eyelids.

"Does she have the data card?" Estelle asked.

Chaz continued to say nothing, and instead ran his fingers across Barber's cheek. It was as if he was saying goodbye.

Dodds saw Estelle mouth several curses, then, "We don't have time for this."

Seeing the man as being disinterested in Estelle's questioning, Dodds once more took the initiative and reached forward to investigate Barber's jacket. Chaz caught him tight about the wrist as he took hold of the zipper.

"I'll do it," he said in a cold voice, without taking his eyes off Barber's face.

Dodds looked up at the big man, knowing that he would not be able to free his wrist from such a solid grasp. He released his grip on the zipper. Chaz took it instead and undid the dead woman's jacket, exposing the white vest she wore underneath. It was soaked with blood and torn in places where it had been slashed. Beneath the ripped material, crimson spots of congealed blood, gathered around lacerated white flesh, were quite visible. They looked like stab wounds. Dodds was reminded of Dean's wounds, as the man had lain dying on his parents' couch.

Chaz started to search the inner pockets of the jacket as the others looked on. After he failed to find anything, he checked the outer ones. Then those of her trousers. His searching started to become more urgent as he turned out more and more pockets and did not find what he was looking for. He then pulled off her boots, though from the way they were so tightly laced it was doubtful he'd find anything there. Whoever had brought the woman in here had decided to dump her body on the first available trolley and leave it there. The boots turned out to be empty and there was nothing in the socks either.

"What's wrong?" Estelle asked as Chaz let an empty boot fall to the floor.

"Isn't it obvious? I can't find the card," Chaz said, acknowledging his commanding officer for the first time since entering the morgue. He began to dump more items on the floor and the gurney as his search continued.

Knowing that his help was not wanted Dodds left the others to continue sorting through Barber's possessions and pulled back a sheet that was covering a body on another gurney, opposite that of Barber's.

"Chaz, how did she die?" Dodds asked, looking down into the scar riddled face of the dead man he had uncovered.

There was a pause, then, "A man killed her," he said, his voice bitter.

"This man?" Dodds asked, indicating the body. Chaz and the other three *Knights* glanced around, seeing the exposed body with its long coat and clothes even more bloodstained than Barber's vest.

"She killed him at the same time. That's all I know," Chaz said.

The answer was good enough for Dodds. "This is our man. This is the guy who blew up *Cardinal*." He began to rifle through the pockets of the man on the table. Enrique and Estelle hurried over to join him in his quest to locate the data card, but after a thorough search they failed to locate anything. Just as Chaz had done they also checked boots, socks and other possible hiding places, to no avail.

Kelly caught Chaz's eye as she stood out of the way, still quite unnerved by the dead bodies. He gave her a look that emphasised his utter frustration.

"Want me to take a look?" she offered, although she asked only out of politeness and courtesy, and not because she wanted to be involved. She regretted it seconds later when Chaz walked back from the body.

"Go ahead," he gestured at Barber's body.

Kelly approached and began her own search, rechecking everywhere that Chaz had already, though much more gingerly and with added caution. Whenever confronted with a dead body she couldn't help but think that at any moment the eyes would fly open and stare straight at her, or that a sick smile would crawl up the face, the grin directed at and meant for her, or that a cold, dead hand would shoot out and grab her wrist...

She shook the images from her head and tried not to think about it. Dead people did not miraculously come back to life. Once dead, they stayed dead.

Dodds, Estelle and Enrique were on the verge of giving up with their own task, preparing to accept that Barber was in possession of the card, and not the man whom they searched.

"Do you think someone else might have taken it from her?" Dodds said.

"Well they didn't take anything else," Estelle said, nodding toward the numerous belongings Chaz had removed from the woman. "If they couldn't be bothered to take her gun, then why would they bother with something like that?"

"Maybe she's hidden it in some secret compartment? How carefully did you check her boots? There might be a false bottom or heel?" Dodds looked over at Chaz.

"There are no hidden compartments in her boots," Chaz answered.

"Gloves? She's a spy, after all, so there's bound to be at least one secret hiding place..."

"There aren't any," Chaz said through gritted teeth.

"Maybe it's in the lining of her jacket? Or around the collar? Could even be tucked into her bra..."

"Can it, Dodds," Estelle said, patting at the raider's long coat.

"You sure she's not just holding it in her hand?" Enrique asked.

Dodds gave him a look of disdain.

"No, seriously," Enrique said.

"She *is* holding something," Kelly said. She was staring at Barber's right hand that, unlike the left, was closed up. Dodds and Estelle left the raider's body and came to stand by Barber once more.

Dodds took the woman's hand and inspected it. "Looks like plastic." He tried to prise her hand open, but found it so stiff as to be unable to even move one finger. After a while he was able to push his own little finger between the gap in Barber's grip and poked the object out. It fell and bounced gently on the floor. He retrieved it and held it up for the others to see.

"What is it?" Estelle asked.

"Some kind of tiny bottle," Dodds said, turning the clear container in his fingers. It felt slimy in his grasp and he noticed a small amount of fluid still clung to the inside. Estelle took it from him, almost dropping it as it slipped between her fingers.

"It's... it's lubricant," she said, sounding more than a little confused.

"Ah ha! I've got it!" Enrique said, the four others turning around to the man. "My grandfather once told me that spies sometimes don't keep really important stuff directly on them; not in their clothes anyway, it's too risky. So, instead, they'll do what drug mules used to do and..."

He stopped talking. Dodds noted the horrified looks on Kelly and Estelle's faces, a mirror for his own. The anger had left Chaz's eyes, his face had fallen. Dodds' eyes went back to Barber as Enrique solved the mystery of the card's location.

"So basically she's swallowed it. It's inside her." The enthusiastic tone was gone.

At the words Kelly's eyes grew wide and she yanked her hands from where they had been worming their way into pockets and feeling the lining of Barber's jacket. She hurried backwards, putting distance between herself and the gurney.

Dodds found he was unable to tear his eyes away from Barber's stomach. "I really, really wish I hadn't gotten out of bed this morning," he said.

Natalia Grace had, over the course of the last three weeks, suffered from fitful dreams, fraught with terrible memories of what she had borne witness to. Images of packed Imperial troop transports sweeping over crumbling and almost defenceless cities haunted her vision. She found herself trapped on their streets, all alone.

The transports landed and started to deploy their cargo: dozens of heavily armed black clad soldiers, carrying all manner of weaponry. The Enemy. They turned to look at her. Fingers pointed. Natalia ran.

She ran as fast as she could, but the ground she covered was minimal, as if her legs were moving in slow motion. She looked behind herself as she tried to escape, seeing the city now gone and the black suits of the Enemy swarming behind her like so many thousand scurrying black ants, spread out across a wide open plain that went on forever to the horizon, with nowhere to hide.

Amongst the sea of black shone innumerable pairs of ruby-red oval eyes, set into the grooves of helmets, the only window into what resided within. She tried harder to run, but her legs moved as if she were pulling them through treacle. She fell down, trying with all her might to crawl herself forward, but finding herself as immobile as ever.

The ranks of black suits began to close in round her, their faces hidden behind their ominous masks. She looked around for another way to escape, turning to the sky, then the ground beneath, but seeing nothing save for the swells of black, glints of knives, and glow of digital weapon counters.

Hands caught her upper arms, then her fore arms, then her legs, pinning her to the ground. The suffocating black enclosed her, muzzles of rifles pushed into her face, mixed with flashes of white from emblems borne on the suit. Her attackers spoke not one word as they prepared to deal her fate.

Natalia shivered in her stasis capsule, so intense were her dreams. But they did not plague her forever and soon the darkness departed, allowing the woman to return to a peaceful, undisturbed sleep; the nightmare having lifted like a veil, as if moving on to trouble another.

Within a small corridor of Arlos starport, interconnecting an airlock, a dozing man awoke as he heard the door's control panel emit a short bleep. He looked up to see the red light that had once indicated that the door was locked had now changed to green. He blinked himself further awake just as the door slid open, and his heart almost stopped as he saw his worst nightmare step on through.

Clad in black suits, helmets covering their heads and faces, the six new arrivals to the port paused for but a moment to assess their surroundings.

Bright ruby-red eyes fell on the man sitting on the floor, only feet from where they now stood. They drew their weapons.

The man started to struggle to his feet, his eyes wide as saucers. A scream lodged itself in his throat, as if it itself was unwilling to expose itself to the invaders. A shotgun levelled itself at him. There was a sound of thunder and tremendous pain ripped through his chest. He toppled backward and gasped as the pain mixed with shock and disbelief. He turned a pleading expression to the ruby-red eyes, begging them to spare his life. He tried to speak, but the scream was still blocking his throat. A thin gasp was all that was permitted to pass.

He had been safe here! They had all been safe here! Just a few more hours and he could have gotten away! He should have made a bigger effort to get on that last ship out! It wasn't fair! Why him? Just a few more hours...

A second round finished him, and as his vision faded, he saw the invaders start forward, preparing to deal the same fate, via a multitude of different weapons, to the other refugees sharing the corridor. They would cut down everyone that stood before them, taking no prisoners and sparing no lives.

"We're going to have to cut her open," Estelle said, unable to wrench her eyes away from Barber's face. The thought was already starting to turn her stomach. She turned to Kelly who was still backing off, a hand on her own stomach, as if attempting to quell the churning within. Their eyes met.

"I'll keep watch," Kelly said and darted out of the mortuary without waiting for any acknowledgement from her commanding officer.

"I'll go with her," Enrique volunteered, before he too bolted out the room after Kelly, leaving Estelle, Dodds and Chaz standing over the body.

"Right... right," Estelle said, snapping out of her trance. Though she had tried to deny it, Enrique was right. All the evidence was there right in front of her. The thing they had come for was inside the dead woman lying on the gurney and there was only one way they were going to get it out. She turned away and began looking around the mortuary. She found what she was searching for at one end of the room. Her fingers brushed over a number of different stainless steel medical implements before they closed around the one she needed. Grasping it firmly in her hand she returned to the two men.

"No!" Dodds said in response to the question that did not need asking.

Estelle thrust the scalpel towards him, ignoring his protest. "Dodds..." Estelle said, her voice a little shaky.

"No! No way!" he said again, retreating to the other side of the gurney, putting the dead woman between the two of them. He pointed to the scalpel. "And certainly not with *that*, that archaic tool! Isn't there a laser cutter?"

"No, we have to use this." She heard it come almost like an apology.

"Why? Cutters are good enough for organs..."

"It could damage the card. Now, come on Dodds." She made to walk around the gurney.

"No, Estelle, stay there! No, Estelle, stay! You'll have to do it. I can't." His voice was shaking, his face showing unmistakable signs of distress.

"I'm not doing it," Estelle said.

"Why not?"

"Because I'm your superior and... and I'm ordering you to."

Dodds' distressed expression disappeared for a fraction of a second, to be replaced by one of disbelief. "You're *ordering* me to?" he said, incredulously.

"Yes, Dodds, I'm ordering you too." Her voice was shaking again, as was the scalpel she held. She could see part of her own face reflected in it. It did not look confident.

Dodds gave a tiny, humourless chuckle. "Well, then I guess I'm going to have to disobey that order, Lieutenant."

"Dodds!"

"What are you going to do about it, Estelle?" Dodds said, throwing his hands up into the air. "File a report that said I refused to cut open a dead woman, upon your orders, because I was too scared? In that case you'd better prepare to add yourself, as well as Kelly and Enrique, to that list."

Estelle said nothing, not blaming Dodds for refusing to do as she said. She had merely chosen to flex her muscles as the commanding officer and delegate an undesirable duty on to another. The idea of cutting open the woman lying on the table was no more appealing to her than any of them. But if she could pass on the responsibility... She looked to the last person in the room that had not yet expressed an objection to the task.

"Chaz?" The big man looked around at her, his focus having still been on Barber, his expression remorseful. "You were keen to get here and get this done."

The scalpel hovered in front of him, still held in Estelle's hand, the light catching it in places as the woman's hand shook. Chaz looked once again to Barber and then back again to the scalpel, before he plucked it from Estelle's grasp.

Yes, he had been keen to get here, but not to do this. He had not believed what the little boy, Ben, had told him. He had to see the truth for himself. Even now, with the evidence lying in front of him, it was difficult for him to believe. He looked again at Barber's peaceful face and thought back over the memories.

You were just doing your job, he thought to himself, before he buried his sorrow deep within him.

Dodds and Estelle gave one another a worried look as the big man held the scalpel, acknowledging neither of them. He stood with his eyes focused on Barber's face, as if stuck in his own world.

"Chaz?" Dodds prompted him after a time.

"Just give me a second, okay?" Chaz said in a quiet voice.

"Whenever you're ready," Estelle said.

Sweeping into the central hall the six black clad soldiers were given the same reception as they had in the airlock corridor. Even though the refugees here had had some forewarning of what was to come, hearing the gunfire and cries of the earlier victims, most were still quite unprepared. The screams and shouting began at the first sighting of the black suits and, as one, people rose and tried to escape. Even before the soldiers began their slaughter there were casualties: limbs were tangled, bones were snapped, and heads were crushed in the stampede.

Their weapons already drawn the lead soldiers fired upon those immediately in front of them, bursts of plasma bolts burning through clothes and ripping into flesh, repeated hits opening up gaping wounds and spilling blood. Bullets performed to a lesser degree, but were no less accurate as they were deadly. In the space of just a few seconds the area around the soldiers was splattered with blood, torn clothing and burnt lumps of flesh that had been torn from their victims.

Behind the front row two other soldiers each pulled a grenade and threw them deep into the crowd. The explosions had their desired effect of killing many, maiming others and causing even greater panic.

With their dramatic entrance over the soldiers advanced after their prey. No one was to be spared: infants, children, men, women and the elderly were all fair game. There was no return fire from any of the refugees, not even the slightest attempt to defend themselves; the men and women well aware of the futility of such actions.

Okay, you've had a good run. Ten years of service, a couple of major operations; one colossal one. You've nearly been killed, let's see, three or four times. Today may as well count for another ten. Plenty to talk about and inspire others with. Could probably spin out two or three books from it. I think I deserve to take the rest of my life off now. At least I don't have to witness the amateur surgery. Thank God for small mercies...

Kelly sat on the floor, hugging her knees and reminiscing over the past.

"You okay, Mouse?" Enrique said.

"Please don't call me that."

"They'll be done soon. Just try not to think about it."

"Then stop bringing it up."

In their bid to get away from the goings-on in the morgue, the two had retreated back to the main entrance to the medical unit, Enrique having taken point at the door.

"Sorry," Enrique said, then, "What's wrong?"

Kelly saw him looking at her with concern. She had been rubbing at the side of her head. "My head still hurts," she said.

Enrique left his post at the door and knelt down beside his friend. "Want me to look?"

"Yeah, see if you can see anything. Here," Kelly indicated to the side of her head that she had knocked in the cockpit. Enrique parted her brown hair in the area she had shown him, looking for signs of trauma. She was not entire sure what he should be looking for as she had not found anything herself; no cuts and no bleeding, although there might be a bruise. He persevered until she winced and turned her head around to escape his exploring fingers, taking hold of one of his hands with hers.

"Sorry," he said once more, as she looked around to face him.

"Anything?"

"Nothing on the surface. You might have bruised your brain."

Kelly smiled and let out a chuckle. It sounded funny. Enrique smiled too.

For a moment they both became aware of how close they were to one another, their hands holding on to one another's. They stayed motionless for a few moments looking into one another's eyes, neither speaking.

"Enrique, I think you should be keeping your eyes on the *door*," she said after a while, breaking their gaze and turning away to look down the corridor in the direction of the morgue. Enrique released her hand and returned to his post.

"I don't know about you, but I just want to get out of here," Kelly said. "This day has been too long. Do you think they'll be done soon?"

Enrique didn't answer her.

She looked up to see him staring fixated out the door's small oval window. "Enrique?"

"People are moving," Enrique said. He then swore loudly.

"What?"

"We've got company!" The man had frozen.

"What's going on?" Kelly asked, starting to get to her feet so she could see for herself.

"Don't move," Enrique hissed, waving her back down. He remained where he was for a few more moments before he pulled back from the door and grabbed Kelly's hand, hauling her up off the floor.

"Enrique, what's happening?"

"Soldiers!"

"What?" Kelly said as he dragged her down the corridors and back towards the morgue. She tried to stop him pulling her in its direction, but he was holding her hand tight. "I'm not going back in there!"

"Given the choice, I don't think you'd prefer to be out there either!"

Enrique answered as they continued running. Moments later they reached their destination.

"Imperial soldiers!" Enrique shouted, as he and Kelly sprinted in through the mortuary doorway.

Kelly saw her other three companions, still standing around Barber's body, jerk around. Chaz was holding something small and silver. It appeared to be a scalpel.

"What?" Dodds said.

Enrique gave Kelly a look that said he was tired of that question. "Imperial soldiers have just entered the port!" he panted. "They're armed and firing on the refugees! One is coming this way!"

"Imperial soldiers?" Chaz said. "You're sure?"

"Positive," Enrique said. "Saw them through the window. He looked straight at me. I'm not sure if he saw me, but they were..."

"What are they wearing?" Chaz demanded, not waiting for Enrique to finish.

"Huh?"

"Enrique, *what are they wearing*?" the big man raised his voice.

Recovering her breath, Kelly saw something that made her feel the most unsettled she had all day: it was the look on Chaz's face. It was a panicked expression. The man was worried. Very worried.

"Black uniforms," Enrique said. "Completely black, with these bright red visors or eyes, and..."

"Hide!" Chaz said, putting the scalpel down on Barber's belly, gathering up the sheet and hurling it back over her body.

"But, there are five of us..." Estelle started, sounding confident that all of them would be able to handle the new threat.

"Believe me, Lieutenant, we should hide," Chaz said, in a grim voice.

Dodds glanced around the mortuary, before turning back to Chaz incredulously. "Where?!"

XII

— Dead Man Walking —

P ushing open the last examination room door before he came to the mortuary, the black clad soldier scanned the interior from the entrance, keeping his shotgun raised. After confirming there was no immediate opposition he stalked into the room, to carry out a closer inspection. He checked under the examination table, up against the wall; within the wall high storage cabinet; and then above him, looking for air vents and other out of the way hiding places. Just like the other rooms this one was empty, no one seeming to having fled in here.

He backed out of the room, spinning around as he stepped back through the entrance, anticipating an attack from the corridor. None came. He then started towards the mortuary. He was confident that somewhere in the medical unit he would find his prey. The doors to the medical unit itself had been locked from the inside, though a single shot to the external control panel from his pistol had been enough to grant him access.

The sight that greeted the soldier as he opened the door to the morgue was nothing out of the ordinary. Six bodies, covered in sheets, lay on gurneys lining the walls. Two were bloodstained.

Keeping his shotgun raised, he inched through the door, halting as more details of the inside of the mortuary came into view. Several roused his suspicions: the first was the presence of five objects that resembled propulsion packs, bundled into a corner next to a locker; the second, a small pile of random items, including two pairs of boots and socks, stuffed under one of the blood stained gurneys; and the third, a round reflective object resting under another. It looked like a flight helmet. Still, he saw no one.

He turned his attention to the bodies on the gurneys, moving to the one with the many items deposited beneath it; the one closest to the door. He reached down and snatched aside the linen cover, momentarily distracted by a tinkling sound as he did so. Discovering the source of the noise to be nothing more than a small surgical instrument, he trained his weapon back on the body on the trolley. The woman's eyes were closed, her skin pale. Her face seemed to lack warmth. He studied her for a moment, searching for signs of life, before then nudging the face with the barrel of his gun. There was no reaction; the woman was indeed dead. Even so, he would check the others. He circled around the woman's gurney, coming to stand by the next in the row. Shotgun still poised, he extended a hand to remove the pure white sheet...

A bumping from a locker at the far end caused him to swing around and he returned his outstretched hand to beneath the shotgun, steadying it in preparation to tackle the threat. The sound appeared to have come from the same locker the propulsion packs had been dumped next to. The locker, however, now stood still and silent. He nonetheless watched it closely. Moments later there was another sudden bumping sound, followed by a soft groaning.

He paced forward, keeping his weapon trained on the locker the whole time, ready to counter any attack that might come from within. He took up a ready position in front of the door and flung it open, his hand flying back to steady his shotgun as he saw the figure hiding within lunge forward to attack him.

He discharged the shotgun at point blank range, sending the man back into the locker from whence he came. The man crumpled down like a puppet that had just had its strings cut, stiff limbs dropping. The soldier kept his eyes on the man, preparing to fire once more if there was another attempt to attack him, or if the first shot had not done its job of downing his opponent.

But the man made no further movements, and the soldier bent down over the body to examine it. Like that of the woman he had seen lying on the gurney, the man's skin was pale and there were no signs of respiration, the blank eyes already staring ahead. He realised that his attacker had been dead all along, and that he had just shot a corpse. With the deception uncovered, he rose and turned back just in time to face a new attacker.

* * *

Dodds lunged for the shotgun the black suited invader still held tight in one hand, attempting to disarm him, just as the soldier made to fire the weapon once more. With the element of surprise on his side Dodds succeeded in directing the shotgun into the air, where it discharged harmlessly into the ceiling. This it did several more times as the pair tussled, before the soldier responded to Dodds' attempt to separate him from his weapon by releasing his grip on the shotgun and catching the young pilot with a powerful swing of his fist across the face.

Dodds fell to the ground, disorientated by the blow, his vision filling with stars. As he tried to make sense of his world, he heard a short, sharp click, followed by the clatter of several spent shell cases bouncing on the floor close to him. The soldier had begun reloading his weapon, the rapid clicking of fresh shells slotting into place making clear warnings of what was to come.

Dodds was just starting to his feet when he heard the soldier load the seventh and final shell, snap the gun shut, and then cock it. Time seemed to slow. He looked up into the bright red eyes of the eerie black helmet as the shotgun was swung in his direction. A moment later he found himself staring down the barrel.

He heard a bang, followed by a grunt. The shotgun fell away and the soldier stumbled backward. Three further explosions followed, accompanied by a number of cries of pain from behind the black helmet, before the solider fell backward and crashed down on to the floor. Dodds saw blood glistening on the black suit as it began to pour from wounds and on to the floor, creating a small pool. Despite appearances otherwise the soldier was clearly not wearing any form of body armour, and the suit had provided him with little protection.

Dodds looked around to see Estelle, panting and steadying a pistol in both hands. He recognised it as the gun that had belonged to Barber and remembered Chaz removing it from its holster inside the woman's jacket, during his search for the data card. Estelle must have picked it up during the scramble to hide. She looked down at him as the others emerged from their hurried and uninspiring hiding places. Her eyes held a mixture of feelings; his, only an apology.

● ● ●

As Enrique had relayed the warning of the soldier's impending arrival to the mortuary the *Knights* had wrenched off their propulsion packs and hidden beneath the sheets of the spare gurneys, feigning their own deaths. Their packs had been thrown into a corner, next to a locker, and each of their flight helmets dropped under their respective gurneys. There had only been four empty trolleys, and Chaz had pulled the raider's body off his table and pushed him into the locker. Though there had been no time to hide any evidence of their recent activities, Dodds, Estelle, Kelly and Enrique had hoped that the soldier would take one look around and then leave; though, from his behaviour, Chaz seemed to have expected otherwise. Their saving grace had come in the form of the raider Chaz had put in the locker. His hurried bundling of the man's body into the storage cabinet had resulted in it crumpling down, knocking against the insides as it did so. The soldier had gone on to mistake the corpse's sliding for someone trying to hide themselves away.

"We've got to get out of here," Chaz said, throwing off his sheet. He glanced in the direction of the fallen soldier lying still on the floor, on top of the body of the raider. He hesitated, for a time caught up an internal debate as to which task he should be attending to first. He then headed back over to the gurney on which Barber's body rested, snatching up the scalpel from where it lay on the floor as he went.

The jacket already undone, he used the scalpel to cut apart Barber's blood stained vest, but stopped short of cutting into her flesh. He once again stared down at Barber's smooth white skin, finding it too hard to carry through the task laid before him. He felt how cold she was as his fingers brushed her stomach.

"Chaz," Estelle started again, fiddling with the pistol she still held. "If you can't do it..."

"I can. Just give me a second," he answered.

"... I can do it instead," Estelle finished.

"I SAID GIVE ME A DAMN SECOND!" Chaz shouted back in frustration at his pending task. He stood breathing for a while, concentrating hard and searching for the will to begin. After just a few seconds of mental preparation he found it, and immediately plunged the scalpel into Barber's belly. He began cutting downwards, working fast and making jagged sawing actions with the blade as he went. The world around him seemed to disappear. He heard nothing and saw nothing but the knife; almost slipping into a trance.

"I'm sorry," he said under his breath. "I'm so sorry."

"Hey, you okay?" Enrique asked as Dodds struggled to his feet.

"Yeah," Dodds said, even though he was not so sure.

"Your face is really bruised," Kelly said.

Dodds touched the side of his face, feeling it hot and a little swollen. The power of the blow had been tremendous and he found himself amazed that the force had bowled him over. He was counting himself lucky that he had not been knocked out. He recalled during his struggle with the soldier over the shotgun that his feet had almost been lifted off the floor.

He looked over to where Estelle and Chaz were standing over the gurney. Chaz's hands were already covered in blood and, though she was overseeing the task, he could tell that Estelle was fighting the urge to turn away. Chaz's eyes appeared to be glazed over as he drove the knife deeper.

Dodds found himself compelled to investigate his opponent and wandered over to the soldier's unmoving body. The man still held the shotgun in one hand and Dodds kicked it away before he squatted down. He noted that the soldier's suit, which he had originally mistaken to have been a construct of ceramics, was in fact composed of little else but leather. It was thicker in some areas than others, extra smooth, hardened padding on the shoulders, elbows, knee caps and other parts of the body, giving the impression of armour plating. The texture varied in places, most often around where one part of the plates joined to another, as well as around joints.

"What are you doing?" Kelly asked in a suspicious voice.

"I want to see what this bastard looks like," Dodds said, eager to see what lay beneath that ominous looking black helmet. It was round in shape and all encompassing, betraying none of the wearer's appearance to the world outside. Two tubes and a thin black cable ran off the back, feeding into the main suit. It looked as though the tubes existed to aid with respiration, although since Dodds had never seen anything like it before they could have existed for any purpose. He found they were all easily unclipped and, after doing so, slipped the helmet off the soldier's head.

"Wow," Kelly said, drawing closer.

Dodds could not say what he had been expecting to find beneath the mask, but he had not anticipated this: the peaceful looking face of the man that he looked upon was - in a word - beautiful. The man's skin was flawless, with no moles, scars or even any signs of stubble present anywhere; not even the tiniest of cuts or imperfections. The skin was so smooth and healthy looking that the man could well have been wearing make-up. The man was dark skinned, the hair on the top of his head short and almost unbelievably uniform in length. He looked more like a model than a soldier.

"What's that?" Enrique asked, drawing Dodds and Kelly away from the man's face. On the left breast of the soldier's suit was a white emblem unlike anything they had seen before: contained within a circle was an outline of a man holding a spear in front of him. Both of the man's hands gripped the shaft of the weapon, his left higher up the shaft than the right. The spear was set at a shallow angle, the tip pointing to the top left of the circle. A sash, tied at the top of the shaft just below the point, curled its way around the man's body. The man himself was bald and appeared to be naked, apart from where the sash preserved his modesty; though the man was depicted more or less from the waist up so it was difficult to tell.

Dodds stared at the emblem for a moment and then ran his fingers over it feeling the raised outlines of the image.

"That's not an Imperial insignia I recognise," Enrique said, his own fingers working over the emblem.

"No, I've never seen that one before either," Kelly added.

Neither had Dodds. Like most he was more accustomed to the noisy Imperial Coat of Arms, being a clutter of swords, laurels, felines and just about anything else the designer had been able to cram into the space the design afforded. This symbol by contrast was a lot simpler than that, though not as simple as the designs of the CSN, UNF, or indeed the INF themselves, those being composed of nothing more than the disjunction of a few basic shapes.

"There's another one on his right arm," Dodds said, comparing it to the first and discovering them to be identical. He looked over at the helmet he had removed from the man, but discovered that it was devoid of any such markings. He peeked inside, unsurprised to discover its main purpose being to serve as protection for the wearer's head. He noted the eye sockets within, the insides being clear unlike the red exterior. Two circular grilles on each side at ear level appeared to aid hearing. What looked like a small inset, unmarked button resided on the left temple. He put the helmet back down, more intrigued with the strange white pictorial image on the suit.

As he and Enrique continued to try and make sense of the emblem, Kelly reached down to the man's right leg and removed the weapon holstered there.

"What you got there?" Enrique asked the small woman.

"Think it's a plasma pistol," she said wandering back towards Estelle and Chaz, turning it around in her hand as she examined it. "Looks like a high power version." There was a low, high-pitched whine as she switched it on, a small digital counter on the side lighting up to display the number of shots remaining in the energy capsule. "Got a full clip too."

"*Careful!*"

It was Chaz. Dodds looked over to see that the sound had broken his concentration and that he had stopped cutting, turning his attention from Barber's stomach to where Kelly stood holding the gun. The big man's hands were even more blood sodden now, covered up to the wrists. He was looking at Kelly with an irritated expression on his face.

"What are you two doing?" he asked of Dodds and Enrique, who were still knelt over the unmoving body of the invader.

"Just taking a look," Dodds said.

"Then make sure he's actually dead!" Chaz said.

"Huh?" Enrique said. He met Dodds' eyes.

That was an odd thing to say. Dodds glanced about to see all eyes were on Chaz, the three other *Knights*, like himself, a little bewildered by his strange comment.

"What did you say?" Kelly said.

Just as Dodds was about to press Chaz further with a question of his own, a strange noise beside him drew him back to the body. Something clattered, bounced and then rolled along the floor. It was followed by another very similar sound and this time the "something" rolled into his fingers. Looking down he saw a bullet. Dodds picked it up, and discovered it to be wet and sticky as he rolled it around between his fingers. The bullet, just like his fingers now were, was covered in blood. His eyes followed the faint splotches of blood on the floor from where he had retrieved it, tracing them back to the soldier's body.

"What the hell..." Dodds said.

"Oh my God! Dodds!" Enrique cried.

Dodds looked back in time to see the eyes of the soldier fly open. The very next moment, and with incredible speed, a hand shot up and grabbed him tight around the throat. Dodds choked as the soldier easily got to his feet, still maintaining a tight hold on him, even as Dodds tugged against the hand holding him.

The soldier's other hand fumbled about his right leg, closing several times around nothing as he tried to locate his missing gun. Realising it had been taken from him, he looked about until he spotted it in the hands of Kelly. He also caught sight of his shotgun, hidden beneath a gurney where Dodds had kicked it.

With minimal effort he threw Dodds from him, attempting to knock down the small woman that was staring open mouthed at the unfolding scene. The woman reacted much faster to the incoming body than she had to the incoming Imperial fighter earlier that day, and Dodds crashed to the floor, skidding along past where Estelle and Chaz stood over Barber's gurney, still trying to discover the whereabouts of the data card.

Enrique saw Dodds land, roll and then remain still before he turned back to face the man who had just got back on his feet. He raised his guard.

With one of his opponents out of the way, the soldier turned his attention to Enrique, the blonde haired man now the only thing that stood between him and his armaments. Weaponless, but not altogether outnumbered, the soldier fell back on his fists.

Enrique avoided the first blow, as well as the follow up, before returning three of his own into his opponent's face. He held back none of his power as he struck the man, the blows he dealt enough to floor many of those he had sparred against in the past few years, almost certainly knocking them out.

The combination over he hopped back, only to see that his opponent was still standing, the strikes not having had the effect that he desired. No blood, no sweat, not so much as even a grunt. Nothing. The soldier had not so much as even reeled from the blows. Enrique suddenly felt as though he were a featherweight boxer pitched against a super-heavyweight.

It was then that he noticed just how big and tall the soldier actually was. It seemed that even Dodds, who had tackled him earlier, had not found the time to appreciate the height of the man. He was just as big as Chaz and also as stocky, but with something else added. Enrique had sparred with Chaz many times and, on more than one occasion, the big man had called time outs when Enrique took it too far. Enrique knew there would be no such call here, however; not because the pair were fighting for their lives, but simply because the soldier did not need one.

The soldier once again swung at him, as if nothing had happened. He managed to parry the attack, but failed to land his own counter attack. The two then engaged in a more serious fight, fists flying, legs attempting to connect kicks, grapples made and broken. Enrique's face betrayed his situation, stunned at the fact that the soldier was still standing. He knew he was not going to be able to hold off the soldier for very long.

"Estelle, shoot him!" he called, ducking under a swing and looking to his wing commander for assistance.

"I can't, it's empty!" Estelle shouted back. She looked back at the clutter of items next to the gurney, unable to recall seeing any more magazines; although they might be in there somewhere. She did the only thing she could think of: with all her might she threw the pistol at the soldier's head. It missed.

"Thanks!" Enrique said as the gun bounced off the wall and clattered to the floor.

The soldier caught Enrique's leg as he attempted to deliver a kick to him, tipping Enrique backward. He crashed into the gurney behind him, overturning the metal trolley and causing it to smash onto its side.

Estelle ran, seeing the shotgun exposed and anticipating the soldier's next move. Reaching it first she kicked it further back up the room before then attempting to take the man on herself, hoping to give Enrique a chance to get back to his feet.

Their plight had not gone unnoticed by Chaz, who was working faster than ever now that the urgency of the situation had reached new heights. Just as he thought he wasn't going to find anything, his fingers closed around something small, solid and cylindrical. Drawing it out and wiping away blood, he discovered it to be some sort of tiny plastic capsule. Inside was something thin and blue. That was good enough for him.

Stepping back from Barber's body he saw that the soldier was starting to overcome Enrique, the black clad invader landing two successive punches across the man's face. Enrique cried out with the blows and stumbled backward. Estelle was lying on the floor behind him, the wind knocked out of her from a boot to the stomach, her reward for coming to Enrique's aid.

"What are you standing there for?" he shouted at Kelly, who had remained rooted to the spot following the soldier's miraculous resurrection. She did not seem to even hear Chaz or be aware of anything until he wrenched the plasma pistol from her hands and shoved her aside, lining himself up with the soldier.

"Enrique, get down!" he barked at the man up front. Enrique did not need to be told twice and fell backward, away from his enemy.

Chaz proceeded to fire the pistol three times: the first bolt struck the soldier square in the face; the second tore straight through his right temple; the third shot struck the soldier in the forehead, almost taking the top of his skull off. The man's lifeless body tottered for a fraction of a second before it slumped down on to the floor.

Chaz strode forward, ignoring everyone else and knelt over the body, keeping the pistol trained on it the whole time. After some inspection he was satisfied that the soldier was now dead. He then started looting the man's suit, pulling out all of the various items that were contained within and about it.

Dodds pulled himself to his feet once more, his back sore from the landing. Enrique flipped over and started to stand, moving to help Estelle who was still trying to draw breath. He caught Dodds' eye as he did so, glancing at Chaz and then back again, wanting to know, as Dodds, the same thing: *Where the hell did he learn to fire a gun like that?*

His short known team mate had handled the firearm as if it was second nature to him; as though he had used it every single day for years and years. Whilst Estelle had held Barber's pistol as though it burned her hand, Chaz had wielded the gun with total confidence. And the accuracy of the shots he had gone on to fire had more than asserted his marksmanship.

Dodds rubbed the back of his head and looked on at the carnage in front of him. What he had just seen was impossible: Estelle had shot the invader four times, landing all the bullets in the torso. Yet a few minutes later the man was back on his feet as if nothing had happened. He spotted one of the bullets that he believed had been embedded in the man, now resting on the floor close to the body.

Had the bullet missed? No, it couldn't have. There had been blood, the man had fallen. He had heard the cries of pain behind the mask. The bullet he had picked up had also been sticky with blood and the man's suit had been torn where the projectile had entered. Surely he couldn't have imagined all of that. *And the strength!* If it weren't for the pain in his lower back - he considered himself lucky he could still walk - he might not have believed how far he had travelled with the throw either. He felt at his aching throat. It was painful to swallow. He was certain that beneath the lining of the flight suit there would be some rather pronounced bruising.

"That man was dead! Estelle shot him down! How the hell did he get back up?!"

Whilst Dodds was silently considering everything that had just happened, Kelly was voicing her opinions aloud. Enrique made his way over to reassure her, as she pointed at the still corpse of the solider Chaz was plundering. She looked a little hysterical, as if her worst fear of dead bodies had at last been realised.

"Is he really dead now?" Kelly said.

"He's dead," Enrique said.

"Are you sure?"

"Yes, he is, calm down."

"How do you know he's not going to get back up again?"

"I don't think he'll be getting up after that."

"Yeah, but we thought that after Estelle put four damn bullets into him..."

"Are you okay, Enrique," Dodds asked above Kelly's ramblings, as he stumbled forward.

"Fine. Are you all right?"

He looked in the direction of the two corpses on the floor by the locker. "I meant what I said earlier: should bloody well have stayed in bed."

"What was that all about?" Enrique wanted to know.

"Don't know. I've got about a hundred thousand questions, but answers that I could count on one hand." He realised his voice was shaking. But then, so was everyone else's. "Did that really just happen?"

Enrique nodded, an arm around Kelly, rubbing her back. Dodds left them to it and made his way over to where the solider had fallen. He caught a glimpse of what remained of the man's head before turning away. He spotted some more red-stained brass coloured objects on the floor. Two more bullets; that made three. He had no idea what might have happened to the fourth. Ten thousand and one.

Chaz was still removing things from the soldier. He had so far collected what looked like four grenades and a fuel cell for the plasma pistol. Other items were being tossed aside.

"Chaz, where's the card? Did you get it?" Estelle asked through sharp intakes of breath.

Chaz continued to search, ignoring her question.

"Chaz?" Estelle asked again louder, rubbing at her stomach.

"*What?*" he roared, looking back at her, anger and impatience clear in his eyes.

"Do not speak to me that way, Lieutenant!" Estelle said, the stress causing her own temper to flare. "Did you find the data card?"

Chaz tossed the capsule in her direction. She caught it and wiped the remains of the blood away, revealing the contents. She caught Dodds' eye and held it up as if requiring a second opinion. He nodded; he could see the small blue card within was marked with the Confederation insignia.

"Right, we've got what we came for," she stated, and began to secure it in her flight suit. "I think what it might be worth us doing is trying to contact..."

"What we *have* to do is get out of here, *now*," Chaz said, snatching up the items he had removed from the soldier's body and stuffing them into various compartments and pockets of his own flight suit. "Enrique: how many more did you see?" he asked as he set about retrieving the shotgun from where it lay under a gurney.

"Four, maybe five," Enrique said.

Chaz swore, then looked around the morgue, his face becoming quite grim. "Doesn't look like there is any way out of here except for the way we came in." He glanced at the shotgun in his hand and then turned back to the group, his eyes flickering over each of them. He then turned back to Enrique. "Do you know how to use one of these?"

"Sure," Enrique said. "I've done my fair share on the firing range."

Chaz tossed the shotgun to him.

"Magazine holds seven rounds, but it has a low effective range so anything over about twenty-five meters is hardly going to be worth shooting at; especially if you don't have a steady aim. Don't waste it on pot-shots, it won't do us any good. Only use it when I tell you."

The tone in his voice let Dodds know this was far more than just a mere suggestion. Enrique nodded as he began to familiarize himself with the handling of the weapon, turning it over and bouncing it in his hands to feel the weight. Dodds looked at Chaz in confusion. It seemed that the big man knew a lot more than he was willing to let on, but quite why he didn't know. His usual silent and steady demeanour had abandoned him, and Dodds wondered if they were now seeing his true colours.

Dodds pointed at the body. "Chaz, that guy..."

"Do you really want to stand around and talk about this now?" Chaz said.

Dodds didn't.

"Right, everyone ready?" Chaz asked, as he started off to retrieve his equipment. "We're not exactly going to have an easy time getting out of here in one piece."

"Lieutenant, what the hell!" Estelle snapped, a furious expression on her face. "Don't make me remind you who is in charge of this mission, Mr Koonan! I am a *first* lieutenant, you are a *second* lieutenant; I am the wing commander of the *White Knights* and I won't have you giving orders to my team whilst..."

Dodds reached out and took a grip of her shoulder, prompting her to stop talking.

"Estelle, I really feel that right now we should be listening to Chaz," he said.

Estelle glared back at Dodds before her eyes strayed to the body of the dead soldier on the floor. She stood in silence for a time, looking from Dodds to Chaz to the body. She then shrugged Dodds' hand from her shoulder.

"Fine, we'll follow your lead, Chaz," she said with reluctance. "For now. But once we get out of here you will have a lot of explaining to do."

Chaz acknowledged her with a mere nod of his head before the *Knights* retrieved their gear and made their way from the mortuary. On the way out Chaz paused, and then turned around and walked back to Barber's gurney. He picked the linen sheet off the floor and spread it back over her body, bending down to give her a kiss on the forehead before covering her completely.

Dodds studied him as he did all of this, but Chaz gave no explanation for his actions; and neither did Dodds seek to ask.

XIII

— The Fate of an Empire —

T he infirmary lay still and quiet, and as Dodds continued his slow, crouched walk towards the main door he was confident that they were alone. At Chaz's request he and Enrique had sneaked forward, leading the group towards the medical unit exit. Chaz had covered their backs, keeping Estelle and Kelly with him. Dodds and Enrique moved to either side of the door, signalling the all clear to Chaz, who hurried forward with the two women.

Dodds noticed that the light on the control panel on this side of the door was blinking on and off and guessed that the lock he had engaged earlier was no longer in effect. Judging by what had just happened in the morgue it would not have stood up to anything more than a shoulder barge from their attacker.

That whole sequence was still quite vivid in his mind: had it really happened? Were they all really here, crawling out of a morgue where they had just cut open a dead woman and fought a man who had somehow come back to life?

"See anything?" Chaz asked Dodds and Enrique in a low tone.

Dodds rose and took a cautious peek out the circular infirmary door windows. The central hall appeared a great deal darker than when they had first arrived.

"Nothing," he said, choosing not to linger by the window any longer than was necessary. "But it looks like a number of lights have blown."

"No, the soldiers have shot them out," Chaz said with a shake of his head. "They do that so that it makes it harder for their enemies to see where they're going."

Dodds nodded, quite willing to accept just about anything the big man told them. Questions could wait until later.

"Take a step outside carefully. Keep low and don't make any noise."

"OK," Dodds nodded. He pushed at the door, but found it almost impossible to move, as if there was a lot of weight in front of it. Enrique came to his aid and between them they managed to open the door just wide enough for Dodds to squeeze through, the bulky propulsion pack on his back making it more awkward than normal.

As he stepped out into the darkened main hall his boot slid on something. He looked down and saw he was standing in a pool of blood. The mass that had been holding back the door was a rather large woman who had died as a result of multiple plasma wounds to the torso. Her dead eyes gazed straight ahead into the rest of the main hall. The hall was not as dark as Dodds had first thought and as he followed her gaze he became aware of the fate of the refugees. What he had first believed to be the random scatterings of abandoned coats and luggage were in fact dead bodies. Dozens of them. Men, women and children lay all about the floor. If it were not for the terrible wounds and the blood, Dodds might have thought that they had all fallen victim to some mysterious plague. As the hideous smell of burnt flesh started to fill his nostrils, Dodds pulled himself back through the door.

"What did you see?" Enrique asked in a low voice.

"They're all dead," Dodds said.

"Who?"

"The refugees. They've all been killed."

"Did you see any soldiers?" Chaz cut in.

"No," Dodds said.

Chaz forced himself out the narrow gap to take a look for himself, before returning back to the corridor and confirming that the hall was clear of danger, though there was much evidence of the slaughter that had taken place. At this point Chaz concluded that they would simply have to make a run for it.

He slipped through the door and then beckoned for the others to follow, telling them to stay low and stay quiet. In a line, headed up by Chaz, they walked as fast as they could in their crouched positions, keeping the wall of desolate coffee shops and other stores to their backs. The air was heavy with the stench of burnt materials and flesh, and all five of the *Knights* did their best not to gag and cough with every breath they took.

They looked all about themselves as they moved, keeping an eye out for any sudden appearance of the soldiers Enrique had mentioned. Glass and plastics crunched loudly under their feet as though wishing to expose their position on purpose. They did not have all that far to go to return to the airlock, but out in the open they would have little hope of surprising their enemy as they had done in the morgue. And this time they would be facing off against more than one of them.

Halfway to the airlock the sound of running feet came from close by.

"Down! Get down!" Chaz hissed, waving a hand to the floor. "Keep still and don't move!" The group dropped to the floor, lying on their stomachs among the dead, the propulsion packs on their backs making it difficult to assume any other position.

As Dodds lay in wait, his eyes fell on two faces that were within his line of sight. One was that of a young woman, the other an older man, somewhere in his late thirties or early forties. Dark patches of blood were splattered about their expressions, mixed in with the woman's blonde hair and the man's black. Their eyes were wide, their faces twisted in terror.

Dodds was reminded of a scene from not long ago. He found himself thinking of Poppy and Stefan, and a feeling of guilt rumbled up his spine. *Don't look at them*, he told himself. But he did anyway, and for a time he was unable to tear his eyes away from them. He found himself wishing to tell them he was sorry; that it had been a terrible accident; that if he could turn back time he would do things differently. He blotted the thoughts from his mind as the sound of hurrying feet grew louder, and before long the source appeared.

A man and woman came running down a non-moving escalator from the first floor, where a number of other restaurants, bars and sleeping areas existed. The man was half dragging, half pulling the woman along behind him as the two attempted to escape their pursuers. They would have been better off running without holding hands, but it was clear that the man wanted to keep the woman with him, fearing that they might become separated. They stumbled a number of times on their way down the static escalator, but managed to keep themselves on their feet; even at the great speed they were descending, taking the steps two or three at a time.

Loud voices followed and then a pair of black figures appeared by the first floor railings. Two of the soldiers! One raised a rifle and fired with clinical accuracy, two blots of plasma striking the escaping woman in the back as the couple tried in vain to flee. She screamed and tumbled to the floor, her partner losing his grip on her hand.

Out of the corners of his eyes, Dodds saw his fellow team mates tense as he did, though they remained motionless on the floor, reluctant witnesses to the scene.

With their pursuers bounding down the escalator after them, the man attempted to pull the woman to her feet. She wobbled as she tried to stand, and as she did so she revealed that her clothing had been burnt away around the two spots on her back where she had been hit, hideous blackened and charred flesh visible beneath. The man could not help her to stand quick enough and he looked up to see one of the two soldiers bearing down on him. He was hit square in the chest by two rounds of his own and was dead even before he hit the floor, the bolts carving their way straight through him. Having ignored the woman in preference to taking out the man the soldiers finally dispatched her, seemingly unmoved by her sobs and pleas for mercy.

A few moments later there were more hurried footsteps and the remaining three soldiers that Enrique had described seeing came running into the scene, to join with those standing over their latest victims. They began to converse, one pointing back the way they had come, others examining their weaponry.

Dodds studied them as they spoke to one another, listening to their words. It was not a language he had ever heard before and a nagging feeling grew within him that it wasn't normal. He tried to convince himself that it was an Imperial dialect that he was unfamiliar with, but the characteristics of the tongue were all wrong. It sounded almost angry and mechanical, even though there was a strong central Imperial accent present in each spoken word.

These five soldiers all sported a number of different armaments, like the one they had encountered in the morgue. As well as the weapon each held in their hands they also had a rifle slung over their backs. Some also had an additional pistol holstered to their right legs. Again, like the soldier they had fought in the mortuary, they all appeared to be a lot taller than normal and in excellent physical condition. There also appeared to be two women in the group. They were more slender than the three others, but just as tall. Something in the back of Dodds' mind told him that they were also as strong and dangerous as the men. Their suits hugged their bodies well, showing off all their perfectly-proportioned curves. They too looked like models.

Dodds hoped that the soldiers would leave the area now that they had eliminated their targets; or, better still, that once they had finished speaking they would depart the starport and head back to where they had come from. But as they spoke one of the soldiers gestured to the bodies on the floor and then pointed in the direction of the medical unit.

You're missing your friend! Dodds thought. *He hasn't checked back in!*

The troops began to scout the area, nudging and kicking over bodies as they went. For a moment Dodds wondered what they were doing. Understanding then hit him like a sledgehammer and he had to stifle a yelp, forcing himself not to panic. He fought the compulsion to turn to the others and work out a plan.

As it was kicked one of the corpses let out a grunt, the noise telling all within earshot that it was in fact playing dead. The "corpse" then rolled over and the man scrambled to his feet. Its investigator reacted quickly to the sudden movement and shot him down. The man cried as a second and third shot struck him, and then fell down silent. The four other soldiers paused for a moment in their own hunt, before returning to their rounds.

"Oh my god..." Dodds heard Kelly squeak.

He concurred. The black suited soldiers continued to nudge and kick the fallen, drawing a pistol every now and again and shooting a body to guarantee it was not also playing dead. Their persistence met with success on another two occasions.

Dodds shifted his eyes to where Estelle lay next to him, seeing her almost as stiff as a board, though shivering ever so slightly. He couldn't be sure whether it was due to fear or the cool of the station; though, from the way he felt, he was certain it was the former. He then shifted his eyes over to Chaz, wondering what suggestions the big man was going to make.

Chaz studied the dark troop as they moved about, making a full evaluation of the situation before making his move. From the looks of things it would not be long before they made their way over towards where the *Knights* were concealing themselves. He would have to act soon. Chaz re-evaluated what he had removed from the downed soldier in the morgue: to their name the five Confederation pilots had one shotgun, with only a handful of shells; a near full plasma pistol, but with only one spare fuel cell; and three smoke grenades and two regular ones. This did not bode well for them; not in comparison with the enemy's armament of numerous shotguns, plasma rifles, pistols, grenades and God only knew whatever else. He had been quite stunned at how poorly equipped the invader had been. Either he had been acting as a scout, or he had exhausted much of his ammunition before coming in search of them.

Chaz noticed that Estelle had shifted her position and was looking at him.

Chaz, come on! What do we do? her eyes cried. *We have to get out of here! NOW!*

He made a swift decision.

"When I say move, get into that bar over there - The Lodge."

Dodds almost jumped at the sound of the big man's voice.

"Find decent cover, away from the entrance." As Chaz finished speaking one of the soldiers' heads snapped around to face in their direction, a pair of ruby-red eyes falling upon the group.

He could not *have heard that!* Dodds thought. *He's too bloody far away!* The big man had spoken just loud enough so that Enrique and Kelly would not have difficulty in hearing the whole sentence, but not enough to project his voice to the five black suited soldiers. To his mind it was not possible to have heard him over that distance. Even so, it appeared he had.

"Enrique, you ready?" Chaz asked out of the corner of his mouth.

"Just tell me what to do," Enrique said.

"Get ready to shoot."

The tall soldier had broken off from his systematic sweep and was heading over in their direction. Dodds watched as the soldier walked towards them, holding his breath and not even daring to blink. As he approached, the soldier tapped at the side of his helmet, around the same area that Dodds had noticed the button like indent. He scanned over the bodies for a moment and then appeared to focus on something. He was looking at the flight helmets. After a few seconds he tapped his helmet again and hoisted his weapon.

"NOW!" Chaz shouted. The noise caught the soldier off guard and he swung his weapon around toward Chaz.

At the same time Enrique brought himself up into a prone position, raising the shotgun off the ground. It had been a long time since he had used a weapon like this and that, coupled with the lack of time to aim, did not inspire him with much confidence. The proximity of soldier and nature of the weapon, however, meant that he had little to worry about. His finger pulled back on the trigger, discharging the shotgun and sending pellets flying straight into his target's legs. The soldier roared in agony and buckled down, the sudden and intense pain making him lose his grip on his own weapon.

"Move!" Chaz ordered, springing to his feet as the sudden noise and activity focused the attentions of the other soldiers. Dodds, Estelle and Kelly snatched up their flight helmets and dived into the bar as Chaz capitalised on the surprise attack. He fired the plasma pistol randomly at the other soldiers, causing them to scurry for cover.

Residing in the middle of the central hall was a large oval desk, that at one point in time had served to provide visitors to the port with information, help and a point of contact for the port's management and security. They ducked behind it, the solid structure of the reception providing them with protection against the Confederation pilots.

Chaz began to fall back to the bar, still firing on the four soldiers and preparing to move a lot faster once they decided to return fire. Enrique was on his feet and moving back to join him. In front of them their first target had regained his composure and was bringing his weapon back around towards the two men once more. Enrique took note and emptied another round into him, knocking him down on to his back.

"Don't waste it!" Chaz urged as they retreated into the bar.

They took up positions close to the front, using the walls for cover against the rain of return fire. Bottles and glasses that had not already been broken and looted by the refugees shattered behind them as they were struck by bullets and plasma bolts. Chaz chanced a glance around the pillar he stood behind and snatched back as plasma fire slammed into it, inches from his face.

"What's the plan, Chaz?" Estelle called from her hiding spot behind the bar's counter.

"I'm working on it," Chaz said through gritted teeth, taking a hasty look outside the bar.

Another of the soldiers had hurried forward to aid his fallen comrade whilst the others laid down suppressing fire. Chaz risked a number of pot shots, but it did little to disperse them. He saw the soldier take hold of his ally by the forearm and begin to effortlessly pull him backward, bumping over and parting the bodies of the refugees that lay in their way.

"Enrique, those two!" Chaz said.

Enrique leaned round the pillar wall and took a snap shot at the two retreating men. He did not find as much success as he had before, only winging the rescuer on the shoulder. The man staggered back, releasing his grip. Though only a few seconds following the interruption the soldier continued to pull his ally out of the way with his other arm, unphased by the attempt on his life.

"I'm nearly out," Enrique announced as he sank back down against the wall and checked his ammunition. Chaz tossed him over the remaining shells.

"He's getting up!" Dodds said. From his own hiding place Dodds had a good view of the scene within the central hall, and watched in horror as the man that Enrique had emptied two shotgun rounds into began getting to his feet. Dodds had only just convinced himself that the first soldier they had downed in the morgue had received nothing more than flesh wounds, the bullets Estelle had fire being slowed by the man's leather suit.

The reality of what they were up against had finally begun to sink in, and the cries of the pilot that Estelle had shot down three days ago came rushing back into his head. The pilot had begged not to be sent back, that if he went back he would die. Now that Dodds thought about it the man had spoken with an Imperial accent. He had thought nothing of it at the time, but now... Was this what those three had been running from? Had they been so desperate to escape from this nightmare that they would risk going head to head with seasoned Confederation starfighter pilots? The odds of their success had been low, but no doubt higher than their odds against these soldiers. The "rumours" he, Enrique and Chaz had heard the previous night no longer seemed to be just that.

Something else occurred to him: was this how *Dragon* had been so easily overcome? From what he was seeing even the several thousand strong crew of *Dragon's* full complement would be no match against such unrelenting foes. What other secrets were the CSN keeping from them?

He looked to Chaz, who was sheltering from the bullets and plasma that continued to fly into the bar, ripping plaster and chunks of concrete from the walls; splintering wooden chairs, tables and the counter; shattering bottles, glasses and decorations.

He caught Chaz's eyes. The man looked stressed.

"Chaz, seriously, who the hell are these guys?" Dodds asked.

There was considerable pause, then, in a grim voice, "They're the result of the Senate's desire to control the Empire. They're a mistake."

"What?" Dodds said. "They're a *mistake*?"

More wood and plaster flew. Enrique swore, his voice loud above the other noise.

"What do you mean? Are they human?" Dodds said.

Dodds was staring at him, but Chaz took no notice, lost in thought as to how they were to escape from their current predicament. He checked the counter on his plasma pistol and saw that only two shots in the current fuel cell remained. Shooting down the enemy was now not an option - if it had ever been. He ducked out of hiding again to loose off the final two shots before crouching down behind the wall to reload the pistol. He tossed the empty fuel cell away, the little splash it made as it hit the floor grabbing his attention for the first time. It was then that he noticed the thin liquid that covered the floor, as well as the strong smell of wine.

"Estelle, what you two got back there?" he shouted to the two women taking refuge behind the counter.

"We don't have any weapons or ammo!" Estelle said.

"Not unless you want to start throwing beer glasses at them!" Kelly added.

"Anything with a high percentage of alcohol?" Chaz said.

"They're starting to come around!" Enrique cried. At their current range Enrique's shotgun was not going to be as accurate or effective against the soldiers as the pistol. He fired it none the less, in an attempt to keep the soldiers together, though they had already split into two groups and had begun to circle around to take the bar blind sided.

Chaz took a chance and fully exposed himself, firing off several shots at both groups to drive them back. The gamble paid off and the soldiers once again pulled back for cover. He sought cover once more himself, knowing that he would not be able to pull off such a move again. He counted himself lucky that he had not been shot to ribbons even for those brief few seconds. The soldiers were not only very accurate, but also possessed incredible reflexes. He assumed they must have already used up their more powerful armaments dealing with the refugees; he would not be safe behind the wall otherwise. It had bought them a little time, but even that was already beginning to run out.

"Found anything?" Chaz called.

Estelle and Kelly were ransacking the lower cupboards, looking for anything that might be of use.

"Vodka," Kelly volunteered, her eyes resting on some large clear bottles of liquid labelled *Velda*. "Lots of it."

"Bring it here - and hurry!" Chaz said.

Estelle thrust two of the large bottles into Kelly's arms and the woman somewhat reluctantly crawled towards Chaz, pausing under wooden tables as she went.

"How many are there?" the big man said, as she pulled herself up next to him.

"About two dozen or so under the counter," she said. "Maybe more if..."

"Toss them out there," Chaz said. "Take the caps off and try and make sure they break. Make sure you get a good spread. Estelle, Dodds pass her the rest. Enrique and I will cover you."

The others started to follow his request, without question. Chaz fired the pistol sparingly as they did so, keeping a close watch on the ammunition counter as he and Enrique continued to lay down a suppressing fire.

As the bottles were thrown out, smashing on the white marble floor, the black soldiers ceased firing and held their position behind the massive desk. They seemed uncertain of what was going on and why their enemy had resorted to such a bizarre tactic. Such feelings were shared by Dodds, Estelle and Kelly who were, at this point, willing to try anything to get out of the port alive.

"Only got one shot left," Enrique said, at the same time that the bottles of vodka ran out. All the bottles had shattered where they had been thrown, the alcohol spreading out across the floor and soaking into the clothes of the dead.

"Pass it over here," Chaz said, still not willing to explain or discuss his train of thought with the others.

Enrique ducked down and slid the weapon across the floor to the big man who let it come to rest next to him.

"When I give you the signal I want you all to get out of here and head towards the airlock. Don't wait for me, I'll be right behind you." He produced the three smoke grenades, double checking they were what he was after. "Hold your breath."

Taking hold of the first, he pulled the pin and let it roll away from him. The canister immediately began to billow thick green smoke, filling the inside of the bar. Setting off another he tossed it just outside the entrance to the bar, yellow smoke belching forth and beginning to cover the surrounding area. He then threw the third in the direction they would need to take to reach the airlock, purple smoke spewing out of the canister.

"Go! Now!" Chaz said.

He watched as his four allies made their way past him, the air all around them filling with multicoloured gas. The combination of the three grenades in the small area was already providing an effective screen for their escape, but Chaz knew this was not enough. Dropping the plasma pistol into his flight helmet, he tossed the shotgun outside the bar where he could more easily retrieve it following the final phase of his plan.

As the smoke screen covered the *Knights,* the soldiers tapped at the side of their helmets, changing the internal visor settings; a tactic they had used whilst hunting down escaping refugees in the near darkness that the soldiers themselves had perpetuated. They had since returned their visors to normal.

But with the thick blanket of smoke now obscuring their vision, they chose a setting that allowed them see thermal radiation. The smoke screen that had been providing the *Knights* with cover for their escape was undone, and their forms were revealed as silhouettes of red, yellow and blue-green hues, running as best they could from the bar in the direction of the airlock corridor, skipping over bodies.

All that was, except for one, who remained outside the entrance of the shot up bar. The silhouette did not stay in that position for very long, however, making a sudden throwing motion and then beginning to run itself, grabbing two objects off the floor.

Training their guns on the figure, the soldiers prepared to open fire when their vision exploded, overwhelmed with an intensity of reds, oranges and yellows. The definition of their surroundings was lost. They did not need to switch off their thermal vision to realise that a fierce blaze had sprung up between them and their quarry. It was now spreading fast, the fire setting alight to clothes and other flammable items that had at one time belonged to the refugees.

The combination of thick, multicoloured smoke and flames provided the *Knights* with adequate cover and the group reached the airlock unscathed. Reaching the door first, Dodds started to work the control panel, opening it and allowing the others through. He remained in front of the panel as the others made their way into the chamber, lest it close and leave some of them on the wrong side of the thick doors. He saw Chaz bringing up the rear and waved him through. With him the big man carried the shotgun that he had originally entrusted to Enrique, as well as his flight helmet.

"Dodds, get in here!" Estelle said.

Dodds released his finger from the button and started forward, only to feel something latched onto his leg. He looked down to see that one of the soldier's previous victims was not yet dead and was now clinging on to him for dear life.

"Hey! Let go!" he started, trying to shake the man off him. Despite his efforts the refugee held on tight, refusing to do as he said, the desperation to escape and reach safety all but closing his ears to any such protest. Dodds began to swear profusely, and reached down in an attempt to pry the man from him. He could feel that he would topple over at any moment.

"Pandoran! Pandoran..." the man said, looking back around him in fear, hearing, as Dodds, the sound of the soldiers' heavy boots on the floor.

"Help!" Dodds said, looking around to his allies in the chamber who were affixing their helmets and checking their gear. The refugee was attempting to pull himself up, repeating the same word over and over. It sounded more like a name.

Chaz came rushing back out the airlock chamber, coming up beside the grappling pair. The big man struck the refugee with the butt of the shotgun, making him release his grip, before grabbing Dodds by the upper arm and hauling him in to join the others.

"Close the damn door!" Chaz barked, as the five black clad soldiers rounded the corner at the end of the corridor and hammered towards them.

As the airlock doors began to close Chaz raised the shotgun for one last time and discharged it. The soldiers did not even halt as the gun was fired, the front most persuader being winged by the spread of pellets. She fell backwards, but the others simply stepped over her, forming a defensive line between their adversaries and their fallen team mate. Through the diminishing gap Chaz threw the shotgun back into the corridor, just as the doors bolted before him. Picking up his flight helmet from the floor he extracted the pistol he had stowed within it. The big man then proceeded to don his helmet, though he did not turn his back on the scene on the other side of the door.

Dodds did likewise, powerless to do anything but stand and watch the fate of the refugee that tried to come with him: with few options open to him the refugee made a vain attempt at rushing the soldiers. The lead did not bother to respond to the threat with his held weapon, but instead grabbed the man around the top of his head with one massive hand. Drawing a knife from his belt he cut his attacker's throat in one fluid and powerful movement, before letting him to slip choking and gasping to the floor. The remaining soldiers ran up to the closed door and stood in front of it, the foremost raising the plasma rifle they held and training it on Chaz through the airlock door window.

Dodds watched in wrapped silence. Even though the soldier could have killed Chaz with a couple of shots, he was not about to pull the trigger and break the glass. To do so would risk exposing the entire port to the vacuum of space the moment the outer airlock door opened. But the soldier waited still. If the outer door did not open, for any reason, whether because of a mechanical failure or security violation, then Dodds was certain he would not hesitate to pull the trigger. Even so, Chaz remained where he was, acknowledging no one else, his back to his fellow *Knights*.

A warning alarm started in the chamber, signalling both the impending depressurization and Chaz's victory.

"Here we go," Enrique announced to the sound of the outer door locks' release. Dodds felt himself start to drift out and he made sure he had a good grip on the control of his propulsion pack. He noticed how Chaz continued to stare at the soldiers on the other side of the glass, even as he floated out beyond the chamber. Dodds slowed himself, catching sight of the big man's expression and noting it to be one of pure hatred for the invaders.

He looked back to the corridor and saw the soldier who had been marking the door snap their gun back and turn back down the corridor with his team mates.

"They're coming after us," Chaz's voice came in his earpiece. "They're not going to give up that easily."

"Oh, hell! The freighter's gone!" Kelly said.

Dodds looked all around himself seeking to disprove her. Unfortunately she was right. The only visible vessel was one bearing the Imperial coat of arms, docked on to the side of the port; likely being how the soldiers had entered. They had all been relying on the freighter's presence to help them get back into the cloaked ATAFs. But with their point of reference gone, finding the invisible craft now seemed like an impossible task.

He tried to think. He looked back to the starport and tried to trace a line from the airlock to where the freighter might have been. But for all his effort, he couldn't judge the distance or the heading; it was too hard.

"Chaz, what are you doing?" he heard Estelle ask. He saw the big man was aiming the plasma pistol, a small green bolt already streaking away from him. There was no answer from Chaz, who seemed to be concentrating at the task in hand.

He fired several more shots, in seemly random locations. The three shots sailed unhindered out into space. The man adjusted his aim to target a different region, but, as before, the next two bolts also failed to land a target. The next shot he fired also disappeared into the depths, then, with his next attempt, his plan revealed itself to all.

The plasma bolt found its mark and, just as Parks had warned, the unmistakeable form of an ATAF lit up before their eyes, the shielding reacting to the hit and looking as if someone had thrown luminous green paint all over it. There it remained but for a scant few seconds before it began to fade from view.

"There!" Chaz said, drawing everyone's attention to the withering green ripples outlining the fighter.

"Stay here," Estelle ordered the others and sped over to the fighter before starting to ease herself through the shielding. Despite the need to re-enter the fighter as quick as she could to assist the others, she had to take her time pushing herself through the layers of tough protection; a task that could not be accomplished without patience.

Before long she disappeared from view. A short while later the fighter she entered was lit with waves of cyan ripples, blue bolts streaking out from the nose of the craft. They hurtled forward, striking objects not far away, revealing themselves to be the four other ATAFs. Estelle was using the mag cannons; she wasn't about to dare using the main guns – they could do more harm than good.

Dodds sped over to the nearest visible craft to him and, just as Estelle had done, started pushing himself through the starfighters' shielding, all the while glancing uneasily back at the Imperial lander that was still latched on to the side of the port. At any moment it could detach itself and start after them. He was surprised it was taking them this long.

He guessed that the soldiers...

What was it that man called them? Pandora..? Pandoran?

... had encountered refugees that had escaped their attention before and wanted to finish the job before giving chase, even if the airlock escapees were of a greater threat. He was soon settled back into the seat of the ATAF and began stabbing at the buttons and controls in front of him, bringing the systems back on-line.

"Everyone ready?" Estelle said. There was a resounding confirmation from all and, as one, the *Knights* turned their still veiled ATAFs around and moved away from the starport, and back towards *Griffin*.

An explosion reflected off Dodds' canopy and he looked around to see the transport craft that had been attached to the port had been destroyed. The port began to vent air, bodies and other materials as it depressurized. A black body spun out of the hole that had been ripped in the side of the port, in wake of the transporter's destruction. The figure made futile attempts to stop itself from drifting further into space, but was unable to do anything about their slide.

Dodds caught the green outline of an ATAF just as it faded from view, swinging around to rejoin the group.

"Just making sure," Chaz said.

As they hurtled away from the port, Dodds looked back around to see that the black suited body of the soldier was still moving, a lot longer than should have been possible. In his mind's eye frightening images were painted:

Though the ATAF was invisible the soldier began to swim through space towards him, gaining on him despite the incredible speed of his starfighter. After all, what was the lack of oxygen and warmth to one who had survived injuries that would have killed an ordinary human being? Latching on to the ATAF's canopy it punched straight through to him, the shields and the canopy itself no match for its incredible strength. The soldier grabbed him by his flight suit, wrenching him from his seat and out into space, the buckles doing nothing to save him. Drawing again on its unimaginable strength, the soldier punched easier through his flight helmet, shattering the tough visor and draining away all his oxygen. There it held him in an unbreakable grasp, waiting for him to die; until finally releasing him and leaving his lifeless body to float through space forever, his friends able to do nothing more than look on in horror.

The soldier's limbs did eventually cease their flailing, but by then Dodds was not surprised by what he had seen. It would not have been a shock to him if it had made an attempt to chase them, cloaked or not.

"He would make an excellent politician," Estelle said to Dodds. She had spent some of the journey back to the carrier questioning Chaz and attempting to ascertain an explanation for his behaviour at the starport. As expected he was not very forthcoming with answers and Estelle had soon given up. She would get the explanation she was after once she had submitted a report. No doubt senior command would be very interested in Chaz's actions themselves and in the end she would get closure; even if it took several months.

"Managed to answer the question without actually answering it?" Dodds said.

"Precisely."

"I'm just grateful to get out of there."

He too had many questions of his own, none that he knew would be answered any time soon. Most worrisome of all, Chaz's statement: *They're a mistake.* If that was a mistake, he didn't want to think what the original intention was supposed to be. The past few hours had been unlike any he had experienced in his entire life.

The journey continued in relative silence, the five pilots happy to take a breather from their recent experiences. Heading back to *Griffin*, Dodds felt as though he was waking from a terrible nightmare; albeit one with many memorable cuts and bruises.

XIV

— Friends Like These —

"**C**aptain."

Parks looked up from his musings to see Liu swing around in his chair, wearing a relieved expression.

"Scanners are indicating that *CSN Ifrit* has just jumped into the system and has started making its way toward our position. Based on their current velocity they'll be with us in a little under thirty minutes."

Parks joined the helmsman by his console. Sure enough the medium range radar was showing a green triangle moving towards the centre of the display.

"Thank God," Parks said. He felt some of the pressure that had been weighing down upon him starting to lift. In the hours following the *Knights'* departure, Parks had overseen the crews' efforts to bring the ship back up to a manageable, working condition. It had not been easy, but with a lot of effort they had managed to restore shields, engines, jump drives, and some weapons systems. And whilst they would not be able to fend off any major attacks or launch fighters, they were at least in a position to return home.

With the advent of *Ifrit's* arrival all that now remained was to await the *Knights'* return and they could at last leave Phylent and begin the journey home. Parks may not have managed to secure the recapture of *Dragon*, but he would have prevented valuable information from falling into the hands of the Enemy. That at least was something to be thankful for.

He turned to Weathers, who had taken the place of O'Donnell on the bridge. "How are the comms systems?"

"They should all be functioning correctly, sir," Weathers said. "We are still experiencing limited performance with shielding, weaponry and engines, but communications are operating perfectly."

"Good. Once *Ifrit* is close enough send them a welcome message on short range broadcast only. Relay our current situation to them and let them know we are ready to leave as soon as the *White Knights* return."

"Yes, sir," Weathers said.

Parks returned to his seat to await *Ifrit*'s arrival. Their fellow Confederation carrier was travelling towards them head on and, from his seat, out the main viewport, he was able to see various aspects of the ship springing into detail the closer it grew to them.

But as *Ifrit* bore down on *Griffin*'s location Parks started to grow uneasy and could not shake the feeling that something was wrong. The carrier was well within visual range, now less than a twenty kilometres out, and devouring the distance at a rapid pace. From the looks of things it would be on top of them much sooner than Liu had at one time predicted. He subconsciously sat a little more upright and further forward in his seat.

Parks looked to Weathers, "Karen, has *Ifrit* acknowledged our HELO?"

"Not yet, sir. Should I send it again?"

"No," Parks shook his head. "First recheck the comms systems. Mr Liu, perform a full system diagnostic. Let's be sure that our message was transmitted in the first place before we begin bombarding them with repeat broadcasts."

"Yes, sir," Liu said, then a minute later, "All tests have completed successfully."

"Comms are still functioning correctly, captain," Weathers added. "Though, it might have been a glitch in the system."

Parks wasn't so sure. Something wasn't right. "Send the greeting again," he said.

Weathers complied, but there was still no answer. *Ifrit*'s form continued to grow larger as it closed the distance between the two carriers, showing no signs of slowing. It was barely a few hundred meters from them now.

As Parks rose from his seat and walked to the front of the bridge, he heard consoles up and down the deck begin to whine, and knew right then that his worries had been confirmed. He looked to Liu at the same moment the man turned to him.

"Captain, *Ifrit* is readying weapons!" Liu said, the former look of relief wiped clean and replaced by a picture of panic.

"Red alert!" Parks said. "Full power to shields, now!"

The words hadn't even left his mouth when *Ifrit*'s guns opened up, the full barrage directed straight towards its almost defenceless former partner in battle. Bright green light from bolts of plasma intermixed with thick red beams of laser fire, the tiny blue and cyan particle trails of missiles almost lost in between.

The opening volley hit *Griffin*'s shields hard and the already damaged power generators were quick to buckle to the intensity of the onslaught. Parks found his seat just as an enormous spray of bright blue splinters erupted from *Griffin*'s bow, signalling both the collapse of the shielding and the vulnerability of the vessel to the hail of fire that followed.

"Return fire!" Parks barked. *For what it's worth.*

Griffin's own cannons trained themselves on *Ifrit*, but their efforts were futile at best, the carrier never having made a full recovery from the battle hours earlier. The rate of return fire *Griffin* was able to muster was nothing compared to that which *Ifrit* continued to pour on.

Explosions scorched the bow and top-side of *Griffin*, the impacts of concentrated plasma fire ripping holes in the already vulnerable hull. All about the ship crew were thrown to the floor as the carrier jerked with the unrelenting attack, Parks himself only just managing to remain in his seat. The captain witnessed one of the two plasma accelerators affixed to the front of the carrier explode, the turret snapping apart and the mount breaking free and spinning off into space. Green and blue chemicals vented from the shaft. Missiles exploded all across the hull. Debris tumbled about from where the attacks had shredded the more exposed and less well protected parts of the vessel.

If Parks had considered his ship a mess before, then it was nothing compared to what he was looking at now: the emblem of the griffin residing across the topside of the carrier, stretching out away from the bridge, was scarcely recognisable, now blackened and charred.

Parks braced himself. He wondered how it might all end. Would he see the frontal viewport shatter and be pulled from his chair out into space? Would he feel himself engulfed in flames for a few moments as the bridge exploded? Or would he hear only a sudden loud bang, see his world go black, and then no more? Whatever it was, he was sure he would find out soon...

And then, for the second time that day, *Griffin*'s lights shut off, plunging the ship into near darkness. Computer arrays and consoles followed in their stead. Some exploded, adding to the causalities that had already built up during *Ifrit*'s barrage, smoke once again threatening to fill the bridge and suffocate its occupants.

Half light spilled into the bridge from the emergency systems, relieving the crew of the momentary darkness. It was aided by the small electrical fires that had sprung up from some of the consoles, creating a smoky orange ambience about the bridge; pockets of flicking blue light from sparking electrics dancing across consoles. Crew members darted about to find fire fighting equipment.

With their power cut *Griffin*'s weapons fell silent and Parks braced himself for *Ifrit*'s impending finishing blow. It was then that he noticed that the carrier had stopped rocking and that missiles and cannon fire no longer rained down on the ship.

"Mr Liu..." Parks started.

"They... they've stopped firing," Liu said, staring out at the Confederation carrier that had moments before threatened to bring to an end *Griffin*'s long service.

Why? Parks wondered. When *Ifrit* had ignored their greetings but continued forward he knew something was amiss. Though he had been grateful for the carrier's arrival, going by the information that Turner had relayed to him *Ifrit* was many hours late. By now he would be expecting to see *Leviathan* instead. *Dammit, Aiden, where are you?!*

"What's our status?" he asked Liu.

"Power outage is temporary and is only affecting certain systems, Captain," Liu said, working at his console. "It can be restored in a few minutes."

Parks hesitated for a moment before responding to the news. "Don't bring us back on-line, Lieutenant," he said. Something told him that it would not be wise for them to stop playing dead just yet.

Weathers' console started to jingle in front of her. "Sir, *Ifrit* is attempting to establish communications," she said.

So, now they want to talk, Parks thought. "Put them on."

The holographic screen sprung up at the front of the bridge, the quality of the picture and sound comparable to how it had been just after the

Imperial fighter had crashed onto the flight deck. Parks heard a number of intakes of breath as he stood up and walked closer to the projection of *Ifrit*'s bridge. Whilst the image was blocky, jerky and suffering from a crackling audio, it lost none of the impact it otherwise stood to deliver.

Zackaria sat in the captain's chair like a king upon his throne, his face serious and stern. Just ahead of him, on his right hand side, stood Hawke, his expression deadpan in the face of his former ally.

"Anthony…" Parks began, the genuine shock in his voice clear even to him. With *Ifrit*'s attack Parks had thought of only two people who could be commanding the carrier: Admiral Zackaria or Commodore Rissard. The thought of Hawke alive and well, and unharmed aboard the ship had never occurred to him. And now the sight of both Zackaria and Hawke stood side by side, as allies, almost floored him.

"This is where we part ways, Elliott," came the scratchy voice of Hawke from the holographic image. "I just wanted to take this opportunity to bid you farewell."

His face had changed a lot since Parks had seen him hours before: his skin looked fresh and healthy, his eyes were bright, and his facial hair was completely absent, as if he had just had a clean shave.

"My God, man! What are you doing?" Parks said, flabbergasted.

"My part to ensure the continued success of the Mission, Commodore," Hawke said with a clean expression. The man spoke in a matter-of-fact manner, as if there was nothing unusual or surprising about his nature.

"The *Mission*?"

Hawke nodded. Or, at least, what appeared to be a nod. "The Mission - For the honour of the Senate. For the glory of the Empire."

As Parks continued to stare, open mouthed at the image that jumped, froze and tore, the pieces of a great puzzle began to fall into place.

"You gave them *Dragon*, didn't you?" Parks said. "That's why you survived. You tried to bargain and they took it. They wanted a man on the inside."

Links formed in Parks' mind, everything finally starting to make perfect sense: the Enemy had intercepted and boarded *Dragon* - how was not important - but he hazarded that at that time it was not with Hawke's consent. Though they had fought hard to hold back the invaders, *Dragon*'s crew had succumbed to the boarders and the Enemy had made their way to Hawke himself. Something else had happened then, a point that Parks still struggled on, but in the end it had led to Hawke's treachery. The man had then been beaten, starved, and thrown into an escape pod, where he was left to drift in Independent space for the allied forces to find him. It was meant to look as though he had run away, or had been saved by his crew so that he alone might be able to tell of the fate that had befallen *Dragon*, and therefore aid the Confederation in its recovery. But instead he had been working against them.

How much information could he give them now, Parks wondered. What had he told them already? That didn't matter; the Enemy had tricked him and they had *Dragon*.

"That is correct, Commodore," Hawke said.

Parks' mind raced, searching for a way out. The Enemy had *Dragon,* and now they have *Ifrit. Dragon. Ifrit.* Something occurred to him; he had to stall for time.

"Anthony, listen: we can talk this through," Parks said. "Please; allow me to come aboard and speak with Admiral Zackaria. We can work something out. We can end this without any more loss of life. I throw myself upon the mercy of the Senate." He knew it sounded absurd; so very melodramatic.

"There will be no discussions," Hawke said in a flat voice. "There has been too much talk already." The holographic image had stopped updating, and whilst the audio was still quite clear, the video transmission had ceased.

Parks couldn't be certain the same loss would be true for *Ifrit*, but he had to risk it. He was sure that Hawke would continue his gloat undeterred by the sudden loss of visuals. He just had to lure him in.

"Your plans won't work, Anthony," Parks said. "There are too many flaws, too many assumptions. We're already well prepared to exploit those weaknesses..." He started to back away from the static holographic image, beckoning towards Liu with one hand. The man rose from his seat and prepared to assist the commodore as soon as he was prompted further.

"It will work just as Fleet Admiral Turner described it," Hawke said. "The ATAFs will join our front line forces and we will use them to fulfil the Mission."

"It's not *your* Mission, Anthony!" Parks retorted. "Listen to me: you are not one of them." He shuffled Weathers out of her seat, gesturing to the woman to keep quiet. He quickly took her place, his fingers racing across the surface of her console, Liu giving him visual prompts as the man's plan began to come together.

"You are an enlisted officer within the Confederation Stellar Navy," Parks said. "You have spent a good part of your life with the service and your time and dedication to serving the Confederacy has not gone unnoticed. You have a wife and one daughter, who has recently been accepted to study law at Cambridge University, thanks to your own efforts to never give up on her and motivate her to achieved her dreams."

"The Mission is more important than any of those things," Hawke's voice came. "All of those who oppose the rule of the Senate must be eradicated, as decreed by the Senior Magistrate. It's time for you to accept it: you have failed, Commodore. You never were the man that Fleet Admiral Turner believed you were. Too much store is put into the weak, into the lenient, into the modest and the humble..."

Parks did not hear the rest, he was working too feverishly. He was thankful that Hawke had taken the opportunity to gloat, though he knew that time was short, and at any moment *Ifrit* would finish *Griffin* off. He heard a new voice speak over the comm link's still active audio channel. The words were unrecognisable and seemed not to be directed at him.

"Time's up, Commodore," Hawke announced.

"Captain, *Ifrit* is readying accelerators!" Weathers said from her position at Liu's console.

From where he sat, Parks did not need computer readouts for that kind of information: at this range he could quite clearly see the green lights, running the length of the weapons' turrets, beginning to illuminate as they charged. *Griffin* was mere seconds away from destruction.

Parks looked up from the console, towards the carrier ahead where he knew both Hawke and Zackaria would be staring back at *Griffin*, preparing to witness its final few moments of service. Parks, however, was not quite willing to give them that pleasure just yet.

"You know how the saying goes, Commodore: fool me once, shame on you; fool me twice..." A single confirmation request lay on the console's screen, Parks' fingers hovering just above it. "... shame on me!"

Parks' fingers tapped the screen, executing the command he had taken the opportunity to set up. *Ifrit*'s plasma accelerator stopped charging, the lights along the turrets extinguishing as if they were flames doused by water.

"Karen?" Parks looked to Weathers for further confirmation of his actions.

"*Ifrit*'s shielding, weaponry and engines have all been disabled, sir," she said. "Life support still functional, but..."

"Bring us back on-line, Mr Liu and get us out of here!" Parks interrupted, rising from the console.

"Where?" the uncertain navigator said. "Jump engines are likely to be extremely unstable since the last attack..."

"Just put some distance between us, man!" Parks said. Whilst *Ifrit* couldn't return fire or give chase, Parks wanted to get *Griffin* as far away as was possible. Not that he knew where they were going to go or what they would do once *Ifrit* recovered. He was buying time; clutching at straws.

Griffin's engines engaged and the carrier started forward, maintaining its same heading and slipping beneath its antagonist, though it was clear that the engines were lacking the power they had possessed at the time they had departed Spirit.

I can't believe that actually worked, Parks found himself thinking. The idea had come to him in a flash: upon seeing Zackaria sat in the captain's seat on the holographic screen, he had become angry at how the man had taken not one, but now two of the Navy's most prized vessels. He had gone back to the fateful start of the day, to when, during the preparations, he had been certain they would return home with what was once theirs. He then recalled how, prior to the commencement of *Operation Menelaus*, *Griffin*'s databanks had been loaded with the security credentials for deactivating *Dragon*. The data bundle had, however, not been restricted to their mission target and had also contained the protocols to link to other Confederation capital ships; including *Ifrit*. With the realisation that Hawke had inadvertently handed him the advantage, Parks knew he had only to keep his former ally talking until he could locate *Ifrit*'s details.

Though he thought his plan to be quite inspired, he was unable to revel in the victory; it looked far too short lived in his eyes. To Zackaria and Hawke this was only a temporary set back and one way or another they would be on *Griffin* once more. And when that time came they would not hold back until the carrier was reduced to nothing but a burnt out shell.

Zackaria rose from the captain's chair, joining Hawke where he stood at the front of the carrier, and ordered him to prevent the enemy's escape. Hawke followed the orders through, assuring the admiral that *Griffin* would not get far. Though *Ifrit* could not follow or fire upon Parks' ship itself, the Confederation fighters ready and waiting on the flight deck were unaffected by the power outage.

Black clad figures leapt up into fighters that were quick to be taxied towards the catapult; the speed and efficiency of the pilots and deck crew as clinical as always. Within minutes the first wing were starting to hurtle down the launch tunnel, more and more fighters lining up behind them.

Hawke watched as the first group of fighters shot out in front of the carrier, knowing there was little chance that *Griffin* would be able to outrun or fend off an assault from close to one hundred simultaneous attackers.

Even so, Hawke was taking no chances and sent out further requests for backup.

The TAFs, Rays and Rooks began to spill fast from *Ifrit* and wasted no time in giving chase to the fleeing *Griffin*. They closed the gap quickly, the first wing soon bringing themselves into weapons range. The carrier was not moving fast, but even if it had been in perfect working order it had no chance of outrunning those pursuing it.

With missiles already locked onto the kilometre long vessel ahead of him, the lead fighter pilot poised over the trigger, waiting for the confirm that his target was in range. The seconds and meters ticked down; the range confirmation flashed up on his HUD; he squeezed the trigger; his TAF exploded.

The TAF next to own fell at the same time, as did one of the following Rays and yet another TAF, not far behind them.

The pack of hijacked Confederation fighters scattered like a frightened school of fish as five sleek black craft appeared before them, seemingly out of nowhere, and rushed straight at them, the tips of their cannons blazing like flaming torches on a dark night.

Heads snapped around, tracing the path of the mysterious craft and seeing them fan out as they hit the rear of the pack.

As *Griffin's* pursuers attempted to reform their wing and once again focus their efforts on the fleeing carrier, the new arrivals arced up and around, and raced straight back at them, cannon fire spraying the squadron indiscriminately. More of the TAFs, Rays and Rooks fell, despite the pilots' attempts to evade the shower.

With their allies dropping all about them, the squadron made a collective decision to eliminate the threat before dealing with *Griffin*, and broke off their pursuit. It was not long before they realised what they were facing off against, many having seen them before, only hours earlier.

The news came quick to Parks.

"*Griffin*; this is Lieutenant de Winter, reporting mission accomplished," Estelle's voice came over the bridge's comm system. "Returning with five ATAFs, five pilots, and one mission target."

"*White Knights!*" Parks said, almost unable to express the relief he felt at hearing that the five had not only returned safe, sound and successful from their mission, but had also stepped up to pull *Griffin* out of the fire.

"I must apologise for cutting that a little fine, Commodore," Estelle said. "I wanted to better assess the situation and attempt to get the drop on *Ifrit*; but I got a bit over-zealous, at your expense."

"There's no need to apologise," Parks said. "Your timing could not have been more appropriate. I think it's fair to say that our present situation speaks for itself. *Griffin* needs cover whilst we retreat and work on a plan of action. Jump engines are currently in an uncertain state, so an immediate evacuation is not feasible." *And even if they were we're not leaving just yet. Not without bringing Hawke and* Ifrit *back in.* "Go to it, *Knights.*"

Dodds was suffering a range of emotions from the events of the day: he was hungry from not having eaten since the breakfast he had picked at that morning, weary from the lack of proper sleep, and sore from the encounter at Arlos.

The sight of *Ifrit* opening fire on an allied carrier had resulted in all those emotions clustering together and expelling themselves as pure anger.

No one could have convinced him that Hawke was not in some way connected with the attack. The urge to break away from the others and focus his rage straight against *Ifrit* had been almost uncontrollable. But he had bitten his lip and remained veiled and radio silent, as they had made their way back towards *Griffin*; until at last letting everything out the moment Estelle had given them the order to attack. He had raced forward, like a dog out of a trap, surging headlong into the wing of *Griffin*'s unsuspecting attackers and taking down the lead with his opening salvo.

"They learned to fly those pretty damn quick," Enrique said, pulling up to continue the pursuit of his chosen target.

"They probably had a lot of time to practice with the ones that Hawke loaned them," Dodds glowered, noting how the flyers of *Ifrit*'s fighter complement were operating the Confederation craft with the expertise of any seasoned CSN pilot.

The *Knights* carried through Parks' orders, driving back the waves of fighters they had earlier that day battled alongside. A hail of fire was exchanged on both sides fighting between the two carriers, plasma bolts drowning out the subtle cyan hues of the micro-missiles the *Knights* loosed against their opponents. And though their opponents made an admirable show of fighting back, their efforts with the TAFs, Rays and Rooks proved no more successful against the ATAFs than they had with the Imperial Mantises, Jackals and Sphinxes.

"Are these guys even *thinking* about retreating?" Enrique wanted to know as he downed yet another fighter.

"I don't think they know what that means," Kelly said.

Dodds brought himself around to look upon *Ifrit*. Fighters were still launching from the catapult and it appeared as though the carrier's hijackers were prepared to throw everything they could at the ATAF pilots in order to take down their targets. Despite the enemy pilots having incurred great losses they were undeterred in their task, and it felt like no matter how many fighters Dodds brought down, several more would appear to take their place.

"*Ifrit*'s gotta be exhausting its complement soon," an exasperated Enrique said several minutes later.

"Not even close," Estelle said. "I don't think we've even hit the half way mark yet."

"How many more of them are there?!"

"Doesn't matter," Dodds said. "We'll keep taking them on until there is nothing left but Hawke himself!"

"*Knights*, concentrate only on the fighters. Do not open fire on *Ifrit*," Parks cut in. "We're not leaving here without *Ifrit*. I want to do everything in my power to bring her back home with us."

Dodds suppressed a growl and plunged forward into another wing, ignoring the hail of fire that sped towards him.

Several more exhausting minutes of battle followed when, at last, the streams of fighters leaving *Ifrit* began to abate. They were no longer launching from the carrier with as much gusto as they had at the beginning of the fight, and Dodds could only guess that it was now taking longer to prep what remained of the complement. It came as a relief; at last it looked as though the day was finally won.

He was about to ask how Parks wished for them to deal with the still dead-in-the-water *Ifrit* when a flash close by caused him to swallow his question. He then swore as he saw Hawke's backup arrive.

"Didn't think it would be long before we saw that again," he said, as out of the portal slipped the enormous bulk of *CSN Dragon*.

XV

— He Who Fights —

S tanding at the front of *Dragon*'s bridge, Commodore Rissard looked first to the ATAFs striking down *Ifrit*'s fighter support, then to the escaping Confederation carrier far beyond, still putting distance between itself and the battle area. He gave no further thoughts to the whirling starfighters and ordered *Dragon* forward. *Ifrit* needed no protection; not from the ATAFs and certainly not from *Griffin*. He knew that *Griffin*'s captain would never seek to risk irreparable damage to the vessel, a point that had been made clear to him when Hawke had called in *Dragon* to assist them.

"It's going after *Griffin*!" Estelle said, as *Dragon* powered forward.

"*Ifrit*'s back on-line," Chaz added.

Dodds noted that running lights were once again dotting the carrier, and that the ship was turning to begin pursuit of its former ally in battle. He brought his fighter about to look over the hulking mass of *Dragon*, never before having been so close to battleship in his life. He was granted a close-up view of the graphic of a blue Chinese dragon that spread itself across the hull, claws sunk in deep, jowls pulled back, teeth snarling. The bow was already beginning to split, in preparation to use the anti-matter cannon. He saw that the hijacked Confederation fighters were breaking off, evacuating the target area so that they would not risk being caught up in the fallout from the assault.

He felt powerless. There was nothing he could do to prevent *Dragon*'s advance. His comms popped; it was Parks.

"*Knights*, what I'm about to ask is going to sound absurd... but I'm going to have to request that you engage *Dragon*."

Dodds swore, though his words were lost within the collective gasps and words of disbelief from his fellow wingmates.

"You all witnessed the power of that battleship's main gun earlier," Parks said, undeterred. "We cannot allow it to gain a lock on us. If it does, then it's all over. I'm going to enable the accelerators. Target and sweep the hull across the vector I'm sending you."

"Sir..?" Estelle's concerned voice came.

"Don't panic, de Winter: you will be targeting power systems only. There is no danger of you destroying that ship."

That's not what she's worried about, Dodds thought.

"The combined power in those accelerators should be enough to break through the shielding," Parks added. "If you hit it right then you'll knock it off-line until the Imperial forces can effect repairs."

Dodds looked over the colossal battleship. Chaz's words came into his head, of how the number of fighters the allied forces were bringing to the table were no match for it. Back then, during the commencement of *Operation Menelaus*, there had been several hundred. Now there were five.

But Parks was clearly convinced that they had a chance of tackling *Dragon*. Either that or the man was clutching as straws. And very brittle ones at that. But what else could they do? They had to at least try. It seemed that as much as the commodore wanted to recapture *Dragon* with the minimum of damage, he no longer had a choice. The man had long given up on the main objective of the operation that had begun that morning, resigning himself to the fact that he would not be retaking the Confederation flagship today.

Dodds' console jingled. The restriction on the accelerator had been lifted and Parks' coordinates had been received. He glanced again to *Dragon* and set to work utilizing the data and preparing the cannon. He then swung his craft up and around to bring himself in line with Estelle and his fellow wingmates.

Rissard watched as the ATAFs changed their heading, breaking away from their engagements with the Confederation fighters and brought themselves into a staggered horizontal formation toward the battleship.

Unperturbed by their sudden interest in his ship, he ordered that they be ignored, his focus remaining on *Griffin*. They could be captured once the carrier had been destroyed. He prepared to give the order to fire, but found that his eyes were inexplicably drawn back to the camera tracking the black Confederation fighters. The ATAFs came into range...

Moments later a thick, bright green stream of plasma erupted from the belly of the lead, striking the broadside of *Dragon*. Beams from the four others joined it, aiming for the same point. There was a call from somewhere down the bridge - the shield generators were struggling. The lead changed their heading, sweeping the beam along the hull. Its path was followed by the four others, who banked hard to trace the line. Against the concentrated plasma beams the shield quadrant held for only a few seconds before it collapsed. Bright splinters erupted from *Dragon*'s broadside, as though someone had just shot a cannon ball through a huge stained glass window.

With the shield gone, and with nothing to protect it, the beams proceeded to cut straight into the hull, tearing open the armour as they went.

The black suited crew of *Dragon* fell about as the battleship lurched violently from the assault. Lights and operational computer arrays failed. Then the gravitational systems failed. Rissard felt his feet lift off the floor of the darkened bridge and he found him floating around helplessly.

By the time the ATAFs had concluded their sweep a large scar ran deep across *Dragon*'s starboard side, venting gases, chemicals, and the splintered remnants of protective armour plating. The graphic of the magnificent Chinese dragon had become a shadow of itself former self, a sordid blackened mark running across it.

A short time later the emergency systems engaged and *Dragon*'s occupants were sent crashing back to the ground. Rissard picked himself up as the ATAFs swooped past the bridge's frontal viewport and ordered the crew to resume their pursuit of *Griffin*. His request was denied, reports coming in detailing the state of the ship in wake of the attack: the main cannon lacked the power it needed to fire, shielding and weaponry were now in an unreliable state, the flight deck had suffered significant damage, and the power generators were in need of repair.

Rissard glowered as he watched the five starfighters pass by and ordered the repairs be made at once.

"That's enough!" Estelle said, as they completed their run. "Get back on the fighters!"

Dodds' scepticism of Parks' plan had been high. He couldn't see any way in which it could actually succeed. And yet it had! And as he pulled away from *Dragon* it looked for all intents and purposes that the battleship was no longer able to participate in the battle.

He had watched as the accelerator beams had hit their target's shield, promising to do little else but prove just how well protected the legendary vessel was. And then, as he had followed Estelle's lead, he had seen the shield give way to the beams which had cut through into the hull. They had sliced and torn and ripped their way through the armour, cutting it apart like thin fabric.

He found it almost impossible to tear his eyes away from what they had just achieved, and again the questions about just what this craft was he was in command of began to rise within him. Twenty-four hours earlier his world had been a very different place.

But now was not the time to contemplate such things. He pushed them to the back of his mind, turned away from the crippled battleship and started back towards what remained of *Ifrit*'s fighter complement. Now the battle *was* won! The day was theirs! He was just separating out a target when a number of flashes drew his attention. He caught his breath; his jaw dropped. From out of the fresh jump points emerged six Imperial frigates, accompanied by a multitude of Imperial starfighters.

"oh my god," he gasped.

"We could be about to become unstuck here, guys," Enrique said.

Dodds' eyes darted from *Dragon* to *Ifrit* to *Griffin* to the frigates to the fighters. He felt his world collapse, not sure of how to begin dealing with the reinforcements.

"Dear God, there's a lot of them," Kelly breathed.

"Doesn't matter," Estelle said. "We need to keep them away from *Griffin*! Go to it, people!"

Dodds did as his wing commander ordered, but his own personal feelings on the matter mirrored those of Enrique and Kelly. The incoming Imperial fighters squadrons was made up of almost everything the INF possessed: Sphinxes, Mantises, Jackals, Scarabs... He had never seen anything like it. And the numbers! They were insurmountable! This was not an Imperial force that he knew of.

With a burst of speed the fighters accelerated away from the frigates they had been escorting, aligning themselves with the sleek black starfighters and almost defenceless *Griffin* beyond. Weapon struts deployed from the egg-like body of the Mantises, locking into place and presenting fully loaded missile hard points below.

Dodds drove himself into the huge squadron of fighters, the pack looking like so many birds, migrating all at once. He could not count the odds stacked against them, suffice to say one thing was all too clear: the *Knights* were now heavily outnumbered.

The front line Imperial fighters opened up with a full barrage against the five approaching ATAFs, multicoloured light from various weapon fire reflecting off the starfighter's armour as it passed by them, all five of the *White Knights'* crafts' shielding rippling with the impact of the shots. Missiles from the back line followed.

There are too many, Dodds thought only minutes into the fight, feeling his zeal beginning to slip. Even so he kept his mouth shut, trying to focus himself better. The swarm of fighters on his radar and outside his cockpit had become overwhelming. His intercom was exploding with chatter, and every one of the voices was frantic, urgent and very, very worried.

Many of the fighters were striking *Griffin* now. The carrier was making a valiant bid at protecting herself, but with only its rear cannons still undamaged, the cracks in its defence were all too wide.

Dodds broke off his engagement, pushing back through the cluster of adversaries and towards the bombers that were the greatest threat to the survival of the carrier. His HUD tagged them with missiles and he loosed them the instant they were locked. They were joined by a hail of plasma fire from another ATAF that was quick to enter and leave his view. He gave no thought to whom it may have been; nor did he seek to ask. There simply wasn't time.

The bombers fell. He swung back around to the cluster of Imperial forces, trying hard to overcome the sinking feeling that was consuming his every being. But he couldn't shake it: this was it; this was where it was going to end...

● ● ●

Watching the bombers fall and the *Knights* re-focusing their efforts on keeping the next wave away from his ship, Parks found himself stuck between a rock and a hard place. For *Griffin* to remain here would almost certainly lead to its destruction in the face of such overwhelming odds. On the other hand, fleeing the system would not only be risky in *Griffin*'s current state, but would leave *Ifrit* in the hands of the Enemy; there was little doubt in his mind that it would also condemn Meyers to the same fate when he arrived with *Leviathan*, coming to Parks' rescue.

As he saw the *Knights* trying to cut down what seemed like an unending supply of Imperial fighters still surrounding them like a swarm of angry wasps, Parks came to a reluctant conclusion: he had lost. He would not be bringing either *Dragon* or *Ifrit* back home with him today. His priority now was to ensure the safe return of the ATAFs, the *Knights*, and the plans to Confederation space. As of now they were the most important thing, more so than anyone else.

"*Knights*, fall back, we're going to jump back to Spirit immediately," Dodds heard Parks over his fighter's intercom.

"Sir, the enemy forces could follow us..." Estelle started.

"I'm well aware of the risks, de Winter!" Parks interrupted. "Fall back, now! That's an order!"

"Yes, sir," Estelle said, then to the team, "You heard the Commodore - Fall back! Prepare to jump back to Spirit!"

Dodds complied, ceasing his attack on the Imperial fighters and starting back towards *Griffin*. The others followed, plasma and laser fire chasing the retreating ATAFs.

But as he headed toward the carrier, seeing enemy fire streak past him and striking both himself and his friends, he was reminded of a very similar situation that had occurred some months back; and something inside him snapped. He slowed and swung his fighter back around to face the pursuing enemies, *Griffin* and the other ATAFs falling out of his cockpit view.

"Dodds, what the hell?" Enrique said.

"Dodds, get back here, now!" Estelle called out to him.

Dodds ignored her, as well as the calls from the others to turn back around and return to *Griffin* so that they might all depart the system whilst they still could. He started to weave, dodge and twist his way through the swarm of Imperial craft, surging closer to the six gathered frigates and the enormous form of *Dragon*. And it was not long before he was well within range of his target: *Ifrit*.

With the cumulative enemy fire focused on his ATAF alone his defences had taken a considerable beating during his approach. Not that it now mattered - he was right where he wanted to be.

"Dodds." Hawke did not need to be told who was piloting the ATAF that was streaking towards *Ifrit*'s bridge; he instinctively knew that only one man could be so arrogant as to pull off such a manoeúvre when everyone else was falling back. He barked an order to the crew to concentrate the carrier's fire on the fighter, as the ATAF aligned itself with the bridge.

For a moment, Hawke's eyes widened. It was going to ram them! At the same moment a barrage of fire issued from beneath the ATAF's wings and sped towards the bridge's viewport, almost right where the Imperial admiral and the former Confederation commodore were standing. The bolts slammed headlong into the bridge's frontal shield quadrant, at first striking it like rain drops upon a sheet of glass. A number of seconds later the shield collapsed, unable to withstand the continuous hail of fire being directed at it. The ATAF pulled away from its collision course, its work done.

Hawke saw the bridge's shield quadrant splinter for an instant before the remaining bolts crashed unhindered into the bridge's main viewport. Huge web-like cracks began to sprout at the points of impact, and both he and Zackaria turned to evacuate the bridge while they still could, the black clad soldiers that occupied seats and consoles springing up to follow them. The next instant the last set of bolts shattered the frontal viewport.

Hawke managed to steady himself for but a fraction of a second before the tremendous force of depressurisation yanked him backwards. He crashed into one of the forward control consoles, fingers scrambling for purchase about the long edge. A warning sounded on the bridge and a pair of large blast screens starting to close to contain the exposure.

Zackaria tumbled over backwards, straight through the middle of the shattered window and out into space, the blast screens coming too late to prevent his departure. Hawke followed, losing his grip on the console that had at one time promised to spare him.

More than half of the bridge crew were condemned to the same fate as Zackaria and Hawke, unable to prevent themselves from being jettisoned from the bridge.

Liu looked up from his console. "Sir, it appears both Admiral Zackaria and Commodore Hawke have been spaced. Enemy forces have also ceased attacking." He sounded confused.

"Bring us about," Parks said, wanting to see for himself. The carrier turned back to face the enemy forces and as the numerous capital ships and fighters came into view, Parks saw that the scene had become a good deal calmer than the chaos and savagery of the battle that had proceeded it. A tremendous amount of debris and wreckage tumbled about, but now guns on both sides were silent. It was as if they had all at once reached a stalemate.

Dodds slowed and looked about from his run to see a number of flailing bodies tumbling out across the surface of *Ifrit*. A small feeling of satisfaction welled up within him as he made out what appeared to be the unprotected body of Hawke amongst them. In their current state Dodds gave them all only a couple of minutes before they succumbed to the vacuum; although after what he had witnessed back at Arlos, he would not be surprised if they survived a little past that. Whatever it was, they would not last very long.

As he continued to watch the bodies floating along, Dodds became aware that he was no longer being fired upon; and nor was anyone else. The enemy forces had ceased their attack on him, the other *Knights*, and *Griffin*, and were instead milling around close to where the bodies tumbled. He remained where he was, watching the Imperial and stolen Confederation fighters breaking away and turning back towards *Ifrit* and *Dragon*. He saw a Ray ahead of him slow, turn and accelerate away, without any intimidation of the ATAF before it.

"What's going on?" It was Kelly, sounding quite bewildered. "Why did they stop attacking?"

"I... I don't know," Estelle said, sounding just as bemused by what was occurring.

"They're worried about hitting Zackaria," Chaz said. "They don't want to risk their leader being killed by a stray shot."

"Speaking of which, good shooting, Dodds," Enrique said.

"Yes, good shooting," Estelle added.

Dodds had half expected her to lecture him, but his wing leader had decided to pass on the verbal slap. He brought his ATAF down to where Hawke and Zackaria tumbled, reducing his speed to that of a crawl so that he could examine the bodies up close. He moved unopposed, passing by an Imperial fighter so close that he could see the occupant within the craft. The pilot, clothed in black and wearing a dark helmet with ruby-red eyes, paid him no attention whatsoever, their focus on the commodore and admiral who were so very close to death.

Dodds came within just a few meters of Hawke, seeing the commodore's face contorted in a mixture of pain and disbelief. Even with the twisted expression, Dodds noticed just how smooth, healthy and young looking Hawke's skin appeared; like that of the soldier whose helmet he had removed only hours earlier. The man's eyes were shut tight. Dodds guessed that he had already lost consciousness.

He then glanced to Zackaria and gave a start. The admiral was staring at him with an expression that Dodds would not soon forget: something had fought itself up from deep inside the man, something angry. It was a threatening look that almost spoke to him through the vacuum of space.

My God! He's still alive! Dodds thought. *But... that's impossible!* He then recalled what had happened at Arlos. So was that. Dodds noticed how, unlike the soldier's and Hawke's faces, Zackaria's was neither youthful nor unnaturally healthy looking. And though he did appear old, his face had more of a distinguished and reverent appearance to it. It demanded respect.

Zackaria never took his eyes off Dodds as he went by and the young pilot could not help but think that he was studying him, marking him, remembering him.

Dodds' comms were chattering with the sound of many different voices, all four of the *White Knights* trying to get his attention. He ignored all of them watching as, in the sudden still of the battle, a number of transport craft passed by him, stopping to pick up the soldiers that had been jettisoned from the bridge. One slowed close to Hawke and Zackaria, the two men being drawn inside.

"Commodore..." Dodds started.

"Stand down, Lieutenant. Return to *Griffin*," Parks said, pre-empting his question of whether he should destroy the transports or leave them be. Dodds did not argue with Parks and fell back towards *Griffin*, coming up alongside the other ATAFs.

Together the team watched as the transports flocked back towards *Dragon*, the huge battleship turning itself away from the Confederation forces with their approach. Then, one after another, *Dragon* and the frigates opened jump points and sped away from the conflict zone, leaving *Griffin* and the *White Knights* all alone.

Meyers arrived in the Phylent system less than half an hour after the Imperial naval forces had departed. He apologised profusely to Parks for the time it had taken him to reach *Griffin*, despite matters being well out of his control. Parks had waved away the apology and together the two men began to organise repairs to *Griffin* and the inspection of the state of *Ifrit*.

"How are things looking?" Parks asked Wyatt, as the head of security returned to *Griffin*'s bridge.

"Aside from some minor damage to the bridge, as well as a few other areas of the ship, *Ifrit* is in perfect working order," Wyatt said.

"Any sign of hostile forces?"

"No, sir. We performed a full sweep of the entire carrier and didn't find any. It looks like they all abandoned the ship. I'm guessing they only manned *Ifrit* with the minimum amount of crew they needed to operate it in the short term. We did, however, manage to locate some survivors..."

"Have them arrested," Parks said without waiting for Wyatt to finish.

"Sir?"

"Attend to any injuries and then hold them in the brig. If they try to escape you are to shoot them dead. Do you understand?"

Wyatt frowned. "But, sir... with all due respect, they are just galley hands and..."

"You have my orders," Parks said, not prepared to argue with or hear the man out. "Now - Is the ship secure?"

"Yes, Captain. *Ifrit* is ready for command."

"Thank you," Parks said, dismissing the man before turning to Meyers. "I don't know about you, but I've had enough of this system for one day."

"I can more than appreciate that, Commodore," Meyers said. "I will return to *Leviathan* and nominate some personnel to help bring *Ifrit* home." The man saluted and left the bridge, leaving Parks alone to think for a moment.

Parks walked over to the captain's chair and slumped down, feeling both mentally and physically exhausted. He planned that once they were in jump he would retire to his quarters and get some sleep.

Whilst he waited for Meyers to give him the all-clear on the skeleton crew he was assembling, Parks reached into his pocket and withdrew the small plastic capsule inside. The usually clear casing was somewhat stained, possessing a light red tinge. He guessed there was a long story to be heard that explained its condition, yet he had not bothered to ask the *Knights* what they had been through in order to get it. The five men and women looked more than just a little exhausted. For now he was happy to see the tiny, thin data card safe and undamaged within.

A little while later Meyers and *Ifrit*'s acting captain contacted him, confirming that they were ready to leave. Parks concurred and requested Meyers open a jump point back to Spirit. The route was formed and together the three carriers started the long journey home.

XVI

— Too Little, Too Late —

N atalia awoke, at first not remembering where she was or what had happened, suffering a brief period of morning amnesia. She became aware that she was lying on a soft, padded beige bed of some kind. Another lay across from her. It was then that she noticed that the acrylic glass cover of the stasis capsule was open. Fear gripped her and she sat bolt up right.

Looking out the front windows of her escape pod she saw that she was no longer in space; the inky blackness now replaced by what appeared to be the interior of a starship hanger. The light level was very low, appearing intentionally so. Other vessels, including what appeared to be starfighters, lined bays, with various pieces of loading equipment and tools just visible. Whilst everything she saw bore all the hall marks as being of Independent design, her experience told her not to trust anything; she could well have been found by anyone.

She leapt out of the stasis capsule and scrabbled around for a place to hide. But where? It appeared nothing within the escape pod could provide her with an adequate means to secrete herself. To attempt to hide in the stasis capsule itself would only give her the option of pulling a blanket over herself. Under them? No, there was barely any gap between the capsule and the floor. The storage cabinet? Far too small; only an infant could fit in there.

The tiny cockpit area was her only option. There might be room to squeeze into the recess at the front, between the control panel and the chair. It became evident to her long before she started over, and had begun crawling into the gap, that she would be hiding in plain sight. But she really had no other choice. Her alternative would be to await whomever had found her escape pod and attempt to fight her way out, in which case she figured she would last maybe five or six seconds at most. Less if she had been found by a hoard of black suited soldiers...

Natalia sat, still and silent, in the alcove under the control panel, her back to seat, unable to see the rest of the pod. As the seconds ticked by she found herself wishing she had some sort of weapon to hand. For a moment she considered jumping out and raiding the storage cabinet, to see if there would be anything she could use. There might be something she had overlooked, despite having dug through them on a number of separate occasions.

My jacket! My reports! Natalia thought, remembering that she had thrown it over the back of the cockpit chair. She turned around, seeing it hanging but an arm's reach from where she was hidden. She leaned forward to retrieve them. The sound of locks releasing made her pulled her hand back quickly. *No! Too late!*

She heard the door at the rear of the pod open and a number of search lights were shone into the dark interior. She watched as they danced around the surfaces, holding her breath and wishing that she could make herself even smaller. She imagined numerous pairs of ruby-red eyes shining just behind them.

"Come out," a female voice called. "You; at the front!"

Natalia's heart jumped at the sound, though she remained where she was, desperately trying to work out what her next move would be. A short period passed as Natalia's mind raced.

The spokeswoman then issued a threat: "If you don't come out we will fire. I'm going to give you to the count of ten. Seven..."

"No, wait. I'm coming out," Natalia protested as she crawled out from the recess. The voice had never declared they would start at *one*. "I'm unarmed." She walked towards the rear of the pod, hands held high in surrender, at the same time shielding her eyes against the glare of the light that was being shone right into them.

Ahead of her stood five people, each armed with a rifle outfitted with a touch strapped to the underside. They were dressed in military fatigues, Natalia making out the light grey and brown colour schemes of their shirts and trousers.

One of the women lowered her rifle in surprise. "Natalia?"

"Nel," Natalia said. She felt tears start to well up in her once more, her legs beginning to shake. She was safe; really was home.

STEPHEN J SWEENEY

The woman named Nel raised her hand, looking all about her. "We're clear. Passengers are friendly," she called out. A couple of seconds later the lights rose to normal levels.

Natalia noted gangways above her where a number of men and women, now visible in the restored light, were lowering weapons. It was a wise and natural precaution to finding a pod drifting in space, the UNF becoming wise to that Enemy tactic now. Nel then indicated to her group that they no longer needed their weapons. The men and women lowered their aim, though they still kept a watchful eye on the woman before them.

"Could someone get my clothes?" Natalia asked, dropping her arms and wrapping them around herself. She was wearing nothing except for the underwear she had on when she had stepped into the stasis capsule. Though confronted with a half naked woman, the faces of the men in the group remained deadpan, as though they had, and still were, expecting to be met by something far worse.

"Suresh," Nel instructed a man who trotted past Natalia and into the pod to retrieve her clothing, whilst Nel herself came forward and embraced her friend. The two women hugged for a while, then Natalia burst into floods of tears.

"All right, all right," Nel said, rubbing the Natalia's back. "You're safe. We saw your pod drifting and decided to risk a pick-up. You're aboard *Cratos*, so it'll take something sizeable before you need to worry again."

"Thank you," Natalia sniffed, squeezing Nel in a tight embrace.

A short time later the man named Suresh returned with Natalia's clothes and she gratefully began to pull them back on. The bay was not very warm and already she had begun to shiver.

"Where... where is everyone else?" Nel asked, glancing behind the unkempt blonde woman and into the empty pod, although from the look in Natalia's eyes she believed she already knew the answer.

"They... didn't make it," Natalia said. She reached into the jacket she was in the process of zipping up and handed over the id card that had belonged to Porter, along with a few others.

"I'm sorry," Nel said, shaking her head.

"We did manage to complete our mission. We hit and destroyed all the targets," Natalia announced, and once more handed over a number of small data cards containing her own and other peoples' mission reports.

"You mean you hit all the targets that we knew about," Nel said. "The situation is far more dire than any of us could ever have imagined. We've essentially shut the gate after the horse has bolted," she added at the sight of Natalia's face.

"How many more..." Natalia began.

"We'll discuss that later," Nel said, gesturing for Natalia to follow her. "Let's get you cleaned up and checked out first."

At the news that her mission had only been a partial success, Natalia felt her world collapsing around her. She had been through so much, had lost so many friends and risked everything to accomplish her goals. And now it seemed to have all been for nothing. A sense of despair washed over her and she felt as though she might vomit and pass out. Sensing Natalia's anguish growing Nel attempted to comfort her and then, after taking one last look back at the escape pod, the pair left the hanger.

* * *

The Grace Report - Summary

The galactic state that was once known as the Mitikas Empire is no more. All that remains of their once glorious empire are many crumbling, dead and lifeless cities. All of these cities displayed the same characteristics: signs of intense battles, with bodies and other human remains left to litter and rot in the streets. All manner of vehicles have been stripped for parts and the bodies of the dead looted for their weaponry, ammunition and other consumables. The destruction ranges from street level combat involving troops and tanks, to mass destruction from nuclear strikes. The only life that appeared to be present in previously human occupied areas were stray animals. Most ran away from us, but every so often we would be attacked by a former resident's pet; the animal either very distressed and confused, or having turned feral.

Extermination has occurred on a planet wide scale, even the smallest of towns and settlements in the most remote of areas being thoroughly cleansed. If there are any survivors I did not see them, and it is doubtful that they would survive very long without core dependencies.

Although my mission priorities prevented me from approaching the Imperial home world of Kethlan, I have been able to determine that the bulk of the Pandoran's force is still concentrated in and around the adjoining star systems. They appear to now be executing a mop up operation before, I suspect, moving on to their next target of Independent World space.

With the information I have gathered from studying the movements and behaviour of the Pandoran forces I now feel I can build an accurate picture of what we are facing: unlike traditional military systems there does not appear to be anything in the way of a chain of command or ranking scheme within the Enemy, aside from the notable exception of Admiral Zackaria and Commodore Rissard. Command is assumed within smaller detachments of personnel on either an ad-hoc or best-fit situation. They all cooperate and mutually agree with this arrangement, with no challenges ever made for leadership. Lower ranking personnel (that is to say anyone below Zackaria and Rissard) could be described as being ant-like, since they work very much as a team for the overall benefit of the entire structure. No task is too big, too small or too demeaning for any of them. They all go about their duties in a very uniform, regimented and almost mechanical way. They do not slouch, swagger or ever slack off.

To add further to this structure there does not appear to be any kind of law (military or otherwise) at work. One does not seem needed since, as already stated, everyone works together as one cohesive unit. There is no stepping out of line and no misbehaviour apparent. No one acts out of personal gain, but only to benefit the whole. Having said that there is neither punishment for failure nor reward for success. There is no apparent social structure - They do not make friends or enemies within their own ranks, and both men and women, young and old are equal in all circumstances.

Physiologically the Pandoran soldiers are nothing short of incredible. Damage to skin and tissue is repaired with amazing speed; seconds rather than days. Broken limbs can be mended within a matter of minutes. Even small imperfections in the skin are repaired, leaving all the soldiers with perfect features. They could almost be described as beautiful. This miraculous healing ability does not, however, extend to extreme conditions. Severed limbs, for example, cannot be re-grown. Severed body parts such as fingers, noses, ears, etc. are repaired as well as can be, and the affected area is then grafted. The reason for this has not been determined, however it is the Enemy's one Achilles Heel. A shot to the head, through the brain, or even a well placed shot into the heart is enough to stop them. It is my current belief that, whilst repairable, the accuracy of repair may be within doubt and therefore not within the scope of the Enemy's healing abilities.

I have also been able to confirm that all Pandoran soldiers benefit from physical argumentation. In hand-to-hand combat all combatants display incredible strength, far greater than normal. Their outward appearance is deceptive of this strength, with all soldiers appearing to be no better built than ordinary ones. This incredible power is present within both men and women with little to no difference in ability. They also display unbelievable dexterity and exceptionally fast reflexes. In addition, all Pandoran soldiers benefit from greatly increased height - six foot five inches being the approximate average. At this time I cannot offer an explanation for this and can only assume it is a psychological attribute aimed at intimidating the opposition. I can confirm first hand that if this is the case it is truly effective. A charging, hundred strong regiment of these soldier, fully armed, would strike a degree of unease into even the most hardened of opponents.

Psychologically the Enemy are, once again, remarkable. Their knowledge of how to command and operate all manner of Imperial weaponry, vehicles and vessels appears to be without limits. A soldier can know all they need to about a weapon without any prior experience or the need to practice with it beforehand. They are able to maximise the weapon's full potential whilst at the same time compensate for its limits. So far we have not been able to clarify whether or not this knowledge extends outside the bounds of Imperial engineering, and it could well be that a period of learning would be necessary in order to operate new and unfamiliar technology. I would hazard that this period of learning would be considerably shorter than normal.

They are code talkers. This makes it near impossible for us to decipher what they are saying to one another, whether it be in a combat situation, a standard communication or otherwise. The cipher code itself seems to also shift on a regular basis. The schedule for this change has never been determined, since it itself seems to be subject to a form of encryption. It is doubtful that we will ever be able to crack their tongue, and whilst they are all able to speak English, they do so only in extreme cases.

Their primary goal is not to conquer, but to destroy without prejudice. With what I have garnered so far we should be very, very concerned about the Pandoran's desire to press on from the Imperial systems and into Independent World space. They are beginning a mass salvage operation and will favour disabling or crippling their adversaries in combat with a view to killing the occupants of the vessel and adding it to their ranks.

They do not appear to have the knowledge of building spacecraft themselves, but are very adept at repairing and modifying craft. Because of this, a large number of their forces will remain planet bound for the foreseeable future but, as stated earlier in my report, the number of mobile forces are not insignificant. Unless we can find a way to slow the speed of their advance then I anticipate that they will be ready for a full strike against neighbouring IW systems within the next six months, if not sooner. And when they do I think we can expect the same approach that they took to the Imperial worlds: prisoners will not be taken, lives will not be spared. They are heartless, cruel and without pity; the perfect killing machines.

A conflict with the Enemy is both inevitable and unavoidable, and for such an eventuality we should immediately prepare. Some will believe that we are facing an alien invader, and that humanity's first encounter with an extra terrestrial life form will be our last. Others will think that the dead are walking as the Enemy rise from wounds that would have killed an ordinary man.

But as we now know the truth is far worse than any of those, and a side of the story that we should endeavour to keep from as many as we can, for as long as we can; including the ATAF pilots, who may well represent our only solution.

And the less they know, the better for all of us.

XVII

— The Honour of the Knights —

*S*imon Dodds ran down the corridors of the medical unit, reaching the door at the other end and finding it locked. He looked out through the oval window to see refugees lying, scattered and unmoving, on the floor of Arlos starport's central hall. The hall was dark and somehow foreboding; as if the gloom itself was responsible for the fate of the men, women and children that lay dead on the ground.

Movement caught his attention. Out of the corner of the window he could see the backs of his fellow Knights as they darted among the corpses, attempting to get back to the airlock. He opened his mouth to shout, but no matter how hard he tried no sound came out. He banged a hand fiercely against the glass, hoping to attract their attention, but they did not seem to hear him and disappeared from view.

He backed away from the door before giving it a hard kick, causing it to fly open. It banged shut behind him as he crossed the threshold, an echoing clicking sound telling him that it had locked once more.

Running out into the central hall he could not see his friends, even though they had been there a few moments earlier. The refugees who covered the floor lay still and unmoving, but their eyes seemed to be locked on to him, following his every move.

He started off in the direction of the airlock, skipping over the bodies as he went. Something grabbed his leg. He looked down to see one of the dead holding him fast, the other arm flailing as it tried to find something else to grab on to. He tried to shake it off, but for all his efforts he found he could not. As he continued to do so he heard the echoing click again and, with a terrible sinking feeling, he turned his head in the direction of the noise. The medical unit door creaked open.

A woman wandered out, looking confused and rather dishevelled. She was tall, with shoulder length lank, black hair, and wearing a torn white vest that was soaked with blood around the belly. Her face was pale, her hands hung by their side, her mouth a little open.

Dodds recognised Barber at the same time she seemed to recognise him, and the woman began to lurch her way over to where he remained trapped, barely lifting her knees and dragging her feet in a quite horrible and unnerving fashion. At her approach, Dodds struggled harder against his captor. He tried to cry out for his friends, but again he could manage nothing but a hoarse whisper.

As Barber approached, Dodds noticed the corpses on the floor beginning to crawl towards him, becoming a sea of dragging bodies. All were silent, save for the sound of body parts slapping on the ground. Another hand closed around his leg and the owner tried to pull themselves up. He took the only action he could and began punching wildly at the faces of those that held him. Grips were released and he sprang free, resuming his journey back towards to the airlock to join his friends.

He rounded the corner and saw them standing, with their backs to him, in the chamber. They were affixing helmets and ensuring they were ready for the evacuation into space. The doors were already sealed.

Dodds sprinted up to the door and began thumping on the thick glass, shouting as best he could. Still there was no sound, not from his throat and not from his hand hitting the glass. His wingmates remained oblivious to his presence. Dodds looked around, back down the corridor and saw a throng of figures lurch around the corner. Dozens of ruby-red eyes fell upon him as the group turned, the refugees having donned the round head gear of the black clad soldiers. Their clothes were blood soaked, their limbs perforated from multiple gun shots, and they had him cornered.

Pandoran, Pandoran, Pandoran.

The words came as a flat, eerie chorus, reverberating off the walls and seeping into his bones, threatening to draw out his very soul.

Dodds realised there was nowhere for him to run; his back was against a wall. He panicked and turned around. He banged on the window again, harder than before, but both he and the glass remained as muted and uncommunicative as ever. The chamber was bathed in flashed red hues and he watched in horror as the outer airlock doors opened and his fellow

Knights *drifted out into space, their backs to him the whole time; never once turning to see their friend; never once offering to help him. They had left him.*

He turned back around and a strong hand closed around his throat. Barber held him in an iron grip, staring at him with a kind of perverse fascination. The black helmeted refugees began to cluster around behind her, their numbers creating an impenetrable wall.

As Barber held up a blood stained, rusty old scalpel, Dodds desperately tried to wrench her hand off him.

It wasn't me! It wasn't me! I didn't do it! *he tried to say. Barber lowered the scalpel toward his belly and moments later he felt the warmth of blood running down his stomach, as the blade drove deep...*

Dodds woke, finding himself on the top bunk of the bed he had fallen asleep on. He was sweating profusely. He had no idea of how long he had been asleep, nor how long it might be before *Griffin* and the other two carriers returned to Spirit, but right now he was happy to lay where he was and wait. Although it had only been a dream, in light of what he had experienced that day it had not seemed all that far detached from reality. He rubbed the sleep from his eyes and decided he would rather remain awake for the remainder of the journey home.

He glanced down at Enrique and Kelly who were both sleeping deeply on their beds. His eyes wandered across the other beds, seeing that Estelle and Chaz, too, lay in the same positions they had when they collapsed on to the mattresses. It looked like he was the only one suffering from bad dreams.

Following their titanic and exhausting final battle the *Knights* had landed back on *Griffin*, where Parks had seen to it that they were given their own private quarters, so they could rest undisturbed. No more cargo holds for them. They had all taken a short nap before being called to eat a meal, before heading back to their quarters to sleep for the remainder of the journey.

For all they had witnessed that long day, no one spoke one word of their experience. They ate in silence, the failed retake of *Dragon*, the fight aboard Arlos starport, and the treachery of Hawke remaining unbroached. Whether it was due to exhaustion Dodds could not say.

He exhaled and stared up at the ceiling. Today had been one of the hardest and most testing days of his life. But he had emerged from it unscathed. Thoughts turned over in his head. Two months ago he had made himself a promise: he would return to duty and put things right, no matter how long it took. And although he had made errors along the way, he considered that today he had done a few things right. He had saved lives, lots of them; he had done everything that had been asked and required of him; and this time - this time - he had seen to it that when taking matters into his own hands, the ends had justified the means.

But the question remained: was he redeemed? Of all the questions in his head, this was perhaps the one that was easiest to answer: No. No, he was not. Poppy Castro and Stefan Pitt were still dead, and no matter what he did he could not bring them back. He had taken their lives unlawfully and that was a fact that he would have to live with for the rest of his life. Maybe one day their families would forgive him, and then at last he would be able to forgive himself.

He closed his eyes again; but still their faces remained.

The three carriers exited jump space and arrived back in the Temper system, not far out from Spirit. Estelle and Chaz woke first, sitting up and trying to shake off the sleepiness in their heads. Dodds clambered down from his bunk as the announcement of their arrival back at Spirit repeated itself over the carrier's PA. He woke Enrique and Kelly, letting them know they were almost home and would soon be able to disembark.

But as the five attempted to leave they were once again asked to remain where they were by a number of familiar looking personnel, who stood guard outside their quarters. After being stuffed into the cargo hold for several hours earlier, the *Knights* knew better than to object. Whilst they waited they sat around in a group and made lazy conversation about anything but black clad soldiers, traitors and refugees.

Sometime later Omar Wyatt arrived to escort them away, leading them to what remained of *Griffin*'s flight deck where the group would be transferred to Spirit Orbital. *Griffin*'s corridors were quite empty, the vast majority of the surviving crew having already disembarked. The deck was just as quiet, only a handful of service personnel in attendance. The five boarded the transport alone, still saying very little to one another.

Dodds wondered to himself what was next for him and his wingmates. After proving themselves in real combat situations with the ATAFs, would they now go on to take on the role that had previously been assigned to the *Red Devils*? Or would they just go back to performing their routine patrols around Temper and other Confederation border systems? As the transport docked with the station, Dodds decided that his questions were best left to be answered in the next few days. He had far too much to think about as it was.

The rear door of the shuttle opened and the *Knights* began to depart the craft, seeing the flight deck of Spirit Orbital swamped with men and women. Several dozen heads whipped around to see who the occupants of *Griffin's* final transport were and at once a cry went up. "There they are! It's them! Look!"

Stepping out of the transport the *Knights* were met by an enormous crowd of people, all eager to meet the mysterious fighter pilots that had fought back against almost impossible odds. With some hesitance the *White Knights* walked towards the throng as hands thrust forward to be shook, whilst others clapped them on the back in thanks and congratulations.

Parks watched the scene unfold from an observation room, reluctantly aware he would not be able to keep the *Knights* a secret forever. Whether he had brought them off first or last it was doubtful that someone would not have recognised them. He watched as the coast guards – the orbital's security staff - that had been assigned to clear the flight deck and sneak the *Knights* away were overwhelmed by the crowd. One looked up towards Parks, a defeated expression on her face. She shrugged. Parks made no gesture. At least the *Knights* were safe.

Turner stood behind Parks, at the back of the room away from the windows, waiting for Parks to present him with the data card the *Knights* had retrieved from Barber. Turner had waited at Spirit for his return, so that he too could confirm the plans were safe before at last notifying the President and her Office. Aside from the two senior officers, the only other occupants of the observation room were a team of six other coast guards, five of whom were well armed, the sixth holding a large metal case.

"How the hell did we miss Hawke?" Turner asked, sounding angry at both himself, Parks, and the CSN in general.

"None of the signs were present to begin with, sir," Parks said, turning away from the window towards the admiral. "They only appear to have fully manifested themselves within the past few hours. It may well have been a result of being in a combat situation with the Enemy, although it could have been some kind of dormant sleeper system."

"If that is so then it's very worrying. How many more could there be who have slipped through the net?"

"All the standard tests came back negative. There was nothing in his blood and the retina and brain scans were as expected. There was nothing unusual about him; he was perfectly normal," Parks said, repeating a belief the two men had at one time held.

Turner tutted and shook his head. "When we pulled him out of that escape pod my gut feeling was to suspend him immediately or, at the very least, hold him back from direct involvement in critical operations. But as you know we need every good man we can get our hands on and I couldn't risk removing someone like that from service." The admiral started to pace, looking down at the floor. "Aside from his refusal to co-operate during the operation, did he do anything else to rouse suspicions?"

"No, he even went as far as to destroy an Imperial frigate commanded by the Enemy," Parks said.

"Did you get a good look at that frigate?"

"There wasn't much time. Hawke destroyed it almost as soon as it arrived."

"Then it was probably part of the ruse. I'd bet good money that it was worthless to them anyway. Was probably completely unmanned, in a poor state of repairs, and ready to fall apart any day now. You're going to have to sharpen up about these sorts of issues, Elliott." Turner continued pacing back and forth in a small area. "Was Hawke acting alone on *Ifrit*? Was anyone else involved?"

"It's difficult to be certain. From what we've been told by the survivors, Hawke surrendered *Ifrit* to the Enemy and allowed them to come aboard. After that the Enemy started to systematically kill off the crew. We found the survivors hiding in the ventilation units near the power cores. They weren't even aware that Hawke had survived."

Turner grunted his dismissal of the survivors' statements.

Parks went on. "The Enemy abandoned the carrier when Zackaria and Hawke were spaced. They picked both of them up in transports and fled Phylent, along with *Dragon* and the frigates that had joined it. It looks like he's been held in high regard for quite some time; certainly up there with Rissard."

"You didn't think to destroy the transport before Hawke and the admiral could escape?" Turner stopped pacing and looked up.

"I... hesitated, sir," Parks apologised. He had indeed held back on destroying the transport since, leaving both men to escape was, in his opinion, the lesser of two evils. Allowing Zackaria to live would permit him to continue with the anticipated assault against the rest of the galaxy, whilst killing him would extinguish all hope of halting to Enemy's advance for good. At the end of the day, it came down to numbers.

Turner nodded. "I'm sure it was not without good reason, Commodore. I may have acted in exactly the same way had I been in your place. Whilst there is no reason to believe that upon capturing Zackaria we could expect him to cooperate, there is no harm in trying. It would have made everything that much easier though. For now it is important that we establish whether or not Hawke was acting of his own free will."

"I will have a full background check made against him immediately, as well as the survivors from *Ifrit*," Parks said.

"We need every detail, Commodore. If there is even the slightest shred of evidence to suggest that this thing no longer affects pure bred Imperials then everything changes: we'll have a full blown galactic pandemic on our hands and we need to be sure that we are able to control this thing."

Both Parks and Turner looked to the six other men occupying the room, aware they should conduct the rest of the conversation in more private and secure surroundings.

"Someone should probably tell his wife too," Turner added.

Parks nodded and glanced back down to the flight deck where the *Knights* were still receiving praise and admiration for their day's work, the five pilots having twice overcome next to impossible odds in the space of just a few hours.

"I never doubted their potential, Elliott," Turner commented behind him.

"Neither did I." Parks turned his back on the scene below him and walked over to Turner, fishing the data card out of a pocket and presenting it. Turner picked up a portal device that lay on a table next to him and inserted the card into a slot in the base. The device jingled and the screen informed him that it was accessing the card, then set about decrypting the data. Before long it displayed the card's content.

Several dozen text options ran the length of the screen, along with options to manipulate the card and its data. The device itself was little more than a screen, the surface touch sensitive. With his finger tip Turner tapped the only piece of text that mattered to him,

Operation Sudarberg

More words filled the screen. Amongst the text present were sections entitled "ATAF", with subsections detailing "Overview", "Schemas", "Phase Analysis" and "Implementation".

Parks stood in silence by Turner's side, watching as the admiral continued to tap through various sections and subsections of the data. Images of the ATAF, concepts and blueprints flashed across the device's screen and Turner moved quickly through them, not lingering long on the overview, schemas and phase analysis sections. Neither of the two needed to see it all in detail. They knew what they was looking at, having seen it almost every day for the past four years.

Finally Turner tapped through the "Implementation" section and watched as an animation played on the screen. It showed an overview of Imperial space. Five star systems, Mekel, Carthege, Haylahe, Atlante, and Codexa, were highlighted. They were positioned close to one another and situated near the centre of Imperial controlled space. As the animation played through the galactic map zoomed out to reveal all of Imperial space and a small number of Independent systems, running the border. Five pale yellow spheres expanded from each of the five highlighted Imperial systems, engulfing all of the Imperial occupied territory and the handful of Independent world systems. Statistics and other various items of information began to fill the screen, though Turner did not wait to see it all.

"Good work, Commodore," he said, powering down the device. He removed the card and placed it into a small plastic container. He then beckoned forward the coast guard holding the large metal case and placed the data card within it. The size of the case was absurd for the tiny object that it had been brought to carry, but the data was deserving of the protection; for the time being at least. Both Parks and Turner knew that it would be kept safe until its retrieval was confirmed by government officials, after which it would be destroyed. The security officer stood back with the others and awaited further instructions.

"We have also obtained full combat statistics for the ATAFs," Parks said. "They are currently being correlated on *Griffin*. I should be able to have them sent to you within a few hours."

"Everything?" Turner asked in surprise.

"Everything."

"If that is the case then we have all the information we need," Turner said, walking over to the window and looking down at the celebrations and cheers that continued below him. He looked over at Parks who had joined him. "We now have only one hurdle left to overcome."

Parks nodded his understanding and together the two men left the room.

A man took back a bottle of tequila that he had previously thrust into Dodds' hand. He whooped and waved it around in the air before noticing that the flight deck had fallen quiet. Dodds and Enrique looked over at the parting crowds to see Parks and Turner walking towards them. Personnel stood to attention and saluted the two men that walked between them, the admiral's expression one of slight irritation at the rowdy behaviour of the spontaneous celebration.

"At ease," Turner muttered, stopping in front of Estelle and her team mates. "Lieutenant de Winter, you and your team have had quite a day from what I've been told."

"Sir, yes," Estelle answered, swallowing hard, her eyes straying over to Dodds and Kelly.

"Answering the call to stand in defence of your carrier, your squadron and allied forces against overwhelming and uncertain odds; risking your lives to go well above and beyond the call of duty at a moment's notice..." Turner reached into a small box that Parks held, removing a medal from within it. He fastened it carefully to Estelle's flight suit. "... whilst all the time acting within the full interest of the Confederation Stellar Navy and her government. Congratulations, Lieutenant Commander." He shook Estelle by the hand.

Kelly gasped. Dodds' jaw dropped and, meeting Enrique's eyes, saw the man mouth the admiral's last two words to him.

It took Estelle a moment for the realisation of her promotion to sink in. "Th... thank you, sir."

"The paper work will be officially dealt with at Mandelah," Turner said with a wink and a smile, as the shocked woman shook Parks' hand. The admiral stood back and began clapping, starting applause that ran the length of the deck. Turner then shifted his attention to Dodds and Enrique, presenting each of them with a medal of their own, before shaking their hands and applauding them. They too were promoted to the next highest rank, moving from second to first lieutenant, the rank Estelle had previous held. Kelly followed suit not long thereafter and then the two men came to Chaz.

"Congratulations, Mr Koonan," Turner said as he affixed the medal to the big man's suit. The applause and cheers grew louder now that the final member of the team had been presented with their promotion. Chaz, however, was not smiling, and as Parks took his hand to shake it Chaz leaned forward.

"I thought you said you had the situation under control, *Commodore*," he said in hushed tones. Parks met his eyes and for a brief period there existed some extreme tension between the two men, each of their grips tightening on one another's hands.

"We *do*, *Lieutenant*," Parks answered him. The two men released their handshake and, putting on his best poker face, Parks applauded Chaz along with everybody else.

Turner and Parks stepped aside and people surged forward to hoist the *White Knights* up on to their shoulders. As he was picked up Chaz glared at Parks, who continued to applaud undeterred, the entire exchange going unnoticed by everyone except for Turner, who had seen it all before.

The bottle of tequila was once again doing the rounds as the merry troop began to make their way from the flight deck and towards the space station's bar. Kelly passed the tequila on without drinking, something playing on her mind. Though she was smiling and feeling rather jubilant in light of her promotion, she was still concerned about seeing one of her father's company's ships docked at a port in Imperial space. She would be speaking to him about it the first chance she got.

But for Dodds, Enrique, and Estelle there was nothing that could bring them down, the thought of a celebratory drink very welcoming indeed.

"Lieutenant Dodds," Turner called, his voice clear and recognisable above the din of song, applause and chanting.

Those carrying the freshly promoted first lieutenant stopped and turned him around to face the admiral. "Sir?"

"You did a good job today."

Dodds grinned back at him. "Thank you, sir."

Acknowledgements

To Mum and Dad, for all their love and support. To Wes, Faye, Ceri and Em for putting up with me over the years. To Ian and Rob for all their encouragement and for being such good friends. To Cheryl for always being there to talk to. And to my brother, Richard, for always being willing to support every project I undertook, no matter how steep or daunting the climb. We always got there in the end.

Printed in the United Kingdom by
Lightning Source UK Ltd., Milton Keynes
142499UK00001B/149/P